MW01591777

Between the Devil & the Deep Blue Sea

A

Novel By

Darline Dorce-Coupet

ISBN 0-9774126-0-1/ 978-0-9774126-0-0

Library of Congress Control Number: 2006921220

Cover Art by Jean Claude Bienaimé

Published by:

FireFly Publishing & Entertainment

Printed in the United States by Morris Publishing
3212 East Highway 30
Kearney, NE 68847
1-800-650-7888

To my very handsome and awesome cousin,
Jivonn,
the only person who figured out the clues.
And to my new muse and inspiration,
Christopher,
love and friendship always.

Contents

Prologue

"**D**o you know who killed your wife and her cousin, Mr. Courage?" The detective's words hung in the air, stark and lethal as a scorpion as he hovered above him. Glancing up with a blank stare, fear lodged in Cedric's throat like a swollen glob of acid as he wondered for the dozenth time that morning if this man understood what it was he was asking. Hesitating for a second, Cedric's entire body went rigid as the detective's piercing, hard eyes peered down at him, studying him as if he were dissecting a bug. Had he the minutest idea, the foggiest notion the devastation he was causing? As shock surged into sudden anger and revulsion, Cedric gave him a nonverbal cue and shook his head slowly, movement minimal. As if any movement he made at all might break him, shatter him into a million pieces.

He had never known a colder darkness or greater emptiness such than he felt at that very moment. He had never realized heartache could pack such a wallop. His worry was quickly building into a torrent of grief, remorse, and panic. Except, he could not let this imbecile standing before him know this. Steadfastly, he refused to say a word.

***

The detective blew an exasperated sigh, and briskly started towards the door, storming out of the room for the fifth time that morning. His other partners had given up long ago, except he was more tenacious. Detective Tanner felt sure he could crack Cedric, get the story...maybe even a confession. *Oh yeah, that would be real nice.* Except his confidence was now failing, wearing thin, dwindling before his very eyes as Cedric sat there tight-lipped. Comatose. This was proving to be a lot harder than he had expected. Apparently Cedric Courage did not plan on divulging any information at all. Cocky little sonofabitch too. Oh, he wasn't overt with it, but you could tell he wasn't used to taking orders but used to giving them.

Scurrying to the door, he let it slam behind him with a loud thud. He'd let Mr. Courage cool his heels for awhile longer before recommencing the interrogation. Some interrogation, he thought grimly. It wasn't like Cedric had said a word all morning. But the sixth time could be the charm. He wouldn't despair...not just yet. He'd let him sit there for a little while longer in communion with himself—and then, once the silence got to him—a*nd by golly, it always did get to them*! Soon, he'd be singing like a birdie.

It was only a matter of time. That was all it usually took. Time...time was his friend. Give a man enough time with his conscience and you wouldn't believe how easy that made police work.

Although Cedric seemed collected enough, the detective observed that his eyes were red-rimmed and that the young man seemed to be suffering from some type of shock or perhaps it was profound sorrow. *Poor chump,* seeing his wife with her strong, virile cousin could not have been easy. A crime of passion it must have been. Yes...but a crime all the same.

Yet he kept insisting he hadn't done it. And he was behaving very peculiar too—like an innocent man. Of course, it could be all an act. Cedric could just be a good actor. He was after all a *performer*, an *entertainer*. Used to getting his way. General grief didn't leave lingering consequences on these Hollywood types in any case—who loved lightly and regretted even less.

Visions of OJ and Robert Blake danced in Detective Tanner's head. These Hollywood types really thought they were above the law. Oh yes, they did...with their fancy attorneys and all their glory and money. He'd have to try again, he decided, but first he'd give Cedric a little more time to reflect on the situation, time to contemplate his actions and wrestle with his conscience.

He prided himself on his fine, detecting skills. He was a master interrogator, not to mention, a very patient man. He would nail Cedric, he vowed. He wasn't about to let him slip through his fingers. Miami was going to teach the rest of the nation how a great investigation was conducted. Just like the Versace-Cunanan incident, they'd crack this case too and show Denver, New York and L.A how the rich, famous and infamous all went to jail. There'd be no OJ Simpsons, Jon Bennet-Ramseys, Michael Jackson or Puff Daddy/Diddy get-aways here.

Entertainers—bah! In Miami, they were treated like everyone else!

Part One

God is Love

*I believe as I did as a child, that life has
meaning, direction and value;
that no suffering is lost; that each drop
of blood and every tear counts;
and that the secret of the world is to be found in
St. John's "Deus Caritas est—God is love."*

--François Mauriac

1

Torn Asunder

What could I say about her death or life itself that hadn't already been said? And now all I could see, all I could feel, taste, smell or hear was the silence busting my eardrums. The illimitable silence pressing me ever so deeper into myself, until I felt myself growing less human. I was Cedric no longer, but this thing. Not a "he who," but an "it that," this thing, a star. A creature of my own creation, but which I wished to be no longer.

It was disparaging, a terrifying journey. One where I delved deeply inside myself. Except, I had learned my lesson thoroughly and well, or so I had thought. I had always been a good student, a quick study, a fast learner. Yet how could I not have seen this shit coming? There were too many holes, too many questions, too many rude hopes piercing the dark, desolate hours that stretched endlessly before me. I felt too much rage in the face of futility, too widely desperate staring in the face of a cruel, indifferent world.

What charm or challenge—if any—did the world hold for me now?

My eyes swept over the room where I was sitting. It was a cold, white sterile room, which fully reflected my mood. One perfect and soundproof and excellent for the ricocheting silence echoing through my brain. It was an interrogation room—yet there was no questioning taking place. Just me inside my head...and it was a terrifying thing. She was gone and my heart was a void over sullen gray skies—over dull, unrelenting silence.

I sat there perfectly still, my mind tumbling over itself. I knew pain like an unthinkable horror. I felt pain. I was pain. The pain and I were one—locked in a fierce, powerful embrace. I felt tortured, as I sat there trying to be cool, trying to remain clam. But moment by moment, I could feel myself losing it. My balance and composure were nearly nil.

Even though all my instincts were to flee, I felt gripped by this weird lethargy. It was a struggle to move a muscle. Even my lips.

After I had sat there and carried on an interminably agonizing conversation with four detectives, several officers and a host of miscellaneous people, I just stopped talking. Stopped trying to explain. It was of no use.

I had tried not to be rude, to be intelligible...yet, I could see how nothing I was saying was sinking in. The same questions were being posed, albeit differently, so as to trip me, so that there would be disparities and variations in my story. They were vying for a confession, and seemed to want an admission of guilt. So... I stopped talking and asked for my lawyer, which was what I should have done in the first place.

Hours had passed and now, still sitting there, waiting for them to decide what the hell they were going to do with me, my gaze fell on what I knew was a two way mirror. But of course in it, I could only see myself. I knew I was being observed on the other side and wondered what they saw? My reflection probably looked no different than it had a day or so ago. Yet I had changed irrevocably, becoming a totally different person where it counted most. Inside.

I gazed straight ahead, studying my reflection, searching for the changes on my face. But amazingly, I looked the same. A tall, lean figure with chestnut hair, streaked with gold, worn in dreads framing a strong-boned, defiant face. One that well suited my arrogance.

Yes, arrogant. That was me.

I smiled. Almost. But caught myself before it had formed fully on my face. I had no right to smile. How dare I smile? How dare I feel smug? How dare I feel anything at all? Bling was gone. My wife was dead. And I had no idea how I was going to go on.

Anger threatened to flare again, and I was doing all I could to try and squelch it. I couldn't afford to be angry. Not here and definitely not now. I had been trying so hard to hide my scorn, unsuccessfully, I felt sure. But I was doing the best I could, regulating my breathing, trying to compose song lyrics in my mind. Anything at all to keep my sanity. I needed not to think of the gravity of the situation and all the ramifications. But worse than that, I didn't want to think about her...about my heart.

That she was, *my fucking heart.* And that was how I felt—like my goddamned heart had been ripped out of my chest, being fed to a pack of wild dogs.

So I created. Yes, I had to create something or go mad. I saw the written lyric's in my mind's eye as I sat there:

Torn asunder by compelling forces,
Buffeted by demons and desires I could no longer contain,

Encouraged and discouraged all at once.
Satisfied, yet feeling horribly empty
Stretched to the limit and then stretched some more
Grab a breath before being pushed under again,
I feel helpless, hapless,
Not at all sure I can go on.

"Wait! Stop! No!"
I scream from the ragged insides of my beleaguered brain.
Who was in charge here?
Why did it have to be this way?
I thought I was making choices
I was invincible and had the ability to change the world,
But is this what I really thought I wanted?

A cry in the darkness
A sigh in the emptied space beside me
The world outside my window
The beat of my own heart in the dawning light
What would this day bring?
How could I gain control?
As I watch myself drowning
Submerged in a wretched, cold, desolate, lethargic sea...

And all I can think
All I can feel
All that I am
Keeps telling me the only thing I can not accept
Arielle is no more...
Arielle is no more...

Arielle was no more.

I looked all around me, as if awakening from a deeply demoralizing, yet strangely satisfying dream. Wondering if my time with her had happened at all—or had it all been my imagination. Had I dreamt her up? Had she really been here, shared in my life, been my wife, given me a son? Had she lifted the doom, the darkness that had always soaked my heart, pervaded my soul? I felt a profound dread. Disparaged. This stank. To high heaven. It was putrid, rabid, rotten to the core. This was fucked!

I fought the urge to cry out NO FAIR. That would be foolish. Childish. Even if that was what I was feeling in my heart. What did it matter? Fate was cruel and struck without mercy. Without flinching. And this wasn't the first time it had cruelly struck me across the face. You'd think I'd be more hardened, more willing to accept.

Except this time—with her—I couldn't.

I could feel the tears prickling the back of my eyelids. I sniffled as they threatened to well up and roll down my face. I pushed them back once again. I refused to cry. Stifled the wail that wanted so desperately to escape my throat. I couldn't let myself cry. Not here. Not now. I fought hard. I had to be strong. Couldn't let these bastards see me break down. Fuck no. Never! Never let 'em see you sweat. Stiff upper lip and all that shit. I was like my old man after all. Nordic. Oh, shit!

My mind turned to my pops and my strict upbringing. Everything I fucking hated. Among them his doctrine of cleanliness and righteousness and timeliness and everything else he stood for. My father and the rest of his kind would scour the world, scattering relics or collecting them. Ruining the earth and indoctrinating everything in their path. Yet somehow, she had mended the rift, bridged the gap between me and the old man. In her own special way, she had brought us together. Somehow.

She had been like that. Before her, I swore I had known myself so well. I thought there was nothing left for me to learn. Until I met her...again.

It was the night of the concert at Club Indigo. Little had I known that night that I was about to come face-to-face with my destiny, the love of my life. If only I had known...if only...I would have made each day count.

That evening had been a whirl of colors, noise, wild applause. There had been hordes of fans all shouting out my name, and unbeknownst to me, she among them. Then backstage, she had found her way into our dressing room. And the rest...well, the rest was history. A history I couldn't bear to think of. I groaned as suddenly, I felt this inexplicable anger, this unbearable rage. So much anger that I felt my internal organs shift, melt, my flesh searing off my bones.

Jesus! There was so little beauty in this world. So little...and she had been so beautiful. So outta sight! She was mad, crazy, sexy, cool. Lovely and so fucking intelligent. Sometimes I wasn't sure what I admired about her more.

Why, oh God, why? Why was there so much suffering? Was this really what You intended? That is, if You even existed at all.

I winced, remembering that I didn't believe in God. Except

moments like this, you wanted to believe. You clung to a glimmer of hope and recognized it wasn't the idea of God you rejected so much, but rather the concept as a whole. Belief in God for me took away responsibility. It meant someone other than yourself held your fate in the balance. However, not believing was just as dangerous. You were then completely on your own. Alone. All alone.

Yet, perhaps there was really nothing. Nothing at all in this vast, endless universe but us and our thoughts. Us and our damnable, fucked up thoughts.

I closed my eyes. Jammed them shut. I was so very frightened. So fucking scared I could scarcely breathe. Didn't want to believe she was actually gone. Even as I felt she might come walking through the door any second...in her long, lithe, sexy stride.

Arielle, my goddess, the wild child, the mother of my son was gone, and I hoped fervently there was an afterlife and she was there. Hamming it up, as vivacious as she was in life.

I stifled a moan then winced in pain, summoning all my faculties and strength to deal with the desperate task before me. Christ! I had to get through this blasted day, but already I missed her so much...

Street Talk Miami, Monday   Final Edition/April 15, 2002
■■■

Sex, Lies, and X-rated Photos
Lurid details showcases high-profile Aventura double-murder case of slayed wife of prominent celebrity, anointed hip-hop superstar.

By: Rebecca Moore

It's the worst Miami scandal since Cunanan shot Versace on Ocean Drive. It's Miami Confidential.

He's an American icon, huge in the music stratosphere, but today Cedric Courage, rap/hip-hop superstar is not sitting on his throne but is cooling his heels at Miami-Dade PD, where he was taken in for questioning and may possibly be charged some time today for the slaying of his beautiful wife, Erin Arielle Symonette-Courage, 26, a South Florida journalist and her cousin, Danyel Champion, 32, a local WEB designer and entrepreneur.

The bodies were discovered at 6:15a.m. yesterday at a posh marina community in Aventura aboard the yacht, *The Kitten,* which served as a second home to Mrs. Courage's first cousin, Danyel Champion, who only recently relocated to Miami from New York. A concerned neighbor discovered the grisly sight as she was going on an early morning run. Noticing that all the lights were on and the door ajar, which was not a normal sight at that time in the morning, she ventured aboard.

Karen Blackmore explained, "I thought I had heard some shots fired this morning, around four or five. Tired and sleepy, I had dismissed them. When I woke up for my early morning run and saw the lights on and the door wide open, my suspicion was piqued. I've never seen so much blood in all my life. It was horrible."

Apparently the two used the watercraft as a love nest and were seen there all the time, cuddling and walking hand in hand around the marina. "They seemed so in love and could hardly keep their hands off each other," Blackmore said. "I always thought they made such a gorgeous couple. But she only came during the day. Never at night."

According to police sources initially on the scene, the couple had been shot multiple times. Police reports actually state cunnilingus as the position in which the bodies were discovered. The cadavers were taken to the county examiner's office late yesterday morning and are now undergoing autopsies. Mr. Courage, who could face the death penalty if convicted of these murders, was taken to the Miami-Dade Police Department where he is undergoing questioning.

The details to this murder case are so lurid that the entire country is already whispering about it. "This is a highly emotional, horrible travesty," said Mr. Courage's manager, Stanley Capella. "Cedric did not do this. He would be incapable of this crime. He was so in love with her." Apparently, Cedric Courage's fans agree. Already, they are holding vigils, camping out on the grounds of the police department and at the marina where the murders took place, still shocked about what has occurred.

"We are showing our support any way we can," said Jaleesa Melville, who claims to be Cedric's number one fan. "I adore the man. He has done so much for our generation and for this community. He has a strong, positive message and I love him. Everyone under the age of twenty-five does. He's our hero. And I don't know what happened between him and his wife, who seemed to be a beautiful, positive role model too, but I pray that everything for him is going to turn out all right."

Linda Phillips, Editor-in-Chief of *Mecca Miami Magazine*, Mrs. Courage's past employer and close personal friend commented, "We are all saddened. It was not an easy thing to digest, waking up to this gruesome news this morning. I, personally, was totally unprepared. She was a very beautiful and vivacious young woman, one who I respected quite a bit. She was involved and extremely committed to this community and she had been considering coming back and becoming the Editor-in-Chief of *Mecca* magazine. We at *Mecca* have suffered a huge loss but our prayers are with their family, who no doubt, have suffered a tremendous loss. This is most unfortunate."

From a tactical standpoint, Miami Police Department is doing their best to handle the situation. Prosecutors are contending that this was a crime of passion, that the murderer executed Mrs. Courage and her cousin in the midst of a fit of anger so brutal, the room where they were found was splattered with blood. "This was a horrific scene, and one that does not sit well with this community," said Police Commissioner Harold Burger. "Every effort is being made to secure the area. Our forensic team worked for over 16 hours yesterday investigating the crime scene and will be there again this morning."

However, the area surrounding the Aventura marina is growing dense, the crowd developing and growing by the hour, and may soon grow out of control. The media circus has begun. "The press is coming in droves, out the woodworks," said Carlos Ferrari, another neighbor from the marina. "It was awful waking up to all the police and yellow tape yesterday morning, and today is no better. Now with the press and the crazed fans, it took me thirty minutes just to get out of the parking lot."

No doubt we will be hearing about this in every newspaper, magazine and on television for weeks. This is already turning into a media frenzy. And the fans are not helping matters either. People are crowding the posh, normally quiet marina area, trying to take pictures and are building a shrine at the scene. A profusion of cards and flowers and candles are being placed all around the marina, near the boathouse where the murdered couple conducted their romantic tryst.

There are so many rumors circulating, regarding the nature of the relationship between Cedric, his wife, and her cousin. There is a question of whether theirs was an open relationship or whether they were a threesome. There are many allegations and rumors permeating the grapevine regarding the circumstances surrounding this illicit affair. Certain pictures were found in the

Courage's penthouse apartment. Pictures which are alleged to be very pornographic in nature, which show very inflammatory evidence of the nature of the relationship between the late Mrs. Courage and her cousin, Danyel Champion. A situation which her husband had to have been aware of since divorce documents drawn up by the firm, Blackwell and Associates, an Orlando-based law firm just two days before were also discovered.

Only recently, the couple was featured on the cover of *Rolling Stone* and looked to be very happy. They had also been prominently featured in other magazines such as *Essence, In Style, Vanity Fair, Spin* and *Vibe* where their in-depth interviews received rave reviews. Karen Kramer, the correspondent who interviewed them for *Rolling Stone* said, "They were one of the most down-to-earth, sweetest, most introspective couple I had ever interviewed in my entire career. They seemed to have it really together and had a deep respect for one another. I can't imagine what happened."

"So far, no weapon has been found," said Police Commissioner Harold Burger during a press conference yesterday. "No arrests have been made and right now, we are simply gathering information, asking questions, and assessing the facts."

Cedric Courage's publicist, Veronica Carrington, could not be reached for comment. The slain victims' family, grandparents who reside in Bonita Springs, Florida and Mr. Champion's parents and brother, who reside in Laurelton, New York, have declined to comment as well. "We would like to be left alone, we are grieving and are very hurt. This is an awful, horrible time for our family. Please respect our privacy," Bailey Symonette, 23, the victim's surviving younger brother has urged.

2

The Longest Day

FBI Headquarters, New York City

She was going back to Miami. Returning home and could hardly believe that her transfer had gone through. FINALLY! Standing at her office window, Kendra Jade adjusted her blinds and gazed twenty stories below at the manic traffic circling around Lincoln Center. Half-smiling, she contemplated what a struggle it had been at first to adjust to the constant motion of Manhattan. But as with every challenge, Kendra had stood her ground and tackled it. And after five years, she almost considered herself a New Yorker and might even now require the energy and faster pace of the city that never slept.

Kendra continued gazing out the window but little of the street scene registered with her. Rather she was already seeing the tall swaying palmettos and smelling the sea salt and heady scent of jasmine, which grew in abundance in her parents' yard in Coral Gables. *Oh, Miami,* she thought in earnest. She was finally returning home, but could she handle it? Would she be able to deal with simple drug-traffickers and petty larceny taking place there to the global conspiracy she was now used to?

For years she had begged to be transferred, and now that she had gotten her request, she was suddenly unsure. Doubting the wisdom of it.

Then too, she had to also consider the fact, there might be a catch to this transfer. The instructions had been cryptic at best but adamantly demanded for her to get down there today. In fact, this morning. She was booked on American on the next available flight to Miami and would be leaving out of LaGuardia at 10:00a.m. Her SAC (Special Agent-in-Charge) had assured her that there would be time in the foreseeable future for her to come back to New York and pack and say her good-byes. However, there was something major going down in Miami and her services were needed there pronto, on the double. She had to leave asap.

Yes, cryptic details at best, but that was the FBI. Kendra took all he was telling her in stride. She wasn't surprised. Nothing at the FBI was ever simple or cut and dry. And nothing was ever fully explained, nor was anything ever handed to you on a silver platter. Oh, she was sure there was a catch all right. A huge one if it meant her getting her transfer the way she was getting it. Being a long time member of the School of Hard Knocks, her only concern was how thick would be the shit that was about to hit the fan?

She smiled slightly. Better get out my galoshes, she thought, knowing for sure that she was about to be wading knee deep in it—just as soon as she got there. She closed her eyes, said a small prayer of thanks, regardless, because no matter what happened, she would be back home with her family. All of whom she'd miss sorely. Being back home in the bosom of her family would have to make up for all the shit she was sure she would have to face, she thought assuredly. After all, home was where the heart was and hers had been missing now for some time.

Before long, her smile brightened and grew, as she welcomed the challenge. Long having turned her back on the behavior that made her who she was, she was now an agent first and foremost, and whatever awaited her she'd tackle it like every other obstacle she'd encountered in her life.

***

WQVC-TV, Miami

Leander Murphy sat back on his plush chair and ran his large, brown hand down his hair. He was still reeling from the news. *Oh God, Arielle.* Arielle had been murdered yesterday morning.

Daviah, his secretary brought him some coffee. "Here you are, boss," she said cheerfully, then saw his face. "What's the matter," she asked in alarm. "You look spooked. Like you've just seen a ghost."

He shook his head. "I'll be all right," but his voice cracked. Upon hearing the news it was as if he had been kicked in the stomach. As he raised his coffee mug to his mouth, his hand shook considerably, causing the hot coffee to slouch over the rim and spill on the papers on his desk. Although he hated to admit it, that little chit had never been far from his mind. And Lord, how he had missed her.

Over the years, he had thought about her all the time, always his fantasy lady. Except fantasy had once been a reality...oh yes, those were the days. His hey-days, which seemed like only yesterday...

She had definitely been more than a pretty face. Unlike the interns of late, Arielle had been no stranger to work. He liked how she gave every assignment 150%, how she'd been so meticulous about details, and how professional she had always been around the office—never betraying or eluding to the romantic relationship they carried on outside the office. For someone fresh out of college, she had displayed a consummate maturity, one which he had appreciated and admired.

Arielle had been talented. Beautiful, with remarkable intellectual abilities and unparalleled sweetness. Truly, she had been the perfect woman.

Was it possible that he had been her first lover? Those torrid memories of her at the Jockey Club, his beautiful, sexy little mistress sprung unwillingly to the forefront of his mind. Yes, he had been more than bedazzled by Arielle's sheer physical perfection. But of course, Arielle had had no idea she was his mistress, and had physically attacked him at a fancy restaurant the day she found out. Her temper was legend, and one didn't cross Arielle and not suffer the consequences. He shook himself, and smiled slightly.

Perhaps he shouldn't have taken advantage of her youth and inexperience. Except now she was gone forever and there was no way he'd ever be able to see her again...even if it were to just apologize for what he had done to her. It felt inconceivable that she was dead and he still alive. She had seemed so young and invincible. How could this be?

It just didn't seem right.

No, he drew in a deep, shaky breath, this just didn't seem right. Picking up the phone, he wanted to dial and order flowers for her himself. Not even trusting Daviah, who was a very competent secretary to do it for him. Some things you had to do yourself...and besides, he hadn't realized until today how special she had actually been to him, how she had stolen a large chunk of his heart. This was the last gesture he would be able to do for her, and he wanted to do it right.

Sweet, sexy, gorgeous Arielle. *What a fucking waste!*

***

Bally's Gym, New York

Veronica had been at the gym in Tribeca, toiling away on the Stairmaster, listening to Howard Stern on her Sony Walkman. After her workout, which usually lasted two hours, she'd catch a cab to work. When she first got there, which was somewhere in the vicinity of 6:00a.m., she'd do some warm-ups before attending the advance yoga class at 6:30 and then did her own thing from 7:15 on. By 8:00, she was usually showered, donned her work clothes and was out of there by 8:30a.m. Next she would catch a cab to Carrington & Associates in Mid-town. Even though it was her company and she was the boss and didn't have to be there 'til 10:00, she liked to set a good example and showed up early. This showed her employees that she was willing to go the extra mile, worked even harder than they did. Besides, she also liked to relax a bit first, liked meditating before actually turning on the phone and the noise and starting to work.

Today, just as she turned on the tube to catch the morning news on CNN, her heart nearly stopped when she saw the screen fill up with Cedric and Arielle. The story already had a name and everything and was being covered by a global media. She nearly choked on her coffee. A good portion of it ended up on her lap and collar.

The story, Miami Confidential, had already blown up way out of proportion, growing more and more, sensationalized by the second. The press was having a field day!

Under the glare of the white-hot spotlight, Veronica's mind whirled, as visions of 9-11 flashed through her brains. That had been a catastrophic day, and today had much the same feel for her. This was a virtual wipeout. Cedric was her biggest client and why on earth hadn't she been notified? Oh, heads were going to roll! This had all been going on since yesterday. For heaven's sake! You'd think someone, some bloody person in her firm would have had the fucking foresight to call and let her know!

Yes, she had gone to visit her parents up in the Hamptons. And yes, she had asked not to be disturbed. But you would think that her staff would be competent enough to know that for something like this—she needed to be called, her holiday interrupted! She should fire them all!!!

Veronica tried to temporize, but failing to do so, she seethed with uncontrollable rage. God, she abhorred incompetence—of any kind. And as far as she was concerned, everyone on her fucking payroll was incompetent. The whole lot of them!

Moments later, she was on the phone. "I need the next flight you have to Miami." Then the next, she was on the Internet. She had two hours to learn all she could, not to mention verbally abuse and possibly fire her entire staff.

***

FBI Headquarters, Miami

It was past 1:00 in the afternoon when Kendra arrived at the SAC office in Miami. Appreciating the big rhododendron bushes or the green lawn and flora sprawling the length of the office building, Kendra basked in the perfect Miami weather, noting the puffy clouds skidding across the azure sky. The sunshine was incredible and it was a postcard perfect day. How pleasant to come home on a day like today, she thought entering the glass complex on Cloud Nine.

Yet her euphoria was immediately shelved as she entered the hustle and bustle of the SAC Office. Almost immediately, before she could acclimate to her surroundings, she was ushered in to speak to the SAC himself. "SAC Peterson is expecting you," his aging secretary informed her, handing her a manila-colored dossier and pointing to a large oak door.

"Sorry to be so abrupt," the SAC apologized, greeting her at the door just as she was about to enter. "You're Kendra Jade."

"In fact, I am," she smiled putting out her hand. "Delighted to meet you. SAC Peterson, I assume."

"In fact, I am," he responded in turn.

Kendra's sherry-colored eyes quickly scanned his face. He seemed pleasant enough. Thank God! Tall, about six feet two with a powerful build, he SAC looked to be in his forties with sandy brown hair, large gray eyes and well-bred face and demeanor.

"Sorry, Agent Jade, but I'm going to have to rush you off. You've met Senior Special Agent Neff..."

"Yes, yes, in New York." Kendra smiled, shaking Agent's Neff's hand, whom she had in fact met in New York a few months prior during the September 11th crisis. It seemed every agent in the country had been there then. Agent Neff she had found intelligent and friendly, but had looked so much like Agent Mulder from the *X-Files* that it seemed almost a joke. He was much less imposing than the SAC, but tall with a more book-smart and cultivated appeal.

"I'm your new partner," he said in a low voice and smiled sweetly at her. "SAC Peterson has made me promise to give you a personal tour of our fine offices as soon as I have a minute, but I'm afraid right now there's a situation that must be dealt with right away."

Kendra nodded. "All right." She was no shrinking violet and in any case had been prepared for the very worse. Her mind veered to terrorist activity. Lots of that going on now, especially in South Florida, seemingly a hotbed for this type of activity. After all, most of the 9-11 terrorist had resided here and gotten their flight training around the state.

"Ever heard of Cedric Courage?" SAC Peterson barreled in.

She was a little taken aback at first, but tried to not show it. "Yes, of course. He's a popular rap artist."

"Well, you may not have caught the news yet…"

"Actually, I did—albeit briefly. His wife was just murdered this morning. Or rather, discovered this morning with a relative, I think the report said. Sounded pretty sordid and the homicides themselves rather gruesome."

"Good. So you're aware of the situation."

"Somewhat, but what does that have to do with the FBI," Kendra asked puzzled.

"Nothing, actually. But Cedric has been the target of some death threats of late and has had this on-going stalker situation. For months we've had him under our protection and have been trying to crack this case, but to no avail. Here's his dossier." He handed her a thick, brown manila folder.

"So far, every agent we've sent in to protect him, well, he's sort of…um, I suppose you could say hasn't been very cooperative. And his old man has major connections. If anything should happen to Mr. Courage or any other member of his family, we're going to look pretty bad. In fact, this might just be part of the conspiracy against Mr. Courage…we can't rule that out. While the police will most likely go full throttle in setting Courage up as the prime suspect, our job will be to do everything in our power to clear him…if he in fact, didn't do it."

"So there's a possibility, you think, that he's guilty," Kendra questioned, trying to feel him out. But he didn't bite.

"Not my place to call. We've been on the case for several months now, but so far no leads. We can't penetrate. This guy has pretty tight security and a huge entourage. He thinks he's safe," the SAC continued, taking a seat and leaning back on his desk chair. "There's a big possibility this might be connected, and so here's the complicated part—we need you to go in. Infiltrate. Find the stalker—if there really is one. Protect Mr. Courage, keeping in mind though, this may be a set up, an elaborate hoax with we, the FBI, as the pawns. Courage may be as shrewd as his father and could be just using the FBI as a cover to get away with murder."

Kendra remained silent, not even capable of feigning enthusiasm for the assignment. Sounded jacked-up. "Where is he now?" she managed to verbalize.

"He's been taken down for questioning. My bet? He's at Miami PD."

Kendra let everything he had just told her wash over her. From every vantage point she could see, this assignment was going to be extremely complicated.

"You're bound to meet up with lots of hostility when you go to the station to pick him up," the SAC informed her. "And as far as I know, he's not under arrest—at least not yet. More than likely, he's being interrogated. You know the drill. Go in there like gangbusters, and if they're not charging him—and hopefully he's been smart enough to keep his mouth shut and not incriminate himself—then you leave with him and stay with him. He's now in your charge. You and Neff both."

Kendra smiled at Neff, happy to have someone with whom she was acquainted.

"His father is on his way down here now," Neff informed her. "I spoke to him this morning, and more than likely, he should be busting through the doors any minute."

"He's a shrewd one, that one," the SAC said, "not to mention connected to the hilt. He's going to be expecting a full report on what we've done thus far, what we're doing now, and how we're going to handle this from here on out. And quite frankly," he chuckled, "I haven't a clue what I'm going to tell him."

That's where I come in, I suppose, Kendra thought .

"We want the tide to change in our favor. Get real cozy with Mr. Courage. Make him like you and trust you. We have a real advantage, because none of the earlier agents had your demographics or background. And the way you look, it shouldn't be too difficult," he said with a chuckle.

Kendra visibly blanched at the SAC's blasé attitude. Was he being serious? Did he honestly think she was going to use her body or looks to bring down a suspect? Did he really expect her to be cool with this?

"By whatever means necessary, crack this case," the SAC

urged, causing her stomach to do a triple flip. "Know what I'm saying. We need answers and I know...it looks very messy. And it probably will be. Yet, I think you can handle it, Agent Jade. Am I wrong in my thinking?"

"Not at all, SAC Peterson," Kendra said, feeling a sudden flash of guilt, knowing she wasn't being completely honest. Though she would try her best to get the job done, she wasn't about to compromise her values to deliver anyone to the FBI. She would do whatever was necessary up to a point. But yes, by golly! How right she had been. She had known what this transfer had meant. *Time to pay the piper.*

"Great!" The SAC beamed and next turned to Neff. "Agent Neff, make sure to get Agent Jade supplied with everything she'll be needing—like her cell phone, credit cards, weapon, car and so forth. Then I need you both on the Courage case—pronto."

***

Miami Police Department

Breathe, Cedric told himself. Just breathe. It was hard, every painstaking, agonizing breath.

He'd been trying all morning long not to freak out and go berserk in this all-white, cold as fuck, godforsaken place. He wanted to be cooperative. To be nice to the officers, who were only doing their jobs. He had tried to be patient and understanding. After all, there was so much at stake. He knew the media was having a field day with this. And he couldn't afford to add fuel to the fire or give them any more ammunition. Nonetheless, his patience was wearing thin.

Borrowing a few lines from a fellow rapper and friend, Earl Simmons, also known as DMX: *Y'all gonna make me lose my mind, up in here...up in here...*So far, repeating those lines like a mantra was the only thing keeping him sane.

Though he was quiet, these people had no idea how very close he was to committing violence. Was there no end to the disrespect black folks had to endure from the 5-0? Were they disrespecting him because he was black or because he was in the rap world or both?

They wanted to stick him for a crime he hadn't committed but he was very close to committing murder up in there...real close...and on that despicable little man with the horrible toupee and putrid breath.

Sure enough, he came in again to resume his questioning, a cold, tight smile playing across his thin, chapped lips that in no way reached his pale, silvery eyes. Cedric could hardly stand the sight of him, so stared straight ahead when he addressed him.

"Look, am I under arrest?"

"No," stated the horrible little man again. Cedric had only asked the question a dozen times throughout the course of the morning. And it was now late afternoon.

"Well, can I leave?"

"Mr. Courage, if you'd only cooperate—"

Cedric stared ahead, not acknowledging the man in the least. He was a suit, probably a detective, but it hardly mattered. Cedric had nothing to say to him or any of these clowns. He knew his rights and he wasn't stupid.

"Mr. Courage, we need to ask you a few questions, like where were you last night? Were you with anyone who might provide an alibi?"

Grateful for his skill in controlling his expression, a skill he had learned well from watching his father, he didn't even give the guy a side glance—showing no emotion whatsoever. Cedric knew this unnerved most people. Being able to completely ignore someone was an art, one he had perfected having had the perfect teacher—his father.

"Oh, Mr. Courage," the detective sing-songed. "I'm growing impatient, and I am talking to you."

Cedric said nothing.

"Look, no one's accusing you of anything. And all lawyers ever do is complicate the issue. We just need to know where you were between the hours of—"

Cedric laughed. It was a deep, rumbling laugh he couldn't seem to stop. Great day, he was going to lose it. BIG TIME. If this man didn't get his foul-smelling breath out of his face, he was going to hurt him. There was only so much he could take, and he was tired of holding his breath!

"Do you want to explain—" the little man started but stopped abruptly, taken aback by his laughter.

"Look, I may be a rap star and a black man and I know in this goddamned place that means less than shit, but I know my rights. About five hours ago, I believe I asked for a fucking lawyer. And since then, I've seen about twenty fucking people none of which I think have stepped a foot into law school. Just what the hell's the problem here?! Do you people speak English—or are the fucking

Constitutional laws different here in Miami like everything else?"

"Mr. Courage, this is hardly necessary," the detective said civilly, trying to calm him down. Except he had had enough, and wasn't about to stop now.

"Now, I may be wrong, and tell me if I am, but I think you're going to have a custodial issue here if you don't let me go soon. You damn sure already have a Miranda problem—trust me on that. None of you clowns took a moment to read me my rights—"

"Well, Mr. Courage, like I've been saying, you're not under arrest."

"I can leave then?"

"No, I'm afraid not. This is simply a detainment. A question and answer-session, but we need some answers. And you've been most uncooperative, which is unfortunate."

"Unfortunate for you or unfortunate for me?"

"Look—"

"No, you look," Cedric said cutting him off, "I don't care what you want to call it. If all the years I spent watching cop flicks served any purpose, I believe anything I say at this point will be impermissible should this go to trial. You know, fruit from the poisonous tree. So, I don't know, you decide...you tell me. But your fucking scare tactics don't intimidate me one bit. I know my rights, and I'll have your badge, detective. Understood? "

"So you wanna be a tough guy, huh, Mr. Courage?" The detective asked bristling up, his feathers now nicely ruffled. "Okay, fine, my friend, but it's your ass!" the detective exclaimed, all civility gone.

"Thank you so much for your kind concern," Cedric said sarcastically. Smiling, he stood up now. "All right then, if you're quite through, either you read me my rights and arrest me or I'm walking out of here!"

The detective stood up as if he meant to restrain him. "No, Mr. Courage. We're not done yet. This interview isn't over until I say it's over!"

"Really? So you're telling me I'm not free to go?"

"No, that's not what I'm saying. I'm saying it would be in your best interest to speak to me now. Perhaps, we could strike a bargain..."

Cedric smiled. "You'd like that, wouldn't you? That would make your life so much easier. You'd like nothing more than a confession. Whether I did it or not—that's really none of your concern, is it? God forbid you should have to go out and actually do some detective work to track down this murderer. The person who actually killed my wife!"

"Look, I'm not saying that you did anything, Mr. Courage. And if you didn't do it, I want nothing more than to clear you! But for the love of God, answer some questions to clear yourself so that if you didn't do it, we can start focusing on other leads before they fade out and grow cold! This doesn't have to get all tangled up and complicated. If you'd only answer a few basic questions. Questions we ask as a matter of course."

"Okay, straight up, Detective, I don't trust you. Don't take it personally though, I don't trust anybody. Cops in particular. So, the way I see it, we have nothing at all to talk about. I'm through. And I can't say it any plainer than that. You want to talk, speak to my attorney. So our business is finished here, as far as I'm concerned."

The detective shook his round, badly toupeed head and smiled sardonically at Cedric showing crooked, coffee-stained teeth. "Mr. Courage, like I said before, we're not through here until I say we're through. You don't dismiss me, I dismiss you," he stated unevenly. It was more than apparent he was losing his composure, close to blowing his cool.

"Speak a little louder, won't you," Cedric sneered. "Hope this is all being recorded. I'm sure my counsel is going to get a kick out of this when he subpoenas your department for these tapes! I'm not under arrest, yet you detain me for questions that I have no intentions of answering. You say I'm not under arrest, which means I'm free to leave whenever I please, but then in the same breath, you're telling me I can't leave. Make up your fucking mind!"

Detective Tanner was turning several shades of red. Cedric could feel his anger building too, but he could care less. He was way past that point.

"Now, if you'll excuse me, Detective, with all due respect, I plan on walking right through that doorway," Cedric said starting to stroll towards the door, "and guess what? You'd better not try and stop me."

But the detective rushed him. "All right. Let's get something straight right now, you little fuck," he howled getting all up in Cedric's face. "I don't give a fucking shit who you are—"

"And I don't care that you're just doing your job!" Cedric howled back, close to shoving him off. "Just don't bullshit me," he said with jarring force. "I'm not fucking answering any of your goddamned questions, so get the fuck outta my face right now!

That or fucking arrest me. If not, then get your grubby little hands off me and get out the way!"

"Just who the fuck you think you're talking to," the detective asked bristling up to his full height of five feet four. He had been posturing all morning and Cedric knew they were about to come to blows.

Still he couldn't hold his tongue. "Ah, do you really want to know...a straight up punk-ass 5-0 idiot!" He shouted with fury. *With stank breath,* he wanted to add, but stopped himself short. *Christ, he was in enough trouble as it was.*

"Yeah, well, fuck you," the detective spat. "We're gonna nail you! Nail your punk ass to the cross! You and all your kind," he shouted. "You think that just because you're big, a rapper probably with more money than God, that the law doesn't apply to you?!! The whole lot of you swear you're above the law, that you can do anything you want! But we'll see about that, Mr. Courage. I'm gonna see your butt fry! And this is Miami. Not L.A. or New York or Denver. Don't think you're getting off like O.J. or P. Daddy or Diddy or whatever he's calling himself these days. Or like those rich folks did out in Denver. Your ass is mine, Cedric Courage, and it's gonna fry, fry, fry, like bacon, baby!!!"

Just then a few other people walked into the room just in time to hear that fry-threat.

"Well-well-well," said the tall, attractive black female who sauntered in, along with two other suits. "How nice. Police brutality in the making."

The detective rolled his shoulders back, cracked his neck, and attempted to straighten out his tie—like he had been about to do something, like take out a can of whoop-ass for him. And for the first time that morning, Cedric really wanted to laugh.

The horrible little detective was probably now assessing the impropriety of the situation. He had been caught in action. Oh, there was a God after all, Cedric thought smugly, wondering how much of that tirade they had actually heard.

"Just who the hell are you people?" Tanner bristled, staring down his intruders, still trying to be a bad-ass.

"FBI," the woman said flipping her badge—just the way they did on TV. "I'm Special Agent Kendra Jade, this is Senior Special Agent Neff, and he's one of yours."

The other suit introduced himself as Detective Kramer.

"Well, what can I do you folks for?" Detective Tanner said more warmly then, adjusting his attitude now that he was dealing with the Feds.

"Well, we're here to pick up Mr. Courage," the woman responded.

"Pick him up? What for?" Tanner asked.

"Precisely," she said with a smile. "Is he under arrest?"

"No."

"So how come you've had him here all morning," Special Agent Neff asked pointedly.

"And why are you harassing him?" the woman followed in, bombarding Tanner with their questions. "And it was more than apparent you were very close to physically restraining him when we walked in."

"This doesn't look good, Detective," Neff rejoined. "If you're trying to build a case, you might be looking at some rather serious custodial issues."

"I'm not harassing him. And I told him since he got here that this was totally voluntary and he could leave at any time."

Cedric didn't even bat an eyelash at the boldface lie. He always knew that most cops were underhanded and played dirty. This only confirmed it.

"Really?" The woman asked with some amusement, as if she knew better.

"With all due respect, Detective, that's not what it looked like to us," Agent Neff parried, as if this was his usual humorous banter.

The woman smiled coolly at the flustered detective then threw Cedric a friendlier smile—one that seemed to say they were on his side. "Mr. Courage will be coming with us, Detective Tanner. That is, unless you're bringing him up on charges."

Detective Kramer, who had walked in with the agents looked a bit uncomfortable. Turning to Tanner, he agreed, "I'm afraid I have to side with them, Tanner."

"Since when does the FBI have jurisdiction?" Tanner demanded, posturing again. For whose benefit, Cedric had no idea. Must be the height, the man had a Napoleon-complex for sure.

"Since Mr. Courage received a death threat. One sent to his home and one to his family's home in Orlando. Obviously whoever's behind these threats have close personal ties to Mr. Courage and knows the inner workings of his life. Therefore, it is imperative that we take every precaution—especially in the light of what has just happened to protect him, Detective. He's now in our charge," Agent Jade explained with such fake civility, Cedric came very close to chuckling.

FBI protection, he thought with much amusement. Hell, he'd been playing games with those clowns for months. Yes, he had received a death threat, but he got stuff like that all the time. There were so many lunatics out there. Overzealous fans. People willing to do anything to meet him. He was also aware that there was a stalker, but his staff and security had been handling that kind of bullshit for years. Since he got into show business, he'd had to deal with threats, people deliberately picking fights so they could file lawsuits. It came with the territory. Just why the FBI was so interested in this particular threat, he hadn't quite figured out. Except that the threat was not only against him, but his entire family. The past few weeks or so, the Bureau had laid low. In fact, hadn't bothered him at all. But today, here they were again—two new ones this time—coming in like the goddamn Calvary. Fine! If they could get him out of here and since his attorney had yet to make an appearance, sure, he'd play along.

Nothing to worry about though. Graydon Stone, his hotshot, very expensive and *expansive* lawyer showed up seconds later, apologizing profusely for the delay. Cedric rolled his eyes upwards and perked up then, dusted off the back of his pants in a totally arrogant manner, and took his leave. "Later," he told them all, and strolled out of the room like the big Honcho, as they all began talking amongst themselves.

He was more than ready to get the hell out of Dodge.

Taking out his cell phone, he speed-dialed Deuce. "Yo, man. Is the 5-0 there yet?"

"What, they gonna come search the place?"

"No doubt. You know what you gotta do, right?"

"Yup," Deuce replied. "I'm on it. But look, man. The whole crew is here. Everyone's just here milling about, waiting to hear word. So what's goin' on with you, bro?"

"I'll have to talk to you about it later, but for now, don't worry about picking me up at the station. Just take care of business, know what I mean."

"Word... Yo, man, you sure you aw'ight?"

Cedric sighed deeply. "Yeah, as well as can be expected, chief. I'll be with Graydon for a little bit. But tell the crew, it's all good and everything's gonna be fine. I'll be there soon."

"Cool, and don't worry, man, I'm on it," Deuce promised and clicked off.

Seconds later, Kendra Jade, the female agent strolled up to him as he waited for Graydon Stone, who had gone off to get something or another—except he was growing tired of waiting and wanted desperately to get out of this police station already.

Damn, he thought as he watched her move towards him. She was a tall bitch, very close to his height, with eyes the color of scotch-whiskey behind hideously ugly glasses, which he suspected she wore to purposefully down play and camouflage her beauty. Her shoulder length hair was pulled back tight in a straight sleek tail down the back of her neck touching the slate-colored two-piece suit she wore with low-heeled pumps. When a woman was as tall as she was, there was no need to add inches with high heels, he supposed. Anyway, he checked her out, making it obvious that was what he was doing, deliberately trying to piss her off. A woman like her, he sensed would not appreciate that at all. She smiled amicably at him regardless, but he knew it bothered her. Yet like habit, good manners were always a convenient crutch.

"Uh, so where do you think you're off to," she asked, looking composed and smart. His initial impression of her was that here was a tough woman. But like most first impressions, he knew it would only be partly right. In any case, she seemed thorough and very professional. Too professional, perhaps, and not warm at all. It was like you knew she took her job much too seriously.

Purposefully cheeky, he responded, "Out of here, most definitely. Beyond that, I don't know." And at that, he casually strolled away, hoping to get as far away from her and this goddamn police station as possible. The farther the better.

"Well, I hope you realize that wherever you're going, I have to come along too," she countered, hurrying after him.

But Cedric did not even give her a backward glance as he hurried through the winding corridors of Miami-Dade PD. She could have no idea how little her comment meant to him.

***

Kendra quickly caught up to him, keeping pace with his brisk gait, while she endeavored to maintain a pleasant expression, attempting to politely explain again.

"Mr. Courage, as I was saying before, I've been assigned to protect you. I'm afraid you're stuck with me for the next few days. Possibly weeks. It's an FBI directive. I apologize for any inconvenience this may cause, but I'm afraid you have no choice in the matter."

Cedric continued his brisk pace as his lips curved into a sweet smile, which didn't reach his eyes. "That's very interesting, Agent—"

"Jade," she supplied. "I'm glad it amuses you."

"Oh, it does. It's laughable. You're telling me I've been assigned protection and I have no choice..." he chuckled. "This whole day is becoming more and more surreal as it progresses."

"I see you have a great sense of humor. That's good to have—especially when the FBI gets involved," she quipped, keeping up with his fast clip.

"You're going to protect me?" He asked sharply and paused momentarily.

His tone froze her and for the first time, she stopped smiling. Her eyes flicked over him with barely concealed annoyance. "Why would that be laughable?"

"Oh, sorry," he mocked. "Now I've offended you."

"Hardly," she replied a bit too quickly, definitely too harshly.

"Nonetheless, I apologize." He stopped abruptly to face her, his gaze intense and unreadable. "My problem, though is I have no idea who or what exactly you'll be protecting me from. Besides, what if I already have protection? How can you say I don't have a choice?"

"Mr. Courage, I do not make the initiatives. The Bureau does, and you've been assigned our protection. That's all the information I've been given, so that's all I can tell you at present. Simply put, my job is to protect you, and that's what I intend to do, I'm afraid."

"I see," Cedric deliberately taunted her, his face thin and gaunt. It was not the high-gloss appearance that usually graced magazine and CD covers, but one shrouded with light stubble and eyes that looked weary, a bit pale and washed out. "You know, for a special agent, you're afraid of a whole lot of things. But as for myself, you need not worry. I'll be fine on my own, Agent Jade," Cedric added silkily. "I have a whole team for protection and won't be needing your services, thank you very much. But tell the Bureau, thanks for the offer, but respectfully, I must decline."

Kendra gave an involuntary groan of disbelief, her face and stomach simultaneously tightening into a knot. She stood quite still in the middle of the lobby as she watched him stroll away from her, trying to absorb the reality of the situation—realizing that Cedric was going to fight her on this at every turn.

"Look," she said with exasperation as she quickly caught up to him again. She could not allow him to get away. "Mr. Courage, I've been assigned to protect you, as I stated before. And I intend to do just that. I won't be deterred," she said forcibly, dropping the gauntlet.

Just then Graydon Stone walked up to them just as an epithet almost left her mouth. "Cedric," he called in his high-handed tone and manner, "I don't want you talking to her or any of these people. Understood? I don't want you saying a word!"

"Counselor, sir," Kendra politely interjected, with a forced, awkward little smile, "I've been assigned by the Bureau to protect your client. You can call and check it out. It's a legitimate directive."

Graydon Stone smiled, as if her words amused him. Staring pointedly at her, his eyes cold and piercing, he said, "Agent—"

"Jade," she supplied. "Special Agent Jade."

"Look, Special Agent Jade," he said grimly. "I don't know what tricks your agency has up its sleeves, but you screw with my client and I'm going screw up the whole case you're trying to build against him. Why don't you call up your AUSA and find out about me!" he huffed, bristling with indignation.

"Counselor, I've been assigned to protect this man. That's all," Kendra said evenly. "I'm in no way associated with any of this. We're here to investigate and get to the bottom of the death threat, and I'm requesting your professional courtesy and Mr. Courage's cooperation to do my job."

"Professional courtesy my ass! I wasn't born yesterday, and I know very well how the Bureau operates. Come on, Cedric," he said dismissing her. "Let's get you out of here!"

Cedric winked at her, "Peace out, my sistah," he had the nerve to say, and followed Graydon out the doors.

Kendra was furious, already disgusted by this case.

"Better luck next time," Graydon Stone tossed over his shoulders.

For a moment she stood frozen in her spot, unable to move, trying to decide what to do. Neff, who had still been talking to the detectives came up to her now. "What happened?" He asked nearly in a panic. "Why aren't you with Cedric?"

"He just left with his attorney," she offered and temporized. "What an asshole!"

"Cedric or Graydon Stone?"

"Both of them," she spat and then laughed bitterly. It was either that or scream, she felt so flustered. "But especially Stone."

"Ah yes, that he is," Neff agreed. "He's tough as nail, best in Miami. Probably why Cedric hired him. And from the look of things, Cedric Courage will need the best defense."

"Doesn't look good?"

"No, not at all. Tanner's piping mad, and is working on

getting a search warrant as we speak to go search his penthouse in Aventura. I have a few more things to discuss with them, but you'd better tail them though before they get away. Here, take the car," he said handling her the keys. "Later, maybe I'll hook up with you again, but for now...if you need anything, you can reach me on my cell. I'll call you to leave the number. Now hurry, Kendra! Don't let him get away."

Kendra rushed out of there to catch her mark, but was instead greeted by a hoard of Cedric's screaming fans, and a platoon of photographers and journalist. Kendra blinked as the cameras clicked and whirled, temporarily blinding her. And now she was being shoved and grabbed as the paparazzi descended on her.

It was mad and chaotic. Like some scene out of a movie. This couldn't be happening. Kendra tried to protect herself as the swarm of newshounds and fans seethed around her like flies on a rotting carcass. Instantaneously, two dozen or so flashbulbs exploded inches from her face. The fact that her face was about to be splashed on every front page and magazine cover from Miami to Madrid and seen on every supermarket tabloid and newscast suddenly dawned on her.

"Are you involved in the case at all," an eager journalist asked excitedly.

"We saw you talking to Cedric. Who are you? Are you a friend?"

"A girlfriend?" Another one said shoving a microphone in her face.

"What's your relationship to him," yet another badgered, wanting to get the skinny for their newscast.

Shoving their mikes back and away from her, Kendra ignored them all, seeing if she could raise on her tippy-toes to try and catch a glimpse of those damnable dirty blonde dreadlocks, which was probably not too far ahead of her. Except the paparazzi was so thick, she couldn't see a thing.

Why didn't the police have this crowd under control, she wondered despairingly. This was a damned police station, for crying out loud! And it was obvious that this crowd was waaay out of control. What was going on here? She had watched mob scenes like this on TV. And now here she was living through this horror. It was a nightmare, one she was already longing to wake from.

Suddenly, there was a great commotion. She could see the crowd start to dissipate, all running towards the street. They must have made it to the car, she thought. Shit! She'd never make it to *her* car on time to follow them, she thought helplessly.

The long black limousine parked in front of the station pulled off, nearly running over some of the more parasitic photographers. Several cars were lined up behind the limo, already in hot pursuit. It was turning into one huge mess.

Kendra ran a good ways on her pumps, attempting to get to her RV to follow them, but traffic in the parking lot was at a standstill. By the time her Range Rover pulled out of the lot, the limousine and the cavalcade of cars and news vans following of it were long gone.

Closing her eyes, she breathed slowly and deeply, calculating her next move. She had to get things into perspective and not let other people's negativity fight their way into her consciousness. What was her next course of action? Where would they go to talk? Graydon's office? Cedric's home? Definitely not a public place. The South Beach studio perhaps? Flipping through the thick dossier she had been given, she skimmed through it.

If Graydon Stone and Cedric Courage thought they could deter her, steer her from her job, they had another thing coming. She was a special agent of the FBI and in a better position to deal with the wrath and vagrants of society than most people. Besides, she was thick-skinned, not easily intimidated or deterred and was prepared to handle whatever they threw her way.

3

Forever is a Very Long Time

It had been a madhouse outside the police station. The press and paparazzi had been out in full force. People were waving, calling out my name, and then the photographers were snapping the cameras like crazy all around me. Once in the limousine, for several minutes, I had been temporarily blinded. I had been pushed and shoved and stepped on. People had bumped into me, shoving microphones in my face. One fan had even shoved her hand down my pants. It was unbelievable, the shit I had to suffer. It was as if being a celebrity gave people the right to do whatever they pleased to you. It was the price of fame, I supposed. But sometimes I wish people would respect my boundaries.

But I was alive, though. Still breathing.

No matter the fucking behavior of the press. No matter what I had been put through or was about to be put through, I was at least alive. But Bling was gone. How could I even complain or feel sorry for myself?

I was aboard Graydon's yacht on Key Biscayne, this real nice cruiser, fully equipped. Graydon had wanted to talk and felt that his place would be more private, a lot quieter then my place in Aventura. From what I had heard, it was a real mess over there and shit, the condo association was going to toss my ass out for sure. With hundreds of journalists and cameras all about, the world media covering this story, I, of course, wanted to stay clear too.

Leaning my elbows on the wooden rail of the deck overlooking the bay, I stared down at the water rolling in, as it gently rapped at the cruiser's edge. Closing my eyes, I fought to squeeze the pain that was threatening to rack through my chest, making me flinch. My frozen heart had begun to pound again against my rib cage.

All morning long, I had felt this unspeakable terror, of my heart lurching and stopping. It was nice to feel a regular heartbeat again, but I shrank into the bench as the horror of what had happened came crashing down on me like lightning, illuminating the calamity I now faced. There was the real possibility that I might be prosecuted for this. As well as the real possibility that I might be found guilty.

Dad and all his power and influence might not be able to save my ass from this disaster. I didn't have an alibi. Not one...

Sure, I could get Deuce or Rico or a number of other friends to say I was with them. And they'd lie under oath for me in a heartbeat. Any number of them would gladly perjure themselves in any court—if it meant getting me off this rap. I knew that with absolute certainty. But would it have to come to that?

I stared out at the marina, looking far off into the sea, thinking about how Arielle had been murdered aboard a yacht probably much similar to this one. Could it had been less than 24 hours ago that I had learned of the tragedy? I was going over the entire thing in my mind. Replaying yesterday morning's events.

"We're so sorry," one of the uniformed officers had said, "Mr. Courage. We apologize for waking you up so early and for this intrusion, but we have some terrible news."

"What is it," I had asked sharply, feeling my heart begin to pound.

The taller officer, who was wearing a hat, took it off and looked down to the floor, while the short, stocky one coughed nervously. That was when I noticed that he was holding Arielle's handbag, along with her driver's license. I nearly collapsed and would have, had I not been holding on to the doorframe.

"Can we come in?"

I nodded and invited them in.

I felt as if all the blood had drained out of my face and had gone racing down and out of my limbs. My heart was hammering so loudly, I had to strain to hear them confirm what I already suspected. She had had an accident? Maybe she was in the hospital and badly hurt, I then thought feverishly. God, what was I going to do if something horrible had happened to her, I thought next. But the thought that she had died—was dead—never even occurred to me.

"This is one of the most difficult tasks we have to perform," the taller one started solemnly. I don't believe I heard anything else. Snippets of information maybe. I heard the mention of "morgue" and "identify." Even heard something about "police station for questioning." I snapped back to full alert when I heard "search warrant to inspect the premises."

And I could do nothing but just laugh. I actually laughed. "Did I hear you correctly? Did you say you have a warrant to search the premises?"

"No, sir, not at the moment. We only mentioned that it is coming," the same one responded.

"But first thing's first," the other said. "The rest will come later."

I bit my lips feeling like all the oxygen had just been ripped from my lungs. What could I even say at that point? What would I ever be able to fucking say? *Why even lay that trip on me,* I thought wanting to kill—something!" In one breath you tell me my wife is dead, and in another that I'm the suspect."

The shorter officer with her handbag shifted uncomfortably, cleared his throat and handed me her driver's license.

I whimpered a little as I took it. "This really SUCKS! Jesus Christ!" I swore.

They both nodded and were real somber or I would have really lost it.

Although it was real quiet, I could hear bells. Distant bells, probably Arielle's wind chimes rattling in the wind outside on the terrace. It soothed me for a few seconds. But only for a few seconds...

"What the hell happened?" I asked despondently. "Can one of you please tell me what the fuck happened?"

"She was shot," the tall one answered. "Along with someone else."

"Danyel?"

"Oh, you know him?"

I shrugged and then thought better of it. I wasn't stupid. I wasn't about to answer any more questions. "Am I under arrest, a suspect? You already mentioned the search warrant to search my place."

"No, sir. This is all voluntary. Standard procedure stuff. This is how we handle homicides these days. We apologize for any convenience this may cause, but now a days, the spouse has to be cleared first before..."

His partner continued as he cleared his throat. "It's just a sign of the times, Mr. Courage."

I was floored. It was almost like I had just been whacked in the head, rammed in the gut, hit by a train with this wretched news, but had to quickly face the fact that I might also be accused of doing this dastardly deed.

I couldn't believe I was still standing. I shouldn't have been, but I stood there probably looking a lot braver than I felt, amazed by my strength. "Well, as you can see, I've just waken up. I need to shower and change, etc..."

"Yes, we understand," the shorter one said.

"No problem," came the other's response.

"Would you like to come in, have some coffee and do you two have names?" I asked inviting them from the foyer and into the living room.

"Officer Dixon and Lieutenant Griffen. I believe we identified ourselves earlier."

"Of course, you probably did," I managed to smile. "Please, have a seat."

They were kind enough to wait. Then right in the middle of attempting to get dressed, Bailey arrived, like the fucking Calvary and saved my ass from the total miserable chore of having to go identify my murdered wife and her cousin-lover alone. I had never felt so relieved to see anyone in my entire life. I'll never forget Bailey's face. He had never looked anything like Arielle, but on my life, I saw Arielle walking in. He was himself and fucking Arielle at the same time.

All of the sudden, I was overcome by this rush of energy and couldn't do enough for Bailey. It was like I felt the need to comfort him. After all, he had lost his fucking sister, someone he'd known and loved and been close to all his life, and his cousin, who was his closest friend. Losing both of them on the same day and under these illicit circumstances couldn't be easy.

However, Bailey seemed to be in such control. I kept staring at him the whole time, waiting for him to give me one smidgen of the turmoil I knew he had to be feeling, but it never came. It was because of Bailey and his strength that I didn't fall apart completely. He accompanied me to the morgue and together, we identified both the bodies. And I stood there in amazement. He was so fucking unbelievingly strong.

It was also because of Bailey that I wasn't taken in for questioning that same morning. "Give the guy a break," he told the officers. "He's just lost his wife. Give him a moment to breathe, to at least wrap his head around it. He'll come down first thing Monday morning to answer your questions. But for today, please bear with us and try to understand."

Bailey spent most of Sunday morning with me, leaving late in the afternoon to go be with his grandparents. "Grandmère is devastated," he confided. "I'm not sure this isn't going to kill her.

So is Grandpère, who now swears there's a curse on the family."

I wasn't sure this wasn't going to kill me!

Thinking about her, though, I couldn't help remembering the last time I saw her alive. All gorgeous and glamorous, a spoiled princess...but my spoiled princess who was threatening to leave me for another man, her cousin.

It was one of those days that you wished you could live all over again. There would be so much you would do—so much you wouldn't—too many things you would change or have done differently. I was beating myself up, wishing I hadn't let her leave that night. I could have stopped her if I had tried. I knew I could have. But I had been too damned angry and too proud.

I thought I could just let her have her fun, and let her come to her own senses. Cause there was no way the two of them were ever going to work, and so I'd allow her to come back to me on her own. Just like I knew she would. What we had was too potent and strong. Too special. She was mine. And I was hers. We belonged together. I felt this in my soul. And well...Danyel, he was a momentary phase, a temporary pleasure that would fade and pass. No one was ever going to come between us. Not seriously. And not for very long. Also, I knew Arielle and knew she required a life of unparalleled luxury that I could easily give. With Danyel, there'd be a struggle, and she'd be back—even if it was just for the lifestyle—I felt sure.

Yet what on God's green earth could I have been thinking when I let her just waltz out of that door without so much as a word to stop her? She was on her way out the door. Going into the arms of another man. Possibly walking out of my life forever and I just let her. Without a fight. Allowed her to just stroll out of the door. With no regrets and little words. And now she was dead.

Couldn't help feeling like it was somewhat my own fault that she was now gone. I should have tried to stop her. I could have made things right...

Deuce picked me up from Graydon's later that day and I barely spoke a word to him. I had no energy to speak, nor to even suffer through all the interminable solemn conversation that people would expect me to take part in. I felt drained. Numb. Empty. Though I had put on a brave face earlier, I could do it no longer.

I felt awful and hated to do it, but I asked Deuce to call ahead to the penthouse and ask everyone to leave. I didn't feel much like company. And although I knew everyone would go out of their way to be kind, to be positive and supportive, wanting to offer their strength and encouragement, I just wanted peace and privacy right now.

The last thing I wanted was anyone's condolences, nor did I want to have to politely accept all the well-meant sympathy and good wishes. Damn it all to hell!!! No one could possibly understand how I felt and I was incapable of responding with the required courtesy when at that moment I wasn't sure I cared to live or if anyone else did.

Also, there was that niggling little feeling that I was trying my best to avoid feeling, but quite possibly, many of those well-wishers might even think I had actually done it. That I had committed that awful crime and murdered my wife and her lover. The suspicion would of course be there. *Did he or didn't he? And if he had, who could blame him?*

When I got to the penthouse, gratefully, it was empty. Thank goodness everyone had followed instructions and gotten the fuck out there. Going straight to our bedroom, I asked Deuce not to be disturbed at all. By anyone. For any reason. Didn't matter who it was or what it was about, I told him. I wanted to be alone. In fact, turn the phone off, I instructed him.

CJ was with my dad and Margot, safe in Orlando and other than him, there wasn't a fucking person or thing on earth I cared about at the moment. I wanted to have my own pity-party, which was long and coming. Wanted to get high and rip-roaring drunk. Deuce nodded, looking somber and grave, seeming to understand the solitude I now required.

Deuce had been with me for nearly a decade, and I knew he had to be thinking how I had never been alone. For years! It was like once you attained stardom, you signed this contract of having no privacy. Absolutely none. There were always people. Always a team, a posse. But I was tired, and just wasn't having it anymore.

Enough.

Upon entering our bedroom, I let myself drop into our bed, not having to pretend anymore for anyone. Felt this black terror, like my whole world had shifted, crashed and burned, and I wanted nothing more than to just allow myself to wallow in desperation, in this doom-filled gloom.

I sensed this ominous clang like the barred clatter of a cell door slamming shut. I didn't want to believe she was gone. Didn't want to think how fragile life really was. Didn't want to give in to my embittered fury, dwelling just beneath the surface, underneath all the sorrow and pain. Even though it was bubbling, and threatening to overtake me if allowed it so much as an inch, I couldn't afford to get angry. Knew my temper, knew how I got when I allowed myself to get angry, which wasn't often. But when I lost it, all hell and heaven broke loose. Couldn't afford to allow myself to go there. Had to stay clear and rein it in, keep my anger in check. For everyone's sake.

I looked over to the nightstand and my gaze rested for a moment on our wedding pictures. My gaze lowered as I stared at one she had taken alone where she was smiling widely, with that sensational knock-out smile of hers that used to drop me right on my ass. I stared at her for a long time, and she stared back at me. Preciously. And yes, that she was. That was exactly what she had always been to me. Precious.

My heart was pounding, a primal reflex of pure fear. How was I going to live without her, I asked myself again for the hundredth time that day. I wanted to berate myself for my own folly. How could I have let her leave that night? Why hadn't I stopped her?

Why? Why? Why?!!

And it wasn't like I hadn't had a strong premonition. That night as she started to leave and she stood there before me—tall, regally beautiful and so much alive—I had felt fear. The fear of losing her—except I had dismissed that fear as my cowardice for losing her to another man.

I remembered the night we had had our showdown, the night I had confronted her about Danyel. She had me so gone, I had truly lost it. Seeing those damn pictures made me go berserk. Except, even at my wildest, I would have never hurt her. How could I hurt her when I loved her so much?

My pride wouldn't let me grovel or beg, nonetheless. Much as I wanted to hold on, the last thing I wanted was to give her an inkling of how much her betrayal and infidelity had gotten to me. So I turned it all around, and made it about CJ and money. Hindsight is 20/20, though, because I was willing to beg now. I would supplicate, implore, beseech, and beg and beg and beg some more. I'd never stop begging if that was what it would take to bring her back.

I took a deep, unsteady breath.

It was still daylight, and the full luminescence of the Miami sun was glaring, blinding me as it flooded through the room. Somehow it wasn't right that it could be such a beautiful day, that the sun should shine or the world continue to spin so nonchalantly when she was no longer here. I got up to draw the drapes.

I couldn't handle the sun's intensity. I wanted darkness. Blackness. Nothingness. I drew all the curtains, obscuring the panoramic view of the city we had once enjoyed from our bedroom. Then came back to the bed to stare at her picture again, this time in the dimness. I reached out and grabbed the gilded frame, hugging it to me as I clutched the scented pillows she had slept on only days before.

I sobbed as I breathed in her scent. Then took several deeper, agonizing, calming breaths. *Christ, I could still smell her...all over the covers.* I gathered the sheets up to me and breathed them in, inhaling her fragrance, her scent, which had always been uniquely her own. No one smelled like her, and the painfully sweet scent was incredibly intense, sweet torture inflicted upon an already tormented man.

This was only the calm before the storm though, and I knew I was about to have my own emotional "perfect storm." But the pain, the pain was good. I wanted to feel the pain; I needed to feel the pain.

Pain was good...the pain felt so good. This was the only way I could purge my soul.

I rushed to her closet, feeling I could now stand to look at her stuff, all the designer clothes I had kept her outfitted in lined neatly before me. I wanted to touch the garments that had once draped her body. One by one, I started to tug and grab at her clothes, pulling them all around me, strangely comforted by the linens and silks, leather and fine wools that hung in her walk-in closet. Pilling them all to the floor, I dropped into them, snuggling deep into her familiar fragrance that still clung to the fabrics. Burrowing myself in like a wounded animal, I marveled at how her memory could hurt this much. Her death was like a gash, a wound that I knew would never heal. She would be unforgettable, impossible not to miss, and I was never going to get over her.

The tears started to seep slowly as I reflected back on our relationship, drawing on the more poignant memories. The night she agreed to become my wife. The day we got married in Vegas. The morning she had CJ at Mount Sinai. Our Vizcaya wedding. Then my mind reeled to the night I let her walk out, and yes...it had felt like goodbye. But what I couldn't acknowledge—not even now—was that it was goodbye forever. And hell, forever was such a long time, *such a fucking long time!*

I wanted to believe that even though Arielle's had ended on earth, that her spirit still lived on. I wanted to cling to that hope that someday, I might meet with her again. It would have made it much easier for me if I was inclined to believe that. Except my dad was a devout atheist and had drilled it into my head from age two that there was no God and no afterlife, and that we were responsible for our own actions and needed to live our life to the fullest here on earth. Cause there was nothing else.

Nothing...nothing...Arielle was no more.

From day one, I had been totally besotted with Arielle, and it seemed like every day that passed I grew more and more in love with her. She was the deliberate coquette, who had always gotten what she wanted. And I, the arrogant man that had had the nerve to want her, I thought feeling a big lug in my throat. Except, I was not her only victim. Danyel had been just as smitten with her as well.

My mind, dazed from the whirlwind of thoughts and flashes of all the times we had all three been in the same room. All the heated looks he used to throw her, and my thinking he was in love with her—but it was all innocent on her part. Several times, I had mentioned my suspicions to her, and she had played it off beautifully. And now, they were at the morgue. Side by side, she and her lover. Seeing her in my mind's eye zipped in a black rubber bag, with a toe tag. Seeing her frozen features and the ashen lips, *oh God! I wanted to die too!*

I understood on a rational level that people died every day, but when you're young, death is somewhat surreal. You know it happens, except it was something that happened to other people, people you didn't know. And even though death had claimed my mother when I was a fairly young age, and I had grieved and mourned her for what had seemed like interminable years. Still... until this moment, I had never before experienced the bottomless depths of despair I felt now. Would there ever be a moment or day when I wouldn't think of her? Would it always be thus, where every breath I took, every second of the day or night I'd think, *I'll never see her again! I'll never see her smile. I'll never hold her in my arms. She's lost to me. Gone forever...*

The trickle of tears that had begun soon became a flood of uncontrollable weeping, where tears cascaded like a river down my face. Giving way to great gulping, gut-wrenching sobs, I balled like a goddamned baby with my body burrowed in her clothes in a fetal position, curled in a pitiable cocoon of pure misery.

I wanted to accept reality, but was still incapable of doing so. I kept expecting her to walk in and tell me how this was only a dream. *Wake up Cedric. You're having a nightmare, and all you have to do is wake up, baby. Wake up, sugar, and you'll be just fine. See, I'm right here. Right here beside you. I'm not dead. Kiss me, lover.*

But then the image of her cold, lifeless body would come to haunt me. The ashy gray lips. The lifeless, horrible, ashen expression. It hadn't even looked like her, the corpse. It looked like a doll, an empty vessel. She was gone. And the only thing left was this vagueness. A body which looked a little like Arielle's except that raw vitality she had always emanated, what had made Arielle "Arielle" was gone and lost. Forever.

My sobs fell into the dark silence of the small room, once her walk-in closet. I couldn't stop crying. It was pitiful. My head felt like it weighed a ton and my breath stifled in my throat to the point where I started hiccupping. I hadn't cried so much since I was a kid. And I felt so stupid.

After a time, though, I closed my eyes, exhausted from crying so much. Except sleep eluded me and wouldn't come.

I would never be happy again.

Booze, music, limos, private clubs, women, drugs, nothing would ever make me happy. It was done. I would never, ever be happy again.

Not a second after that horrid thought, my cell phone rang. And all I could do was just stare at it—thinking not for the first time—what a horrible, awful, invasive instrument that ubiquitous cell phone had become. I should have followed my own advice to Deuce and turned off my own damn phone.

Christ! What had people done before the advent of cell phones? They used to fucking wait, right? Until they could get to you, but no more!

People no longer had any qualms about interrupting, irritating, invading your fucking privacy anytime they pleased. It didn't matter what you were doing. You could be sleeping, praying, showering, fucking, meditating, hell, it didn't matter what the fuck you were doing. Mother-fuckers would ring your phone for any reason, anytime they saw fit. *Even when you told them you desperately needed to be left the fuck alone!!!*

4

Round Midnight

Much later that evening, Kendra strode into the SAC's office determined to beg off the case. Oh no! She wasn't going to deal with this. There was no way! She didn't want to deal with Cedric Courage. Couldn't they assign someone else? Why her?

"Look, we don't like it any more than you do, but his dad has major connections. Apparently, he was a purple heart, major top-notch CIA agent," the SAC informed her with a stiff smile. "This guy was like the real James Bond—with the British accent. From what I'm hearing, he was so undercover, not even his kid knew about it."

"Almost like that Arnold Schwarzenegger movie, *True Lies*," Agent Neff who had been with him in the office when he stormed in threw in for good measure.

"Anyway, he's a real hero and very well respected..."

"Not to mention well-connected," Neff added.

"Thank you, Agent Neff. I can finish my own sentences," the SAC said testily, turning back to Kendra. "Spoke to the man earlier, real sharp. Very personable, even reasonable. He has no illusions about his son. Said he knows he's been giving us a hard time, but he thinks this stalker means business. He feels it in his bones, he said, and always trusts his instincts. He thinks the stalker is somehow involved in the murder of Arielle and her cousin.

Kendra's eyes rolled upward while as she gave a dire sigh. "Yeah, right...you believe that? He's his father, of course it's his duty to be loyal. Look, I—"

"Agent Jade, I don't have to tell you how major this is. This is real sensitive and I'm trusting that you're the top-notch, well-qualified agent New York said you were, and hope I can count on you to fulfill this mission. I have every confidence in your abilities to handle this assignment. Yes, he's a bit full of himself, a rebel, a loud-mouth. I know. And he's probably going to be hitting on you every second. I'd suspect that much too. But you're FBI, remember that. You're made of tougher mettle. You can handle Cedric Courage, Agent Jade. I know you can."

Kendra listened carefully to all the bullshit, feeling a sudden surge of uneasiness wash over her. She was actually quite replete after the steady spoons she had been steadily fed. She was trying real hard not to tell him where to stick it—he had no idea! But remembering FBI training, good manners, and still very grateful about her transfer, she was willing to suffer the stakes—no matter how foul they might be. If this was the price she was going to have to pay to be with her family again, so be it. So she'd have to deal with Cedric. Yes, but she definitely wouldn't like it. No matter what, though, she was going to have to find a way to make this work.

"I trust nothing is wrong and that you'll be able to handle this assignment, Agent Jade," the SAC stated in the confident tone of a man with enormous power and influence.

Kendra gulped, next nodded, not trusting herself to say anything more. It was at times like these that she wished she were a man. Yes, most definitely. As an FBI agent, in a field dominated by males, she was always getting the short end of the stick. And besides that, she hated what other people—namely men— perceived as her weakness, the fact that she *was* female. Cedric certainly would not be treating her like this if she were a *brotha* and not a *sistah*. She was sure of it. But she'd soon show him that under her gentle, feminine veneer lied a cool, seamless, practical if not ruthless heart. He'd come to respect her, she vowed, and to depend on her.

These idle thoughts flitted through her mind as she left the office parking lot once again. But by nine o'clock when nothing had panned out, she decided to wave the white flag and give up. Veronica Carrington had not been able to help her. Neither had Stan, his manager. She suspected they were being deliberately evasive. Of course they knew his address and probably knew where he was but had refused to cooperate. She had gone to the studio in South Beach. The people there had directed her to another studio he frequented in North Miami. No luck there neither. Actually, she had had to get in touch with his old man. But she was pretty pissed off when he had not been there and had yet to return any of her calls.

Where the hell was the asshole? Was he even in the country? For all she knew, he could be on a yacht off in the Caribbean somewhere sipping tropical drinks. She thought about calling his cell phone again but then thought better of it, afraid she would lose it completely if she heard his silky, arrogant voice telling her in his mild manner to go to hell. So instead, she called Neff, who agreed that she should give up the search and go home. After all, she hadn't even gotten a chance to go to her parents yet, where she'd be staying 'til she could find her own place. Even though she had talked to them at length over the phone between chasing Cedric, she had yet to see them in person.

The crisp April breeze whipped through the open windows of her Range Rover as it skimmed down the road headed south on I95. Kendra could feel the vibrancy of the city as it came alive and had always appreciated the color and edginess of the he Miami skyline at night, an array of laser and neon light. And so she focused on the sights to clear her thoughts, happy once again and grateful as hell to finally be back home. Getting off on US1, she made her way to Ponce De Leon Boulevard, heading towards her parent's Coral Gable home.

Although she had to admit she felt a bit defeated and more than a little furious that she hadn't caught up with Cedric. She was a perfectionist and normally tenacious as hell. She hated giving up. Loathed the sick feeling of failure she felt having to do it, but what could she do? She certainly was not going to let him or this case start driving her crazy. It was too soon for that, no nervous-breakdowns on the first day. Beside, she was a lot more competent than that.

Still, she couldn't help calling him just one last time. She felt compelled to do so but knew better as her fingers pressed the redial button. She simply had to throw in a final plea before driving through her parent's carport. Cause once there, she was not about to leave—for anything in the world! Cedric Courage be damned!

"Cedric, please. It's Kendra. Kendra Jade, the agent. Would you please return my call?"

Damn, she had lowered herself to begging but the thought of anything happening to his obnoxious ass on her watch gave her the creeps! But hey, if he didn't call, his problem...

Turning her thoughts now back to her family, she soothed her ruffled feathers satisfied she had finally returned back to her beloved Miami, back into the bosom of her family, all of whom she had missed so much. Affectionately, she thought about her older sister, Sophy, whom she was going to be able to hang out with again; her brother, Jason, who was also in law enforcement, he was with the Florida Highway Patrol. Not to mention the fact that she would get to know her niece and nephew, Sophy's kids, and get to spend time with her wonderful parents. Yes, it would be great to be back in the fold.

Cruising down Ponce de Leon, she navigated the RV through the deserted streets, happy she no longer had to deal with the endless flow of traffic and pedestrians of Manhattan. A small smile touched her lips as she noticed a lone pair of lovers cuddled close, trying to stay warm in the jasmine scented breeze mixed with sea salt that reminded her so of Miami. Just then her cell phone rang.

Her eyes darted immediately to the number on the caller ID, but it read "private."

"Hello," she answered.

His now familiar, smooth voice came on, "Yo." Mixed with the relief of him finally calling was also irritation. His tone irritated her, grated on her nerves. His whole attitude and demeanor did. Like she was supposed to know who he was. Like he didn't need to identify himself. Now she understood why the detective at the station had been reading him the riot act when they had first entered the interrogation room. Cedric could be infuriating.

"All right. Let's get something straight right the fuck now," she said forcefully. "I don't give a damn who you are. I'm here to do my job—so don't BULLSHIT me!"

"Just who the fuck *you* think you're talking to?!"

"Cedric Courage. Cedric fucking Courage! Yes, I know who you are. All of the free world does. But I don't give a damn! Understand? You want to tell me where you are?"

"Nope!"

"Fuck you too," she said and clicked off. This time she had hung up on *him*. She started to laugh then when the realization hit her of just how childish and immature—not to mention how unprofessional that was. Great day! What was going on with her? She had never behaved so inappropriately on all her days on the force. And she had had some trying days. But in just one day (afternoon really) Cedric Courage had her in this tirade. *You are not going to get the better of me*, she longed to tell him, but let it go. Forget it, he wasn't even worth it.

Only heaven knew, she thought and laughed again, why she was behaving so. But she also felt much better all of the sudden that she had in fact told his ass off. She still couldn't believe she had done it, but she was glad she did.

***

The foyer was dim. It was late, way past midnight as Veronica made her way through the dark halls of Cedric's William Island penthouse. Finally, she had gotten a call back from Cedric who had asked that she come over. Deuce let her in and told her she could find him in rec room.

He had to still be reeling from the news. She had been trying to get a hold of him all day, but had been unable to get through. Finally he had answered her call after leaving her to cool her heels in a hotel room, watching the news and stressing out over this without a single word. She felt furious, but she was trying to understand what he must be feeling. But hell, she might as well had stayed in New York!

Assuredly, she had been in constant contact with her office that had been bombarded by phone calls, email and telexes from everywhere. Shit, she really should have stayed in New York to handle this crisis, but had also wanted to be here for him, to be nearby in case he needed her. And he had to be needing her, his family and friends now. God, Cedric needed everyone surrounding and supporting him right now. That was why she couldn't understand where everyone was. Why was Cedric alone tonight of all nights? Where was everybody?

"Cedric," she called out as she made her way down the long, stretching hallway to the rec room. The lights were dim in the foyer, as well as in the hallway and she couldn't help the spooked feeling of uneasiness that enveloped her. She felt eerie, uneasy. Where was he? "Cedric," she called out again.

The rec room was dim also, as she made her way through its French doors. From the corner of her eyes, she saw a movement and breathed a sigh of relief as she saw the mass of thick, blond locks and the dark figure sitting at the bar. He was dressed in his usual black—except it was more appropriate on this night—sitting on a barstool nursing a drink. She approached him from behind. He had still not answered, nor had he turned around. Sauntering over to him, she came up behind him and placed her head on the back of his shoulders. He pulled away abruptly, nearly causing her to fall as she struggled to maintain her balance. He turned around and glared at her belligerently.

"Cedric," she said again, not knowing what else to say. How to react. What could she say? "I'm so sorry..." she started.

"Are you?"

She bit her lips, knowing she could not lie convincingly. No, she wasn't sorry. Not at all! Not for her. But she did feel very badly for him. "Cedric, I don't know what to say."

"Then perhaps it's best not to say anything at all."

He sounded so bitter. His normally chocolate for the ears voice was raw with emotion. She had never heard him so...so...she didn't even know how to describe it. "I don't blame you if you're angry. I understand."

"Do you? Well, I'm glad I have your blessing."

"Cedric, please don't."

"Don't what?" He goaded.

"Please don't shut me out."

"Is that what I'm doing?"

"I want to be here for you," she said sounding a little desperate—even to her own ears. But she felt so dreadfully bad for him. She knew firsthand how much he had loved that harlot. If only she could erase the sadness, the misery that was so very evident in his voice and face. Tonight he looked so much older than his 28 years. This was a nasty business, this dying thing. How did you comfort, what did you say to someone who was obviously in so much pain?

"Well, you're here, aren't you," he was saying now. "Do you see anyone else here?"

"Probably because you wouldn't let anyone else up."

"Well then, that must say a lot about you," he said coolly, his gaze remaining fixed on her, unnerving her. Even though his voice carried a touch of irony, his expression was totally serious. He was wearing thin wire-framed reading glasses, which emphasized the slight obliqueness of his Oriental-cast eyes and the elegance of his dark, expressive brows were so striking. With admiration, her gaze swept over his skin, golden from Miami living, blending so well with the high desert color of his long, roped dreads.

They were quiet for several long seconds, both assessing the other—her feeling totally unnerved by his appraisal. His thoughts closed to her, she had no idea what he could be thinking.

"Why did you agree to see me? Just me?" She asked intent on breaking the ice.

His brow arched high over his expressive eyes. "Now that's getting right to the point, isn't it?"

She shrugged. "You brought it up."

"Why do you think?" His mouth quirked into a chilly smile.

Veronica stood there, not knowing what to do or say. Cedric was making her feel sooooo uncomfortable and she didn't want to say the wrong thing, make the wrong move. Basically she was at a loss, uncharacteristic for her. "I don't know why, Cedric. That's why I'm asking you."

"Well, then I think you'd better leave," he said simply, lifting his lowball glass and taking a gulp.

Veronica couldn't move, standing rooted to the spot, standing so close, almost between his parted thighs. She wished so much she could move a few steps and embrace him, comfort him, but she knew he would misconstrue her actions for lust or pity and hate her for it, whichever way. So she stood her ground, ignoring her instincts. The last thing she wanted to do was alienate him.

"Didn't you hear me? I asked you to leave and now I'm telling you to," he said more forcibly.

"No," she said steadily, trying hard to leave out all the emotion she was feeling.

"Excuse me?"

"I'm not leaving!" She uttered with false bravado, standing her ground.

With lightning speed, his hands shot out and caught the scarf at her waist and hauled her against him really hard. The impact drove the breath out of her. Then just as quickly, he twisted the scarf around his fist, roughly grinding his hand against her stomach, while his thighs gripped either side of her hips. His jaw was rigid and tight, and his mouth was hard and set. "Don't play games. You know why you're here." For several seconds he stared intently into her eyes unflinchingly and then he closed his eyes, swearing fiercely as he expelled a breath. "Bitch," he whispered silkily, as if it were an endearment.

Veronica's blood was on fire, as she stared longingly at him, her heart beating wildly. Was he being serious? "Cedric, look...I-I, I don't know what to say. How to help you...

"I'm sorry, Veronica. I'm sorry," he sighed deeply and then laid his head against her breasts. "Yes, I'm angry. I'm angry as fucking hell, but not at you." Veronica tried to hush him by putting two fingers over his lips. He kissed the tips, then brushed them aside. "I'm angry at her! And him! Not you. But there's nothing I can do. There's no way I can get them back," he whimpered. "They're dead! She's dead! Hell, she's gone, Vee! And there's no way to release this rage inside me..."

Veronica raised her arms and cupped his face, removed the glasses and then wiped away his tears. He groaned softly and let go of the scarf belt, wrapping his arms around her waist instead.

Then snaking them up her back, he pulled her to him, holding her real close.

"Cedric, I'm here for you. Any way you want me. I'm right here, my darling. Right here," she murmured softly.

She was hoping that Cedric would kiss her, but when he made no move to do so, but turned his head, snuggling his face into the crook of her neck, she relaxed a bit. Apparently, all he wanted was some comforting, and she was prepared to comfort him in whatever way she could. He was holding her so tightly, quite desperately, and yes, the fact that she was the only one he let near him tonight spoke volumes. Maybe she was starting to mean something to him again. Maybe now that Arielle was gone, she would once again hold her rightful place.

That bitch. That incalculable bitch had hurt Cedric so much. That filthy slut! That low-down disgusting whore! She had always despised her. Never liked her! Maybe instinctively she had known she was no good for him. She had seen right through her. Yes, she may have snowed everyone else, but not Veronica. She was too smart, too good of a judge of character for that. Too bad she hadn't been able to convince Cedric how awful she was for him. Oh, and he was so right—had every right to be angry with her. And yes, she'd help him find a way to release all the anger that was raging inside him. She wished to God there was some way to make that bitch pay. Paying with her life really wasn't enough.

As she held Cedric in her arms, she noticed how there were books and journals everywhere, spread out across the bar on the coffee table and couch and overstuffed chairs. What had he been doing? Reading himself to death? She noted too, how this was all *her* stuff. Her books, her journals. She pushed his head back then, tucked a lock of his hair behind his ear, moved her fingers slowly across his jawbone, across the plane of his beautiful face. She adored his eyes, slightly Oriental, tilted marginally with dark, sweeping long lashes. But more than the eyes, she adored the man.

"I'm here for you, Cedric," she ventured again. "Nothing you want, nothing you ask of me will be denied. Please remember that. I'm at your complete disposal. At your beck and call. Nothing's too big or too small," she reminded him. She wished she could add that he was her heart and soul, but she wouldn't push it. Despite everything, she knew that Cedric really loved Arielle, and that he'd need time to grieve. But she really meant it. She'd be there for him, however he wanted. And maybe with time, she could make him forget Arielle. He had loved her once, maybe he would learn to love her again.

***

She felt so warm. So incredibly warm. And he felt so cold. Too cold. She was like a hot latte on a cold winter's day. So good and warm. She was just what he needed right now—exactly what he needed.

Holding her tightly in his arms, he needed what she was willing to give him. Needed to give of himself. That or go crazy. He needed that vibrancy, that energy to surge from her to him. He needed to feel. To feel something, anything, because right now all he could feel was the numbness, threatening to imprison his soul.

He continued holding her, feeling the warmth seep out of her and into his chest and arms. And before long, he realized only the comfort of her body would appease him. He needed relief, a physical relief that only sex would bring.

She clung to him so sweetly and smelled so good. Too good! Taking several, deep, painful breaths, he buried his face between her breasts, relishing her perfumed, musky scent. Pressing his lips to her soft, smooth flesh, he could feel her shudder her surrender as her hands swept up to his head, her fingers burying into his mass of soft, wooly dreadlocks. Trailing his mouth up to her collarbone to nuzzle gently on her ear, she hugged him even tighter.

Caressing the curve of her hips, he gripped her ass in his palms, kneading it, remembering how this woman used to like to keep him on his toes. Oh yes, she had liked him always off-balance, out of focus. And for awhile, that had been all right. He had traded that for all the excitement he felt when she would let him in, allow him to feel the texture of her skin and kiss the blonde ringlets nestled between her pale, creamy thighs.

Yes, he remembered her by taste, by smell, by touch. He longed now for her intimate touch, relishing the memory of how her mouth would curl around his shaft, how she used to suck him like she needed his cum for sustenance, and swallow all his juice, making him forget everything.

His drowsy eyes rose to meet hers briefly, but he quickly broke contact—feeling too exposed. Her eyes were an astounding shade of blue, and her skin the color of pale cream with a sprinkling of freckles across her nose and shoulders. She was beautiful, like the sun after a long, dark storm. And he really needed her to save him now. He didn't want her pity, but he did want her comfort. He wanted the temporary forgetfulness making love to her would bring.

"I want you," he murmured, breathing in her fragrant, expensive perfume, letting his senses delight in the feel, sight and smell of her. Feeling his body warm up and come alive, he was aroused and knew if she was unwilling, he would have to beg her for it. He needed the comfort of her body that badly. He needed to feel...something...anything! Whatever it would take to soothe the numbness, to warm his soul, so he could stop feeling so damn cold!

He brushed his lips with hers, but couldn't bring himself to fully kiss her. He wanted to, but resisted. It had been so long since he had kissed anyone else, or touched anyone else. He felt odd, but he let the feeling slip away. He would kiss her, but that would come later. Much later. After he had been soothed, comforted...yes, perhaps he'd kiss her then.

He got up and brushed past her, grabbing her hand briefly then let go and left the room, walking up the steps past the sitting room, into to the bedroom. For several seconds, Veronica stood there perhaps not knowing exactly what to do, but then she got the message and started to follow him up. Going up the steps and walking slowly into the bedroom behind him, carefully stepping inside, she stood at the threshold of the door, looking uncertain. Although she had been over to the penthouse countless of times, she had never been inside this bedroom. The master suite. His and Arielle's room, once upon a time.

Cedric tried not to think of how this was really *her* room. A room *she* had decorated personally. A room *she* had been in only days ago. A room *she* had spent a great deal of time in. And yes, the room where he had made love to her not more than a week ago. Yes, making love to Veronica here would be totally desecrating to her memory.

Good.

He planned on having as much booty here as possible. Right on the very bed they had shared. A bed he was sure she had shared countless of times with *him*—her cousin-lover! He shook himself, not wanting to think how many times they had gone for broke here, in his absence. He shuddered to imagine, but decided then not to think on these things, concentrating on Veronica instead. His beautiful blonde publicist who was standing there looking so gorgeous, luscious and fine. He took her hand again, and led her to the bed. He sat down, letting her stand in front of him, in between his legs and then stared up at her, smiling. He sought the colorful scarf tied around her waist, catching it between his fingers and tugged on it, and made it come undone. Slowly, he unbuttoned her silk blouse, moving with deliberate slowness, inserting his hands underneath the small lapels, easing it down her back. Kissing her flat stomach, he popped open the fly of her pants, unzipped them then pushed them down her hips, peeling them off her. Once clad only in her lacy Victoria Secret style underwear, he let his eyes roam all over her, skimming the creamy flesh of her breasts, the flatness of her stomach, the sheer perfection of her pretty, shapely legs before bringing her down to him. A small sob tore her throat.

And that was when he noticed the tears and saw her distress. Pain knifed through his heart as he clutched her to his chest. "You don't have to do this," he told her hoarsely.

"I want to," she said fiercely. "Make love to me, Cedric. Oh, God, I've missed you so much!" She gushed, holding on to him just as tightly.

Cedric closed his eyes and took a long, deep, shuddering breath, feeling a temporary bout of sublime contentment, feeling relieved that she wanted him just as much as he wanted her. He explored her by touch, like a blind man who could only see by touch, remembering every curve of her well-formed body—the slenderness of her back, the slimness of her waist and soft fullness of her ass and breasts. He cupped the mounds of her hips gently, squeezing, pressing, arousing both her and himself to a frenzy.

"Cedric, Cedric," she said breathlessly. "Kiss me. Please," she begged prettily. "Kiss me, my darling. I want your tongue. I've missed that ring on your tongue and your cock. Oh, God, how I've missed you!"

Cedric grew more erect by her deliberately chosen words but didn't do as she asked, but instead coiled his fingers around her silky, straight almost white blonde hair, tugging her head back gently, kissing her throat and neck roughly, thoroughly, making her crazy when he bit down on her shoulders. Her hips were undulating, caressing his hardening groin, while her breasts bobbed up and down, caressing his chest. Her normally clear, cornflower blue eyes were dark and smoky now as she moaned with pleasure, *"Oh, Cedric!"*

She arched against his hardness, continuing to bounce up and down above him, writhing upon him in a sexual frenzy. Cedric undid his pants, bringing her hands to him, silently instructing her to touch him as he continued planting hot and moist little kisses on her throat and chest and peeled off first her bra, then her panties.

Now naked, Veronica moved over him and straddled him again, opening her body up as she slowly and steadily sat back on him, taking him in an inch at a time. Once impaled and buried to the hilt, she started to ride him—gently at first—but quickly went buck, riding him mercilessly. Just the way he liked it. Like a jockey trying to win a race.

Cedric's hands glided up and down her back and hips, then cupped her breasts, his fingers kneading her nipples. Then replacing his fingers with his ringed tongue, he started kissing and nuzzling her breasts, tracing the pattern on the very swollen nipple of her small left breast until she was nearly delirious.

Her moans and sobs and screams fell on deaf ears as the pounding of his own heart obliterated everything else. She arched her back in splendid rapture at the same time giving him greater access to the inner core of her body, slamming down hard, riding him at a fast clip. She was whimpering and clutching his hair, emitting desperate little cries of pleasure until he fell back, grabbed her by the hips and started thrusting up deep inside her. She let out a sharp, loud wail as she started to come. Cedric let her ride it out but then quickly took her down, rolling her over on her back. Levering himself above her, he pulled nearly all the way out of her before he violently slammed into her over and over, savagely, bringing her ever closer to her peak again and again— but not allowing her to, changing the pace on her, teasing her unmercifully, wanting her to work for her orgasm until his whole body started to strain for relief.

He closed his eyes and for a fast second, Arielle's face flashed before him, the way she looked right before she climaxed. Groaning, he almost cried out her name. Almost. He kissed Veronica's lips now and tasted his name on her lips as she groaned his name as if in terrible pain. Filling her completely now with tongue and cock, he let go and filled Veronica with sperm as her warm, velvety softness surrounded him, comforting him in a sublime caress.

Soon after though, instead of the euphoria that usually followed sex, Cedric was suddenly panicked. Shit, in all his distress, he had forgotten all about using a condom—and apparently so had Veronica, who was usually very sensible about these things. He collapsed on top of her, into her welcoming arms, sated and spent, but felt total distress. She was still shuddering, holding him, and staring up at him with so much tenderness.

Maybe he shouldn't bring it up—the condom thing. But next she said something that totally floored him.

"I love you, Cedric."

He tried not to react, but his body of its own volition recoiled, and he couldn't get away from her fast enough. Abruptly, he moved off her, rolling away from her. Those words were like anathema.

"You shouldn't," he said simply, fighting to overcome his repulsion.

Veronica, still trembling, moved back into his arms. Snuggling up against him, she laid her mass of silky hair across his chest. "But I do, Cedric. I do."

"Love is an emotion and emotions aren't real. They're only make-believe," he snapped.

***

She visibly flinched as he recited something she had told him numerous times. Too many times! Though she had once believed this wholeheartedly, it was hard hearing him repeat this philosophy to her now. *Give me something I can hold in my hands. Something I can touch. Can you touch love? Can you see love? No. It's not real, I tell you. It's something people imagine and make themselves believe so they won't have to feel so alone. But it's only an illusion. Nothing but a fantasy.* How many times she had given him that speech? That lecture. Now it had come back to haunt her. To bite her in the ass! Of course he had the incentive now to throw it back in her face.

If you reap the wind, she knew the saying.

But God, how she wished she could take everything that had happened in their relationship back! How she longed for time to turn back...

"Cedric, I was wrong. And I was cruel too. I realize that now."

"No, you were right," Cedric replied unenthusiastically—like he had to force himself to speak to her now. "You were absolutely right. The heart is a muscle—only a fucking muscle that pumps blood into our bloodstream. Love isn't real. Feelings are bogus, pure bullshit and you can't trust them!"

***

Tears welled up in her eyes and started rolling down her face and Cedric could feel them soaking his shirt. He was still dressed, he realized then. Raising himself up, he gently untangled her out of his arms, stood up and pulled his trousers back up. Zipping his fly, he excused himself. Even though he knew she was still crying, he couldn't hold her. He couldn't find it in his heart to comfort her. Now that he had fucked her and gotten what he wanted, he only wanted peace and quiet. He didn't feel much like talking and it looked like Veronica was going to run her mouth all night if he let her.

Hell, he needed to get of there! After all, he was the one who needed comforting. He was the one who was fucking hurting. What was she crying about?! Although he never thought he'd ever see the day he could make Veronica cry, tough as she was. But he couldn't deal with that nonsense now, and he couldn't be so rude as to ask her to leave. Not after what they had done. His best course of action would be to go back to the rec room, perhaps then, she'd get the message.

Once there, he poured himself a shot of Scotch whiskey, went to his safe beneath the false wall, cracked it open and took out his stash. Deuce had done good and hid his stuff well. All of his shit was still there, undisturbed—his pot, his revolver, everything was still there. Yeah, *fuck them*, he mused silently, rolling up a nice, fat blunt as he contemplated how he didn't like cops. *Hated them actually.* And his attitude had deep roots and did not just stem from the notion that cops didn't like rap stars or that most Black men had to spend a lifetime dodging them, outrunning them or generally just being hassled by them. But more than that, his problem was that he had a problem with authority, period. He didn't like being told what to do. He couldn't stand being in any situation he couldn't control. And he hated how cocky any asshole with a badge and gun could get. Like it was their God-given right to tell people what to do.

His gorge was up as he took a deep drag off his joint and leaned back into the leather sectional. He searched for his remote and turned on his sound system. God, it seemed as if he hadn't had one of these in a long, long time, but tonight he needed it. Veronica had provided temporary comfort but now he needed something a bit more lasting. He took several more deep drags and got more comfortable, sinking into the overstuffed leather couch and closed his eyes until the feeling of *no worries* came over him, listening to sweet soothing sounds of Sade. Yes, Sade could lull him to sleep anytime. He closed his eyes, as a peaceful smile formed on his face.

***

The doorbell rung rousing him. Had he fallen asleep? It didn't seem like it. Had his eyes finally closed? He couldn't be sure, but he felt like shit now. That was when he noticed he was still sprawled out on the leather couch and still in the rec room. Shit! He wondered if Veronica was still there in the master bedroom. *Their*...that was the operative word. God, he was still thinking about *her and him being a them*. To him it was still her room too. And yes, last night he had made love to another woman on their bed, but this morning he wasn't feeling too proud of that.

The doorbell rung again. Fucking hell, who could that be this early in the morning coming over unannounced?! And where the hell was Deuce, he thought crossly as he sunk even deeper into the buttery leather couch. Probably still sleeping. This visitor was the one who should be tarred and feathered. Who the hell came to someone's place before eight in the morning? He had a good mind not to answer. Maybe whoever it was would just get the message and go away. His mind turned to the million and one details and things he had to do today. He was hoping that Veronica *was* still here because honestly, he did need her help.

The person at the door persisted on ringing the doorbell. Soon Veronica emerged from the bedroom and peeked through the archway. She was in a robe—in one of Arielle's skimpy Victoria's Secret silk robes.

He let his eyes roam over her, and didn't hide his displeasure, fixing her with a quelling look. He had a good mind to tell her: *Bitch, you done lost your mind!*

"I hope you don't mind," she had the nerve to say next.

"I do."

"Fine," she said shrugging the robe off and now stood there in all her naked glory.

Cedric sucked his teeth at the trifling gesture. "Oh, just keep it on," he snapped.

"Aren't you going to answer that?" She motioned towards the door.

The doorbell continued to ring steadily.

"No."

"Don't you even want to know who it is?"

"Not really. Nobody I want to know, I'm sure. But what I want to know is why nobody's called from the guard gate downstairs. That's strange!"

"Maybe it's the police."

Cedric shrugged. Not wanting to even think about the fiasco he went through yesterday. It better not be the police! It was fucking harassment if it was.

"In any case, the person is not going away," Veronica pointed out, "so I think you'd better answer that."

Cedric groaned and stood up reluctantly. "You'd better get dressed." Picking up his cell phone, he speed-dialed Deuce, who had to be up by now with all that knocking, ringing, and ruckus. "Who's at the door?"

"Some bitch claiming to be FBI."

Cedric blanched. It must be Special Agent Jade come to pester him again. He supposed putting up with her shit yesterday hadn't been enough. There was more to come. "Let her in," he said decisively.

"You sure, man?"

"Yep."

Cedric was scowling at her as she took a tentative step through the threshold. There she was once again, glaring her disapproval of him. "Bright and shine, there's lots of work to do," she told him, looking all professional in a navy pinstripe suit, reminding him of Arielle who had a Chanel suit very similar to it. In fact, physically Kendra Jade reminded him of Arielle period. They were both tall and statuesque. But their style and mannerism were very dissimilar. Ms. Jade was all polished and very professional. You could tell she was a by the book, no-nonsense type of person. He doubted she'd ever flirt—not on the job anyway. She'd be strictly business—always. She was still wearing her hair pulled back and those atrocious glasses, downplaying her beauty—although unless you were blind—you could still tell she was quite a looker. Whereas Arielle never made any bones about her beauty, going all out to dazzle you! And maybe it was personality too. Kendra Jade didn't seem to have one.

"I hope that work doesn't involve my having to do anything," Cedric informed her.

"Oh, it might. I just have some questions I came up with last night, and there are some things you could get me that might help me out. I know the place was searched yesterday by the police, but I may have to do a search again."

"Whatever for?"

"Well, yesterday, the police searched for evidence. Items that would serve to indict you. But what I'm looking for are any clues that might exonerate you, which at that same time may give us some insight into this person who's threatening you. My hunch is that this is the same person who killed your wife."

***

He was staring at her. She could feel his invisible appraisal again. Intense. Disapproving. She could see the dark circles around his eyes, the harrowed tautness of his skin. She bothered him, she knew he definitely didn't like her.

"How could you possibly know that," he asked sharply.

"I said that it was a hunch. Not that I know it for a fact."

"Lady, I don't care what the hell you said. Just don't bullshit me! Okay?"

"Look, Mr. Courage..."

"Look, nothing. For all you know, I killed my wife. You don't know a goddamn thing about me, my wife, or anything, understand. So don't come in here like you know shit. You'd better come correct."

Kendra stood there, her eyes flicking over him, speechless. She didn't know how to respond or how to react. *Was he serious? Joking?* She couldn't be sure. "Mr. Courage, did you kill your wife?"

"If I did, I certainly wouldn't be confessing to your sorry ass."

She was immediately furious. "Look!"

"No, you look! Don't ever come to my place again without calling first. Got that?!"

Just then Veronica came waltzing down the steps interrupting the verbal attack they were exacting one each other. Thankfully, she was dressed. She approached them, sizing Kendra up with her eyes. "Hi, I'm Veronica Carrington, Cedric's publicist. Can I get you some coffee, orange juice, anything to drink?"

Kendra stared from Cedric to Veronica for several seconds, assessing the situation. Then she responded somewhat stiffly, "Ah, yes. We spoke yesterday. No, thank you on the drink. I'm Special Agent Jade, pleased to meet you."

Veronica took the hand she offered and gave her a limp handshake, still looking over her as if she were measuring every inch of her, counting her pulse, devouring her brains. "Sorry, I couldn't help you yesterday, but I didn't find him till much later," she said cryptically.

Apparently so, Kendra thought with derision. Although that didn't explain why she hadn't called her as soon as she *did* find him—she supposed there were other more important things they needed to do.

"So you've been assigned the case?" Veronica went on curiously, coming to stand next to Cedric, hooking an arm possessively around his waist.

Kendra looked from one to another again. "I'm sorry," she said tilting her head and affecting her voice in a condescending manner. "You're his publicist, right?"

"Yes," Veronica answered, not understanding Kendra's attitude or perplexity.

"Then you must know how badly this looks."

"Excuse me," Veronica said a bit ruffled, trying to distance herself from Kendra's measuring gaze, trying to look away.

Kendra went on nonplussed. "You two being here together, alone, this early in the morning. Well, I don't need to tell you, the spin the press could put on this. Or Miami PD. You realize that the world is watching very closely. Cedric has to be really careful about the messages he's sending out. And this, I'm afraid, even to me, does not look very good."

Though she had not been talking to Cedric, she was very surprised when she heard an "Oh, no! I know you're not gonna go there," he lashed out suddenly, wild and explosive. "Don't tell me you're going to start dictating to me how I live my life too!"

"Look, I've been assigned to protect you, Mr. Courage. To find out who's sending you those death threats, who's trying to kill you. Now I figure, since you're also in this big legal bind, that I'd use some of my expertise and try and help clear you of any wrongdoing as well. But if you don't want my help...if you want me to butt out...all you have to do is say so."

"Butt the fuck out," Cedric raged.

"Have there been charges," Veronica said throwing Cedric a quelling look, then looked at Kendra with genuine concern. "Do you think they've found enough evidence to charge him?"

"Not as of yet, but they're working on it, I assure you. And if I don't develop any other viable leads real soon, they're going to charge Cedric. That's how the police work. They have their suspect and they go for it. Find whatever will stick, and right now, Cedric is their number one suspect."

"Okay, so what do you need us to do," Veronica asked earnestly.

"Well, for one thing, lay off each other for while. Lay low.

Cedric's wife was just murdered. There hasn't even been a funeral. So try not to be with him just as of yet, if at all possible. Propriety is very important right now.

"Okay, we understand," Veronica said nodding. "I agree wholeheartedly."

Kendra looked at Cedric who was standing there still sulking. "Is that fine with you, Cedric?"

He shrugged, starting to stroll away. "I suppose so. Why don't I let you two figure it all out. You seem to be doing such a great job, planning out my life. Don't mind me. Carry on, continue. Veronica should be able to get you whatever you need."

Veronica flashed him a look, "Now Cedric, you know I have no idea where your wife's things are."

"Anything to get away from me, right, Mr. Courage? Do I offend your sensibilities that much?!"

***

Actually, you do, he thought solemnly. *You remind me of my wife a little too much,* but he didn't dare tell her that. Instead he resorted to browbeating her again. "No offense, Agent Jade, but my body and mind don't quite function until after two o'clock in the afternoon. I'm a fucking musician, remember? And, it really would have been polite of you to have called first, you know what I'm sayin'."

"But you were expecting me. Remember our conversation last night?"

"Nah, I don't remember a goddamn thing about last night except you cursing my ass out—for no good reason—then hanging up in my face! That's the only thing I remember."

She looked at him piteously. "You're trying to break my chops," she said with a dry chuckle. "Is that it? You have to be the bad-ass. I get that. Cedric's big and bad. Cedric's laaarge! Okay, Mr. Courage, I got it. But what I'd like more than anything else is to start over again. I know that things...things have not gone as smoothly as they should. And I realize that we don't have to like each other, but let's at least be civil."

Cedric smiled slightly with amusement now glittering in his eyes. "You think we could do that?"

"What?"

"Start over."

"Where there's a will..."

"There's a way," he finished for her, genuinely smiling now. "Okay. So where do we start, Agent Jade?"

She looked at him for a moment before answering. "Well, we can start on friendlier terms. Please call me Kendra."

"Only if you'll call me Cedric."

She smiled. And Veronica looked on baffled by what was taking place. "Could we get down to business," she interjected. "Friendship is overrated. What we need is some professionalism here," she said looking pointedly at Kendra in a she-wolf, standoffish manner that told her in no uncertain terms that Cedric was hers.

Kendra quickly recovered and said, "Well, I need to look at your wife's personal stuff. Did she have a journal? Photo album? Keepsake book or things of that nature?"

He shrugged and headed for the kitchen, allowing Veronica to field Agent Jade's questions. Taking some sliced bread and popping them in the toaster, he tried to have some toast not remembering the last time he had had a bite to eat. But he couldn't hold it down. For the past 48 hours, he had been living on the sugar from his Scotch. And even now, the sight of food made his stomach queasy.

Last night, he hadn't slept a wink. Didn't even come close to closing his eyes because all he could see every time he did was that serene, sleeping Arielle. The one at the morgue.

He left the kitchen and went to the bar in the rec room and fixed a drink and overheard Kendra and Veronica discussing what would be said in the formal statement.

"Yes, yes, we'll have to make one soon," Veronica was saying.

"Choose your words carefully," Kendra warned.

"Why, of course. Of course. Still, I know the tabloids are gonna have a field day."

"Well, it'll be your job to squash it as much as possible. Do whatever you can. I don't have to tell you that these days trials are almost determined by public opinion."

"Yes, yes," Veronica said absently, excused herself and next followed him into the rec room. "Are you sure you want to do that. It's only eight in the morning."

"And..."

"And perhaps you should have a bite to eat first."

"I guess you didn't see me gag on the toast in the kitchen? Anyway, what are you now? My mother?"

"Hardly. Just making an observation."

"Point well taken. But please, mind your own business."

"I'll try."

Ignoring her stare, which was boring through his back, he continued fixing his drink. Sneaking a peak at the mirrors on the bar, he noted how his eyes were red rimmed. He hadn't shaven and had a thick shadow and looked unkempt and disheveled. He ran an unsteady hand through his hair. Man, his father, CJ and Miss Penny would probably be here shortly. He had to make himself presentable. Yet he couldn't find the energy.

He took a sip of the scotch. Closed his eyes as the liquid burned down his throat. He closed his eyes and leaned weakly against the bar. He could feel Veronica's eyes still on him and knew he was causing her undue worry. Except it couldn't be helped.

The worst part was, he knew his response to all this was still at the larval stage. He was just warming up. Just getting started. He had somehow managed to isolate his grief. To freeze it back a little. But he could feel it fermenting. Oh, it was coming. And he wouldn't be able to hold it in for much longer.

Even now, with her here watching over him—or with that agent snooping around in the living room, he was trying hard to control himself. He knew he wouldn't be able to fight his urges forever, though. Sooner or later, they would boil over.

He took out a pill from his pocket, and popped it in his mouth, before Veronica could see. He'd need Valium to take the edge off if he was going to be dealing with this funeral bullshit and not to mention, his father and everyone else today.

***

Kendra was relentless in her search. Cedric watched her nearly an hour going through the house, collecting things. She was very through. Very meticulous, probably very good at her job. In the end, she had a box of things she set on the dining room table and starting to go through, listing them on her notepad, constantly talking into this small tape recorder as she conducted her investigation of Arielle's things.

After being sure Agent Jade was comfortable and had all that she needed, Cedric went for a shower, taking an extra long one. Veronica had gone back to her hotel to change but promised she'd return ASAP. Meanwhile, the phone was ringing off the hook. Deuce and Rico were on phone detail, awaiting the arrival of Quentin and Joe. He knew there were a zillion details he had to attend to, but he couldn't do any of it right now. He was hoping everyone would be prepared to roll up their sleeves and really help, because he wasn't sure where to even start.

Shortly after he was dressed, his dad, Miss Penny and Margo carrying CJ came waltzing in and he had never been so happy to see them in all his life.

Miss Penny was the first to take him in her delicate arms. "Oh, Cedric! Oh, my darling! I'm so desperately sorry. So sorry..." Her voice trailing off.

Cedric hugged her fiercely. Then his father. Even Margo. But when he took CJ, whose face lit up like morning sunshine, he could barely breathe. He kissed him hard on the forehead and then gathered him up between his arms, hugging him so tightly. Tears brimmed his eyes as he hugged his beautiful little boy, whom he hadn't seen in days.

"Dad-dy," CJ gurgled as he ruffled his hair. Soon he'd be asking for mommy. Cedric took a deep breath, wondering how he was going to handle things with his son. Of course, he was too young to understand, but he was bound to notice that mommy was no longer around. A lump had formed in his throat as he looked down at his happy little toddler, who was dressed in his Tommy gear. He didn't want to even think about CJ having to live without her. He had to gulp really hard, and really suppress himself not to break down right then and there in front of everybody. CJ was their legacy, the only part of Arielle he had left.

Kendra hearing the commotion stopped what she was doing and came into the foyer. He watched as Kendra introduced herself. Soon after, his family took over, answering the phone, making all the arrangements he hadn't been able to make. Veronica came back and started helping out too. Together, they found some writing paper and started making lists, writing obituary notices, making endless phone calls. They had to find a good funeral home, make decisions on the casket, decide on whether to get a plot or mausoleum. There were also the programs, invitations, the viewing, where, when, what time? Not to mention flowers, musicians, caterers, and a host of other details that needed tending to.

Soon the penthouse was bulging with people, his entourage, his band members and a number of his other friends who stayed till the wee hours of the morning. His dad had hired a caterer who he was paying to stay around the clock to help his personal chef. He told Cedric it would be like this for a few days until the actual funeral. In a way, all the flurry of activity was good, in that it helped to keep his mind off the inner turmoil cresting and gathering momentum deep in his belly.

Cedric wasn't sure how to feel when he saw Bailey, who had become the brother he had never had. Upon seeing him, Cedric hugged him affectionately—real fierce—the way he wished he could hug Arielle. It was only because of him he was even able to speak to grandmère, who he knew was more than devastated over this. This had to be such a hard blow, especially for her, who had been extremely close to Arielle. He felt bad for her...so bad! No stranger to tragedy, this couldn't be easy having lost her daughter and son-in-law to murder and now two grandchildren. What comfort could he possibly offer her?

"Cedric," she had told him on the phone. "It's so kind of you to ring. This is killing me. It's really killing me. I wish I could be there for you, but I can't even get out of bed. I honestly can't. Suddenly I feel so old...so very old. Be strong, my son. Be strong for all of us. I promise to be there for the funeral, but forgive me if I can't be there now. Though you deserve endless, endless sympathy, trust me when I say, I'm praying for you."

"Thank you, Grandmère, and believe me when I say I understand," he grounded out, understanding completely. At first he didn't think he was going to make it either, but having everyone around him and feeling all their love and support had helped tremendously. Grandmère really needed to get here. She really needed everyone around her, instead of just grandpère. But Danyel's mother, Cecille, and his brother, Michel and his wife were on their way down to be with her, he had heard. And so he supposed, she'd be fine. So far, everyone was rallying together— not worrying about all the horrible things being suggested by the press—not listening to all the innuendoes. Yet he knew that so much horror loomed ahead. How much longer would the love and support and understanding hold up?

Surprisingly, not one person had asked if he had done it. Not one. Well, with the exception of Kendra Jade—though he had provoked her and goaded her into asking it. Even though, he was the number one suspect with the police, everyone was being cool. That alone gave him tremendous comfort. Even Kendra seemed to be on his side, despite their showdown on the phone yesterday and their shaky truce of this morning.

It was much later in the day when his dad spoke about something that had been weighing very heavily on his mind. CJ.

5

Reality Check

They say that our childhood is what forms us, that those early years' influences are the key to everything. This spurred me to thinking with a good measure of anxiety about my own life. My childhood, adolescence, teenage and young adult years, and how it had all been dominated and even overpowered by my father. I had never known a mother's warmth or kindness, had been deprived of my mother's love.

I had never felt a feminine touch growing up, not until I started forming alliance and started to have sexual contact with the opposite sex. Remembering the first time I was even hugged by a female was still a wonder to me. And now, just like me, CJ would be deprived of the very thing. I felt embittered by the tragedy of it.

At least CJ had Margo, his nanny. I had had a valet, Jeeves, a gentleman's gentleman. That was before I was carted off to boarding school.

I had been an only child, and for reasons I still didn't know, my mother and father had gone their separate ways shortly after my birth. The little I did know was that she had been from the Philippines and a raging beauty. After her death, people had described her as vivacious, intelligent, passionate and yes, she would have to have been for my father to have been involved with her. Aesthetically, she had to be perfect. My father was very visual and so into perfection, I couldn't imagine he'd settle for less than exquisite.

My mother had been a painter. Had studied art at the École Des Beaux Arts in Paris, where she and my father had met. Other than that, my knowledge of their romance and subsequent disastrous marriage and split was very limited. The reason I knew anything at all about my mom was largely due to some of her watercolors that had decorated the walls of my childhood home.

Not knowing my mother though and the entire idea of who she was and how I had come to be, loomed heavily in my mind for a very long time. That it had affected me and formed the person I am today was definite. Yet, the more I pondered it, the closer I came to the truth. Might not an unhappy childhood be the best preparation for life itself? Wouldn't the opposite be like leading a lamb to the slaughter?

I thought about my dad and how it was being raised by him, who's fundamental credo was his total power of will, a man's greatest asset—or so he had always said. And he had wielded this will with an iron fist. The combination of his unquestioning belief in his own power to dictate his life and mine, and the tall, stalwart physique in which that will resided made him a very powerful man and for me, a most formidable opponent. I was raised for the most part in a very authoritarian environment and had to constantly bend to that will—which I suppose was not a bad thing considering how rebellious I had been.

"Can we speak privately," my father said now, pulling me aside during the course of this impossibly hectic day. "I'm concerned about CJ and what your plans are for him."

I hardly knew what to say and simply sighed deeply. I had been trying not to think about it. Though it arrived with alarming suddenness, horror devours its prey very slowly. And even though I knew I was going to have to deal with everything sooner or later, I thought about putting everything off for later. Time stretched ahead of me endlessly. I'd have a lifetime to deal with everything—or so I thought.

"Look, leave CJ with me. You can't take care for him right now. And besides, he's gotten comfortable over there with me. Has a routine. Of course, we'll have to check with Margo and see if Orlando suits her needs. But for now, son, you have to take care of you. Get your life back together again. Don't feel guilty, like you're doing something wrong—putting yourself first. You have to right now. There's no other choice."

"Dad, there's always a choice. And the way I see it, he's my responsibility—not yours. And no matter what you say, I would feel guilty letting you shoulder the burden—"

"No-no, my son. You're looking at this from the wrong perspective. And what is guilt, really? It serves no purpose, but one thing. It stifles happiness. Trust me on this, son. You're your first priority right now. Remember that. CJ is fine. Cared for. I think he's going to need some stability in his life—especially with his mother gone. So for now, leave him in my charge."

I hated the way my pops always made so much sense. And I resented the fact that he was trying to keep my son. I could just feel him muscling his way into CJ's life, taking over little by little until he took over completely—if I wasn't careful. I knew my pops and how he could woo damn nearly anyone into total submission.

Yet right now, there wasn't much I could do. I knew what my lifestyle was like pre-Arielle. And it had been insane! No place in that life for a child. But things had changed, I had changed. I would never be that insane again. I had a son. Responsibilities. I didn't want the burden off, I didn't want to get off so easily. I wanted to be part of my son's life. To raise him myself if I had to. But remembering what my life had been like the last 48 hours, perhaps it would be best to leave him in Orlando with my pops for a little while longer, who was watching me closely, observing all the doubts and concerns crisscrossing my face.

"Dad, I don't know. I feel...Damn, I don't know if it's right. I know you're thinking about my lifestyle and all, but it's not like that anymore."

"Cedric, your lifestyle is the least of my worry right now. It's you—emotionally—that I'm concerned about. You have enough on your plate without having to care for a small child."

"It's not like the baby doesn't have a nanny, dad. Margo's wonderful with him."

My father snorted. "Do you think a nanny is enough? You're going to let a nanny raise your child, teach him manners, care for all his needs."

"Of course not!"

"Look, Cedric," he said placing a hand on my shoulder. "Leave him with me for a little longer—until you figure out what it is you want to do. I'd like you to concentrate on making yourself better, without any care to CJ. It's going to be a long, arduous road. I know. I've been there. Just know he's in excellent care. As soon as you feel you want to, come get him. Call me whenever you want news of him or to speak to him. Just don't sacrifice his care out of a feeling of guilt or out of some sense of propriety. I'll take good care of him. Just promise me you'll take good care of *you*."

And of course he was right. How could I even argue with that? He took a card out of his pocket and handed it to me. "I have it on good authority that she's excellent. She specializes in grief counseling."

I looked down at the crisp, pristine white card he handed me: *Dr. Kendall Silverman, Psychologist.* My dad placed a hand on my shoulder, squeezed it. "Courage," he said. Yes, and that was our name. And when he said, I also knew it wasn't simply encouragement or candor. He meant it and truly believed everyone's best interest would be served by following his. I also knew he truly believed he knew best, and perhaps in this matter, he did.

***

She prided herself on her aggression and used to love the fact that she thought just like a man. When her girlfriends were crying or complaining about how their men had used them or had screwed them over, she used to feel superior, secure in the knowledge that no man was ever going to make her feel like that. No man would ever have her in the precarious situation where she was willing to do anything for his love. Suffer humiliation. Accept his crumbs. Play second-fiddle. Be his "yes" girl. A booty call. *Never, no way, not me!*

Lesson number one: never say never. An old saying, but one which was certainly true. It was amazing how life had a way of making you eat your word.

You never knew what you were going to do until you were in a situation. In that special circumstance. That was what tested your mettle. Those were the defining moments—when you learned who you truly were.

And many times, all those things you had promised you'd never do, all those things you were so sure of about yourself, all of those brave words became cold comfort—crumbling into the sea! For none of that shit meant a *damn thing* when you were staring adversity straight in the eye.

Veronica felt her body clench with every stroke as Cedric banged into her, his face directly above her, staring intently at her. His eyes were glazed, and she realized he was not even looking at her really, but staring straight through her, past her. His mouth cruel, harsh, unsmiling. He was using her—savagely! It felt almost like he was just jacking off inside her body.

Tonight he hadn't bothered with any niceties and like the night before, he hadn't even bothered taking off his clothes. And tonight, not even hers. Simply, he had gone straight for what he wanted. In fact, he'd asked for it very plainly. "I want some pussy," he had told her the moment he came through the door. No sweet talk. No pretenses. Plain as rain. "I want some pussy."

Amazingly enough, she had felt grateful that he had even come at all. Came to her hotel to seek her out. She had gone into his arms and picking her up, he deposited her a few steps on the bed, lifting her skirt, yanked down her thong panties and with no preliminaries, he unzipped, tore open a condom, rolled it on and just rammed into her without so much as a kiss or a word.

As she watched the tormenting pleasure register on his face as her walls closed around him, she had felt appeased, and that had been enough. She was giving him pleasure, and that had to be enough.

Her fingers brushed his lips and square jawbones, and then wound around his neck, trying to bring him down to her. She wanted to feel his weight, but he strained against her, seeming to want their sexual organs to be their only connection.

Veronica groaned from the frustration, finding a perverse pleasure in being denied. Raising her hips up to meet him, she welcomed his every thrust. Even without foreplay, she was still very turned on. Maybe due to his amazing staying power—not to mention the fact that his cock was just so big, so good, so sweet. No other man could satisfy her like Cedric did. No one had his reach, his stamina, his expertise.

He was enormous and veiny and his cock looked exactly like those way huge dildos they sold at sex shops—except his was real. And right now it was hers! All hers, *yeow!!!*

She was moaning, feeling like she was about to peak. She grabbed his hips trying to press him further into her and he swore, grunting some obscenity as he grabbed her buttocks. Cupping her in his hands, his chest finally came down to crush her breasts. She was coming hard when he whispered naughtily in her ear, "Yes, yes, come for daddy."

And did she, goodness she was coming! She was sobbing too, going all buck, it felt so good. That must have pleased him, because all of the sudden, he started to kiss her, swallowing her moans of pleasure. He plunged his sexy, ringed tongue all down her throat, giving her the affection she had so badly needed. "Yes, yes, oh, yes!" she sobbed. *God, how she loved this man!*

Meanwhile he had still not as yet had his release, but he was stroking her deep—his hips swirling and caressing, just like his tongue. She was getting it from both ends—in her mouth and bottom. She thought she would die from wanting. Could he go deeper?

She wanted him deeper. When she came for him again, she forced him to come himself. Quite loudly. And the moment was too delicious. Even the withdrawal was slow and sensuous.

Veronica was still shuddering long after, holding him protectively between her arms. Mother of God, she wanted to give this man everything—all of her. She had never felt so loving, so tender, so emotional about anyone. *What was up? Why was she feeing him this much?!*

I'm in love, she groaned silently to herself, kissing him fiercely against his temple. She had lost him to Arielle and now she was so grateful to have him back. As she pressed another kiss into his temple, she realized he had already fallen asleep. Almost immediately. She allowed his weight to press her into the mattress for a little while, liking the feeling of being smothered. But then he became too heavy. She had to wiggle a bit to get from underneath him.

She then went to the bathroom, disposed of the used condom, used the bidet to wash off, and came back with a warm, moist towel to clean Cedric off. Next she took off his shoes and socks, pulled off his clothes, removed her clothes and then cuddled him, feeling so protective of him. She was going to care for him these next few days. With all the details of the funeral and the press bombardment, he was tired. She looked at him, tucking his hair behind his ears, kissing the tattoo on his upper arm, which was his name spelled in Japanese and wondering about this new tattoo on his chest. She hadn't known about that one, a small Valentine with the initials *EAS* in it, right on his pecs over his heart.

Hell, he had loved that cunt so much. Damn her for ruining everything, for ruining Cedric. He had loved her ass so much that he had had her initials branded into his skin, on his heart. God, he could be so romantic, she thought ruefully, feeling her heart squeeze in pain. She knew firsthand and wondered where she had gone wrong with him. Even though she knew and knew well.

Oh, how could she had been such a fool?!

She had had him first. His heart once belonged to her. Except she hadn't wanted him then. She'd shunned him. Played all these silly little games. And now she loved him quite desperately— except he was in love with someone else. Someone who was dead and who was so unworthy of his love. Being no fool, she knew where his allegiance was though, and it wasn't with her. It didn't matter that the bitch was no longer alive, nor that she'd betrayed him—with her own cousin. That little guttersnipe still held Cedric's heart and unwavering devotion. She wouldn't fool herself about that. She knew this and knew it well.

How she hated Arielle, Veronica mused. From the moment they had met, it had been instantaneous. She had been totally unable to hide her revulsion, so Arielle was quite aware of it as well. Though it had hardly mattered.

Arielle had been gorgeous in a way that ate away at your insides with either desire or envy. A true beauty. Veronica often thought of her as the goddess of plenty. She had too much of everything—too much hair, too much leg, too much ass, too much tits. There was nothing she was lacking—even brains.

Veronica would never forget their first meeting, how Arielle had looked or how she had watched Cedric stare at her—and practically every man there. He couldn't even help it. And she had known then that Cedric was a goner, dying and pining away for her. But if Arielle noticed, she didn't betray it at all.

She was Veronica's opposite in every way: dark-skinned where she was very pale, with long, luxurious cascading black curls where Veronica's was blonde and short and cut in straight bob. She was tall, statuesque and voluptuous, where Veronica was slight, petite and athletic. She was coy and flirtatious, where Veronica was polished, professional, slightly sophisticated. She had a winning, warm simplicity to her that perhaps made her alluring and inviting, where Veronica seemed brash, cold, and a little calculating, and even perhaps a bit too serious.

Veronica could see how easily she had lost Cedric to her. She hadn't had a snowball's chance in hell after he'd met her. Cedric seemed bewitched by her. He had been spellbound, and she supposed in the sense, Arielle had summoned forth his deepest desires and dreams, making them come alive for him in a way she had not. Especially when she gave him a son, something he had always longed for. Veronica had known that had cinched his undying love forever. Something she would have been too selfish to give. After all, there was her precious career—except none of the things she thought so terribly important mattered that much anymore.

Cedric was fast becoming her number one priority.

When she had first met Cedric seven years earlier, when Cedric had not yet been *Cedric Courage, Musical Sensation*—when he had been an exciting, adventurous, sexually crazed young man—much like most of the young newcomers who owed their careers to her, she was in control then. In the power seat. She had been used to meeting these amazing, talented young men. Whether they were singers, actors, authors or sports stars, they usually had one thing in common—these huge, overblown egos. She'd ruffle their feathers, show them who was in charge, and that was usually that. Cedric, however, hadn't been on that huge ego trip most of the others were on. Oh, he had his quirks, and was a bit of a prima donna when it came to composing and arranging his music, but for the most part, Cedric had always been a nice guy. And though that huge, blockbuster ego seemed a prerequisite to reaching super stardom, Cedric had made it to the apex without donning it.

She had taken Cedric under her wings and broke a cardinal rule she had in all her business relationships, becoming his lover because he was nothing like the others. In fact, he was gentle and humble, willing to learn, patient and long-suffering. He was sweet and genuinely nice person. She had never regretted getting involved with him—at least not until Arielle came on the scene.

From the moment they had said hello, she had thought he was the sexiest man she had ever met. He was the first client she had ever felt an immediate physical attraction to, and she knew she was going to have a relationship with him beyond the professional almost from the get-go. When they shook hands after their introduction, Cedric had held her hands a few seconds too long and then given her this boyish, perfectly white grin. And that was all she wrote, as the saying went. *Game over.* It had been as simple as that.

She had been instantly turned on, and not upset or offended as she had often times been when other male clients had made sexual overtures or advances. All at once she had felt slippery and hot between her thighs and had the suspicion he knew just what effect he was having on her. His eyes were penetrating and caressing, his manner intimate—not mocking at all. She felt drawn to him.

After several months of working together, he never once made a play for her again. It was just at the initial meeting when she had felt that pull from him. But he did nothing else. Yet she understood the invitation was open. Right there. Flapping in the wind.

In the meantime, he was polite, responsive, respectful. And she was damned if he didn't know how much he turned her on. But it was as if he was not going to make any more moves after that first time. He had let her know how he felt, had taken the first leap, the rest was up to her. She would have to initiate anything else between them—even if he was all for it.

It was infuriating at first. A game of cat and mouse—one which she suspected Cedric regularly played with women he fancied. He gave you just enough rope, feeding you just enough crumbs, but kept it innocent and light otherwise, until you felt thoroughly crazed. Ready to scream at his head for him to take you!

Though she had wanted him, she had felt above his game. She knew he had wanted her too—without a doubt. Only problem, she had to do the seducing. He had turned it around, reversed the roles, until she was the pursuer. But she remedied that and thought him a lesson he wouldn't soon forget.

She'd seen *The Graduate*, and took a page from Mrs. Robinson. The second she had his ass in her bed, the moment she put her hands on him, it was over. She made him beg and plead and paid him back in kind for all the frustration he had caused her. She gave him a most painful orgasm, one he'd always remember and hunger for. She never had to worry about pursuing him after that. After all, he was a man, and she'd made it her duty to please him.

They had gotten along fabulously for years. She was the bitch-goddess he adored. And it wasn't just a pretense, she really was that way. He wanted to play games, so she played along with him. She put him through the ringer and he seemed to be enjoying it immensely. More and more he was coming to New York. Coming more often, staying longer and longer on the pretext of business. But it wasn't all business. Hardly business—in the dark of the night. He was trying to woo her, to romance her. And she was thoroughly enjoying it too, having her fun. But then one night, he uttered those three dreaded words and just ruined everything for her.

"Why'd you have to say that," she asked him with so much hostility.

"Because I do," Cedric said with a smile. "I love you."

"You shouldn't."

"Why? Because it's one sided? It's okay Vee, you don't have to say you love me back. I know you do."

She had laughed. Rudely. In his face. "Don't be so sure. Don't you know, love is an illusion. Love isn't real. It's only something you're imagining but it doesn't exist. Can you see love? Can you hold it in your hand?"

"No, but I can show you love," Cedric had said coming to her, getting up real close. Taking her hand, he kissed her open palm and then placed it on his heart. "Do you feel it, Vee? It's right here." Then he pulled her entire body against him, and kissed her on the heart.

Her body shook and trembled uncontrollably remembering that tender moment. But she had pulled away and laughed at him again. "Cedric, get a hold of yourself, the heart's a muscle. A

muscle that pumps blood. Love is bogus. Don't buy into the myth."
She had been 24, full of herself, and stupid. She could see that
now.

After that night, she had refused to see him exclusively,
preferring to date lots of men. Then she had had the nerve to
berate him whenever he expressed his concern or showed the
tiniest measure of jealousy.

"Why are you doing this," he had asked her in earnest after
she had deigned to see him one night. "You know, I'm jealous. You
know how I feel about you. Why are you deliberately trying to
make me crazy with all these men? Is this one of your other sick,
white-girl quirks I can't even begin to understand? Shit, woman,
you need to slow your roll. There are niggas calling you at all
hours of the day and night. Why you spreading yourself so thin?!"

"Cause it's my prerogative to do so," she had told him,
meaning to put him in his place. "If I so choose, I'll have three or
four lying up in here too. You don't like it, step to the curb. Know
what I'm sayin'?"

"Aw'ight, I hear you," he had replied, cool as a cucumber.
"Loud and clear." And he had left it alone, never mentioning it
again except she could see the hurt in his eyes every time a man
called or she spoke to some guy in a room. And she knew how he
was thinking she was fucking this guy or that guy and moreover,
she was thrilled by it. Loved the fact that he had admitted to being
jealous and knew how it was eating him up inside. But even
though, she had remained true to him—except, he was not at all
aware of it. And she had deliberately kept him in the dark, leading
him to believe otherwise.

She had wanted him off-kilter, off-balance. She enjoyed
toying with him. Loved the torrid passion and steamy tension of
their relationship, and knew that keeping him guessing was the
only way she'd be able to keep him really interested. Power was so
sweet—not to mention intoxicating. But she had no idea that life
was about to deal her a losing hand.

She had been cruel. Yes. But back then she had thought men
deserved it. They needed to suffer for all the drama they put
women through. And so if she had the power to engage one in
combat and fight the deadly game of love and attraction, it was
justifiable. Whether or not he truly deserved it, he had to pay for
the sins of his comrades, his brothers-in-arm. And she certainly
tried to make him pay for all the other assholes out there. But now
she realized she had approached love from the wrong angle.

Completely turning it into a game of war.

How could she had been so misled?! All those *Jane* magazines, she thought wearily—and *Cosmo* too. You read enough of those girl-power rags and your mind becomes warped.

At the beginning of 1999, he went to Miami during Super bowl weekend, he was performing at half-time—a gig she had gotten him. If only she had known he would have met *her* there. Arielle stepped into the picture and changed everything. And though things hadn't changed immediately at first, and he was still coming back for more, it wasn't long before their relationship grinded to a stop. Somewhere, somehow things did change. Horribly.

She would never forget how he had told her about it one weekend. He had come up to New York briefly after spending several weeks in Miami and told her over dinner one night, "I met this girl I used to go to school with in Gainesville. She's Haitian-American, born in Brooklyn and works at a magazine down in South Beach. I really like her and want you to meet her. I think you'll like her too."

Of course, he hadn't thought anything of it. And it sounded innocent enough. After all, she had reiterated to him over and over that they were just friends. Friends with benefits—like the saying goes—who happen to fuck when the occasion arose. But that was all. So he had taken her at her word.

The same night he had made this little announcement, she had let him come over to her place and had screwed his brains out royally. And he had enjoyed it. So had she, except he had no idea that she had a hidden agenda, and that was to lure him back.

The next weekend she had found a reason to fly down to Miami. She had wanted to be there for the video shoot they were making for his latest release. So she had flown down that weekend and "met" Arielle. She would never forget the jealous rage she felt when she first saw how stunning she was. The girl could stop traffic! Not to mention the fact that she fairly oozed stylishness, carried herself with an unbelievable grace, and had sparkling personality to boot. Just didn't seem fair she could be this perfect!

Cedric, who could be surly sometimes was laughing his ass off the entire weekend, and couldn't keep his hands off her. Always with his hands around her waist or around her neck or clasped in hers, they seemed to be always connected. Oh, and his eyes. He couldn't keep his eyes off her—especially off her shapely butt, which she seemed to enjoy flaunting in his face. But what was more was the way it was obvious to everyone watching them how crazy he was about her. He hadn't slept with her. That was plain to see. The sexual tension between them was coiled too tight and they had to be touching each other every second. People didn't behave like that once they had slept together.

Veronica was disgusted—sickened by the sight of them.

"So how do you like her," he had asked when they had had a moment of privacy.

"I don't know. But I wouldn't trust her."

"Why do you say that?"

"She seems flighty. Like a social butterfly. How many boyfriends do you think she has looking like she does?"

"Amazingly enough, none."

"Oh, and you believe that?"

"No, baby. I know that. I'm the only one she's seeing. In fact, before I came along, she told me she hadn't had one for well over a year."

Veronica had laughed. "Oh, you're crazy if you believe that. Not that hot little number I met today. No way!"

Cedric had smiled. "What I like is that she is hot. But only for me. I really like that. And God, you have no idea how hot."

Of course, he had added the last part to hurt her. To make her jealous. And it had worked like a charm. She had been as angry as a wet cat. At that time, he had still been carrying a torch for her. Except a year later, the fire had been totally extinguished.

She had hated Arielle with a passion since that time. She had stood by and watched as Arielle came to mean everything to Cedric—eventually becoming his wife and having his baby. Yet she had been vindicated, proven absolutely right. She hadn't been true to him. Arielle had played him. Played him for a fool.

Poor sucker had spent so much money on her. There had been so many presents and expensive purchases. The jewelry, the car, the dream vacations, the penthouse and finally the mansion he was building for her on LaGorce. You name it, she had gotten it. Rings, bracelets, earrings, necklaces. Diamonds, rubies, emeralds, sapphires. At least two strands of black pearls, which he had given her just this Christmas. She had no doubt that she had at least half a dozen or so watches, the cheapest one was maybe fifteen grand. She knew for sure of two Rolexes, one which dripped with ice (diamonds). She had been coveting that one for a long time. But of course, most precious of all, was the joint-bank accounts. She had had access to all his wealth, and he was worth a substantial amount.

All the while, that conniving little viper had been using him as a tool. He was her limitless ATM credit card, her moneybag and access to instant fast cash. Meanwhile the bitch was in heat and in love with her cousin. Served Cedric right, really, for not believing her. She had warned him. Countless of times. But he had scoffed at the idea. Oh yes, he had brought this upon himself.

Yet, she couldn't help but feel badly for him. And now the bitch was dead, Veronica swore she was going to make him forget about her. It wouldn't be easy, she wouldn't deny that. But if there was some small opening, some remnant of love left in his heart for her, she would find it. She couldn't stand seeing him so bereft and sad in any case, so she'd make it her duty.

She continued to watch him as he slept. Looking at how sweet and peaceful he looked, like a young boy with dark, sweeping lashes resting on his hallow cheeks. God, he looked so guileless and innocent. Kissing his lips, feeling it's sweetness and fullness and realizing there wasn't much that she wouldn't do for this man, she shuddered, emitted a groan of displeasure.

Oh, the gods were so cruel! *Why hadn't she loved him like this when he had been in love with her?* Fate was so unkind, so unbelievably cruel. That, or her timing sucked! Remembering how it had felt just minutes ago in his arms, she arranged herself back into that position and whispered, "I love you, Cedric Courage, and I don't care what you think. I'm not losing you again," she finished, before murmuring a quiet prayer and falling asleep.

God help her, she'd make him hers again. Somehow!

***

He was so much better-looking in person than ho was in pictures or on his videos, which did not do him justice at all! Kendra thought as she considered Cedric, whom she found herself studying a lot these days. After all, she was constantly with him due to this assignment. And it was proving not too difficult to do. Good thing he wasn't an eyesore but real eye candy, she told herself—perhaps disturbingly so.

Serious and intent, he had this aura, this persona that seemed to brighten up a room the moment he entered. He had star quality and that something special that set him apart from normal people. He seemed larger than life. She was slowly starting to understand why so many youngsters, his posse and fans adored him so much. He drew people to him like a loadstone. His innate grace and charm—not to mention magnetic personality was admirable. And though she hadn't thought it possible, she was beginning to warm up to him somewhat and his graceful, beautiful life.

Kendra remained intent and watched as he interacted with his friends who were coming over in droves. They had just attended the wake, and everyone was coming by to pay their respects, condolences coming from all over the world. Meanwhile, she observed how he treated everyone, making each person feel special. Even with this crisis at hand he created a gentle flow, a milieu in which others could feel comfortable. It was a lazy river, this environment he created. Leisurely. Welcoming. *Come join me. Drift with me. Come meander and flow with me. Let's float together wherever you want to go.*

Yes, he was completely easy-going, she decided, real mellow. Yet she had seen his dark-side. Had suffered his wrath and knew he could be very cruel and quite unpleasant when he wished to be.

She found herself wondering about him quite a bit lately. Even after hours—when she went home and Neff took over, she'd lay in bed and think about what he was doing, who was he doing, how he was feeling.

Had she actually grown fond of the jackass? Why did she even care? Was she attracted to the bum? And a bum he was, the guy was an absolute dilettante that did nothing but brood all way.

She pondered that for a little while.

Maybe. But he also did so many fine things—like creating music for a world audience and from the looks of it, supported a village of people.

Was it his fame? The mystery shrouding him?

He was definitely great to look at, a very beautiful man. But she had been around plenty of good-looking men most of her adult life, and working at the Bureau where men outnumbered women 10 to one, they had never been in short supply. After so many years of no effect, why was she suddenly so affected—not to mention conflicted? What was it about Cedric that made him a cut above the rest, or that attracted her so?

Sure, it was true she had never been around someone that famous. And granted, he did have star-quality, movie star appeal, what Hollywood had coined as the *it-factor*. Whatever *it* was, he definitely had. But she was never one to have crushes on unattainable men. She might look at Brad Pitt or Denzel Washington and say, *my-my, he's certainly fine,* but she'd never get it into her head that she might get with Brad or Denzel or any other famous dude for that matter.

It was a good thing Neff had taken the nightshift. It was a relief because she didn't want to know what he was doing at night. If he was with his publicist or any other female, she wanted to be none the wiser. For one thing, it only reinforced her bad opinion of men in general and her thinking of them was pretty bad already. And two, she didn't need it reinforced on a daily basis.

As far as she was concerned, they were all dogs. Dogs that should be locked up in a pound, mostly. And if she ever got it into her mind to get into a relationship again, she'd be an emotional wreck—thanks to Cedric and a few other acquaintances she did not care to mention. How was she ever going to trust anyone? His wife was not even in her grave and here he was with another woman. And maybe this woman had always been there. Maybe that was what drove Arielle into the arms of her cousin. Maybe things had gotten so painful that she had found comfort wherever she could find it.

She was trying not to be judgmental, but she couldn't help feeling the way she did. Couldn't help feeling like she was being personally betrayed. Seeing him with that woman. That *white woman*, she thought and blanched. *What the hell was that all about? Why did all the fine, rich, handsome brothers feel the need to cross over?*

Okay, she was going to stop right there, and not get on her soap box. Take a breath. Breathe in, breathe out. Don't get mad. Color was nothing but a thing, but *oh! It ate her up!!!*

Would it had mattered if she had been a sister, she wondered. Would it had made it any more palatable? She doubted it. But it did bother her to the utmost that she *was* a white woman. It was a personal affront. A further indication to the treachery and utter betrayal of the black man to the black woman.

The fact that his wife had been unfaithful didn't even matter at this point. The fact was that someone he professed to love was dead. She was the mother of his child. And her life should mean something to him. No matter what she had done! No, to her Cedric wasn't suffering enough. And she hated being judgmental, but she couldn't help herself. Cedric was a jerk, she decided—regardless of how sexy he was.

It was obvious to her the kind of man he was. His passion was quiet, yet fierce. And several times, she had wondered if he had done this ghastly deed. Was he capable of murder? Oh, she had no doubt that he was. But had he killed his wife and her lover? Of that she wasn't sure. Maybe even doubted. But she'd get to the bottom of it. If she found out he had anything at all to do with it though, he was going down! She'd make it her personal mission in life to bring him to justice. Regardless of the way she felt about him.

Neff, however, didn't share her opinion.

After the first night he had spent with Cedric, she had asked how the night had gone.

"Well, he doesn't sleep much. Told me he couldn't sleep. We drank and played cards all night. Deuce and Rico joined in, and next a couple more friends dropped by, and pretty soon it was nearly like a party, a pretty wild night. You know what, I like him though. He seems real, genuine."

"So you think he's clean?"

"Yeah. You know what? I do."

She was tempted to ask about Veronica. If she had came by. But then thought, no. Maybe she'd better not go there.

She didn't want to admit it, but she was reeeally attracted to him. It had happened instantaneously. The moment she had spoken to him at the station. And that knowledge in and of itself disturbed her a great deal.

Cedric was potent. Sensual. Erotic and possibly lethal. She would need to always be on her guard with him.

Everyone had left. Except for Kendra and Neff, a few of the girls from his entourage who were still cleaning up and the bodyguards, who were always with him. It was a little after one in the morning. The funeral would be early this morning.

"God, aren't you tired? I thought they'd never leave," Cedric said looking haggard and weary.

"Well, why don't you go and try to get some sleep," Neff advised him. "Maybe you ought to break down and take a sleeping pill or something. Cause you need some rest, man."

"Yeah, maybe I'll do that," Cedric agreed, rubbing the bridge of his nose and then asked, "Have you ever had one of those days that you wish you could live over again? Like Bill Murray in *Ground Hog's Day*? That's how I feel about that day she died. Like I wish I could live it over again, and fix things. So that it didn't turn out the way it did."

Kendra wished she could have squeezed his hand sympathetically, but could only mutter, "So what would you have done differently?"

"Everything. Oh God! I would have fought for her. I wouldn't have let her go," he said his voice cracking. "I should have fought for her."

Kendra felt so badly for him. She could understand to a certain extent how he must be feeling. The blaming of oneself. The denial. Whatever the lies your lover had made to you. It didn't matter. Kendra sat there reflecting about Patrick—the first agent she had become involved with at the Bureau who she had been involved with for exactly a year. They broke up on their first year anniversary. On the exact date.

He could have lied about having an affair. He could have lied about his alcohol and cocaine addiction. He could have lied about the missing $10,000.00 from her bank account. But that night, as she sat down with him at the romantic Espalagne where they were having a fancy dinner in celebration of their first year together, he decided at that moment to come clean about everything!

She had felt sick. He had been fooling around with *her* partner of all people. The capricious little bitch she had to work with, who come to think of it, reminded her of Veronica. But it hadn't stopped there. He had felt the need to purge himself of everything. All his crimes. Crimes against society, against God, against humanity. She was thinking perhaps someone had slipped some truth serum in his drink. But no, everything just came pouring forth like a flood, because he said, he realized he was falling in love with her.

Gee, thanks! Just when I realize that I can never love you. Not after all of those confessions. God, and she had to admit, he'd just ruined everything. And later, she discovered she hated him for doing it right then and there—at their anniversary dinner. Couldn't it have waited? Couldn't he have allowed her to enjoy her meal. Lull in the romance of the moment—even if it were a lie. Why ruin the celebration and come clean just then?

She would have preferred the lie. She had thoroughly enjoyed the illusion of being in love—even if it was simply an illusion. But the way he had made her feel on a day she had prepared herself for, decked out in her finest, thinking the night would be perfect. Yet there she sat, the moment gone slack, her mind reeling from all the confessions left her feeling bereft and totally devastated.

To be sure, she could certainly understand how Cedric felt.

Betrayal was such a hard and brutal thing. Especially when there was no way to resolve it. Cedric might beg to differ with her romantic assessment of the situation, but right now, it seemed he was gripped by painful memories.

There was a definite edge to his voice when he turned around and said amiably, but forcefully, "Look, guys, you know, I really appreciate everything you've done. All that you're doing, but I really want to be alone tonight. I mean, really alone."

"Cedric," Kendra started to protest. "It's dangerous."

Neff quickly chimed in his agreement. "Yeah, man. That's not a good idea."

"Look, this is William's Island. There's security up the whazoo over here. The building's completely secured. I'm not going anywhere. I'll be fine. I just really need to be alone. I really, really do," he said getting agitated, "know what I'm sayin.'"

Kendra could see he was going to lose it if they pushed him. "All right," she said looking over at Neff. "But..."

"No, buts. I want to be completely alone. I'm a grown man. And I'm afraid I'm going to have to insist."

"Okay," Neff said. "All right. We can't forcefully protect you. Hope you know what you're doing."

Everyone said their good-byes and left him. She was the last one to leave.

"I'll be fine," he assured her.

"Cedric. You have to let us do our jobs. It's our ass should anything happen to you."

He smiled. "And such a fine ass too," he said flirtatiously.

But she was serious. "Don't leave this apartment. Neff said you sneaked out on him last night."

"I had somewhere to go."

"Cedric, please."

"Don't worry. I'll be fine."

6

Keeping it Real

Walking back to the room, I let Neff and Kendra see themselves out. It had been a real, strenuous, hectic day, and the funeral was tomorrow. *Gulp.* And I wasn't sure I could stand to be around anybody right now.

I stared at her picture again that I had tossed on the bed earlier. I was always staring at her picture when I was alone. As if that would bring her back to me or keep her memory alive. Sometimes I would close my eyes, and I'd forget exactly how she looked—and that scared me.

Staring now at her picture, I found myself remembering the feel and texture of her skin. The ring of her laughter. The way she sometime looked totally mysterious, so hauntingly beautiful after I had made love to her. There were so many little intricate, intimate details about her that I had found totally out of sight.

It was because of this intimacy and passion that had been so overwhelming and compelling between us, that left me raging, when I found out she had been whoring around with Danyel. Yes, it nearly killed me when I found out about her betrayal. And while betrayal of any kind was hard to handle—when it happened so close, in your own backyard, it was even more horrendous.

Even now, though she was gone, and I had what seemed like an eternity to contemplate her lost, it was still hard to wrap my head around it. When someone had you that strung up, it wasn't long before you got delirious to the point where said person could do no wrong.

Yet it was so much more complicated than even that.

I hadn't realized how high on a pedestal I had placed Arielle—not until I had to confront those X-rated photographs, where she had been an eager devotee to *every* base desire and seemed riven beyond words with pleasure. Had she ever looked so deliciously pleasured when she was with me?

Those sordid images of her with *him* could bring my spirit down to wallow in muck. Basically, she had me loving her the way a woman loves a man. I was the one who was all romantic, all-emotional, all hung and strung up...couldn't see the forest for the fucking trees. Shit! Talk about role-reversal. For quite some time, I hadn't known what was up with me. I wasn't myself. I had married her. She had my child, and I just loved her more than life itself. More than I suppose I had a right to. You can't put someone that high on a pedestal and not expect them to come tumbling down.

And from the very beginning, my love for Arielle hit me real hard. At first I thought it was because I had never really loved before. But I was wrong. I had loved. Just not quite like that. Not the way I loved her.

She was unlike any other woman I had ever known. I loved her openness, her wantonness, the way she could be so brash and just say whatever she wanted to me and not give a damn what I thought. In fact, she didn't give a shit what anyone thought. She was definitely her own person. A free spirit. So lusty and positively hot-blooded. I used to tease her about being a dude, she loved sex that much. But a man she was definitely not. She was totally female, every beautiful inch of her dazzling, breathtaking, flawlessly feminine, but with the libido of a man.

Wasn't complaining, though. I had finally met my match.

And I lost myself in her perfection. I liked the way she made me feel too, like I was the only man in the world. The way she made love to me so unabashedly, the way I could make her cry just from loving her. Too quickly, she came to mean everything to me.

After making love to her the first time, I was more than hooked. I wanted to be with her all the time. And when I wasn't with her, I had to block out all thoughts of her from my mind to make it bearable. She was an absolute distraction, someone I could be with in bed for days on end, and never tire. I was never bored, and I had to work like a madman. 'Cause work and Arielle did not mix. Got so much accomplished because I had to—only so I could rush back to into her loving, open arms.

After our marriage and the baby, my desire for her never abated. If anything, it grew fiercer. It used to amaze me that she had actually married me, that I had a wife and child, two people who I could definitely call my own. But the day I opened up that envelope mailed to me by some unknown source and saw those pictures of her banging Danyel in every conceivable position imaginable, it was as though time stood still and everything churned into an upside down state—my stomach included. I had just had lunch and everything came rushing back up.

To say I was devastated would have been putting it mildly. I felt like a train wreck. I was overwhelmed by a tsunami of emotion that left me mortally wounded and from which I knew I would never recover. I was clutching the end of my desk, trying to hold on for dear life as my head spun in dizzying circles, the stench of my vomit making me want to retch. My heart was on fire and beating rapidly and I broke out in a cold sweat.

I can't even remember what I did after that. It was like everything after that was in slow-mo. I went on a three day drinking and drug binge that I really hadn't come out of it until I was slapped in the face with the cold reality of what had happened to her. Being told about the murder served as a bucket of iced water thrown in my face, which woke me up from the self-induced pity party I was wading in.

At some point of that horrific discovery week, I called Rico in to see me, Arielle's personal bodyguard, the one she had never known about, but who had been trained to follow her from afar. I called him into my office at the studio and promptly fired his ass. "Who do you owe your allegiance to, nigga? Who pays your goddamn salary?!" I stormed at him. I swear I wanted to pummel his ass. There's no way he couldn't have known about this!

I showed him one of the pictures. "Swear to me you didn't know about this."

But he couldn't. "You never told me to spy on her, boss. Only to protect her."

"You sonofagoddamnbitch motherfucker," I raged. "I'll make sure you never fucking work in this business again! You goddamn punk ass motherfucker!"

I was a ranting, raving lunatic. I wanted to grab him by the collar and kick his ass, make him feel just a little bit of the pain I was feeling.

I was on a rampage then. Wanting to know for sure how many of my crew, my posse, my boys, the people I called friends knew about my wife's incestuous little escapades. But Deuce, my personal bodyguard brought home the fact that even had any of them known, look at me. I was going berserk. Who in their right mind would have had the nerves to tell me and risk my wrath? People say all the time, not to shoot the messenger, but the messenger—we knew—always gets shot every time.

Snap, and really, I could see his point. I was behaving badly. And Rico, goddamn him, was only doing the job I had hired him for after all. I hadn't told him to spy on her, and it was really amazing that he hadn't told a soul about what Arielle was up to. A juicy secret like that could have earned him big bucks with the tabloids. Loyalty like that should be rewarded, not punished. So I called him back gave him his old job back as my personal chauffeur, and hoped everything would be status quo. Except I should have left him protecting Arielle. Perhaps she wouldn't be dead right now.

Should have...could have...what was the point? Hindsight's 20/20.

I missed her like crazy, though. Every second of every minute of every hour of every day. I was notified about her death on Sunday and even though it was only Wednesday and just three days, it felt more like an eternity. And now tomorrow was her funeral. I realized Sunday would always be a marker. Arielle died just last week. Arielle died two weeks ago, last month, last year. Oh, she died five years ago, ten years, twenty. When would it ever end? How would I ever live without her? When would the pain of losing her ever subside?

My heart sunk as I thought about tomorrow and seeing her in a coffin and having the casket shut. Lord, help me, I thought.

I had the world press camped outside the gates of this island. I couldn't go anywhere. And my fans, great as they were, wanted to devour me whole. I might as well resign myself now to the fact that I was going to have newspaper reporters digging through my garbage, telescopic cameras strategically placed in places I'd never imagine. Had to always be aware that people were observing my every move. Every aspect of my life had changed and gotten a little worse. Sure I had been famous before, but now with this whole situation I was infamous too. Christ, and it sucked!

Then there was my image to think of...making music had gotten so corporate. It was no longer just about your music anymore. It was your whole persona that counted, and some companies might want to distance themselves from the scandal. But there was nothing like a good scandal to sell CDs. Sales had to be soaring. I was on television enough. Day in day out, it was a media circus.

Except this was utterly horrific!

Like almost everything in life, this was a catch 22. While I might be selling more CDs, my biggest corporate sponsors would shy away from sponsoring since my latest image might tarnish theirs. And while I was wealthy enough to finance my own tours, it was not a venture I cared to get into alone. I depended on the sponsors to keep me financially solvent. And whereas my label might pitch in a few dollars, the corporate sponsors and various endorsements I held were the backbone of my touring operation, and like hell, I needed them!

Stan and Veronica were doing the best they could to protect me from a lot of the shit I knew was happening. They had to spin this just right, I understood to appease my record label and all the corporate sponsors. Everything from concerts and movies to clothing and Internet ventures to toys and advertising. Everything was so tied to everything else, and hell, my label was probably having a conniption right about now. There was so much to consider, I knew, but they were trying their best to shield me from as much of it as possible. Yet, I was going to have to face a lot of those things sooner or later.

I gritted my teeth in contemplation of all those things. And then my mind turned once again to Arielle and what a fool I'd been, and here I sat grieving her, not even caring about what a laughingstock I might become.

The press was going to eat this up. Make mincemeat of me. And none of that seemed to matter. She was gone and I wanted her back, and it was simple as that. The desire I had felt for her could not even be explained in words. No, it would be impossible to explain in words or phrases. It existed. Simply, it existed. And even now, it wouldn't falter. It was just as real now. Still as heightened. Nothing was ever going to replace this ache, this void I now felt. No one was going to ever replace her.

She was extraordinary. Magnificent. A pure adrenaline rush.

One smile. One caress.

A throaty laugh. A magnetic pull.

She was a song. My song.

My love. My eternity.

My mind turned to the lushness of her body, thinking about how perfect her breasts had been, and her ass. *Umph*, pure perfection...

All of the sudden, I was totally aroused with nary a woman around. I thought about Veronica and her sweet little body. Except I couldn't keep doing that, using her this way. How many more times would she submit to me—and not expect other things in return? Like a commitment of some sort.

No, I should just content myself with thoughts of Arielle. Of white satin sheets against her dusky, luminescent skin. Maybe I could jerk off thinking of her.

She had wanted for nothing. I had made sure of it. I strongly believed in taking care of my business both personally and professionally and most definitely both in and out of bed. I had made her my queen, and had definitely treated her like one. Except all the while, she had been playing me for a fool.

Fuck! Jerking off was not going to work—not when I was aroused at one moment and then surging with rage the next.

Just thinking about what she had done could rile me up, make my blood to come to a steady ass boil. *Was I pissed?* Much as I missed her, *damn-straight!* I couldn't stop myself from reliving the day I received those pictures again. Those images obsessed me! Even now, I could feel the jealousy, revulsion and anger, *how could she?*

They had played that cousin-trick on me. The one where you told your significant other how the person you were secretly banging on the side, was a relative. Most of the time, said person was a cousin. Except in their case, they really were cousins. First cousins!

More upsetting still was the fact that I also felt somewhat turned on by it in some sick, perverse, totally diabolical way. Regardless of what she had done and how sick it was, I was still very much attracted to her...still in love with her. And I couldn't understand it. Didn't want to believe it.

I was discovering things about myself I didn't care to know. Like there was this whole other side of me I didn't want unleashed. Felt this sick feeling of total depravity when I realized that looking at her, even though she was with him, I could still be sexually aroused, in fact was extremely aroused imagining them together.

For days I couldn't even speak to her. Couldn't say a word but felt this rabid, disgusting lust for her, which I didn't dare act on. Then I realized with more dismay that she didn't even notice how I wasn't talking to her. Wasn't even fazed, that's how oblivious she had become to me and our so-called marriage. For close to a week, I continued looking at those pictures as a daily ritual, stewing in my rage, and Arielle was none the wiser.

The afternoon I chose to confront her was as gray as a bad smile. There was a torrential downpour the likes of which I had never seen. The weather felt like my wrath—heavy, vengeful, unrelenting... More infuriating still was the fact that she would go out in that kind of weather just to be with him. Damn, but he must have had some powerful shit! To have her come out to him through rain, sleet or snow. Hell, she didn't give a damn what the weather was like...she was going to be with her man no matter what!

I took it pretty badly. And by the time she returned home, I was foaming at the mouth. Hadn't she told me just a week ago when I had wanted to get down that she wasn't in the mood, was on her period, or some bullshit!

The confrontation was a damned botched up abortion. It went horribly. I had deliberately gotten high and drunk, awaiting her. The moment she walked in, I could smell him all over her. Then she had the nerve to try and lie about it. So I struck her. Really hard. Right across that beautiful mouth of hers. I'm not proud of that, I had never raised my hand to a woman, but I had fucking lost it with her. Roughed her up real good. I fully expected that she would fight back, defend herself, but for the longest time, she did nothing. Kept trying to reason with me. A madman. She should have realized the second she laid eyes on me that I wasn't rational. I was out of my skull! Jealous and rabid with rage!

Did she have any idea how I felt about her? How much I loved her? I kept thinking the entire time.

She had changed my life in so many ways. Sometimes I thought how she had even saved my life. In fact, I thought of my life in this way—my life B.A. and my life A.A. (before Arielle and after Arielle).

I was a former bad boy, the kind of guy who was getting so much play that I hardly knew what to do with it. Hell, I was a star. Enough said. I met Arielle, though, whom I had known since college except we had not connected there, but after a concert one night on South Beach, we connected like a motherfucker! That was the beginning of my life. The real beginning. Before that, I had been living in this fog. I had been going through life existing, I suppose, rather than living.

I was a dreamer. I loved to daydream. My mind was constantly in the clouds, swaddled and consumed in philosophical thought. Forever preoccupied with what I knew now to be absolute garbage. Things like pondering the existence of God. To what end? What the fuck did God have to do with me? Or I with Him? Did He really give a damn?

I doubted it.

Who the fuck cared? If there was even such an entity, and my thoughts on it, was that it was highly unlikely...but even supposing there was. He was an absolute failure, in my book. Why even associate? Look at the system He had created, though beautiful indeed...moralistically, it was insolvent. There was no justice. No one gave a damn. Not really... I'd often think if God existed and I had the opportunity to meet Him that I would approach Him calmly, remain self-possessed as I listened to all the hypocritical banter I was sure He'd impart, then I would promptly spit in His eye.

Yes, I was bitter. Perhaps I blamed Him for ripping me out of my mother's womb. Maybe I should have been left there. After all, it was warm and cozy in there, which could be the reason why that was where, even now, I most liked to be—in the womb.

Before it hadn't much mattered in whose womb, but then I met Arielle, and her womb became my womb of choice. And damn it, if I wasn't one of those rare creatures. It was like once I had met her, whatever pheromones she had had did me in. It was like I had mated her for life…and beyond.

I tried not to think about the state I was in. I was still debating whether I should take a cold shower or seek out Veronica again.

I smiled. And it was so chill.

Maybe it was His fault too…for making us the way He did. And ultimately, He was probably the cause for my mother and father not getting along, the reason they had fought with one another. The reason we humans couldn't get along no matter what. Yes, He was the reason they broke up and separated and never got back together. And He was the reason my father lied to me all those years. Oh, and I blamed Him too for so many other things as well—including my fucking hard-on that was determined to stay up and not go down all night!

If men were dogs, He made us so. And a man had to do what a man had to do.

Blame it on the rain…. Um-hmm, to me God was the rain, and yes, I was blaming Him for everything!

In addition to God, who had become a major preoccupation, freedom was the second. Ah, yes…sweet blessed freedom. America was based on the notion. Liberty and justice and freedom for all. But were we really free? Free to do what? All my life, there were always people around me, milling about, pestering me. Was there ever a time when I was truly alone? If so, I couldn't remember it. Had I ever felt disconnected or cut off? Lonely? Funny how foreign a feeling that was for me…I understood the concept, but I had never felt it. Maybe in my sweetest of dreams. Maybe.

Yet I felt lonely now. Like the loneliest person in the world!

I thought about life B.A., when I had had this huge entourage. All those people I felt necessary to have around me. All of them may have thought I was happy, mistaking my smile and laughter as a sign that I was having a good time. Only I hadn't been. All those years, I was miserable inside, and didn't give a fuck about anyone or anything. I was a paradox. And I thought too damned much!

But she had seen through all of that, Arielle. Saw through all the smoke and mirrors and all the bullshit. She was a no nonsense hands-on kind of person, and boy, did I find that refreshing. She put her hands on me and touched me in ways I had never imagined. Being with her, something shifted inside me. All of the sudden, I started to care. Started to give a damn, which scared me to my very core. Until she had come along, my life had been a whirlpool and cesspool of everlasting shit. Even the music...much as I loved it had been like everything else, where I only pretended to care. Except it was all a farce.

Only with her, it ceased being a game. Even if that was what it was in the beginning. Yes, then it had been very much a game, but then somehow, it all changed.

From day one, I knew she wanted me. And I toyed with her need. With her emotions. But then one day, it ceased being a game. It burned me how fucking serious things became in just a blink of an eye. Slam-bam, one day it occurred to me I was no longer playing but was knee-deep and wading through this deeply, emotional terrifying sea. Then once it happened, everyone could tell at once. The change was that complete, that noticeable. I was licking this woman's boots, kissing her ass. Quite literally. And loving every portentous moment of it.

How many times did I have to swallow my pride, which wasn't an easy thing considering the size it had become. Fame did things to you, you couldn't imagine. But for her, I'd grovel and do whatever it took to please her. I lived to please her. And to be perfectly honest, she didn't let me grovel too much. It was like a dance, where she'd bend to my will and I to hers. Even when we fought, the vibe was always there, this totally beautiful thing. She was feeling me and I was feeling her. And there was so much drama. So much emotion. She was a pure adrenaline rush. Thrilling to the max...everything about her had been.

Often, I'd find myself pissed off by how cavalier she would treat me. It was like she was pulling a *me* on *me*. Man, how dare she? I was the cavalier one, the one who didn't give a shit. I was the superstar. Except she humbled me, knew just how to put me in my place. Always. She'd call me on it, and didn't take any of my shit.

She was everything I had ever wanted. She was what we in the rap and hip-hop world we called a *dime piece*, a perfect ten. She was my idea of physical perfection. With her sexy curves and a devastating face, she possessed a rare beauty. A lethal combination that was knee-buckingly beautiful. For sure when I first met her, I was in lust, but what amazed me was how quickly my lust would turn to love.

Even now I could recall how gorgeous she looked that first night at the club, when she was all about business. Then on our second date, after the Superbowl, I took her to a private party a friend of mine was throwing where she immediately became the life of the party, enchanting everyone. And that was Arielle, with her heavy hair falling over her shoulders, eyes sparkling with curiosity or mischief. Her lips were frequently curved in a winning smile or open in spontaneous laughter. She was exquisite. Captivating and beautiful and usually had the undivided attention of everyone around her. But beyond her obvious physical appeal, she had this dazzling charm and amazing mind, and though I fought and fought hard, it was too difficult not to fall in love.

After our third date, she had me gone. Long before we had gone to bed. Smiling, I thought about how I had made her wait. Made her wait until the breaking point. I had tortured her, and myself! By the time we hit the sheets, neither of us could get enough. But she was well worth the wait. And I adored her from then on...

There had been times in my life that had been so difficult, I thought I would never be able to share with another soul. A lot of it having to do with my mother and what my father had done to us. Like how he had led me to believe from the age of two that my mother was dead and how I was raised believing that my entire life—only to find out that was a lie. Then when I made arrangements to go and find her, it was too late. She had lupus and died two days before I reached her. For a long time, I had hated my father with a passion. Thought I'd never forgive him, and for the longest, there was no one I could talk to about this until she came along. The day she met my dad, I was finally able to share.

It was on our wedding night and we were at his house when the saga of my father and I came pouring out. I'll never forget how light I had felt after hurling that stone off my chest. It was as if these huge boulders I had been carrying on my shoulders forever had been finally lifted and I wanted to cry so bad from the relief I felt. She had held me in her arms and I had felt her tears on my bare shoulders and I couldn't hold on any longer and had wept uncontrollably.

I'll never forget her eyes, concern etched in their very depths. Eyelids misted with tears. Her quivering lips, her face pained. Did she have any idea, any inkling of what I felt for her? Did she understand the power she had over me? The power of love without limits. Did she understand that she had tamed me? Had tamed the wildness in my heart and made it her own? I had sobbed in her arms as her fingers slid into my hair in a tender, soothing caress. And I was comforted, as I longed to be now.

The day of our confrontation, the day I slapped her with the divorce papers and those incriminating photos, I had frightened myself. Can't imagine how I must have seemed to her. But I do remember her reference that I was the devil incarnate. Slamming out of there, I had to storm out or else I might have killed her with my bare hands. When she threw the fact that CJ might not be my son out in the open—an insecurity that had already sprung to mind the second I had seen those photographs—I knew then that I was capable of murder the second those words hit the air.

I went out on my motorcycle even though it was pouring rain and got soaked. Drenched with the pewter rain that not only battered my body as I drove through it, but permeated my soul. Seeking solace, I rode to Michael's place, who I knew would have or could get me anything I wanted. I needed to get doped up. Fucked up. Smearing and soiling my body, dulling the pain, abusing and filling it with every manner of filth Michael had to offer. Afterwards, I couldn't feel a goddamn thing.

Michael drove me back home late the next afternoon and of course, she wasn't there. I hadn't expected to see her. And then when I did, when she walked in looking more beautiful than any woman had a right to, I felt even more unsettled. I was seated on the window seat looking at the spectacular view we had of Miami. She came to sit next to me, drew close, brushed against me. We were sitting side by side, our faces turned towards one another, close enough to touch. We exchanged a glance, then a long, soulful kiss. Time stopped. I believed our love had returned—or the illusion of it. Yet soon after, something jerked off kilter and she jumped up, as if remembering herself and broke the spell. Next, she was getting dressed and on the phone with him, going to meet him.

I had lost. I accepted defeat. Danyel was who she loved, the man she wanted. There I had said it. I mentioned his name. That was probably good. Healthy.

I hadn't planned on being there when she got back. After she left, I felt humbled rather than humiliated. I was in tears. Crying hard. Had really started to cry as she stood there, tall, regal and beautiful, with legs that stretched up to heaven in that white form-fitting dress fitting her curvaceous body like a nylon glove. No, I hadn't planned to be there when she got back, but felt sure I had sunk a little lower. Felt convinced real love didn't exist at all. Felt certain all other embraces would turn sour—just as ours had.

We had shared some beautiful moments. Nights of lovemaking where we'd both cry out with pleasure. Moments when I was too busy anticipating our time together never even realizing how attached to her I'd become. In the beginning, sex exalted our love, but after we got married and especially after having CJ, the two seemed to merge. And now, I felt quite lost at the prospect of living with neither. My love was bone-deep when it came to her, I doubted seriously I would ever stop loving her. She was hard-wired into soul. Imprinted, and there was no getting over her.

That night, I drank as never before. Slept like a stone. Dreamt of Arielle, who seemed to be consumed by fire. She was gleaming, streaming up like a white lightning streak to the stars. All night long, I tossed and turned, rising and falling as if in water, grappling with this luminous doom. By morning, I was roused from sleep by the incessant ring of the doorbell that was sounding like a five-ring alarm in my head. I was still sprawled out on the couch in the rec room when I stumbled to the front door, intent on answering. Groggy, hung over, totally fucked up, it took me several minutes to register the two uniformed 5-Os who were standing at my door. They were both white and had that upright straight-back stance that cops often had, which made them look as if they had a stick up their ass.

It took me a few minutes to realize I wasn't dreaming. I was trying really hard to register what they were saying, I could see their lips moving, but it took all I was to understand what they were saying.

In my bleary, peripheral vision, I could see one of them holding Arielle's handbag in one hand with her driver's license in the other. It finally dawned on me that he was asking me to come with him to the morgue to identify her body and after that, they'd need me to come down to the station for questioning.

The ground fell from beneath me.

I nearly went on myself when they told me she was dead. Had

been murdered. I wasn't naïve enough to think and wasn't going to even kid myself—I knew I was their number one suspect. Yet, as the next morning wore on and I sat in that damned interrogation room, I started focusing on her. Hell, I felt as if I'd go insane.

Was it painful? Had she suffered? Did she beg for her life? Who could have done this? Why? Why? Why? Oh, God, WHY???

And although I knew she had planned on leaving me, that things were over between us, it started to dawn on me I was never going to see her again. Ever. And I couldn't handle that. Didn't want to wrap my head around it.

She was the mother of my child, the woman I loved more than life itself. How rotten and lousy and hopelessly corrupt this whole goddamned system was. There was no sense, no order, no honor, no humanity. Only chaos. Chaos that humans tried to impose order on—but chaos all the same.

Nothing really made any fucking sense anymore. There was no logic, only the illusion of it. And the fucking saddest part was...no one was immune.

Least of all, me...

7

Image is Everything

Leah gave herself one last quick glance before throwing open the door. She needed to look good and did in a simple black elegant Donna Karan dress, dark stockings, stiletto pumps and wore a beautiful wide brimmed hat with a net that fell over her face. Beneath that, she would wear her black Versace shades to hide her eyes. She knew the media was going to be there in droves and she wanted it written how waify and elegant she looked. She desperately wanted the press' sympathy, along with everyone else's.

The girls would not be attending their father's memorial service. Although it would pull on the heart-strings, they would hinder people from focusing on her, really seeing her—not to mention the fact that they would muss up her clothes. No, for appearance sake, the girls would be left with their nanny. Cause today was her day. She would have the spotlight and would play the grieving young widow with aplomb.

She had studied old photographs of Jackie O and was dressed remarkably similar to her. She looked starched and pressed and didn't need to look all crumpled and wrinkled from holding babies or have spittle and throw-up all over her clothes. She needed to look her best for the cameras. Just then she remembered to add her three-strand string of pearls, which would complete her Jackie O, grieving young widow look.

Perfect.

Danyel's memorial service was this morning and the bitch's funeral would be tomorrow. And although she longed to attend that funeral as well, she knew it would be politically incorrect to do so—or so her mother had told her.

"Why would you even want to attend," she had questioned her. "The woman was carrying on an affair with your husband, her cousin, and had the nerves to call you friend. Why would you want to go anywhere near her? I say good riddance to a bad seed. The bitch had it coming."

Yes, and so did Danyel. But she was going to his goddamn service. He was a jerk as well, but her mother was, of course, not seeing it that way. She had no idea what a rat bastard Danyel had been. How he had been such an ass to her in private, and behaved like the perfect, model husband when other people were around. How he never touched her, preferring that cunt's embrace to hers. He had loved that bitch more than anything in this world. Even more than he loved his own children! And for that, she would never forgive him! Never...ever...ever...

No, she wouldn't tell her mother about all the humiliation she had suffered at that man's hand. How she had begged him once to make love to her, and how he hadn't, but had actually refused her! He wouldn't or couldn't—she wasn't sure which, but his refusal and betrayal and total rejection of her—all because of that Arielle bitch had hurt so much! And she hoped there was a special place in hell for that bastard...and his bitch!!!

She wasn't sorry at all for their plight. They had both gotten exactly what they deserved. Him especially! He deserved every bullet he got, but of course she couldn't tell her mother any of this. She'd never tell a soul all of the things he had done. She'd allow others to keep their illusions about him—even if it was a completely false one.

Even now as she argued with her mother over the phone about her decision to attend Arielle's funeral, she knew how she must have sounded. Crazy. Desperate. But she couldn't be honest. She couldn't reveal her real agenda for wanting to attend.

"But mom, she and I were once friends."

"You still consider her a friend," her mom asked in consternation.

"No, but...she's dead. The least I could do is pay my respects—"

"Respects?! Are you kidding me? The woman had been having an affair with your husband!"

"I know, mom. But I just—"

"Leah, look. It's out of the question! Don't show your face at that woman's funeral, you hear me. It's ludicrous! Totally preposterous! Ridiculous! I know you have more sense than that!"

What she couldn't possibly know was how much it was going to kill her not being able to attend that funeral tomorrow, where all the real action was going to be. That was going to be the real show. With network and cable coverage, all the world's press there. Damn, that was going to be the place to be! Hell, if only she could go, she lamented. If only her mother would let up and try to understand!

The doorbell rung at around 9:30. That would be Bailey. She rushed to the door, threw it open and faced him, Arielle's angelic little brother who um...really wasn't so little anymore. He had grown out his hair, from the last time she had seen him. And she rather liked it. It was wavy and curly at the end, like hers, nearly the same exact texture and parted in the middle. He looked real awesome. He was also a lot buffer than she remembered, even under the expensive black tuxedo he was in she could see the outline of his chest and um..."Well," she said giving him a tight hug, "G-gosh, Bailey. It sure is nice to see you." Feeling his strong, sinewy arms go around her, she realized, she was right. Bailey had definitely been working out and looked incredibly good. Real good.

Bailey broke their embrace and gave her a kiss on both cheeks looking at her sadly. His eyes were glossy with unshed tears. "How are you holding up," he asked softly, his voice squeezing with emotion.

"Okay," she said assuming an appropriately sad tone. Trying hard to cover up her excitement. "Considering..."

He hugged her again, really hard. Then he took her hand and placed it in the crook of his arm. She flipped a curl back out of her face and took a deep breath for his benefit. He smiled gently at her. "Don't worry, Leah. I'm going to be here for you. Just keep taking those deep breaths and ignore the damn press, and just remember, I'm right here if you need me."

"Did you guys pass by the church already? How do you know there's a lot of press," she asked.

"'Cause they've been hounding us at the hotel, and they've just been relentless. I can't believe how awful they're behaving. And Cedric, man. Poor, Cedric. He's just been hiding out at his place on William's Island, he's bearing the brunt of this. He's not even trying to come out of his penthouse. The damn press, they're like flies, everywhere, I swear! They're irritating as hell! I'm surprised they're not camped out at your doorstep."

Yeah, she thought. "I guess Cedric's the famous one."

"Anyway, consider yourself blessed."

Except she felt cheated. They should be badgering her too, cause like her husband was mixed up in this mess as well. But so far, they had pretty much ignored her. But she was going to make sure they knew who she was today. She'd be the elegant young widow. She'd have a story too.

"How's he doing?"

"Who?"

"Cedric."

"I don't know...not too well. I don't think. And then they're accusing him of this awful crime."

"You think he did it?"

"No! Hell no! I don't—"

"Well, Bailey, we don't know that, now do we?"

"Naw, Cedric didn't do it. He loved her too much."

"You don't know. He may have snapped."

"I doubt that."

The chauffeur was waiting with the door open for them and she climbed in first and was surprised to find Bailey's grandparents there. "Oh, hi," she said quickly. "I didn't realize you guys were here. I wouldn't have kept you waiting."

"It's okay," his grandfather said politely, holding unto his wife who was hugging up on him. Her face was buried in his neck. Her eyes were shut with a handkerchief gripped between her fingers, which she was holding to her nose. She was also making these pitiful little moaning sounds—not even acknowledging her. How rude of her, Leah thought, feeling slighted as Bailey slipped into the seat next to her.

"What's wrong with your grandmother," Leah whispered discreetly as the limo pulled out of her driveway.

"I think she's really traumatized. God, she's burying her grandson and granddaughter on the same day, the way she did 13 years ago with her daughter and son-in-law, who were also murdered. That's a bit much to bear, don't you think? Not to mention the fact that she and Arielle, God, they were so close. Super close."

Leah looked at the older woman with some sadness. Yes, it was sad. She had forgotten that Bailey and Arielle's parents had been murdered as well. Shot to death, just as Arielle and Danyel had been executed. That had to be rough for the old woman. But she had to understand that bad things happened to bad people and she had to recognize the fact that her grandchildren had been doing wrong. They had screwed a bunch of people over—namely she and Cedric. And their children. They were both selfish and irresponsible and really didn't care about anyone but themselves. Maybe she wouldn't feel so bad if she looked at it from that vantage point.

Did they deserve to die?

Well, that was unfortunate, but that was the will of God. Or else they would have survived. That was the way she looked at it.

"Is she going to be all right," Leah asked becoming annoyed by the incessant moaning. God, she was hoping she would shut up. She was seriously considering turning on the radio—anything—not to have to deal with this.

"She hadn't been able to even get out of bed until this morning. Ever since she learned of the news, she's been bedridden and hell, my grandmère is one of the strongest people I know. This just crushed her.

Leah looked over to her again, seeing how she was now clutching at her husband's lapels and how she hadn't and probably wasn't going to stop her moaning. And then she remembered how Arielle had displayed that same behavior once when she had gone to a party and ran into an old boyfriend who had shown up with his real girlfriend. She had been humiliated, she had confessed to Leah, crying and carrying on, getting a goddamn nosebleed. She had been a mess, moaning and clutching her much like her grandmother was doing now. It must be a family trait. But then she remembered how good she had felt to feel so needed. That was when Arielle had been so wonderful to her, such a good friend. When they had been close, tight, like sisters.

They arrived at the chapel where the memorial service was being held. Danyel's parents had begged her, begged to have him buried in New York. She couldn't deny them this, his mother had pleaded. They wanted him buried in their family plot where her sister and husband were buried and where their grandparents would eventually be buried. The same had been requested for Arielle but Cedric had flat out refused, saying how Arielle never wanted to set foot in New York, and certainly wouldn't want to be buried there.

"But she needs to be with her parents," came the argument.

"No, he's right," the grandfather had finally agreed. "Arielle would want to be right here in Miami, where she loved."

So Cedric had had his wish. She, on the other hand, hadn't really cared one way or the other. So she let them have their wish. She realized she could have been a bitch and refused. She nearly did, but when she remembered how wonderful and pleasant his mom had been to her, how she had been helpful and supportive—especially when the twins had been born—she couldn't find it in her heart to deny her this one final request. Danyel had been born and raised in New York, and was for all intent and purposes, a

New Yorker. Had it not been for Arielle, he probably would have never moved down here. Anyway, it wasn't her fault that her son was such a sick and depraved bastard—or that her niece was just as depraved and a total slut. *Poor woman.*

Despite the fact that this was a memorial service, there were tons of people there. Friends, family, old college mates, business associates. And the press was thick. THANK GOD! She felt much better once she saw all the cameras.

A lot of people had flown in from New York despite the fact that he was being buried there. Since the burial was going to be limited strictly to family and few, close friends, most came to Miami to pay their respects, and Leah suspected too, to satisfy their curiosity. This was a huge story. *Miami Confidential,* and everyone loved a good scandal.

Leah arranged her face as she saw the crowd of people, feeling in her element, loving the attention she was getting as press and paparazzi alike descended on her like vultures closing in for a kill.

"Leave us be," Bailey shouted becoming irritated, trying to shield her and protect her from them.

Oh God, she was hoping that someone had gotten a decent picture of her. It wasn't every day that she looked this good or that she would make all the papers. Hell, she was enjoying her fifteen minutes of fame. *What was wrong with him?* Much as she liked him, she didn't want him blocking her shot.

But she tried not to dwell on it. There would be other photo opportunities later, as they headed out of the chapel. She was going to deck whoever got in her way then.

Leah sat through the service bored out of her skull as people cried silently, a few of the cousins shouted out. She was sandwiched between her mother and father and Danyel's brother, Michel and his wife, Marcia, and their preteen, twin daughters. She always forgot their names. Everyone looked so incredibly sad, and Bailey's eulogy was exceptional, moving mostly everyone there to tears. But she was only counting the minutes until she could head back out. Sure, she had to shed a few crocodile tears, but really, she felt nothing. Nothing but bitterness.

There was a momentary buzz when people thought Cedric had come in, but it wasn't him. She doubted very seriously he would come. Yet, if he did come, that meant she could go to Arielle's funeral tomorrow. She was praying he would come and pay his respects. Even if it was just out of consideration for her and Danyel's family, also Arielle's family.

He should come, she said to herself. He really should. That would show he wasn't angry and even be a way of showing the police and press that he was innocent and had not committed this horrible crime. After all, he and Danyel had been friends. At least once upon a time. Why doesn't he come, she lamented as the minutes ticked by.

But he never showed.

***

Grief bubbled up into a mixture of anger, frustration and anxiety. Today was the day he had been trying not to face. But there was no avoiding it. No getting around it or under it. He would have to face it, shake hands with it, give it hugs.

But would anyone there understand what he had lost. Know how much she had meant to him? Know how much she still meant to him. She was his weak spot. Had gotten underneath his skin and crawled into this fairly large space which he didn't control. Where he had no control. Where only she ruled. Goodness, she was his heart, his conscience, his memory. Everything he held sacred and dear.

Sunrise, another day. All the days flowing together on an endless journey. And today the funeral. That dreaded day. So final. So gruesome. And it didn't matter that he couldn't accept that she was gone. He desperately wanted it to, but his mind, everything that he was, refused to acknowledge that he was burying her today.

Cedric stared at his bar from the leather couch where he had taken to sleeping. He couldn't even sleep in their room anymore. Now whenever he entered it, all he could think was how it was her room. The entire penthouse felt like hers. This was her place, her house, her things—not his. After all, he had bought this place for her.

He focused on the bar and headed towards the hard liquor—except now as he got there, he realized all the scotch, the whiskey, the gin, the vodka—all the hard stuff was gone. The only things left were a few bottle of wine and some champagne.

Champagne, he thought, sobering up. Arielle's drink of choice. Yes, Arielle had certainly loved her champagne.

Christ, he'd have to have Deuce or Rico stock up on the liquor again. He needed fresh supplies. Everything. Fuck, fuck, fuck and now he needed a drink bad. Okay...so he'd have to make do with the champagne that gave him only a slight buzz but gave him a mother of a hangover.

He walked to the kitchen and opened the fridge. Maybe there was some beer. He opened it and other than the leftovers from the other day, there was nothing in there either.

The phone rang.

That would be Veronica or his pops.

It was his pops.

"Are you getting ready," his father asked.

"Um-hum," he lied.

"Son, are you all right?"

"Yes."

"Where did you go after the wake? Everyone was worried about you."

"I came home. I wanted to be alone. Even though mostly everyone followed me here. They didn't leave until late, so I'm still pretty tired. But other than that, I'm okay."

"Well, I'm glad but I don't think you should be alone right now, Cedric. You need to be around your friends and family."

"Yeah-yeah, pops. I know that."

"Why don't you come stay in Orlando with me for the next few weeks. I think it would do you some good. You'd be with CJ and we'd give you lots of space."

"I'll think about it."

"Good man. So would you like us to swing by for you on our way to the church or do you have own transportation?"

"Pops, this is Miami. You know I have my own car. Anyway, he's scheduled to arrive in another hour."

"Okay. Fine. Then I'll see you in a few."

"Yeah," Cedric said clicking off, feeling depressed as hell, and sick to his stomach."

Just as he put the phone down. It rung again.

"Cedric. It's me."

"Hey, Veronica."

"Where were you last night?"

"Here."

"I called."

"I know. I was busy."

"Doing what?"

"Some of the guys came over and kept me company for awhile."

"You know what I'm asking," she hedged. "I was expecting you."

"Didn't have to."

"Why?"

"I'd rather not say."

"Why?" She persisted. "I waited for you until three."

"Sorry, I should have called."

"Cedric, you know I'm here for you."

"I know that, Veronica, and I appreciate it."

"You don't even have to, but hope you know…understand how much I care…"

"I do. Thank you."

"I want you to know that I'm available tonight. Especially tonight if you need me."

Cedric closed his eyes, not wanting to hear that. Not wanting that to seep in. It would be so easy just to use her—except she was a friend and he didn't want to. He hated using her like this, but she was making it so difficult not to.

"Did you see anyone else last night?"

"I'd rather not say."

"I'll take that as a yes. Who was it?"

Cedric looked at the phone for a few minutes in disbelief, and said nothing.

"Please. Tell me"

"It was no one you know."

"Just tell me her name." She sounded angry. "And you know you have to be careful, Cedric. Remember what Kendra told you. Oh, and by the way, was it Kendra?"

"No! That woman can't stand me."

"Then who was it?"

"A prostitute! You happy? Now you know!"

"WHAT?! You picked up someone off the street?!"

"No, I called a service."

"You what?!!" Her voice went up several more octaves.

"I called a service. It was real discreet. Deuce used his name."

"Why," she said, sounding wounded. "You bastard! You really know how to hurt a woman."

Cedric could say nothing in response.

"I'm coming over," she said next, with a sniffle.

"Don't."

"Try and stop me." She slammed down the phone.

Shit. Shit. Shit. He walked briskly into the bedroom and shook Caitland who was still lying face down on the bed. Her legs were sprawled in a provocative manner, ass pointed up, with one of her tantalizing breasts exposed. He stared at her posture. Smiled gently. CJ slept like that. "Ummm...back that ass up, baby," he said caressing her sleeping form, then curled a strand of her flowing hair with his fingers, shaking her shoulders gently. "Hey...hey...yo baby, you have to wake up."

But she didn't budge. Damn, she slept hard.

She was a UM law student, or so she had said, who stripped and did the call girl thing on side for some extra cash. She had been fun last night. Uncomplicated. He wasn't cheap and didn't mind paying for it. She'd drank with him. Smoked a little weed with him. Entertained him. Didn't want anything from him but money. She was exactly what he had needed.

Pure relief.

They had had empty, meaningless sex, the kind that felt great while it lasted but as soon as it was over, it was over. And that was all he needed right now, no emotional ties. She needed money and he needed pussy and they had both resolved their needs in the most direct, honest way.

There was no guilt. No feeling ugly inside like you were hurting someone who had a weakness for you. He had fucked her supremely and she responded shamelessly, beautifully. And that was that. No emotions involved.

And that was where he was failing miserably with Veronica, who made him feel so awful every time it was over.

Well, it was probably not *her*, making him feel awful. But him simply feeling awful...using her as he did. To make himself feel better. He couldn't just bang her and cut off all his feelings—not knowing how she felt about him. Damn her! Why'd she have to tell him she loved him? Why couldn't she have been the way she used to be before?

But people never behaved the way you wanted them to, did they? Especially fucking women—with all their fucking complications! Had she stayed cool and just enjoyed the sex for what it was, everything would have been cool. Except it wasn't anymore...

Besides that, he worried too how he was fucking up a fantastic friendship and business relationship. He'd known Veronica for years, since he started in showbiz. She was an excellent publicist. The last thing he wanted was to botch things up.

Moreover, he really liked Veronica as a person. She was so intelligent and such a babe. Professional. Great at her job. Good face. Nice body. Great lips and legs. And once—for a brief second—

he had fancied himself in love with her. Except once he had met Arielle, he'd pretty much felt the way Romeo had felt about Rosaline once he had met Juliet. *Did my heart love till now?*

He smiled. It was funny the way things worked out.

Yet Veronica had never seemed to mind. Sure, he knew she was maybe a little jealous of Arielle, and Arielle had been vehemently jealous of Veronica. But he had kept them separate, and everything had been cool. Now, however...nothing was cool. And using her was definitely not cool. Even though she still didn't seem to mind, he couldn't bear treating her this way. She deserved so much more. Using her just for sex made him feel sordid. Dirty.

Last night, he had had Deuce call an agency and had requested they send a pretty black girl. Preferably tall, real leggy with a small waist and nice tits. Fortunately, he hadn't been too disappointed. She was a lot slimmer than he preferred, but her brown satiny skin and baby doll face had more than made up for her lack of voluptuousness.

"Cedric Courage," she had grinned instantly recognizing him the second he opened the door. "I'm a huge fan!" She had a chirped, her voice cheerful and personality positively upbeat—the way only a teenager can be. He felt relieved cause he hadn't wanted anyone who was too professional or too hardcore. She was perfect.

"Come on in," he had grinned, inviting her in.

Deuce had been checking her out and gave him an approving grin, then made himself scarce. Just like old times. Meanwhile Cedric was paying careful attention to every detail of his invited guess, appreciating her slinky red sexy slip dress and matching strappy sling back do-me-baby pumps.

"I think it's awful what the press is putting you through," she said next. "How are you doing?"

"Fine, now that you're here. But if you don't mind, I'd prefer not to talk about any of that stuff."

"No problem. What do you want to talk about," she asked flirtatiously, looking him over up and down, eyes smiling.

He had stared at her like a ravenous wolf, enjoying her down-to-earth demeanor. "Well, about your fine ass for starters."

She giggled and he decided then that she was really pretty, a beautiful chocolate Barbie doll. "Ummm...I always knew you'd be nasty."

"Oh, and you can't possibly imagine how nasty."

"Well, for me, the nastier the better."

"Then you're definitely my kinda girl," he said, scooping her up.

Without missing a beat, she locked her legs around his hips and he slapped her ass, pressed her back to the closed door and it was on. Face flushed and now breathing hard, she gave him a laser gaze and started to unbuckle his belt.

There were no games. No pretenses. No airs. Just unadulterated, hot, raw as hell sex. Then after freaking her in every possible position, he just passed out. She had given him quite a work out, and it had been awhile since he had indulged in pure marathon sex, where his mind wasn't involved at all. Where it was all about the biology and nothing else.

"Hey baby. You have to wake up," he said shaking her harder now. She stirred, turned around and looked up at him. She had that just fucked wild night out mussed-up look with smudged mascara and lipstick he loved. He tried not to think of Arielle and how she used to look when they'd first started out and were partying hard. How he used to nail her every morning just before he let her slip out the bed and get ready for work, loving that wasted, bad girl look.

Caitland smiled up at him, but it wasn't really her face he saw.

'Hey," he said smiling back. "You gotta go."

"You sure?" She grinned, rolling her eyes provocatively.

"Yes," he said staring at her lips, letting his eyes linger on her pretty face.

"God, I must look a mess."

"No, actually, you're slammin' baby. Very beautiful." He kissed her shoulder. "Thanks for everything, but you have to take off like right now," he said squeezing her hips, then smacked her backside. "The money's in the envelope next to your bag."

She glided her hands up and down his chest, caressing him. Then she murmured, "You know, this is the first time I feel guilty about getting paid."

He kissed her temple and then lifted himself off the bed and went into the bathroom to start his shower. He came back to the door. "Baby, do me a favor and close the door behind you."

"Okay," she said slipping off the bed to get dressed.

Then he speed dialed security on his cell phone. "Deuce, if Veronica comes by, don't let her in."

"Aw'ight, boss."

He took a long shower, even though the time was getting short, feeling strangely detached. Taking a deep breath, he let the water run down his head to clear it a bit, then washed down. But as he came out of shower with all the steam swirling about, he could have sworn he saw her, sitting right on the toilet, with her head resting on her arms, staring up at him.

At first, he rubbed his eyes, thinking his mind was playing tricks on him. But then he reopened them and she was still there. He didn't want to believe it.

What are you doing? What are you doing? He heard her saying—except her lips didn't move, but he could hear her voice very clearly in his head. *What the fuck are you doing?*

It was outlandish, some truly freaky shit—to even think that she was actually there—but there she was. Although his heart was racing, he turned around, seemingly nonchalant, and started to brush his teeth. He had to rub the steam off the mirror to be able to see, and he could barely see the apparition, but turning back several times, she stayed there. Seated quietly, staring up at him.

Strangely enough, after the initial shock of seeing her, he found he was not scared. He brushed his teeth vigorously with his electric toothbrush. Washed his face. Then started to shave. Turning around again, he looked in back of him, and she was gone. He started to get distraught then. Where'd she go? He concentrated real hard, then turned again. There she was again.

Cut your hair, he heard her say, inside his head again.

"What?!" He said aloud.

You heard me. Cut your hair. Right here. Right now. Take your shears, and cut it all off.

"Why?"

I never liked it. That's why. I never told you, but I liked my men clean-cut. Cut it off. Besides, back in ancient times, people cut their hair to mourn their dead. You do mourn me, don't you? You did love me, didn't you?

All of the sudden, he didn't like the hair that was clinging to his back and shoulders. His dreadlocks, which he had been growing for the past ten years now offended him. Yes, he would cut it. Cut it all off. Of course she hadn't like them. They displeased her and he wished never to offend her. Quickly, he opened a drawer and grabbed a pair of shears.

How would he even look without them? His hands trembled as he took hold of a lock. Without thinking too much, he cut the first one, which went tumbling to the tiled floor. Then, steadily, he started cutting off all the others. It got easier as he continued, until it no longer mattered. It all came down, all of his hair was down on the floor. And when he was done, he could hardly recognize himself. He looked so *different.* Taking his electric shears, he tapered his hair, giving it more precision, some type of shape, making it neat.

Staring at his face, he thought about how he looked. Like a complete stranger. Goodness, he could actually see his face, his chiseled jawline, his cheekbones looked higher. He didn't look too bad. He looked a little like a Jesus with cropped hair.

Now go, before you're late to my funeral, he heard her say inside his mind again—except she was gone.

Oh shit! The funeral!

Oh shit, he thought feeling giddy all of the sudden. He was cracking up, laughing. He could hear her. It was Arielle. She was speaking inside his mind. And he had seen her too. She had decided to haunt him. "God in Heaven, help me," he said aloud.

Just then Deuce walked in to tell him the car had arrived and was downstairs waiting for him. But one look at him and Deuce looked like *he* had seen a ghost.

"Christ almighty," Deuce exclaimed. "Boss, you done lost it. You done lost your mind!"

But Cedric was standing there, his face wearing a strange expression. Deuce was still staring at him and shaking his head. "Cedric, you're not even dressed, man. The funeral's in twenty minutes. And goodness, what happened to your hair? Lord!"

"Did Veronica come," Cedric asked, splashing water again on his face.

"Yes, and she was piping mad. Angry as a wet cat. She promised she'd have my job."

Cedric smiled, feeling a great burden lift off his chest. Arielle was going to haunt him, and he was looking forward to being haunted. He was actually grinning.

Could be all the crap he was pulling, all the women he was banging...in her house...on their bed. He was now very close to laughing.

"Cedric, what's up, man. Why you grilling like that and why'd you cut off all your hair, man?"

"Life is a beautiful thing, bro," was all Cedric could offer as explanation. Then he balled his fist and touched it to Deuce in a playful handshake. Deuce continued to look at him in absolute bewilderment. "And where's Quentin, man?" Quentin was his stylist. Today of all days, he needed his help.

***

Leah turned her television on two hours before the funeral telecast. Not wanting to miss a thing. The funeral coverage would start at nine o'clock with a look at the back story. The funeral itself was at ten. Leah woke up at seven. Made coffee. Got her newspapers from outside and promptly began to read all the local coverage of the event. Simultaneously, she monitored the television.

The Miami Herald, The Sun Sentinel, The Miami Times, Street, City Link, New Times, every newspaper she could find were all lying on her kitchen counter as she scoured their pages to glean whatever she could regarding the funerals. U.S.A. Today, had a little blurb as well. She smiled when she saw her picture on page 2A. Of course, Cedric was on the front page, but hey, she was happy anyway.

"Morning, Madam," Mercedes, her Cuban nanny said as she walked in with either girls on her sides. But Leah could barely acknowledge them. Dressed in a pale blue floral gown, she glanced absently at them and took a sip of her coffee as she turned her attention back to the TV.

Cedric had arrived late, which was causing quite a ruckus with the live coverage. *Cedric did not show. He's not there. What does it mean? What's the significance?* Leah looked on in angst.

What the hell did that mean?

There was no way. No way at all he wasn't showing up, although she half longed for him not to. What a slap in that bitch's face. Anyway, he was probably late. No way wouldn't he come. He was just late. Only late. Those reporters needed to calm the hell down. After all, Cedric was half-black. Just like her. He was just on C.P. time. He'd be there.

Then when he showed—no one even realized or recognized him. Despite the multitude of journalist and cameras milling about, many of the fans and the elegantly dressed guest filing into the church, Cedric slipped in unnoticed.

Later, they would show tapes of where he had in fact walked in flanked by Duce and Quentin, and show his chauffeur Rico, who was standing on the steps, after dropping him off. He walked in and up the aisle, even though the other guys had hung back, taking a seat at the back pew. Cedric kept going though. All the way to the front of the altar as the priest eulogized Arielle and did not stop until he was in front of the casket. It wasn't until he placed the single red rose he had been carrying in his hand, and bent down and smooched the corpse that people recognized him. And then all hell broke loose.

"Cedric is in fact here and inside the church. He slipped past us. He has cut his hair. Shaved off his famous dreadlocks. Let's see if we can playback some tapes of his entrance," the reporter from CNN rattled off.

Leah quickly flipped to FOX network, which she knew would have the juiciest news. This network carried the news tabloid style.

The chirpy reporter was talking real low, listening to the piece in her ear. "We have a man inside," she reported. "We have someone in there and what he's reporting is very choppy right now, but bear with me and we're going to get it to you just as soon as things develop. He's saying that right now all is relatively calm. Apparently, there's a murmur that Cedric has just entered the church. He says everyone's looking about, but Cedric hasn't made his way to the front yet. He says there's a big hush. People are looking expectant.

"Oh-oh, he says Cedric's in view. He's flanked by his two personal bodyguards. He says the guards have stopped half way as if to pay their respect but that Cedric has continued up the aisle alone. Everyone it seems is holding their breath, he reports. Cedric has stopped in front of her casket and is looking down. There's a single rose in his hand. It's red. It seems like he's crying. His shoulders are moving up and down. He's placing the rose inside, but...

"Oh goodness, he says Cedric has taken a hold of the cadaver and is hugging it fiercely. Pandemonium has broken loose. People are yelling and screaming, tons of people are now trying to pull him off, but he's holding steady.

Leah gulped. "Christ!" Her throat felt dry, raw. She needed some water but she couldn't leave, didn't want to miss a second of this blow by blow account of what was going on in that church.

"Our man is saying that they've finally pulled Cedric off her but that he's dug his heels and has fallen to the floor. He's crying real loud. He's screaming, "Arrriieeelle! Arrriieeele!" The yells are heart-wrenching. Pitiful. Blood-curling, people who were trying to be strong are getting sucked into his grief.

"Someone said to be his father is by his side right now. And the rest of the church has joined in on the crying and moaning. Several of the family from her side have started to scream and are falling out. Cedric's set the precedence and this funeral is going to be a heart-wrenching, highly emotional affair."

Leah felt the tears glossing her eyes. This was actually sad. Real sad. But she wiped her tears away solemnly. She should have been there. She really should have been. Why had she let her mother brow-beaten her into not attending?

This was too delicious. Exciting TV.

"It's chaotic inside," the reporter continued. "There is screaming and shouting. The grief is too much. Too much for the family to bear. There's not a dry eye in that church. The emotion is raw. Our insider says he's never seen anything like this in his life!"

Leah watched and listened intently to everything unfolding with her heart in her throat. It was voyeuristic. Like watching a fatal car crash, you're saddened but riveted to the tragedy. Everyone needed to see the pain. She switched stations wanting to be sure if the other stations were reporting the same thing. Going from station to station, she was desperate to find the one with the best coverage.

She hardly noticed when Sandra, the nanny, whom she had recently hired to help her with the twins came out to join her. The twins were up and with her, but Leah couldn't even help with their feeding, she was so glued to the tube.

Oh the network was really milking it now—playing Simon & Garfunkel's "Bridge over Troubled Waters," that sad, quiet, haunting song while showing montages of fans who were lining the streets showing their support and solidarity for Cedric. They were being kept at bay by the police barricades and what looked like the entire police force. That was what was keeping them from storming the church. They were starting to join in the screaming and grieving too. Then there was the pictures of the church steps littered with flowers and candles, balloons and stuffed bears. There were cards, and letters. It was tense, a spectacle.

"Sweet Lord," she murmured. The ratings must be going through the roof!

The phone rang. It was her mother. "Are you watching this?"

"Of course!"

"Can you believe how they're glorifying that little hussy! Are people forgetting that this little whore was having an adulterous affair with her cousin, your husband? Has the world lost its mind?!"

"Mom, I guess it's just good television. The press doesn't care, so long as they get their ratings."

"But this is ridiculous. I can't believe how much they're

playing this thing up!"

"Well, mom, she *was* married to Cedric Courage, so it's a high profile murder case."

"Do you think he did it? I mean look at this. I think he's acting the way he's carrying on."

"Well, I wouldn't put it past him," Leah said, barely paying attention, still flipping through channels. "Mom, I gotta go! I told you I should have gone!"

She hung up and turned back to CNN, then flipped back to her favorite news channel, Fox's WSVN.

***

Everything about this moment jarred and caused him pain. This was the moment he had been dreading all along. The terrifying moment of finally having to say goodbye.

He stood quietly, staring sadly at the frozen beauty of his beloved Arielle. Noting how the beauty of her face had not as of yet been marred by death. She was a beautiful corpse, a stone statue. Her hair looked so alive and glossy, spilling over her shoulders the way it had when she was alive, but her chiseled features were now more like marble.

He was in a church full of people, with the world press harboring outside the door, yet to him he was all alone. He felt a hand rest on his back then move to his shoulders. It was his pops, and turning, he hugged him fiercely.

His father hugged him back, whispering in his ears all the while: "Don't do this son. Find some dignity. I know you loved her. Loved her dearly. We all did. But this is not how you honor her. You must let her go with dignity and grace. You give her a fantastic send off—one she would be proud of—and show her honor in that way. Now come sit down. Come sit next to me and mourn her with the proper decorum."

He longed to tell his father how there was nothing dignified about the way he loved Arielle. Yes, he had made a spectacle of himself, but he could hardly care. He loved her so much. He was beyond hope, past grief. He sighed heavily, weeping as he allowed his father to take him to his seat.

The organist was playing a rendition of the Beatles tune, "Let it Be," so appropriate for the moment. He sung the words in his mind as he walked back to his place, allowing the service to continue.

Somehow he'd gotten through it. Singing that song in his

head, *Let it be...Let it be...*

Now seated between his father and Veronica who had managed to move towards them, he tried to give the impression that he was all right. That he was going to make it through this with no more eruptions. That he would find the dignity his father wanted him to display. But the truth was, he was slipping every second that went by. His skin felt hideously alive and he wasn't sure if it wasn't due to the Xanax Deuce had so thoughtfully provided on the drive there. But now he was itching to claw at himself—to break skin.

He was trying to look around the church, careful not to take in the altar, in front of which rested Arielle's coffin, the one that he had nearly knocked over earlier. There it was, all that remained of a life he'd loved and still loved quite desperately—now only a body he must bury. He could feel his body sweating like mad. He could feel the pain devouring him, ravaging and eating up his insides—and why did it have to hurt so bad?!

It wasn't until Bailey began his eulogy that he felt any sort of peace. Bailey's tone and words served as the balm he had desperately needed.

"A wonderful person once told me that the birth of a soul could change the world forever," Bailey began. "That person happened to be a clergy, Father Timmons, a priest at our parish. I never forgot those calming words of encouragement, words deftly offered to a child in compassion for one who had tragically lost both parents. Yet, I stand by those words today because my sister was definitely one of those souls.

"Anyone who had the opportunity to meet her or who had the joy of walking close to her knew how special she was. She epitomized beauty, style and grace. Championed great causes. Knowing her means being forever touched and changed for the better."

Cedric could hear people sigh their agreement and sniffling going on all around him. Yes, Arielle was very special indeed. He listened as Bailey continued.

"The Symonette family has lost one of our most precious members, but she has not left us completely. She will be missed, but she will be kept alive, suspended in the hearts of those lucky enough to have been graced by her presence. Once you know someone as genuine and special as her, you can not help but follow her example. And in the end, it is not how you died, but how you lived...who you touched that matters most.

"Although beautiful spirits have a way of wandering off, they don't leave without making a difference. I am blessed to have known her, lucky to have called her sister. Yet, the rest of you who knew her, who understood her and recognized the beauty of her soul will keep her memory intact, and her legacy of empowering others will live on eternally.

"In calling her up by name, we keep her spirit alive. Arielle! Erin Arielle!" Bailey shouted from the alter, speaking directly to her now, startling some of the mourners, causing everyone to start tearing up again, "Sister, friend, mother, daughter, wife! You were all those things. You played so many roles. And you will be forever remembered.

"You were my dearest friend. My sister and mentor, and the most beautiful person I have ever known. The person I am today, I owe it all to you. You molded me by your belief in me. You told me so often, I was destined for greatness. Except it was you who attained that greatness. Your ability to love, nurture and educate surpasses many educators I have come into contact with. You are the great one, the profound one. And it was this way of yours, the ability to show others how to be human, how to love, live and learn. It is that which made you who you were—the embodiment of hope, truth, love, warmth, courage and strength.

"I'll miss you, Erin Arielle Courage," he ended, wiping at his eyes, "but you'll forever live in my memory and heart."

***

"There's some semblance of order again inside the church," the chirpy reporter from WSVN reported. "Cedric is off the floor next to his father, who apparently got through to him. Originally, he was going to say a few words and was even scheduled to sing a song—however, we're not sure if that's actually going to happen at this point. But from what we understand, his brother-in-law, Bailey gave a beautiful eulogy that left not a dry eye in the church."

Leah was going nuts as she blasted to another channel.

"Jesus Christ!" she stormed. "I knew I should have gone! I knew it!!! Aren't they going to televise the eulogy?!"

Sandra, the Cuban nanny, looked at her with some concern.

Goodness, she wished she could have been there to see Cedric screaming and carrying on. She wished she could have seen her family as well, falling out, carrying on. They didn't act like that yesterday. But then again, she'd remained perfectly calm and poised. Towards the end, though, she had managed to squeeze out a couple of tears, but all this melodrama today, well...was pure sensationalism. Absolute pandemonium. It would have definitely been fun to watch.

What she didn't get, however, was that oddly enough, instead of nailing him, how the press was being strangely sympathetic towards Cedric. And the crowd was amassing, growing in the streets. More and more people was joining the melee, it was insane! The press for lack of things to do, since they were shut out of the actual funeral, were now interviewing the fans while the funeral service continued.

"Why'd you come," one reporter asked a Hispanic guy who looked to be in his mid-twenties.

"I don't know. I just felt like I had to come give my support."

"To whom are you giving your support?"

"To Cedric and his wife's family, man, Cedric is the man, the bomb! He rules! I'm sorry this had to happen to him. It's horrible! And then on top it, they're accusing him of killing her. No way, man. No way! He didn't do it."

"No way at all, dawg" a friend he was with chimed in. "To waste that fine ass. Hell, I don't care who she was sleeping with!"

"Even if it was with my own father," his friend said and high-fived him.

"There's no way he would have wasted that. Cause she was too damn fine!"

"Well, there you have it," the reporter said smiling despite herself. Going over to some other fans, some females this time and posed the same question.

"I had to come be here for Cedric," the teeny-bopper with the mid-rift top and low-rider jeans claimed. "He needs us right now. In his time of need."

"Yeah," added her other friends.

"The guy's the coolest, the hottest rapper. I mean, Fifty Cent don't have nothing on him, you know what I mean? He could have gone there all cool with attitude. But instead, he broke down, man."

"Now that's real," one of her friends added.

The reporter thanked them and ran back to the church steps when she realized the service was now over and people were beginning to file out of the church, catching the first person she could find.

"What was the mood like in there?"

"If I live to be a hundred years, I'll never see anything as sad as this," the woman said, still wiping at her eyes.

The next person she asked declared, "If he killed his wife, then he deserves an Academy Award!"

"Although there had been over 300 people invited to the mass, from what I'm being told, only family and close friends will be attending the actual burial. Then the day will end with a very private reception at Cedric's Williams Island penthouse—again for only family and close, personal friends. Although we're restricted to the outskirts of the cemetery and his home, we'll be bringing it to you LIVE whenever we can," the reporter concluded. "Stay tuned."

Leah cut off the television in exasperation. Nobody was going to stop her from going over to Cedric's reception. No one! She was definitely attending that! This was just too juicy to miss altogether, she didn't care what her mother said or thought.

"Sandy," she told the nanny. "I'm going out. See that the twins get bathed and that they have their nap by noon."

She ran to the bathroom to shower and get dressed. Goodness gracious, why had she listened to her mother. To think she could have witnessed all of this high drama first hand! SHIT! Double-shit! She would never listen to her mom again. She never used to. Why start now?

But she would get all the dish from Biandra and Jorge—well, then on second thought, maybe she shouldn't ask them. They might be...well, they had always been so close to Arielle and might get offended. No, maybe Lucy, Arielle's ex-secretary who she had probably driven nuts, would be a safer bet. She wouldn't have missed this, and she must have been invited. Yes, she'd dish the dirt with Lucy later, but now she had to hurry and get dressed so she could at least make the reception!

**

To get out of the church, they had to make their way through a barrage of reporters and photographers—not to mention all the television cameras and thousands and thousands of mourners who had come to pay their respects. It was a media circus, with not only local and American press, but press from all over the world. So diverse and international. Veronica marveled at the spectacle. Who knew this tragedy would have such a widespread, universal appeal? So many people, it seemed wanted to be a part of this. It was crazy, truly extraordinary!

Cedric's bodyguards had to make a human chain to encircle

him, and still they couldn't adequately protect him. The press, his fans, the police, everyone seemed to have gone ape-shit—cluttering around, snapping pictures, shoving microphones all over the place. Not even making an attempt to even appear respectful. Everyone seemed to want a piece of him for their own selfish reasons.

Veronica shuddered at it all. What had America become? We might as well change the acronym to our name. USA should no longer stand for the United States of America, but for United Selfish Assholes!

"Okay, here we go," Veronica told him, trying to strengthen his resolve. She was walking next to him, having her hand firmly clasped in his.

"Cedric! Cedric! Cedric!" They were all yelling.

"Cedric! Please! Can you answer a question?!"

"Cedric, a second please!"

"Please Cedric! Over here!"

"Cedric Courage, did you kill your wife?!" One overly ambitious reporter asked, breaking through the chain.

Veronica had to restrain Cedric, so he wouldn't deck her. Veronica herself wanted that supreme pleasure. *Of course he did*, she wanted to say, *and next he's going to kill you!*

Scavengers. That's what they all were. Sweet heavens, how in the world were they ever going to make it to the cemetery?

***

After her shower, Leah dressed with great care. Choosing a smart but demure, simple Channel little black dress. The look she was going for was classy, but shy enough to win sympathy. Poor little Leah, that was the look and attitude she was going for. The role of victim was a specialty of hers.

So she would go over and offer him her condolences and grieve with them. Meanwhile, she was diligently working on a wrongful death suit to be launched in the event of his arrest. If he was convicted, he was going to have to pay her a staggering amount of money. Yes, and she was going to be filthy rich. As it was, she found out only a few days ago that Danyel's company was merging with another media outfit and going public, not to mention the fact that he had a two million dollar insurance policy that was going to leave her and the girls nicely taken cared of. She would never have to work a day in her life again—not that she had had to in the first place. No stranger to money, she had grown up quite comfortably and actually had a sizable account as it was. But now, she was going to be a lot more comfortable. She almost laughed. What was the saying—you could never be too rich or too thin.

Oh, it was ashamed that Arielle was gone. How she would have loved showing off! Playing the elegant, rich widow. Yes, it was truly ashamed.

Just as she grabbed her bag, she heard the doorbell chime. Who in the world could that be just as she was about to head out? She sprayed a little bit of perfume and walked into it just as she had seen Arielle do on occasion. Then walked out the door. Sandra was already at the door with one of the toddlers on her hip and holding the other's hand.

"Leah, she said softly. "It's the FBI, they say they need to talk to you."

"The FBI?"

"Yes, they showed me their badges, this man and this woman."

"What could they possibly have to talk to me about?"

Sandra shrugged.

"All right. Thanks, Sandy. Take the girls up to their room. I'll handle this." She smoothed back her hair, put on a serene face and went to the door. "Yes, may I help you?"

"Mrs. Champion," the black woman said. She was real tall, not at all what Leah expected. Very attractive.

"Yes."

"Hi," the white male said. "We're with the Federal Bureau of Investigation and we have some questions we'd like to ask you regarding your husband's murder."

The woman looked her up and down and said, "It looks like you were going out or just came back. And we're sorry to disturb you, but this will only take a few minutes."

"Sure," Leah said glancing at her watch. It would probably be another hour before people started heading back to Cedric's. They were probably still at the cemetery. Besides, she was very intrigued to know what the FBI wanted. She had already been questioned by the police. In fact, while she had lain in a hospital bed. She had fainted upon hearing the news and slipped and hit her head. During their questioning, she had been very cooperative, even though her head had been bandaged and she had been suffering from a concussion.

"Please come in," she said graciously. "Make yourself comfortable."

"Can I get you two some coffee."

"No, we're fine," the woman said quickly.

"Thank you though," the man answered. Both of them taking a seat on the couch.

"You have a very lovely home," the female agent commented, attempting to break the ice and put her at ease.

"You know. I don't think I caught your names."

"Oh, our apologies," the man apologized. "I'm Special Agent Neff and this is Special Agent Jade."

"Neff and Jade," she said with a slight smile and settled herself on the love seat across from them. "Well, fire away."

"Well, first of all, we want to let you know that we're aware you've been questioned by the police," Special Agent Jade began.

"Right, I had planned on mentioning that. But what's going on, has this case turned into a federal case now?"

"Mrs. Champion, Mr. Courage's life has been threatened, as well as that of his family's. It is apparent that he may also be getting stalked. Now we don't know if there's a connection between those murders and the threat on Mr. Courage's life, but we are pursuing all avenues," she explained.

"Okay. So where do I come in?"

Special Agent Neff smiled patiently. "We're not sure if you come in at all. Have you received any questionable mail?"

"No, none at all."

"Are you aware of any enemies your husband may have had?"

She shrugged. "My husband was a very charming, very well-liked guy. Did he have any enemies? I don't know. I only met him about two years ago when he moved here from New York. What his life was like back there, I don't know. He never talked much about his past."

"So there's no one you knew who he may have had a problem with? A business partner? A disgruntled customer? An old girlfriend," Neff questioned.

"Well, I don't know, but he seemed to have this thing with Cedric."

"Cedric," the Jade woman said immediately on the defensive. Apparently Cedric's mad appeal was too potent even for the most testosterone-prone females.

"Well...I guess it may have been because he was carrying an affair with Cedric's wife, but he seemed to hate the guy."

"Danyel hated Cedric," the Jade woman asked with more surprise. "I thought they were friends."

"Friends," Leah laughed gently. "Hardly. To me, he loathed the guy. But I suppose it was mostly because of her. I mean it was like she was playing them one hand against the middle. But they were civil with each other, I guess, for the most part."

"For the most part. Why do you say that," Neff inquired.

"Well, I did know of a fight they had once."

"Fight as in duke it out," Agent Jade asked now.

"Why, yes. I wasn't there. I just heard about it. But Danyel went to his studio and tried to kill Cedric with his bear hands when he learned they had gotten married. Shortly after that he married me."

"Interesting," she said, then asked, "What about Arielle? You were friends also. Weren't you? Do you know someone with an ax to grind?"

Other than myself, she thought and half-smiled. "Well, Arielle was a real bitch, you know. I'm sure she had a lot of enemies. But I didn't know all the people she knew. All I can tell you about her is that she thought she was hot shit! She had so much attitude. Always talking about kicking this or that person's ass. She was a bad ass—if you know what I mean. Even slapped Linda, our boss once in front of the entire office one time. And I know of quite a few other people she had slapped—including ex-boyfriends. She just couldn't keep her hands to herself. She was one of those women that was bitchy. The kind you loved to hate."

"And did you hate her," the Jade woman asked casually.

"Me," she said realizing that she had perhaps said too much. "Well, hate would be too strong a world. I mean, she was having an affair with my husband for heaven's sake! But I swear, I didn't find out until the murder. That's why I was in so much shock and fainted. Cause we were like friends until the very end. I just couldn't believe it, you know, her being his cousin and all. Gosh, I knew she was trampy. Hot to trot. But I had no idea she was this morally repugnant, and that she'd stoop so low."

"And how did Arielle feel about you?"

"We were friends—like I told you. I mean, we had our ups and downs. We went through our periods when we didn't speak to each other, but for the most part, we always made up and," she sniffed, wiping away a tear, "I thought we'd be friends forever. Anyway," she said getting up, "I really wish I could help you guys more. But, I was on my way to Cedric's. I want to go and be there for him. So, I have to be leaving."

Kendra stood up first and Neff followed. "Well, maybe we'll see you there. We were on our way there as well."

"You were," she asked puzzled.

"Perhaps we didn't mention it, but we're Cedric's protection. As I mentioned before, he's been getting death threats."

"Oh, yeah...right."

"We're headed to the cemetery now, but maybe we'll see you later there."

"All right then," she said walking them to the door. "Yes, maybe I'll run into you guys again."

Kendra gave her a measuring look. "Well, nice meeting you...Mrs. Champion."

"Likewise," she told her and shook hands with Agent Neff.

BITCH! Leah thought as she saw the woman whisper something the him. For some reason, this broad reminded her of Arielle. They had a similar build, even some of the same mannerism, putting on that same bitch-goddess air. Nope! She didn't like this woman one bit, and hoped not to have very many more dealings with her. She'd have to make today an exception, though. Nothing was going to deter her from attending that reception!

***

Leah arrived on William's Island and was nearly turned away at the entrance gate. There was heavy police security there. Too many people trying to get on the island, trying to get to Cedric's penthouse. This must be a nightmare to the resident's of this posh community. All this media circus couldn't be sitting well with them.

She had to call Bailey's cell phone and he had to come over and escort her in personally since her name had not been on the invite list. She had to show ID, so did Bailey, it was ridiculous. But she was grateful he had come to get her, and felt more comfortable walking into that penthouse on his arm instead of alone in any case.

There were a lot more people there than she had expected. And so much food. The penthouse was filled with flowers—just as she imagined the church must have been. Very tasteful, very expensive. The food was bountiful and beautifully arranged and the uniformed servants walking around with trays of delicious looking pastries, sandwiches and drinks added to the understatement of wealth, privilege and class.

Oh, this shamed the little shindig she had had for Danyel

yesterday at her parent's Coral Gables mansion. Although she had hired a very reputable catering company, it hadn't been quite as lavish as this. This was shaping into a really grand affair. When had Cedric found the time to organize this—but then again, she was forgetting how Cedric had all these underlings who took care of things for him. She was forgetting he had an army of people on his payroll. He probably hadn't lifted a finger to do a thing.

In any case, this was first class, with lovely food stations overflowing with silver platters of lobster, mussels, clams, oysters and cocktail shrimp. There was also a pasta station, where the chef was serving up food freshly cook for the guest, adding whatever you asked for. Not to mention a separate station of fresh-cut fruits, salads, cheeses, pastries and a variety of tasty desserts.

No sooner had she entered, she was immediately asked what she would like to drink. She would have loved to have asked for champagne to go along with the cold seafood and caviar, but she didn't want it to seem like she was celebrating. "Some wine would be fine. White, please."

A number of Cedric's famous celebrity friends were there as well. Leah was trying hard not to gawk at some of the more notable faces. It took a while to spot Cedric, who was sitting on the window ledge a little apart from everyone else. He had his jacket off but was still in his black Armani slacks with his white silk shirt opened at the collar, his designer tie hanging askew, looking pretty damn good with his new low-cut hairdo. Now he looked like a total white boy. With wavy dirty blonde hair, the same color as hers.

Gosh, they could be brother and sister. She excused herself and went up to him. Cedric was sitting at a far off window seat, sitting apart from his guest, smoking a cigarette. Calmly exhaling smoke out of his mouth, he hadn't said anything as of yet and had his back to her. Standing right next to him, suddenly she didn't know what to say.

He looked at her—his eyes were red and moist. Leah took a deep breath and gulped. *Shit. Oh, shit.* A noise came out of her throat but nothing she said made sense. She was trying to talk, but she couldn't. She saw such misery in those eyes. So much raw emotion. Torment.

God, what could she say? No wonder he had separated himself and was still standing apart. Everyone needed to go and leave him alone.

She stood there for awhile saying nothing and feeling dumb until he took heart and took her hand in his, tugging gently to pull her down to sit next to him. Her fingers tingled and she felt really funny holding his hand. She could feel the energy, a heat pouring from his hand to hers. It was odd, because they had never touched before—well save for a few pecks on the cheek in greeting once or twice. They had never been particularly close. But holding his hands felt nice. Felt good actually and looking into his eyes with his long, wet lashes, she was thinking, God, he's beautiful. He was ridiculously beautiful...now that he didn't have all that hair covering up all of that raw beauty. His eyes were so pretty. She loved the Asiatic shape. She had never realized how handsome he really was—before today. The cropped hair was really becoming on him.

Why didn't he say something, though?

Why couldn't she say something?

Maybe nothing needed to be said.

Maybe they alone could commiserate, knowing what they had lost. Except his feelings were real and made her feel like such a fraud. Just thinking about all the foul things she planned on doing to him was making her queasy—like the wrongful death suit she was planning on filing if he was arrested for the murders. She had twin girls with no father, and hell, he had plenty of money. But deep in her heart, she knew he didn't deserve that. He didn't deserve any of it. He had never been anything but kind to her.

Yet she had to do what she had to do. Life wasn't fair, now was it? We were dealt a hand and just had to deal with it, make it work for us.

"You loved him," he asked after awhile.

"Yes."

"So did I."

"I loved Arielle too," she said faltering. And then she started crying, for real. For the first time, because she realized, it wasn't a lie. She *had* loved Arielle. And she was being real. And she had cared about Danyel too. In her own way. Sure at first it was because of some stupid woman rivalry between her and Arielle, that had made him so appealing. Head games...that's all it was at first. But then after living with him and seeing him day in and day out...she had fallen in love...so completely in love. Especially seeing how he had interacted with the twins, the way he had fallen so deeply in love with them. Another bash of hot tears fell quickly down her cheeks—except he had never loved her. He had never fallen for her...How could he when his heart belonged to someone else? Wholly and completely.

And that's the way she had been, Arielle. She ate you whole.

"I'm so sorry," she sniffled, mascara running. "I'm so sorry," she said again and had to escape. Anywhere. Just not there. Just not next to him. His grief was too much to even watch, to even see him bear. In fact, just being in this house was making her crazy...making her remember too damn much! Being there was making her feel things she didn't care to feel.

Perhaps her mother had been right.

Bailey seeing the interaction and watching her escape came immediately rushing after her, catching her just as she was about to enter the bathroom.

"Leah," he said, easily catching up and pulling her into his arms. *Oh, he felt so good, so safe, so warm!* He gave her this great bear hug and she feared she was melting all over the floor.

"Are you all right?"

"No, I'm not," she said, wrapping her arms more firmly around him. Not caring who saw, who was watching, what anybody was thinking. Burying her face alongside the crook of his shoulder, she said, "Please, Bailey, I want to get out of here. Would you come with me? I need...I need someone to talk to...to be with." She tilted her head back to look into his adorably concerned eyes, her lips trembled slightly, her breathing was coming in shallow, short spurts.

"What did he say to you," Bailey demanded, worry etched in his handsome face. "Did he say something mean to you?"

She shook her head. "No-no, nothing like that," she said trying to wipe away her still flowing tears. "I-I just can't stay here anymore. This place is...it just reminds me too much of ...of...I just feel her, like she's here and I..." she wasn't making sense she knew. She pulled away. "I really have to go! Give Cedric and the rest of the family my regards."

But Marie, one of the cousins was standing by the foyer as she tried to make her run, blocking her escape route. "Leaving so soon," she said. "But you've only just got here. I was hoping we could talk. About some things. The girls...are you going to let them—"

Leah ran past her. She couldn't stay there another minute. She couldn't breathe. Bailey ran after her.

"I'll be back," he told Marie. "Tell Cedric we'll hang out later. Something's up with Leah."

"Okay," she mouthed to him as he dashed out the door, trying to catch up with her. He caught up to her at the exit, near the elevator doors. She was breathing a little more easier now, after having taken several large gasps of air. Inside the penthouse had been positively stifling, and she had felt something truly eerie in there. She couldn't explain it, but it was as if Arielle had been there...watching and observing.

"What happened back there," he asked her in the elevator. "You looked spooked."

And she had been. She had been. She had been spooked!

"Look," she said grabbing hold of his lapels, "I don't want to go home right now. I feel...just so out-of-control. And I don't want the girls to see me like this. You mind if we go to your place? I'm tired. I want to lie down. Just not at home. Do you mind?"

He hugged her again. "No problem," he said, stroking her back affectionately. *"Mi casa es su casa."*

Suddenly, she was able to smile again. Yes, she was going to be all right. She had just needed to get away from there. And Bailey was so sweet, *my house is your house,* he had told her in Spanish. Yes, everything was going to be all right after all.

8

Courage in the House

Nearly every day brought even more evidence of her betrayal. New discoveries. One more painful thing to contend with. I hated her at times. Felt total contempt for her. Just being honest about my feelings. Don't hold it against me. She had done plenty of shit to me—especially after reading her journals that I shouldn't have done in the first place. That was a mistake. I'll admit that.

I had violated her trust in a sense. Those journals weren't meant for me to read. Not sure she'd ever intended for me to ever see them, much less read any of the words written there. No, she wasn't that cruel. I was no better than those damned reporters and blasted paparazzi that were making a mockery of her memory. Even Kendra had tried to warn me. She had gone through them quite thoroughly.

"I don't think you should read them," she had warned me. But I had paid her no heed. It only made me what to read them more. Yes, for sure. I could absorb all the hurt and pain. I was strong—or so I thought

There were no more secrets. I was aware of exactly how she had felt. And I was the loser. Danyel, clearly the winner, the one with all her affections.

I started reading about them and the little secret world they had built together. The words took me by surprise. The beauty of her expression. She was a true poet. And reading about the sex and all the torrid emotions, I'd never believe it by the way she had looked at me. How could she be this in love with someone else, and yet make me feel like I was the only man she loved?

I would have never suspected she was false.

The words written in her journals spoke clearly how she had found the love of her life—and it wasn't me. And though she tried to hide the love that she denied by living a lie with me, she had never let me feel it.

I cried a lot, reading those journals. Feeling her despair. And as I go through my life, I'll never believe the emotions, the agony she had gone through...living with me.

Yes, it was hard to come to terms with: I had been nothing but a sloppy second, a consolation prize. Cut to the bone, but facts were facts. And if her journals were any indication, I had been a goddamn fool...and still was now.

All I was for her, really, was nothing but a bank account. The guy who had fathered her child and who took care of her business. But in the meantime, she was all-choked up, hot and heavy and sexually involved with her pretty boy cousin—who I had actually considered a good friend. Christ! How many times had they rolled around on this very bed, laughing at me. At my pure stupidity! If Danyel wasn't already dead, I swear to God I would have put a bullet in his head myself after reading those blasted journals.

I didn't want to believe how badly my woman had had it for this guy. How much she loved him. How she literally adored him. How she was his—lock, stock and fine ass.

I was a laughing stock! Hell, practically every comic in America was ranking on me now. Even people who weren't comics threw in a few licks. And the tabloids were trying me—left and right. I was their main feature for a few weeks straight until the next crisis rolled around. It was a persecution.

But nothing had made me feel as fucked up as this. I felt so played. It was like my whole crew, all the fans, the whole world knew I had been dissed like a piece of shit! Punk ass nigga— straight up. I was feeling so down. Suicidal, even, but I put on a poker face, appearing unaffected. But in the meantime, I was bleeding...all over the place. No one had any idea how fucked up I was feeling.

Now I understood why people sometimes went berserk and just started shooting up a place. It was like you no longer cared. You're drowning, and no one's even there to throw you a life-jacket. Instead, the world seems to be holding your head down, wanting to make sure you swallow more water, enjoying watching you wallow in the muck.

Every second, there was a camera shoved in my face—some asshole trying to get pictures. Telling you how they had twelve hungry kids to feed. Let them take this money shot. The Notorious C.C., they had coined me. Jesus-Lord! And it was all very sad. Life meant so little to people anymore. Two people had lost their lives—tragically—and no one gave a damn really. The press was having a field day. They couldn't report fast enough about every lurid detail. Pictures of Danyel and Arielle were circulating all over the Internet. Somehow or another, they had gotten the copies that had been sent to me. Someone had made a mint on them. More pictures were being auctioned daily on EBay every day. It was perfectly awful.

But the fucking world went on spinning. And the ratings were going bust. Record sales were soaring, and I was actually being advised to go on tour now—cause I would break every record ever set since the fans would come out in droves to see me. It was INSANE!

Security had to be beefed up big time—not to mention the fact that some lunatic was out there threatening my life. I had to have 24-hour police protection. Pops had gotten the FBI involved and this woman I got assigned was just...I'm at a loss for words. But I'm going to try anyway. Overzealous. Overbearing. Stick up her ass, always asking questions.

Everyday, I just wanted to cry: LEAVE ME ALONE. JUST LEAVE ME ALONE. I was hurting so bad. And it was like I was locked in a freaky, carnival sideshow. Couldn't help remembering an old Smoky Robinson song. It truly was, *the saddest little show in all the land.*

> *Let the sideshow begin*
> *Hurry, hurry...step right on.*
> *Can't afford to pass it by*
> *Guaranteed to make you cry.*

Yup, everything was pretty fucked up on the whole. Barely knew where to turn. I felt weary and raw. Totally on the edge.

***

Cedric was sprawled in his rec room, still pouring over more of the journals. It was like he couldn't stop himself. He couldn't stop reading Arielle's memoirs. It was as if he needed to know every lurid detail. Much as it killed him, he just had to know.

Every time he thought of her and Danyel, his guts wrenched so hard it hurt. He tormented himself, going over everything in his mind. All the times they had been together. Their whole life were right there on those pages. She also had little memorabilia to go along with everything. Pressed, dried flowers he had given her. Matches from restaurants they had gone to. Stubs from movies or playbills from shows they had attended together.

He had been gone for four months and they had been living a blissful existence—all at his expense. Then he had came back and ruined their shit. He remembered all the furtive glances, remembered how Danyel had not even been able to disguise his love for Arielle. Not even with him there. He would look at her and just couldn't help how he felt. Cedric remembered very clearly the moment he realized that Danyel was in love with her.

It was the night they had gone to the Promenade after a volleyball game and Danyel had been dancing with her. And at first Cedric had thought nothing of it. They were cousins, so what? They were dancing. But then a song he liked had come on, and rather than grabbing some other woman there to dance with, had cut in on Danyel, wanting to dance with his girl.

Danyel had let him, but then he was fuming as Cedric danced with her. Cedric had purposely dipped her back and pulled her up for a kiss just to see his reaction, he had been scowling so bad. Danyel had walked out not even being able to stand it. He's in love with her, Cedric had thought. He's in love with my bitch. Go figure. And she's his cousin.

Little had he known they had been carrying on big time— behind his back.

He felt anguished, and laughed scornfully at himself. How gullible and what a fool he had been. Oh yes, they had had a good laugh at his expense. But who was laughing now that they were both *dead!*

He took a gulp of the bottle of scotch he held in the crook of his arm. Then in a fit of rage, he threw it at the mirror feeling destructive. The mirror splintered and the bottle shattered, pieces of it flying everywhere, as he crouched low to not get hit by the pieces of charred glass.

"Oh, God!" he moaned loudly, sinking further down to the ground. "Oh God, oh God," he cried. He'd never felt so helpless. There was nothing he could do. Nothing at all he could do.

They had met on the blasted ship because he hadn't been there. Of course they hadn't realized they were cousins then, but life, circumstances, Christ! It was as if that was the way it had to go down. He remembered her passage in her journal:

Saw his face from across the bar,
the way he let the bottle rest just inside his mouth,
I had never felt such lust for a complete stranger.
He was so beautiful to me, so perfect in every way.
All I could think was how jealous I was of that bottle
and how I wished it was I he was drinking from.

We exchanged glances and I knew in an instant,
almost immediately that he'd be someone very dear to me.
Even without talking or touching or anything else,
knew my life was changed forever.
He was my future.

Cedric's lips trembled as he remembered the night they had gone to dinner. Arielle had been acting weird all afternoon. In all fairness, she had begged him to stay in. She didn't feel like going out to eat. Please order room service, she had pleaded. But he wasn't having it. He had met up with the guys in Jamaica and had wanted to show her off, like she was some prize.

Remembering the tenderness he had felt for her when he came to the room and found her there, sleeping instead of enjoying herself, looking all miserable, like she had been crying for days— he had mistakenly thought it was all for him. Except now he knew the truth.

He had come and ruined everything!

His heart thudded loudly and there was a roaring in his ears. Gulping for air, Cedric's eyes squeezed tightly. As hot tears poured down his face, he started to sob.

They had been fucking like rabbits for three days straight. Then she found out they were cousins and it still didn't matter to her. She was in love with him. It didn't even matter, but he refused to be with her and that's where he came in:

I consoled myself with Cedric.
I gave him everything I wished I could be giving Danyel.
All of me. Everything I was, everything I am.
I gave it all to him, all the while wishing he were someone else.

Cedric closed his eyes again, gasping for breath as the words she had so neatly written in her crisp curvy handwriting flashed before him. She had recorded it all down in her journal for prosperity, so there could be no question. It was right there in black and white. Her deception. Her treachery. There was no making any excuses for her. It was all there for him to see.

He groaned, his stomach clenching in pain. If a doctor could read his EKG printout right now, he was sure it would probably resemble that of a person in the midst of a heart attack.

Christ, they had played him for a straight up punk. A muscle hardened his jaw. He had trusted that bitch, that whore, that slut! And this was how she repaid him.

He didn't want to believe he could be this much of a fool, he lamented. And now sitting here agonizing like this…feeling so miserable. She was winning a victory over him all over again.

Yet, like a true masochist, he pushed himself to read more. More betrayal. More of her wickedness, her duplicity, her disloyalty. More, more and so much more. So much suffering…so much deceit. Reading about her fraudulence and utter unfaithfulness until he felt numb, he allowed the pain to redouble. To quadruple, until he could bear no more.

Finally he tossed the journal aside, leaving the page opened to this:

I love everything about him.
Every single thing.
God, and the way he kisses,
let's just say I knew what I was talking about from the onset.
How can I even describe his kisses…
How he starts so gently at first, hardly touching my lips.
Then how they flame with passion.
How they burn, and make me feel exquisite, perfect joy.
Honestly, I could have an orgasm just from kissing him.
And occasionally, he does just that.
Makes me climax, come real hard
Just with his delicious, succulent, luscious kisses.
It's almost like a supernatural delight…

The shame flowed through him like hot lava, making him want to melt into the cracks of the tiled floor in the rec room. Cedric smiled, then gritted his teeth so hard until his jaw ached. Scurrying back to the safety of his master bedroom and letting his body drop into the bed, she was killing him. Just as surely as she was dead, she was trying to take him with her.

He would never read another page, he vowed. It was beyond torture what he was doing to himself. Even now, after several months, her betrayal was still so fresh. His obsession with her had to end. He had to stop thinking of her, dreaming of her, aching to be with her. His habit of drifting through the days in a prolonged stupor and agonizing through nights at the casino and clubs had to cease.

God, he hadn't even picked up his guitar in ages! He had stopped composing music. Too much of Arielle was attached to his songs. He felt completely demoralized. Like he was floundering, losing ground.

She had used him so mercilessly. So callously. She had toyed with his emotions. Why did humans inflict so much pain on one another? And how could we ever love again after being so hurt?

It was no wonder he had put up such a huge wall to fight Veronica's probing interest. To put it simply, people were just fucked-up. They did incredibly foul things to one another because they could—if for no other reason.

Sweet Lord, had someone not gotten to them first, he might have killed them himself. They say, a picture tells a thousand words, but that wasn't true. Even the pictures of them in every conceivable position didn't hurt as much as these words. Her words. The pictures, though graphic, had been just sex. Seeing her with him in the pictures didn't even begin to approach the sting of the words he had read in those journals had accomplished.

She'd been desperately, passionately in love with Danyel. All the while she had been involved with him, it was Danyel she had wanted. All the while.

She had married him knowing she didn't love him.

Cedric moved his legs up, tucking them under his chin, arranging himself into a tight little ball, wanting to make himself as small as possible. Wishing he could make himself disappear altogether.

He wished he could just shrug it off and not feel so furious. Except he couldn't. Swinging himself off the bed, he went to the bathroom into his medicine cabinet and pulled out a small brown paper bag. He tensed up, tightening his fingers around the vial of blow he had stashed there.

Michael had promised it was pure, pharmaceutical coke, and he was hoping it wasn't just a bluff. He needed to get straight-up stoned right now.

Fuck it, he thought as he knocked some of the powder unto the marble counter, arranging it in a neat line then bent down to snorted it up. His nose burned. It had been so long since he had done coke. But he needed it now like never before. He'd never felt this bad in his life!

More power to whoever could take this shit lying down, but he was going to do whatever he had to—to feel okay—even if it was for only for a few minutes.

Moments later, he flung the door open and stepped into the master bathroom, going to start the shower. Slipping off his soiled shorts, he gazed at his naked body. Still in shape, he thought as his mind turned over to that erotic dream he had recently had of Arielle.

He chuckled. "Damn, I can't get over you," he said to no one in particular. Yeah, he was now also always talking to himself. Let's just put that on the long list of the weird things he's been doing lately. Banging ghost, seeing things that weren't there, talking to himself.

Perfectly certifiable.

He had tried drinking himself to oblivion, having empty, meaningless sex. And now he was experimenting with drugs again. Today he had done coke, the night before that, Extasy. Hell, he'd even done heroin. What was left?

Crack?

Crystal Myth?

What hadn't he tried?

He knew his boozing and drugging was destructive. He had tried at first to burn off some steam playing basketball. He used to like to play ball at one time. Play basketball with the boys and play so hard to tire himself out. To the point of exhaustion, where he would pass out the moment he hit the sheets. That had at least kept his body fit, but what he was doing right now was simply crazy. But he could hardly help himself.

He grabbed a towel and threw it on the counter to wipe off with after his shower. Just how much abuse could his body take, he wondered before collapsing. As he stepped into the glass-encased cubicle, he stood there trying to get the water to the desired temperature—very lukewarm, but not too hot. As the temperature turned just right, he started lathering up.

Kendra had suggested he seek counseling and remembering the doctor his dad had suggested (he still had the card), he had actually picked up the phone a few times to make an appointment with Dr. Kendall Silverman. Except, he had never finished dialing. Maybe he should, though. Maybe he should. Anything had to be better than all the drugs he was pumping into his body.

Although the idea of a therapist poking around in his head, getting too deeply into his psyche didn't exactly appeal to him. No matter, he rationalized, he desperately needed it.

He stayed in the shower much longer than he'd intended to, but right as he set his foot out to grab his towel, he saw her. There she was...just standing there. Right before him.

Stopping suddenly, he froze and wondered if he was still dreaming. He hadn't seen her since the day of the funeral. He blinked several times staring at the apparition, real eerie with the steam hovering around the room.

You say you hate me. And of course, you have every right to. I can fathom that. What's there not to understand? I did you dirty. Yes, I'll admit that. Still, as much as you think you hate me, you also miss me, she said in his mind, *so very much!*

Her lips were not moving, and yet she had spoken very clearly. Standing there watching him, maybe six feet away, her warm, brown eyes seemed to sparkle, imploring him not to be afraid. A feeling of great elation poured over him seeing her presence. Had he been hoping to see her ghost again?

He could hear his heartbeat pounding in his head. She had returned. She had come back to him!

Too much booze and coke, he thought next.

Perhaps he was only imagining this. It could be merely a trick of the mind, a hallucination, an all too real dream. He said nothing but held his breath as she drew nearer. Feeling all the hair rise on the back of his neck as she stood before him, he felt real apprehensive too.

He could not move as she circled him, inspecting him. He watched frightfully as she moved her hands, and placed it on his chest, running her fingers up and down in a gesture he remembered all too well. Then she looked down at his groin area and gave him a demure little smile and next touched him in a most improper way.

Sharp intake of breath, heart racing. He had to be dreaming.

"How'd you do that?"

She chuckled. *"Would you really like to know,"* she asked, still in his mind, not once moving her lips. She only had to look at him and he could hear her in his head. *"Did you enjoy that dream?"*

"Oh, you know about that?"

"Mmmm," she said with a throaty laugh. *"I made you have it."*

"You're very...inventive."

"Inspired, actually. I think you enjoyed it very much."

"Too much," he agreed. "But now, I'd like to wipe off and put on some clothes—if you don't mind. I'd feel a little less vulnerable that way."

"Really, that's too bad for me. I like seeing you naked."

"Oh...well, if you'd prefer, I can stay naked for you. Still, I have to wipe off though."

"Be my guest," she said continuing to watch him, like a cat contemplating a tasty mouse. Nothing much had changed. She was still the lioness hunting her prey, perfectly awful.

He reached for the towel and turned, starting to pat himself down, keeping an eye on her out of the corner of his eyes. He wondered if he reached for her what he would feel? He had felt her hand when she'd touched his groin, but he wandered what would happen if he tried to touch her. Would she be solid or would it be like touching air…"Can I touch you," he asked.

"Now only in your dreams," she said, and this time her mouth actually moved.

He turned abruptly and startled her a little, trying to grab a hold of her, but his hand went straight through her. He gulped, and she looked at him sympathetically.

"Yes, I hate it too. But tell you what, let me try touching you."

"Can you?"

"I'm not sure, but I can certainly try."

"You touched me earlier."

She giggled. "I did, didn't I? But that took a lot of effort."

"Some effort," he joked. In fact, he was still aroused.

The more he stared, the clearer she got.

She looked like a hologram. Like a virtual image. Dazzling him with a smile that was a kin to Times Square on New Year's Eve, she stood there, running her fingers through his hair, fanning it out, then shaking it a bit. He stood absolutely still, trying hard to feel her hands on him. She took his hands and brought them up to her hair cascaded wildly down her shoulders, framing her beautiful face, as the rest tumbled to about the middle of her back, looking dark, vibrant, and as beautiful as it had looked that night. She was also in the same outfit, the one she had worn to go meet *him* that night—white short, slinky, he had loved her in that halter dress, cut really low, exposing her beautiful back. But he had been awfully jealous—knowing she had dressed for *him*.

She brought his hands to rest on her hips now and gave him another seductive smile. Her smile was magic! "Can you feel that?"

Cedric shook his head.

"Sssh, concentrate. Imagine it. Remember it."

He tried, but couldn't. Then all of the sudden, he was irritated. "Forget it," he said walking away from her, leaving the bathroom, going to his drawer for his underwear. "This is really dumb. You're not even real. This isn't even happening."

"No," she said, startling him. No longer behind him, she was right in front of him now. It was disconcerting the way she could vanish and appear into thin air. Ignoring her, he quickly pulled on his shorts and went over to the bed. She followed him, coming to sit beside him. Crossing her long legs, she leaned into him. "Why are you so easily discouraged?"

"Why do you find so much joy in tormenting me?"

"Is that what I'm doing?"

"Yes."

"Oh, and here it is, I thought I was helping."

"In what way, might I ask? How is this helping?"

She smiled her achingly beautiful smile. "I think you miss me, can't live without me. I think you're quite desperate from wanting me, and I more than anything, would like your suffering to stop." Moving closer until she was sitting right in his lap, brushing her head against his dirty-blond tightly curled afro, making it actually move. "Your hair grew," she noted.

"Should I cut it again?"

"No, I like it," she declared, quite relaxed on his lap. "In fact, I'd like you to let it grow, but not into dreads. Just let it grow wild and loose, like Bailey's and CJ's. I think you'd look great in that style."

"Oh, and I don't look great now?"

She laughed, and studied him, gazing wonderingly into his glossy brown eyes. "You look wonderful. Good enough to eat."

Unsure of how to react under her scrutiny, he gazed back silently at her, her eyes glistening like chocolate oil in her ghostly face. He was both fascinated and terrified at the same time. That she could be there and be speaking and arousing him this much! How could it be...but it was. She made him burn with her words and image, though she was no longer there in the flesh. She was still the amazing temptress who could seduce him in his dreams, leaving her eternal searing seal on his soul. She was a delicious nightmare, a splinter in his heart that would never go away but would burn and burn. Old flames never died, they only reminded you that you were theirs forever.

"You still cry for me. I know, Cedric. I've watched you do it all the time," she continued, as if she had never stopped talking, her fingers seeming to entwine with his. "And really, I'm touched, but you can't keep mourning me like this. Accept it's over, that I'm gone, and we were never meant to be. Truly accept it, baby, and you'li see how much better it'll be. I hate seeing you suffer. Trust me, I'm not worth it."

"Oh, and I know you're not. Believe me, I do. But...the heart wants what the heart wants." Cedric wanted to grab her, to hold her and squeeze her, to never let her go. Except when he reached for her, there was nothing in his grasp again. Nothing but air. "Oh, God! Oh, God! Arielle, I need you. I don't want to live like this anymore either. I find life impossible without you. Am I mad? I can't stop thinking of you. I can't get over you! And I hate it, I do. But what am I gonna do? Basically, I'm screwed."

"No, you're not. You're not, baby. I'm right here, holding you. Can't you feel me? Close your eyes, close them, and feel me."

Cedric obeyed, really concentrated this time and could almost feel her...almost. He could feel her essence and definitely felt her presence. He knew she was there. An image of a field of wild, fuchsia flowers sprung to his mind, making him feel passionate, reckless, erotic. For a second, an image of them running through that field flashed through his mind.

"I should have fought for you," he said tightly. "I could have won you," he continued tightening his grip. "But I gave up too easily. You're right. I am easily discouraged. That's my character flaw. I'm proud and willful, and don't persevere."

Opening his eyes again, he was staring into her beautiful face, the ghostly apparition, her very image. He tried to get a grip on her again, to stroke her hair. But his hand went straight through her again, frustrating him to no end. This seemed to unnerve her.

"I know. I know. This is no good! I hate this too and wish you could touch me, just as I long to touch you."

Cedric struggled not to cry. "Baby, why did you say I hated you earlier when I love you so much?" This time, when he leaned forward and kissed her, he could almost feel her kissing him back. Probably wistful thinking on his part, but he'd take her anyway he could have her.

Straddling his lap, holding his hand and looking into his face, she said, "I want you to celebrate every day for me since I can't do it anymore. I want you to devour life. Eat it up! Go out there and party and have the time of your life. For me...for my sake, baby.

"You think I like seeing you waste away like this?! I hate watching you suffer," she said bring his hand up to her cheek. "I really do. You see, if you do all the wonderful things you're meant to do, I'll enjoy it vicariously through you. I want you to stop mopping and feeling sorry for yourself. Don't waste another moment being sad, crying for me. I'm dead. Accept it. Besides, I'm not even worth all this anguish."

"Why do you keep say that? Don't even say that anymore!"

"I screwed you over, Cedric. Every chance I got. Trust me when I tell you, I was pretty damned selfish, and you don't know the half of it..."

"Why because of your affair with Danyel?"

"I was unfaithful to you in every conceivable way—with my body, with my mind, with my very soul. You don't owe me this allegiance. You shouldn't mourn me like this, I don't deserve it. I wronged you. And you know what? I didn't even have any remorse at the time. I thought it was my God-given right to behave exactly as I pleased, to have everything I wanted—even if it meant having two men. I wanted the both of you. You and him. I even fantasized about having the both of you at the same time." She laughed. "I wanted it all. And for a while, I had it—even though I knew I would pay the price."

"With your life?"

"Yes, with my life."

"And you didn't care?"

"What could I do? Long before I died, I knew exactly how it was going to happen—except there wasn't much I could do to stop it."

He was silent for a few minutes. "Why couldn't you just stop when you knew it would lead to your demise? Even knowing that, you still couldn't be true to me?"

"Don't you think I tried?!"

"Oh, you tried. You TRIED! I don't know which hurts the most. The fact that you tried and couldn't, knowing you would die or if you had simply told me you didn't care enough to try at all!"

She smiled expansively, showing her glimmering white teeth. She looked absolutely lovely—even as a ghost.

"Who can explain the disturbing pull of desire…It doesn't matter how it gets started, but sometimes one look, one encounter, one smile, and you're finished. Even when we try to squelch it because we think it's bad or wrong or because it simply feels too good, it's still there…lurking in the shadows. Desire is as inexplicable as it is unmistakable." She smiled, seemingly satisfied with her explanation.

"So now I'm supposed to understand, to come correct." She laughed.

"What's so funny," he asked, surprised by her amusement.

"You! Still the same ole Cedric I knew and loved."

"Apparently the one you didn't love enough."

"Oh, I loved you. Just as much as you could handle. I don't think you could have handled the brunt or full range of my love."

"Oh, and Danyel could?!" he rasped indignantly.

"Even he couldn't and told me so regularly. That's why I had to have the both you. Please, forgive me."

"Like I have any other choice!"

"You always have choice if nothing else, Cedric. That's the only thing we do have. Free will."

"So why did you think I couldn't handle the full brunt of your love?"

She smiled, shrugged, and pushed back a strand of her beautiful black hair, tucking it behind her ear. Old habits were hard to die—even when you were dead—he mused. She looked amazing, though, he thought.

"So what are you?" he teased. "The heavy-weight champion of the world when it comes to love? Is your love deadly?"

She became serious. "Don't even kid around like that...look at what happened to Danyel."

"Well, it's not like you killed him."

"Oh, I most certainly did. It's because of me, he's dead. Think about it...Had I been mature enough to leave well enough alone, we'd both be alive right now."

"So you couldn't leave it alone?"

"No, apparently not...I couldn't stop myself from loving and wanting him. It was just one of those things. Some people just love harder than others. And well, my love can be very intense. Totally overwhelming..."

"I'm sorry I didn't get to experience its full intensity, because goddamn it, you certainly got the brunt of mine!"

She moved towards him, trying to press herself against him—except now he was no longer afraid but frustrated as hell that he couldn't connect with her. He wanted to feel her weight. He wanted her in the flesh, and it was a certainty that this was never going to be.

"I love you, Cedric. I want you to know that. And yes, I know when you sit here reading my journals, you feel sullen and used. You think I didn't love you at all, because I was so consumed by him. But I swear to you, I loved you too...and still do!"

A faint chill passed over him as he gazed into her intense brown eyes. He wanted desperately to believe what she was telling him, but the memories of all those words written in her journals flooded back, numbing him, making him feel dark inside.

"Talk to me, Cedric. Please, say something."

Why did she have to bring up those blasted journals?! He'd like to take them all and have a goddamn barbecue.

"Burning them won't make a difference," she told him.

"Oh, and so now you read minds."

She laughed. "Always could. There were a lot of things you

didn't know about me."

"You mean your supernatural powers or the fact that you were getting your groove on with your cousin with me none the wiser?"

She fell silent, staring at him blankly.

She was the kind of woman you wanted to take into your arms and run with, but at the same time, she was also the kind you knew you had to run far away from. With her pronounced cheekbones, soft brown eyes, and lips made totally for sin—especially when they were whispering all those beautiful words you so desperately wanted to hear—Cedric felt he might burst into tears.

"No darling, you mustn't cry. I want you to stop crying, want you to start being happy and live again. Life is too short, baby. Shorter than you think. You blink and game over—it's gone. And there's no way to get it back. Please, Cedric, promise me that you'll go on with your life. I'm begging you. Live because that's what you were meant to do. Live, because you're beautiful, warm, passionate and alive. Eat it up, baby. Eat this life up!"

He clung to her, taking her in his arms. "I love you, Arielle," he said reaching out frantically, wanting to feel her, but knowing he couldn't.

"I love you too, Cedric Courage."

He could almost smell her. There was a faint fragrance of her old cologne. It was sweet and pretty and nearly irresistible. It drew him. "So are you saying there's nothing to look forward to, that all we have is this?"

"No, I'm not saying that at all. What I am saying, though, is there's no place like earth. It's wonderful being alive—touching, smelling, tasting, hearing, seeing—having all your senses. It's limiting but then limits are sometimes good—the feeling of being grounded to something, of having weight. I know it's hard to understand, but enjoy your time here. It can be a treat if you let it. Live life to its fullest and indulge in all its pleasures—if you do nothing else. With no guilt. Eat, drink an be merry. Take pleasure in the little things. All those old adages are there for a reason., Cedric. 'Cause they're all true!"

"God, I'd give anything to have you back, Bling. To be able to hold you in my arms again, girl. I'd sell my soul!"

She placed one of her willowy hands across his lips. "Don't say that."

"Well, that's how I feel."

"Why do you wish for the impossible?"

"I don't know. I just...I just wish there was a way to have you back—even if it were just for one night."

Her grin grew then. "Sometimes, fairy tales do come true," she whispered, kissed him on the temple and was gone.

Cedric sat there for a long moment afterwards—not sure he had actually experienced what he knew had just occurred. Had he been dreaming or hallucinating again? He couldn't be sure *what* was reality anymore. He'd better go easy on the drugs and the booze...cause he was loosing his grip for sure! All he knew was he longed to clash, fuse, and make love to her—just as coolly and thoroughly as if they were an old couple. And she was right...he did want the impossible.

9

Taking a Chance on Love

Cedric was at the Blue Room resting his arms on the bar a few days later when he spotted Kendra making her way to him. Damn, she was worse than a greyhound. She could find him anywhere. His mind had been deprived of sleep, and he was tired as hell. Lately his dreams had been haunted by rampaging and disturbing images of Arielle. And even when he wasn't sleeping, his mind would still conjure her up.

Then there were his showdowns with Kendra. They didn't get along and could barely be civil to each other most of the times. He wasn't sure why except she went out of her way to be a bitch sometimes. It was a constant war, an ever-going battle. Everything he did seemed not to sit well with her. Perhaps they just needed to stop playing mind-games and just fuck each other. He was sure sometimes that was all it was. They needed to fuck.

Cedric took in the dark tailored suit she was wearing. Since he'd known her, she'd never dressed down. Not once. Always the agent, dressed in preppy blazers from Brook Brothers, Gap or the Banana Republic. And always slacks. Never skirts. Forget about a dress. He had yet to see her legs or any skin for that matter. She was a far cry from Arielle who was so comfortable with her sensuality. Who was comfortable in her own skin and enjoyed showing her body. Kendra despite her good looks was not sexy.

"What, I'm beginning to take it very personally, these disappearances of yours," she said dryly as she slipped into the seat beside him. "Are you trying to make my job more difficult?"

"No, trust me. It's nothing personal," he said taking a sip of his drink and then reached for a cigarette. "You don't mind, do you?"

She smiled slightly and shook her head. "Well, you stop disappearing, and I'll stop taking it personally."

She was always so serious—all business all the time. Very

professional and proper, not even a hint of a flirt. Nothing. Totally on the up-and-up. What a waste! And damn those damnable glasses she insisted on wearing. They were perfectly awful, but he suspected she wore them purposefully to make her less attractive—going for the same look with her hair and clothes.

"You should really get new glasses," he advised her.

"Next time I go for an eye exam, I'll be sure to have you tag along. That way I won't go wrong," she replied with zing. He may have touched a nerve, he thought with a smirk. Women got all riled up when they thought you were criticizing them.

"I mean, really...are you intentionally trying to look awful," he bounced back, going for gold. He had committed thus far, he might as well go all the way.

"Gee, thanks so much," she said looking a little hurt.

Cedric beamed at her. "Okay, I'm sorry. I didn't mean—umm, to offend you."

"Could have fooled me, but...okay. No offense taken. Forget it," she replied quickly, brushing off his apology. "Your opinion hardly matters to me in any case," she volleyed back.

"Oooo-kaaay," he said taking a puff off his cigarette. "Great come back."

She gave him a quelling look, deliberately trying to make him feel uncomfortable, but Cedric ignored her mean look. He was not going to allow her to get under his skin today—no matter what!

So far, from what he had gleaned from their conversations, even though she did not talk much, unless he was pestering her about something—she came from a respectable family. Father a judge. Mother, a writer and college professor. Brother was a cop. Sister, a lawyer. Grew up in well-to-do Coral Gables. It was funny but she was really the first person he had met here who was actually a Miami native. Even Arielle, who's family was Haitian was born in Brooklyn. He had come to accept the fact that everybody who lived in Miami was from somewhere else. Miami was the new Casablanca—everyone was a transplant and had their own story—some pretty shady.

Not so with Kendra Jade, though. She was so normal to the point of being weird. For one thing, she didn't drink. She didn't smoke. She definitely didn't get high. In fact, she was really beginning to cramp his style. She didn't party. She didn't listen to music. All she did was read. Read, read, read, and read some more! If she wasn't busy snooping around, *investigating*, she called it, but he saw it as her license to snoop and be a nosy-body. If she wasn't snooping then she was reading. She had a serious schoolmarm-librarian thing going. The girl needed help!

Hell, and he remembered that Arielle liked to read too. That girl's nose was forever buried in a book too—when she wasn't writing. But she'd pick screwing over reading any day. No problem. Not so, he suspected with Kendra Jade though.

Nobody that great-looking should be so a-sexual. That is, unless men were just not her bag. And that might explain *everything*. Although he already knew she was going to turn him down, he always liked to fuck with her just for the hell of it. "So can I get you a drink?"

"No, thank you, Mr. Courage. I don't drink."

She never got upset about it. Never raised her voice. Always polite. Respectful, even. No one called him, Mr. Courage. Every time she called his name, he had to look around, wondering if his father was there or around.

He supposed he could accept the fact she took her job so seriously. It was because of her fine detective work he wasn't sitting up in jail right now. And yes, she was more than capable of keeping him safe. She was sharp, pragmatic and had won his respect. But did she have to be so serious all the time?

"I guess I'm just hoping that one day you'll break down and have a drink with me."

"I'll take some iced-tea."

"Oh, iced-tea. Whoopteedoo! I'm wearing you down though," he teased. "I can feel it. Pretty soon, you're going to break down and actually have a drink with me. Even it's just a glass of wine." This was a step-up. Normally all she would have was water or club soda. He ordered her drink and a scotch-whiskey for himself, then turned and ordered some appetizers too. "Well, I'm thrilled. You actually ordered something other than water."

"I didn't realize you cared what I had. Didn't mean to hurt your feelings."

"A man keeps asking to buy you a drink and you keep refusing. How do you think it makes him feel?"

"Well, if that man understands I'm not supposed to drink while on duty and will be much more alert with better reflexes when sober, than said man would understand my job is to protect him and requires my hundred percent attention and concentration."

"Of course, the man understands. Still the man would like a hint of remorse when he's turned down."

She rolled her eyes heavenward. "Ooooh, g-g-gosh...I really

wish I could," she stammered. "But I can't. I'm on duty...That better?"

"Tee-hee-hee, you're so funny," he said dryly. "So what you're saying is that you do drink. When you're not on duty."

"Well, normally I don't even drink then. But if I go on a date or to some social function, I might have a glass of wine."

Cedric raised an eyebrow. "Whoa! A glass of wine? Christ, what I would do to behold that sight. And a glass of wine must go straight to your head. You strike me like that type."

She laughed. "That's probably not far from the truth."

Cedric looked stunned. Today was a day of first. He had yet to hear her laugh. Ever. She had a real nice, earthy laugh—not at all what he had expected.

Of course he had all these preconceived conceptions of her—most of which were probably untrue. Still, he didn't stop forming them. For one thing, he didn't think she liked men. He wasn't sure she was a lesbian either. But she just struck him as one of those women that needed no affirmation one way or another. She seemed happy in her own, private little universe, and felt completely comfortable with her books. Which in fact, was a type of escapism, he supposed.

"So, why don't you like men," he asked straight-faced when their drinks and appetizers came.

She shot him a look of surprise. Probably a little taken aback about how he had come full frontal. No warming up.

"Why do you say that?"

"Oh, it's just an impression I get. Am I wrong?"

"No."

Cedric smiled with satisfaction. He had been right.

"It's not that I don't like men, rather I mistrust them."

"Humph. I see. So do you like women? Is that your bag?"

"Not particularly," she said lifting her ice-tea to her lips, "although, I have found myself attracted to women at times."

Oh-ho! Cedric was busy staring at her lips now, which she let touch the glass carefully. Then hearing that response, he became very alert. Definitely aroused. Well-well-well, *who knew?* He knew she'd have to have some vice. No one could be *that* perfect! Although, that admission made her more perfect than she could ever imagine.

"How fascinating. Have you ever tried to go there," he probed.

"No."

"Why not? Try it you might like it."

"No, I could never. It's wrong."

"But if that's your nature…"

"It's not," she muttered, looking a little uncomfortable now. She had shared something that she shouldn't have. Something that was way *too* personal. And now…she wanted to rail it back in. "Let's talk about you."

"Me?" He looked her over, taking in her smooth, caramel complexion and soft wavy black hair that brushed her shoulders. Although her complexion and features hinted of mixed roots, her full, sensual bee-stung lips were distinctly and potently African— and they definitely hadn't escaped his attention.

Tonight, he was seeing her in a totally different light. And his anger towards her was softening a bit. Goodness, she had just admitted to being attracted to women. "What do you want to know about me?"

She smiled warmly. "Let's talk about your music."

"What about it?"

"Today, I was listening to one of your songs and…how do I put it delicately…how can you write songs like that? Those lyrics! Can you rappers find some other subject to sing about, rather than a woman's anatomy?"

"Oh, us rappers. I feel an attack coming on."

"Look, you know what I mean. I'm not dissing rap—"

"Dissing? Whoa, I didn't know you spoke Ebonics."

She ignored him. Faltered, not knowing how to proceed. "I'm not trying to put rappers down. Or you for that matter! All I'm saying is that hip-hop, rap, or whatever you call it—most of the male rappers seem seriously angry and pissed off at Black women."

"Oh, now it's a color thing."

"Call it whatever you want. But it's true. I mean, look at the videos, which portray women (mostly the black ones) as bitches and whores, sporting these huge breasts and backsides almost as if they were some fashion accessory—like their merely pieces of jewelry—purely for decoration."

He laughed. "It's all about the bling-bling, you're saying."

"No, I'm asking—is that all it's about? Oh, and you find it funny?"

He shook his head with mock seriousness. "No, of course not! And while I'll admit these allegations of yours are a true revelation, and the industry does to an extent exploit certain aspects of a woman's anatomy, I'd like to point out that rappers are not the only ones doing it, and that everyone's jumped on that bandwagon—including corporate America. Sex sales...it's as simple as that."

"And just because everyone is doing it, makes it right?"

"Next you're going to tell me that rap and hip-hop is the cause behind all of society's ills."

"It glorifies crime and violence—"

"Oh, and Hollywood and the entire media doesn't?"

"Let's not even venture there. That's a given. But that's not what we're discussing here. We're discussing *your* lyrics. You can't point your finger at the media or Hollywood when you're a part of the problem as well."

The food arrived, momentarily stopping the exchange. But Kendra had only just begun. "I'm not even going to get into how much the drug dealer is glorified and praised in these videos. Gangsters and pimps rule! All praises. All praises. It's sick!"

"Oh, stop it," Cedric said stuffing his mouth with food, and after a beat, "You'll give yourself indigestion."

"Your music glorifies everything tearing down our community."

"Christ! You act as if rap and hip-hop have no redeeming qualities. What about the positive things it's done? Like the fact that it's brought our cultures together. Blacks and Whites are listening to the same kind of music, wearing the same clothes, hanging out at the same clubs. It's a beautiful thing. I mean, we're still a long ways off, but finally, we're moving towards one America. One world for that matter. A global society. Maybe rap is responsible for a little of that too. Isn't that a positive thing?"

"That doesn't excuse the message."

"The message hardly matters. It's all about the vibe, ba-by. The groove. And I'm in love with rap and hip-hop. It's what I play and who I am, and so I'm not about to sit here and listen to you dis it. Period."

She laughed, surprising him. "Finally something you're passionate about. Again. You've hardly said two words these past couple of weeks but today..."

He stopped and chuckled. "I apologize. I do tend to get a little heated about this subject. I get sick sometimes of having to defend what I do."

"Understood." She smiled.

It was very nice, her smile. And she had laughed again. She was very pretty, he decided, when she smiled. And her laughter was contagious.

"Truce?"

"Truce, and well, I didn't mean to rile you up. And I swear I'm not dissing your music..."

"Yes, you are."

"All right. I am," she agreed, smiling. "Maybe just a little. It's just...I hate the way certain things are being embraced by our youth. Like single-parenting. That crap is totally accepted now. It's even revered. I hate that song, *That's Just My Baby's Daddy*. I want to scream every time I hear it. And the domestic violence and just the general scorn for the police and respectability are frightening. Law enforcement is constantly challenged, and I feel there's a shirking of all sense of responsibility. I'm just afraid the effect it'll have on the future. I think we're creating a generation of monsters, and by the time I'm old and grey, these kids will be in power, running the country."

"Girl, take a breath and you really need to chill, straight-up. You don't think that every generation went through pretty much the same things we're going through now? You think this is new?"

"I'm not saying that."

"Read your history, girl. This is how it's been from the dawn of time. It'll be another billion years before we destroy ourselves. Don't worry..."

"I disagree. I think we're well on our way. The signs are all there, and it's not like I'm that old—"

"No, just square."

"Hallelujah, then. Cause I can't get into music that glorifies prostitution, or female rappers like L'il Kim who sees herself as a bitch and who in fact, advocates women as bitches and getting what they need with their bodies and sees no problem with it. That said, *bon appetit*."

Cedric laughed. "Baby, I've been eating for awhile now. In fact, I'm almost finished. You, on the other hand, have been so opinionated—not to mention judgmental—you've let your food get cold. That said, *bon appetit* to you too..."

He had no idea how she was going to eat as riled up as she was. And she thought he was passionate about this subject! Smiling to himself, still contemplating her, he watched her pick up her fork and attempt to eat her scallops. God, she was repressed. *Poor thing*...how he'd love to get her drunk or high or both and have her renounce all that repression. She needed some release. *Emancipation, baby!* How he longed to liberate her. Corrupt her. She was way too serious and much too high on herself. He'd love to knock her off her high horse, and bring her down a few pegs, and watch her wallow in the muck. She might find she liked it. In any case, it would do her a world of good. Make her more normal. More real...

She glanced over at him somewhat uncomfortably. "I'm not judging."

"Yes, you are. You think you're better than Li'l Kim and others like her. Just because she embraces her sexuality, you find something wrong with that. You can't accept that maybe she doesn't have a problem with something you do."

Kendra blanched. "Okay, end of discussion. You've purposely misunderstood me. I'm finished. You're going to defend it, and it's not your fault since you're a part of it. So I understand."

"Oh, no, love. I don't have to defend a damned thing. Not to you or anyone else."

"Mr. Courage..."

"No, please call me Cedric. After all that personal, intimate and great pouring of emotion and frustration, I think we can now be on a first name basis. Don't you think?"

"Fine. Cedric..."

"Yes. Kendra?"

When she smiled, she looked really beautiful, he thought again. Despite those whacked glasses of hers. Without question, she didn't want to attract attention. That was obvious. From her way of dress to her mannerisms and attitude as a whole, she was totally uninviting and sent off this vibe to just stay away—except he was pushing—would keep pushing her buttons until he made her explode.

"Why did you ask me those things? Are you toying with me?"

"Flirting with you, maybe. But not toying..." *At least not yet.*

"Flirting? This is the way you flirt?"

"Well, not exactly. It just depends on whom I'm doing the flirting with. With some women, I can come full frontal, no problem. But with you, I think I might have to go to Paris and back."

She laughed again for the third time that evening. She was going like for a record tonight.

"Oh, you find that amusing?"

He could get used to her laughter.

"You can be funny at times. That's all."

"And at others?"

"Totally exasperating, obnoxious and irritating. But then, when you want to turn on the charm..." she let her voice trail off.

He was grinning, "I can do it with amazing ease...right?"

And now she was smiling back. She was nothing if not tough and demanding. But he liked that about her. What could he say? He had a weakness for strong, challenging women.

"Kendra, don't get offended or anything, and I'm not trying to disrespect you. I'm just asking..."

"Yes?"

"Have one drink with me. I know you're on duty and all, but I think you could use it."

"Ahhh...I think you're the devil incarnate. Always tempting me..."

"Just do it. Do like Nike says, Kendra baby, and just do it!"

She shook her head. "In half a second, you've gone from Kendra to Kendra baby. My head is spinning already. That's just a little too fast for me. Maybe some other time..."

Gazing directly into her eyes, he leaned forward, close enough to kiss and murmured, "I'm gonna hold you to that."

She looked a little rattled, but her tone was very measured. "Okay, Mr. Courage...I mean Cedric. One day, I promise I'll have that drink with you. But I have to solve this case first."

"Of course, Miss Jade...I mean Ken-dra. I understand completely," Cedric said still holding her gaze. She talked to him as if he were a child she had to indulge. It could really burn him sometimes but he'd be between those classy thighs one day—having his own drink. Of that he was sure.

***

Kendra leaned against the door and closed her eyes, seeing him in her mind's eye. *Oh God,* she shuddered. Why did she find him so damned attractive? And what was all these unwanted feelings he was bringing forth inside her? Was it lust she was feeling?

Yes, she thought with exasperation. It was sex. And that's all it was!

She flung off her jacket and holster, as she stumbled into her still dark bedroom, turned on the night light, then started to undo her pants.

She had abstained tonight from having that drink with him, and had had to grapple all night for control over her senses—except that had been quite a feat when she had to face Cedric Courage head-on. Of course, she knew he was a fantasy—one she could not indulge in. Like alcohol, he was potent and lethal and she couldn't give in to him.

Sitting at the edge of the bed, she rallied to get herself together. To recover. She felt so shattered. So damned exhausted! Thinking about the night she had just spent, being on edge at every minute, endeavoring not to let her emotions run away with her had overtaxed her. No one should have to go through such torture!

If only she didn't find him so goddamn appealing. So wickedly sexy. Lately, spending any time at all with him—whether it be in the day or night—left her exhausted and spent. He had laughed about wearing her down, except he had no idea how well it was working! All that masculinity and physical beauty slayed her. She was drooling all over herself and lucky for her, she was good at hiding her emotions so he barely noticed. Thank God!

She took several deep breaths to calm down then yanked off her slacks and pantyhose, letting them fall to the floor before heading for the shower. Tonight she needed a very cold shower. She could still feel the heat of his eyes on her skin.

Just before she had left him, he had held her hand a little too long. He had insisted on walking her to her car and had this look on his face that prickled all the hair on the back of her neck. She had almost let him kiss her. She was still trying to figure out if indeed he had meant to kiss her. He had moved in a little too close, invading her personal space. He had also given her this super sexy gaze that had made her gaga.

Standing under the shower, she imagined his broad shoulders and strong back. She had seen him shirtless enough, and knew what was hidden beneath his over-sized shirts. His body was muscled, well-toned, and his skin was so light—so much so that you could see the bluish green veins underneath. His nipples were caramel-colored—the darkest part of his body—and she suspected his penis would be probably the same color.

Amazing! She didn't want to believe that she had even gone there, but she had. She was now even thinking about his penis. Ahhh, much as she hated to admit it, that was her secret longing. How much she wanted that penis between her thighs. Just thinking about it caused her anguish. And of course, Cedric would gladly oblige her if she let him.

Now that Veronica was no longer in the picture, he was looking for her replacement. Most likely, he was looking to score with her. Very convenient. Hey, why not, she thought with venom. If she were willing...why not have her as a personal bodyguard and a booty call too. Made sense!

She laughed bitterly. Well, she wasn't about to be his whore. He could forget it! She knew his kind only too well. He promised nothing. Took everything! She'd never stoop so low and allow him take advantage of her. No matter his appeal, regardless of how gaga he made her, she would abstain from the pleasure. Better to keep her self-respect, she thought. NO WAY! Under no circumstances was she going to give in to her base desires and bed down with him. Uhn-uhn...never gonna happen, she swore fiercely as the cool water poured over her.

Better to get this out of her system now. Better to buy a vibrator, anything, then to have to live with the fact that a man could control her—have his way with her—against her better judgment. Mind over matter. She could do this. She would resist him.

Damn, damn, damn. If only she could stop thinking about him, though. Lately, she could scarcely get him off her mind. Not for food, not for sleep, not even for the fact that he was an arrogant, egotistical, exasperating bastard! When he turned on the charm...HE TURNED ON THE CHARM, and she didn't even want to think about it.

He was so cocky. So totally sure of himself—not to mention full of himself. And yet, strangely enough, he excited and fascinated her more than anyone ever had. He was like rain after a drought. Like a gift dropped at her feet. He seemed so unafraid, even though he was now walking this terrifying tightrope. Despite all that had happened in his life, he was still able to laugh easily and take risks—even though these risks were beginning to wreck havoc on her nerves. He seemed bent on making her job ten times harder sometimes. And though she didn't blame him for it and knew he deserved some freedom, she was constantly afraid for him. Nothing could happen to him. Not on her watch.

As she lathered herself, she contemplated how she was beginning to enjoy this job a little too much. Well, was enjoy even the appropriate word? Perhaps she looked forward to it—a little too much—loving the fact that she was going to see him everyday.

Daily, she wondered what they were going to do. Even what he would be wearing. He looked so good in his clothes, out of them too. She loved the muscle shirts, the leather pants, the funky jeans, his smooth casual chic. He was well-groomed, forever elegant and yet strangely uncomplicated. He was a paradigm.

Man, and she loved the way he could make her laugh—despite herself. He insisted on her having fun whether she liked it or not. Besides his public persona, the glitter and dazzle, there was someone very deep inside. He had integrity too. Style, grace, intelligence, and one of the rarest things, *courage*—not very many people had that and Cedric not only carried it as a badge of honor but sported it as his last name.

She had asked him that night if that was his actual name or a stage name. A name taken for his showbiz career.

"You know. You're the first person who's ever asked me that? What do you suppose?"

"I don't know. Courage isn't a name you hear everyday. Cedric Courage. It sounds too perfect—made up."

Smiling, he said, "Why don't you just marry me so you take my last name. Special Agent Courage, has a nice ring to it, doesn't it? But in answer to your question, yes, it's actually my name, the one on my birth certificate."

He always said something to knock her off balance. It's like one moment he'd say something that made her feel bad, then the next, he'd throw in a compliment—except he didn't make it sound like a compliment when he said it, so that you never really knew what he liked or admired about you. Or whether he was ever serious. It was like a head game, and he seemed to be a master at it.

Every day now she had to keep reminding herself he wasn't want she wanted or needed. He was wild, fun to be around and great-looking, but he was someone to be admired from afar. He was famous, smart, stylish, and fantastically rich. Any woman would be crazy not to want him. But she had to keep reminding herself she wasn't every woman. And furthermore, she couldn't *trust* him.

Yup, that was the crux of the problem right there...how could you fall in love with someone you couldn't trust? She was not going to fall in love with any man that beautiful or that rich, who had the adulation of millions. Besides that, Cedric was seriously in love with his dead wife. She was positive of that.

How could she or any other woman compete with a ghost?

Veronica, his publicist, thought that she could—until he had sent her packing and crying back to New York. She wasn't sure what had happened between them, but one day she came over and Veronica was booking out of a restaurant they were having dinner at with her hand over her mouth, sobbing very loudly. She nearly got hit by a car, trying to get out of there. And Kendra hadn't seen her since.

Cedric had followed her out, looking mean, and like he was

very angry. He didn't follow her, but went back into the restaurant and finished his dinner. Kendra wasn't sure what had transpired, but it couldn't have been good. What could she have done, and why the abrupt ending to what seemed like a budding or rekindled romance?

Occasionally, he had some girls—some of them famous—some on them obviously hired over. And she knew he slept with some of them. Yet for at least a month, he had been celibate. Or, she thought. For the past several weeks, there had been no women. And she was beginning to wonder why.

Yet why should his sex life even concern her? Why should she even care?

She had to admit one thing to herself, though. She did care. Very much. And she did want to get to know him better. Enjoyed their talks and being with him. He was fun. Never a dull moment. He amused her with his self-absorption. Never had she met anyone so totally involved with self. And then to observe so much self-pity and sadness from someone who totally had no right to be. Not that loosing his wife wasn't a horrible thing, especially the way in which it happened. Still, he had to be one of the luckiest people in the world. He had the number one CD in the country, all this success and fame, and even given all of that, it amazed her how he could be so sad, despite it all, because of Arielle.

No one would ever replace her in his affections—no one.

Finishing her shower, she turned off the water, and toweled herself dry. Standing in front of the mirror, she gazed at her body, wondering if he'd find it pleasing. Thinking about what it would feel like to make love to him. Instinctively, she knew he'd be a great lover. He'd probably be real good. Too good. She could sense it was in his nature. See it in his eyes, in his demeanor.

A faint chill passed over her as she looked at herself in the bathroom mirror. What if this attraction was all one-sided? What if he didn't think of her sexually at all? Wrapping the towel now snuggly around her body, she walked into the bedroom to fetch her nightshirt.

Damn, she really needed to stop thinking about him.

***

On Sunday, it rained all day. The rain was coming down in sheets, and Kendra felt wonderful sharing the day with Cedric, whose mood seemed much lighter today. Neff had day entire day off, so she'd be pulling a double, which meant an entire day spent with Cedric Courage. Their work day was divided into 12-hour shifts and if one of them had the day off it meant the other had to pick up the slack. She didn't mind, though. Cedric seemed to be a in a good spirits—even a little playful. Maybe it would be a good day.

She had arrived that morning to find him in nothing but silk navy pajama bottoms. Looking lean and powerful, Kendra couldn't help her eyes from straying to his chiseled chest, ripped abdomen, and sinewy arms. He was buff, all muscle with not an ounce of fat anywhere. He was in such great shape, but she knew he also worked at it.

Quentin, his stylist and personal trainer made sure of it, pestering him to exercise even when he didn't want to. Cedric also played a lot of basketball too and he was very physical. His body spoke to that. And right now, it was certainly speaking to her loud and clear. He aroused her. That was undeniable. And he was making her dizzy, she wanted him so bad.

Every morning, watching him run through tai chi exercises with Quentin and then go through a battery of sparing exercises, where they both tried to show off for her, was something she looked forward to. They had even let her join in on the training—and liking to work out herself—she was greatly enjoying this aspect of protecting Cedric. Of course, it was Sunday, and Quentin was off today, but she was still being treated to Cedric's physical routines.

Kendra watched him as he pranced around the room. He was a bundle of raw energy and was talking to someone on his cell phone while simultaneously trying to organize his CDs, which were strewn all over the rec room. Last night, he had had a small get together with his manager and some of the guys from his band, where they had discussed possibly beginning on cutting a new CD. Later, he had confided to her how that was the last thing he felt like doing, but how he'd make an effort for the guys.

Her eyes swept over him and studied his tattoos then noted the three earrings on each ear, two smaller studs on top and a small hoop at the bottom. Nothing too big. Tiny, in fact. Real discreet, but on both ears. She hadn't realized that straight men were now wearing earrings on both ears. Normally, she wouldn't go for that look on a guy at all, but on Cedric, it looked totally hot! She couldn't believe all the other things she found attractive about him—like his tongue ring, which totally intrigued her. More often than not lately, she found herself wondering how it would feel kissing a man with a tongue ring, as well as how fellatio would feel with that as a bonus.

Her mind was in the gutter when she was around him, as usual. Admiring his face and hair, she smiled as she contemplated his look, potent mix of Viking and African, with a hint of Asian mixed in. The features composing his face were a beautiful, poetic blend, and she could never get over how gorgeous people of mixed heritage usually were. It was like they got the best of all worlds. He was letting his hair grow out, now a riot of tight, glorious curls. After that shocker at the church when he had appeared minus his long, sexy dreadlocks, he hadn't cut his hair again, preferring it long. And his hair grew so fast. He wore his hair like CJ now, and it was attractive as hell.

Shortly after he got off the phone, he placed the last CD in it's slot and then picked up his guitar, something he hadn't done in all the months she had known him and started playing some tunes.

Kendra was sitting on the sofa in a pair of Levi's and long-sleeved T-shirt, pretending to be reading, Iyanla Vanzant, but inspirational as Iyanla was, her eyes kept straying to Cedric and his tattoos. The big Oriental one on his arm and the smaller one of the heart on his chest, and she knew if he turned, he'd have a dragon right in the small of his back. She couldn't see the whole dragon. Only part of it. "Why the tattoos," she asked curiously all of the sudden, out of the blue, breaking the silence. "I mean, they're great! Don't get me wrong. I really like them. But what makes you decide to go off and tattoo yourself?"

He laughed wolfishly. "Oh, no. Not another question and answer session about my tattoos. The first question is always why did you do it? Then the second is, did it hurt? And I always want to say, do dogs have fleas?"

Kendra smiled. "Okay, forget I asked."

"But still, you're curious, right?"

"I am, but it's okay-"

"What would you like to know," he asked, giving her his full attention.

"Well, what makes you just up and do it? Cause like, I've wanted one as far back as I can remember. But I just...I've never been able to just go through with it and get it done."

He looked at her in mock surprise. "You? A tattoo. Can't even imagine it."

She grinned. "Yeah, me. You know, somewhere real discreet."

"Hmmm...you know, I wonder about you sometimes. You must be one of those women that comes off as real straight-laced but who melts like lava when you're in the sack."

She smiled tightly, not liking the turn the conversation had suddenly taken. Sometimes she had to be so guarded with him because he could get so personal so fast. It disturbed her how frank and open he was when they talked. She folded her arms, self-conscious all of the sudden, and dug her heels into the carpet in a nervous gesture, but responded all the same, "Well, I won't tell."

"Yeah, well I think you are straight-up. So what will the Bureau say?"

"The Bureau needn't know. Anyway, times have changed and the days of thinking that tattoos are for degenerates is highly archaic now. Don't you think? Today tattoos are an artistic expression. Stylish."

"Hey baby, you don't have to convince me. I'm all for them."

"I just squirm when I imagine the process. All those needles..."

"And that's your problem right there. You're thinking about it too much. A tattoo is something you think only twice about. Not once because that's not enough. And then more than twice, you won't ever go through with it. Me, once I get a tattoo into my head, I just automatically want it on my skin. Just like loosing your virginity, a tattoo shouldn't be something you plan. It's the heat of the moment. You want it. You do it. Bam, it's done."

She cleared her throat. It was amazing how sex kept creeping up into the conversation. "Loved the way you explained that. Was that the way it was when you lost your virginity?"

"Pretty much," he grinned looking like he was recalling images into his mind. "Ummm...but let me guess. Your first time was planned. Every aspect. It probably happened on prom night. Posh hotel room. Flowers, champagne, totally first class."

She was grinning like an idiot, but of course, it was true. "Yeah, pretty much," she responded then laughed. She felt embarrassed talking about sex with him.

"But you can't approach this tattoo in the same way. You shouldn't try to plan it—not if you really want it. And you mustn't forget this one thing. A woman gets a tattoo and all of the sudden the way she's perceived by a man is totally different."

"Yeah, and what's the impression?"

"That's she's freaky, ba-by. That she's sexy hot."

"Oh, so it's different for men? What about men with tattoos? How do you think that people perceive you?"

"I am freaky. Through and through. I'm not gonna lie to you.

Hell, I have a tongue ring, that should tell you the whole story right there," he said flicking his tongue at her. "I give much pleasure. And I like to receive pleasure too."

Kendra covered her face and giggled. She was blushing, and she felt so silly, reverting to her prepubescent antics. When she looked up, Cedric was grinning at her. "Oh, so every time I see a guy or a girl with a tongue ring or if someone has tattoos or piercings, they're freaky."

"Freaky or adventurous. Call it whatever you like. I just think it takes that person to another level as far as I'm concerned."

"Oh, so it can't be just a fashion statement?"

He smiled. "I'm sure in your case that's all it would be. Or maybe that's what you'd like me to think." He winked at her. "But we both know better, right?"

"And what is that?"

He grinned widely. "I don't dare imagine."

She blushed again.

"Ah, man...I'm embarrassing you."

"No-no. Go on. It's cool."

"The biggest impact, though, about getting your body tattooed is that it's going to be liberating as hell. Basically, it says your body is yours to do with whatever the hell you want. And that personal freedom is where it's at for me. That Devil-may-care attitude of doing whatever you please."

"Thus the basis of its appeal," Kendra agreed. "So was that your reason for doing it?"

"Maybe my first tattoo. I was fifteen, living in Japan. I was rebellious as mother-effer and yes," he grinned sheepishly. "I suppose I was sending out a message to my dad. That was just about the time I decided I wanted to grow my dreads too.

"Bet you were a hell-raiser."

"Girl, you have no idea! If CJ pulls half the shit I did with my dad, I'm gonna jack him up real good. Shit, I'm not putting up with any of that bullshit. I did things that could have landed me in jail or worse, gotten me killed. I was nuts! Out of control. You think I'm wild now," he chortled, "but you didn't know me a few years ago. I'll tell you, I've calmed down a lot! It started with Arielle, she toned me down, but it wasn't until CJ was born that I was completely tamed."

Kendra nodded. "I hear you."

"You know there's nothing like a child to bring it all into prospective for you. The first time I held him in my arms, I finally understood. He changed *everything*. He was my best therapy. Pure love...that's what he brought to my life. And now, it doesn't matter how sad or how mad or how hectic my life becomes. I see that beautiful little face of his, and everything else vanishes. All the hate. All the pain. All the bitterness. I look at him and understand why I wake up every morning."

Kendra shook her head in wonder, despairing how impossible it was going to be not to fall in love with this man. "It must be a beautiful thing...having a child."

"It is, you should try it," he winked.

She beamed at him. "And so now poor CJ can't pull any stops since you know all the ropes. It's gonna be hell, him being your kid."

"In more ways than one," he sighed, as an ironic smile lit up his eyes with a sunny amusement. "He's gonna have to be real tough."

"Would you like him to follow in your footstep and become an entertainer?"

"Hell no! You know that's something that I don't get. You see all these showbiz kids from showbiz family. That's the last thing I'd encourage CJ to go into. This business is insane. Fucked up. Does horrible things to your psyche. Really fucks with your head. But if this is what he has his mind set on...what am I gonna do?"

"Sort of like do what I say...not as I do. You know that doesn't work, right?"

"Yeaaah," he grinned, looking at her measuringly, unnerving her. "Don't I? So long as he's true to himself, I suppose."

She laughed nervously. "Guess you'll have no other choice but to respect his wishes."

"Well, that's life, right," he said earnestly. "What the hell can you do?"

"So what are you going to do when he comes home with his first tattoo?"

"I'm gonna kill him. Kick his ass."

"Ever regret getting that first tattoo?"

"This one. Nah, I love it!"

"What is it?"

"It's my name spelled in Japanese."

"Oh, wow. It does look good. The first time I saw it, I thought it was gang related."

He chuckled. "Yeah, you would think that."

She grinned. "But it looks really neat."

"Neat? Shit, it's *dope*. Everyone likes this one."

"And the one on your heart. Do you regret that one?"

He took a deep breath. "This one I did for love. Got it on my wedding night."

"How romantic."

"Do I regret it? Having a woman's initials carved into my heart. Maybe for two seconds. But it doesn't matter, cause really. I'll always love her."

Kendra was pensive for a few minutes after that revelation. However, soon she asked, "So what's the story with the dragon?"

"Well, that one's recent. I got that one shortly after this whole ordeal started. I don't know, it was strange, but I felt it would sort of protect me, you know. Help me to fight and combat everything that was being hurled at me. I see it as a kind of amulet, protecting me from all the ills of the world."

"Wow, all of your tattoos have a story that goes along with them. They're all meaningful."

"Absolutely. A tattoo should definitely always be that. Meaningful. Otherwise, what's the point?"

Kendra smiled at him. "Well, that was quite an education."

He grinned back and started strumming the guitar again. He looked so boyishly charming, with his hair in wild disarray and his brown eyes glowing with jest, Kendra felt her heart constrict. She found him so beautiful. "You're sweet, you know that," he said softly. "You bring sunshine."

There it was again, where he'd say something and she wouldn't know how to take it. "Why do you say these things?"

"I just call 'em like I see 'em," he said absently, as he strummed the guitar into a tune.

"Is that a compliment?"

"Absolutely," he said staring at her, starting to play a really delightful number. It was real pretty. She had never heard it before.

Kendra was grinning again—like an idiot—she was thinking. Oh, God, but it couldn't be helped. He was killing her, slaying her. Listening to the languorous tune, watching his every move, she saw only the beauty of his Eurasian eyes and a moment after as his head lifted, his disarming smile. "Thank you," she gushed, her own grin replete with contentment.

He grinned, chuckled a little. Then he started singing *to her!* Kendra was tickled. The man who stood before her was a huge entertainer. Famous as hell, larger than life. Was considered a musical phenomenon, a musical messiah, and he was serenading *her.*

Kendra could feel the sexual tension elevate as the performance continued. She wondered if Arielle had been regularly treated to these private sessions, where there were no costumes, no dancers, no light shows—just the man and his voice and the music.

After a while...
You learn the subtle difference
between holding a hand and chaining a soul...
And you learn that love doesn't mean leaning
And company doesn't mean security
that the company of others is only as good as the company you keep.
After a while...
You begin to learn that kisses aren't contracts
And presents aren't promises
And you begin to accept your defeats
With your head up and your eyes open
With the gifts of an adult, and not the grief of a child.
After a while...
And you learn to build all your roads on today
Because tomorrow's ground is too uncertain for plans.
You learn that real love is a gift.
One given from the heart, soul, and mind.
After awhile...
You learn that even sunshine burns if you get too much
So you plant your garden and decorate your soul
Instead of waiting for someone to bring you flowers
And learn that you really can endure
That you're really strong,
And that you really do have worth...
After all...

She was speechless for several minutes. She was enjoying this, perhaps a little too much. Realizing too that more than anything right now, that where she wished she could be with Cedric was in bed, she tried to contain herself. Forget about the foreplay and preliminaries. She thought about how all he would have to do was make the slightest move, the least amount of effort or gesture, and she would be his to do whatever he pleased.

"That was beautiful," she complimented in a hushed tone.

To which he said nothing, but just laying one hand gently against the guitar strings, and placed the other at his temple in silent contemplation. He must be thinking of her, she thought.

Must have written it as an ode to her. But it hardly mattered. Sitting quietly in the presence of this alarmingly sexual creature, she felt golden, luxurious bliss, and he was awesome standing there before her. Powerful, with a predatory grace, as he started another number, a faster one this time, which he was also dancing too.

Allowing him to perform a little more, she interrupted. "You wrote that for her? That first song?"

"Yes," he said simply, then sighed deeply, all into what he was playing now. The music moved him, as he swayed to the melody, and she found herself swaying to, wishing she could join him.

"It was beautiful. Except, I've never heard it."

"Haven't recorded. Won't record it. It's too private."

Kendra smiled, but then he had played it and sung it for her. Listening to the intimacy of the lyrical passages, watching his face, all the emotions racing across it—yes, it had been private. And now more than anything she wished to be even more private...so sure he would be sexuality uninhibited, as she watched him do a slow grind to the music he was presently playing. Sex for him would be as instinctive as breathing.

She wanted to close her eyes and not look at him and just listen to his strong, powerful voice. And listen to the rapturous, sensual music he was making. Didn't want to be distracted as she was now. She wished she were bold, and that she could slip off the couch and put her arms around his neck and dance with him. She wished she could tell him how she felt. Ask him to make love to her. Take the initiative. She wished a lot of things that would never happen...because she wasn't bold. Wasn't brazen, and want as she might, she'd never bring herself to go there. No way...

He finished and she applauded enthusiastically.

He threw back his head and laughed, sweeping his hair behind his ears in a swift, gestured mannerism that Kendra had come to find so appealing. "You liked it?" He strummed the guitar some more, now practicing scales. "Gosh, it's been so long since I've performed. Hell, since I've played music period," he said absently.

Kendra shrugged, thinking how the moment had passed now. How her heart would quicken as something strong and sexual would telegraph itself to her, but how she could never act on it. And she was getting so tired of sitting idly by and doing nothing about it. Yet, it wasn't just the words, the music, but his entire persona. Looking at him, she found herself powerfully excited.

Shit! He was hot, she thought again. Then it occurred to her, if he could read minds, she was so screwed. She laughed at the thought.

He smiled at her laughter. "I'm glad I'm amusing you. Gosh, I know I'm rusty, but I'm not that bad, am I?"

"God, no. You're...you're...I'm at a lost for words. Hey, can you do that number, the one you did on MTV Unplugged?"

He smiled. "Gosh, you saw that show? That was so long ago. Seems like an eternity. What song was that?"

Kendra snapped her fingers as she tried to remember. "I think it was called, *You Complete Me.* His expression immediately changed, his eyes clouding.

Oh-oh.

Damn, it was as if everything had crashed and burned. She had really messed up the groove and his mood was totally altered. Unstrapping his guitar, he let it drop to the couch, looking disturbed, discouraged, and maybe even a little perturbed as he strolled out to the terrace. She followed him out a few minutes later. As her bare feet splashed slightly across the wet tile, he turned and noted her presence, then leaned against the wall, taking out a packet of cigarettes from his pajama bottoms, tapping it on the back of his hand, then shoved it between his lips, letting it hang from his mouth before lighting up.

What had she said? He looked so glum...

She joined him on the wall. They were both now staring over it, watching the wall of rain that was coming down in sheets slide down side of the covered terrace. His back was straight, but his head hung low. Kendra could sense his restlessness. The immense power of his self-control. Like his sexuality, it was coiled tightly, smoldering, fighting for control.

"I'm sorry," she said to his back. "I didn't mean to..." her voice trailed away as he turned to look at her "...say anything..." His eyes glittered, seemingly amused at her lack of words. She hardly knew what to say. "I didn't mean to bring—"

"Forget it," he said waving off her apology, his voice dripping with sarcasm. Or was it contempt? "I doesn't even matter anymore. What the hell does it matter, huh? She's gone. Right? And I need to get over it. Get over myself!"

"No. You have every right to hurt. To—"

He chuckled before taking a deep drag off his cigarette. "I see the way you look at me sometimes. You think I'm crazy. That I have so much that I don't appreciate. You think I'm pitiful, so self-absorbed. What you don't understand is...it doesn't matter how much you have when there's no one to share it with!"

Kendra's surging wave of confidence had evaporated, being preempted by a sudden chill. The rain was suddenly getting to her, making her shudder. So was the way he was looking at her. She felt so embarrassed. She had let her emotions get carried away, and Cedric, well, he really didn't care for her. Not like that. He had made that more than apparent.

His eyes glowered. "You look like you're freezing. Maybe you outta go inside. Make some tea or something," he said staring purposefully at her bosom, at her nipples which were stiff from the cold beneath her thin cotton t-shirt.

"Yes, maybe I'd better," Kendra answered through teeth that threatened to chatter. He had the uncanny ability of making her feel socially inept, ugly and physically repulsive. Yes, she knew she would never compare to his precious Arielle, but...damn him! Did he find her that grotesque?!!

***

The following week, things had gotten much better. She spent one of the best weekends of her life with him—when he had decided to sail to the Bahamas to go gambling at the Atlantis. Even though she was still on assignment and there was no romance or sex, between them, she still felt thrilled. Enchanted. Like they were going on a romantic get-away with the added bonus of having CJ, his adorable little boy as company. The few times she had been around him, he had completely stolen her heart. He was simply to die for! She smiled as she remembered what Cedric had said, "Yeah, me and CJ, we work as a team."

Yes, they certainly did. She was sure to have the time of her life.

However, something warm and utterly dangerous to her self-preservation had surfaced. Actually, it had been steadily simmering for a while, but that weekend it came boiling to the surface. She had lost her distance from this case completely. She had lost her objectivity, she had become too attached.

Though she wanted to indulge, she knew she shouldn't. Cedric was in love with Arielle. It didn't matter that she had died. That was the woman who held his heart, and she knew she'd only end up getting hurt if she agreed to any type of relationship—sexual or otherwise. Yet she had never wanted *any* man so much in her life! And she was ridiculously close to giving in to her desires.

But once more, she endeavored to squelch it, futile as the task seemed. In any case, she still had to do her best to push down all the emotions threatening to bubble to the surface. That had for all intent and purposes come up to the top. But God help her, she couldn't knowingly walk into something that was sure to crush and destroy her.

Difficult and frustrating as it was, regardless of the circumstances, she had to keep her wits about her.

Kendra thought about Darryl, her ex-boyfriend from New York, remembering how she used to have sex with him because she had known that was normal. What two healthy adults involved in a romantic relationship did. But how she had never really been into it. Not really. She could count on one hand how many times she'd had an orgasm with him. Even though he had had a nice enough body, had been handsome and more than physically appealing, sex with him had not been satisfying. She hadn't been sure why.

She had told herself that it was fine. That it was okay that she didn't always climax, that she enjoyed the closeness, the intimacy. He even used to tease her. Told her all the time how she was orgasmically-challenged. But she didn't believe this would be the case with Cedric. Though he had come to prefer masturbation to having a sexual partner because at least that way, she was sure to satisfy herself, she knew she was no longer satisfied with just that.

Cedric had changed all of that.

Sexually, he could bring her straight to the edge. She could more than sense that already. And just thinking about him without a shirt, his flat washboard stomach, those bulging pecs, oh how he thrilled and excited her! They had not as of yet kissed, but already she knew. Absolutely knew how awesome it would be.

Cedric would be her undoing. Sex with him might be too dangerous a thing, so why tempt fate? She couldn't risk it. If only...if only...if only...she could do the deed and satisfy her curiosity without her heart getting involved.

Only problem, that wasn't who she was, and her heart was already well-engaged. And if there was something she absolutely didn't play with...it *was* her heart, which needed to disconnect and disengage before it was too late.

10

Playing With Fire

They put CJ to bed early, the day before their departure. They were staying at the Atlantis on Paradise Island, dining on the terrace. The view was phenomenal, so romantic. The vivid blue sea below, the swaying palms, the mood was perfect and she felt overwhelmed by the beauty. And by this man. Ohhhh...how she wished...she wished for so many things. She found her seat, clung to it and said a small prayer. *God give her strength. Give her strength, cause this was becoming too much.*

And the way he was looking at her...the way he was treating her...like she was his lady. She knew it meant nothing. To him. He was a gentlemen. Well-brought up. Despite his public, rap artist persona, he had class. Lots of it. His warm, seductive voice, the sheer perfection of his face, he was, without a doubt, the most beautiful man she had ever had the pleasure of befriending. And he was ever so sweet too—booking this hotel, planning this entire little excursion for them. No boyfriend of hers had ever been so thoughtful and she should be enjoying this—except she wasn't. It was torture. Pure hell. How was she supposed to fight her feelings in the face of all of this sweetness?

"You know," he said picking up his linen napkin and laying it aside as he began picking at his salad. "I always wanted to bring her here. But she wouldn't come."

As always, the conversation usually reverted to Arielle one way or another. She was still very real to Cedric, still very much a part of his life. She didn't mind it too much though tonight. It was actually better to have him concentrating more along those lines then trying to seduce her. Yes, tonight Arielle would be a fascinating subject, she reconciled to herself. She felt too weak, too willing. Better to figure Arielle into this equation. It was infinitely better this way with the state of things.

"Why wouldn't she," she asked amiably.

He shrugged. "I came here one weekend with someone else

when I was supposed to be in Key West with her. She could never get over that."

Kendra laughed. "Well, can you blame her?"

He laughed too. "I guess I can see her point more clearly now."

"So she wasn't the only one doing the cheating?"

"I was faithful. Once we were married, I never looked at another woman after that. Even before that, really. Once I got serious about her and decided she was my woman, I felt satisfied and didn't want anyone else."

"You really expect me to believe that?"

"No, you don't have to. Except I don't see any reason to lie. What would be the point?"

"I don't know," she shrugged. "Maybe you want to impress me."

He grinned looking her dead in the eyes. "Nah, I think I've already done that." His voice deep and sensual sent a ripple of excitement through her.

Now why had she even gone there? She could feel the air crackle around them with sexual tension. It was true. He had.

She took a sip of her non-alcoholic tropical punch feeling her heart begin to beat erratically, wanting to say something to ease the sexual tension. But her mind was drawing a blank. How could she turn this around? Arielle, she needed to bring the focus back to her. *Yes, Arielle was safe.*

"Did it surprise you when you learned that she had been unfaithful to you?"

He winced at the question. "Kick me in the gut, why don't you," he said with a soft groan. "Hell, just thinking about it still hurts." Then he laughed. "You want to kill a man in love with you—cheat on him. Yeah, that'll hurt him like nothing else." He put his fork down. Like just the thought had caused him to lose his appetite.

"Sorry I brought it up."

"It was like writhing on the emergency room floor with no insurance and nary a doctor around. I thought I would die. I swear to God, I did." He chuckled and shook his head. "It's like I still can't accept it, you know. I still don't want to believe she was... *cheating* on me. But you know, she had a way about her, this winning way that made me feel just oh-so special. Like I was the only one. Guess she made him feel the same way, cause otherwise, why would he accept it? You saw his pictures. He was a pretty good-looking guy. He had no problem getting women. None at all. He had to have been in love to have..." He blew a breath. "God, don't want to believe that Arielle was such an operator." He was laughing now. "She had both of us pretty whipped."

Kendra pulled a face. "Oh, and you find that amusing, acceptable?"

"No, not at all. I just...I just can't believe how we both got played."

"I understand how you got played, but how did he get played?"

Cedric shook his head. "You're trying to piss me off, right? Except it's not gonna work. I don't care what she wrote in those goddamn journals. She loved me. She was in love with me too."

"Oh. Poor baby."

He grinned. "She did. I don't care what she had to say. Maybe he read her stuff and she had to write that. She loved me too, I'm sure of it."

"She probably did. Why not? You're loveable, right?"

"Yes, as a matter a fact, I am."

"I don't doubt it."

He laughed again. "You bitch. You're really trying to piss me off."

Kendra laughed innocently. "God, Cedric. Here I am agreeing with you and I'm teeing you off. What do you want me to say?"

"Nothing. Just listen."

"Okay. I'm listening. Now I'm your shrink. I'll be sending you a bill in the morning."

"Do you want to hear this?"

"No, but that's not gonna stop you from telling me anyway, will it?"

"Nope, if you don't want to hear, I'll stop."

"No, please. Go on, honestly, I want to hear."

"I...I still can't believe it. She was sexually insatiable...if you know what I mean. And I'm pretty much the same way, and so now...I'm thinking. How? When did she have time? Where did she find the strength? Even though I know...I know she made time and had the strength, still, it's pretty unbelievable. At least to me. Know what I mean?"

Kendra closed her eyes, not wanting to see his frustration and the pain. Her heart went out to him. She knew what it was to be betrayed. *You have to see her for what she was. She was double-crossing you with another man. Her cousin. You have to face that. Come to terms with it. That she was in love with another man,* she longed to tell him but didn't dare. He'd probably curse her out, have her head.

He took a sip from his drink. And was silent for a while. "Everything between us was so complicated. The way she felt about him had nothing to do with me. It was totally separate. I understand that now."

Kendra gave him a piteous look, one that said he might be crazy.

He shrugged, tucking a lock of his hair that had fallen to his temple behind his ear. "I don't know. I can't explain it. Maybe it's just wishful thinking on my part. But I think when she was with me, she was really with me. That she wasn't thinking about him. That she was concentrating on me."

"Cedric. Her journals more than prove that her thoughts were elsewhere."

"All I know is how she made me feel and that couldn't have been a... lie...," he said softly, pensively.

"Look, this is going to sound harsh. But I have to say it. You were nothing more than a consolation prize. Now I know, being who you are, that's a tough pill to swallow. But accept that. Face the truth. And move on. Go on with your life. Remember her with fondness, but don't build a shrine to her. Set impossible standards that no other woman will be able to measure to. See her for who she really was and move on."

"Easier said than done. I've tried, Kendra. Believe me." He laughed bitterly. "Hell, I've done everything I can to forget. Everything! Still, I can't let her go! Can't stop thinking about her. Not for a minute. You have no idea."

"Cedric, she's gone. You have to forget her. What are you gonna do, but move on?"

He shook his head.

"You have to. You have no choice. You eventually have to put tragedy behind you. I don't mean to sound callous, nor do I mean to belittle what you're feeling. You have every right to mourn your late wife for as long as it's necessary. Every right. Still, eventually, you have to put it behind you. Or it's not healthy. Life goes on and you have to go along with it.

"Really?" he said, smiling slightly. "Maybe."

"Of course, you do. You have to stop dwelling on her and the past. You need to stop looking behind and look forward. And I know you're argument will be that real love is so hard to find. And I understand that you might have shared that with her. And goodness, it must have been powerful. But even the Bible says, *till death do us part*. You die and it's over, Cedric. And now you have to make a mature decision and choose life. You choose life cause that's all you can do. What else can you do?"

"And where did you get your psychology degree?"

Kendra chuckled. "I'm not psychoanalyzing you."

"Oh, you're not?" He said playfully, picking up his fork and starting to eat again.

Good, she thought. His appetite had returned.

"No, I'm just talking to you as a friend. From one friend to another."

"And who have you loved and lost?"

Kendra tried not to flinch as images of just who that person was flashed before her.

"Like the saying goes, don't give me advise unless you've walked a mile in my shoes."

"I'm not sure the saying goes like that exactly."

"But you know what I mean."

Kendra nodded.

"Arielle's life went suddenly. Just like that," he said snapping his fingers. "Like a light switched off. Her life was snuffed out by some nut who's still at large and roaming the streets and who you say may now be after me. It's hard to accept. That's all. Real hard."

"I know," she said earnestly. "I know it has to be."

"And Christ, you have no idea how much I loved this woman. How insane I was for her."

"I have an inkling."

"No, you don't. You can't possibly." He shrugged. "I don't know if I'll *ever* be over her."

Kendra stared at him and was now shaking her head. "She must have been truly something. Why don't you tell me what it was about her you loved so much? I'm curious to know how a woman...any woman could make a man like you fall so completely for her."

He chuckled. "You say that as if I'm more complicated than other men. But I'm just like any other guy. I'm no more complicated. Men like what they like. That's all. And when a woman turns you on—"

"Oh, so it's all about sex and being turned on."

He shook his head in contemplation. "Nah, not really. But I'm not gonna sit up here and lie to you and say it doesn't have a lot to do with it."

"So what about a woman turns a man on?"

"Shit, what about a woman doesn't turn a man on? Baby, just about everything about a woman turns me on," he grinned sheepishly. "The way you look. The way you smell. The way you stand. The way you walk. It's really everything about you. Most women have no idea how visual men are. How much we enjoy just looking at you," he said looking directly at her. "Especially when you're stripped of clothing, wearing damn near nothing. Why do you think men love porno magazines and skin flicks so much?"

"Cause their nasty Neanderthals," Kendra murmured feeling the heat turn up a notch.

Cedric eyes smoldered. "It's the clothes you wear...and how you look when you're in nothing but your bra and thong, " he said amusingly. "It's how soft and smooth your skin feels when I reach out and touch you. It's how beautiful and perfect your ass looks when it's turned up in offering to me. It's about variety, and being receptive to trying new things when we're in bed. It's about being tough, naughty, raunchy, and totally sexy. About being down for the marathon sex sessions I'm gonna demand every now and then—the kind that lasts till dawn—leaving us dazed, tired, sore and totally satisfied. It's even about how my friends feel when they look at you—how they all secretly long to fuck you."

Kendra raised an eyebrow at that. "So far I haven't heard one thing about a woman's mind. What about the way she thinks? The knowledge she has—"

"So long as that knowledge includes how to suck my cock just the way I like it, then it's a beautiful thing," he said straight-faced. "But you know, most of the times a woman's mind gets in the way of getting down—know what I'm saying. Look at you for instance."

Kendra looked at him in astonishment.

"Oh, don't look so shocked," he admonished, half-jokingly. "I think you more than understand what I mean. Like what's stopping you right now from fucking me where I stand? Nothing. Nothing but your mind..."

"Gosh, you're a caveman. I thought you were more evolved."

He grinned. "God, you sound just like Arielle."

"*Moi*? You're comparing me to the incomparable Arielle?!"

He looked at her for a beat. "Um...in fact, you remind me of her...a little."

"I do?"

"Just a little."

"Well, I can't imagine why. I'm nothing like her."

He smiled a secret, mysterious little smile. "Well, I beg to differ."

The night wore on, they finished dinner and still nothing untoward had happened. They continued to talk. Just to talk. Him sipping wine and her drinking Perrier. Somehow they fell on the subject of his mother. His mother died of Lupus, and he confided since then he had done some research and discovered that four million American had the disease, mostly women. In fact, 90 percent were.

"The disease is so difficult to diagnose and in my mother's case, she was sick and constantly being hospitalized for close to five years before she was ever diagnosed. You know, I never saw her alive. I have this one tattered little picture of her dad allowed me to keep from the age of nine. I was always sneaking it and he used to catch me looking at it all the time. She looked nothing like that picture when I saw her. Would you like to see it?"

She nodded and he pulled out the old photograph out of his wallet.

"I arrived right on time for her funeral. I couldn't believe she wasn't able to hold on until I got there. Her family had been telling her I was coming, to hold on, I would be there. And they said she was so happy knowing I was on my way. Still she died, two days before I got there. I was crushed," he gulped. And it was really hard seeing her lain out in the coffin. That's always the only image I hold of her now, a serene corpse laid out in a coffin."

"Where did she live," Kendra asked handing him back the photograph.

He smiled sadly. "Manila. And the funny thing was that I had lived there a number of years with my old man. That bastard knew my mom was there the entire time, maybe even saw her, and he never once told me about her."

"Maybe you met her and didn't even know."

"Maybe I did. I don't know," he shrugged. "It's just crazy, you know. How people do things, justify their actions to themselves, uncaring of the hurt they might be heaping on someone else. I suppose we're all guilty of it."

She sighed. "I suppose, still, it's awful. Has he ever told you why he and your mother broke up?"

"Never," he said bitterly with so much emotion. "You see, my pops doesn't feel the need to justify his actions to anyone—and especially not to me. He honestly thinks he owes me no explanation. And at this point, I don't even want one, you know what I mean? Cause if it's stupid, something ridiculous," his shoulders heaved, "I'm not sure what I'd do. I might go fucking nuts, you know, really loose it. So I figure, better not to know. Better he hold his peace and go to the grave with it. Just as she did."

Kendra wanted to reach out and comfort him. She wanted to hold him and make everything okay—except she didn't dare. Just the idea of touching him moved her to distraction. Making her feel excited, dizzy, and panicky all at the same time.

He took a deep breath and then chuckled lightly. "God, I really killed the groove up in here."

Kendra shook her head, a big lump lodged in her throat. "No-no, God, you need to talk about this. Get it off your chest." She gazed indulgently at him.

"You're being sweet tonight. Anyway, let's talk about happier things, like the Goombay we attended this afternoon. Did you enjoy it?"

"Did I," she gushed. "It was fantastic, my first one. It was real nice," she said sobering up, wanting to say, *especially since I was with you*. She reached out and touched his hand then, and strangely enough, she didn't feel the rush of excitement she had imagined she would feel, but felt soothed. She thought about how much she feared this feeling, this attraction she had for him. How she feared it might unleash some wildness in her. But holding his hand and feeling their warmth had unfolded no great mystery, nor did it unleash any great flood of emotion. It simply felt nice and comfortable. Just as it should.

***

She was loosing her objectivity and still, she wasn't any closer to solving this case. After they got back from the Bahamas, she begged Agent Neff to take over for a little bit. She needed some time off. Time to breathe. The Bureau understood—thank God! Besides, she had still not as of yet taken time off to settle herself in, hadn't even gotten rid of her place up in New York, nor brought any of her stuff from over there. So she took a whole week off to settle her affairs.

That week, she became reacquainted with her family, her original reason for wanting a transfer to Miami in the first place, as well as flew to New York for a couple of days to tie up loose ends.

Taking some time off helped her to refocus too on the case. Helped her to get some perspective that she hadn't been quite able to see standing so near. She showed up at Cedric's a week later and he seemed real happy to see her. She and Neff had flipped schedules, and now she had the nightshift, since Neff had had it for close to three months. It was only fair, but it put her in a precarious situation. No telling what would happen.

That night, when she went to the guest bedroom that she would be occupying, he told her how her bathroom had flooded earlier and how she could use his master bath if she'd like. It sounded reasonable enough, but then again, she felt this weird feeling of angst and excitement.

She looked into his eyes and she saw this expression in them that she didn't altogether trust. What was he up to? When she gazed at him though she couldn't quite put her fingers on it, his expression was definitely strange.

His master bath was entirely mirrored—great solid sheets covered the walls with little irregular pieces on the ceilings. It was like a mosaic of glorious streaming water.

Kendra draped her clothes carefully over a cream colored stool and stood gazing at her naked body, which was even more trim and fit since moving to Miami because of all the running around she did. It was also a testament to all the vigorous exercise she had been getting regularly with Cedric. She had taken full advantage of Quentin, his personal trainer, since she had to be there regardless to guard Cedric. And Quentin was very good at his job.

Her breasts were small but firm, her waist had gotten much leaner and her hips were nicely shaped and slightly rounded. She looked pleasing, she thought as she caught a glimpse of her face, hazily reflected in the clouds of steam. Except her looks had never mattered much to her—until now. But her looks were of the utmost importance now. She felt self-conscious, embarrassed to even admit this to herself, but she cared because Cedric did.

Cedric had run her a bath and had filled his roman tub with warm water. He had even added some bubble and scent. She sighed deeply thinking how sweet Cedric could be at times, feeling very tired all of the sudden. She was so tired of life and fighting her feelings, and wondered why everything had to be so damned complicated.

She stepped into the tub then lowered herself into the scented, bubble bath. Then wearily, she closed her eyes, leaning back against the edge of the roman tub. Weariness coupled with worry and tension caused her to remain there in the tub much longer than she had intended. She hardly knew when she had gotten up or what had happened. When she woke up, it was morning and she was lying in her room, on the bed, except there was this faint but distinct probing pain in her nether regions. What the hell had transpired? Try as she might, she couldn't remember a thing. Nothing other than closing her eyes in the roman tub.

11

Loving in Metaphors

The first time it happened, he was seated in front of the fireplace, staring into space like he always did with a drink in his hand, a smoke in the other and Kendra, who had been soaking in his tub, just came sauntering up to him. She had just came back on assignment and came out of her room solely in pajamas—with an expression on her face which was not that of Kendra, but totally Arielle. Her smile was like pure sunshine, and she wore that smile like a flag. That beauty-pageant contestant I-need-your-vote-real-bad/don't-hate-me-cause-I'm-so-fucking-beautiful smile Arielle often wore in real life. Cedric sat transfixed as he watched her, knowing full well it wasn't Kendra.

She slowly let herself drop before him, keeping eye-contact the entire time. She said nothing, but Cedric, unable to even help himself immediately gathered her up in his arms, understanding everything all at once. Their lips touched and Cedric thought he'd explode from sheer happiness.

After discovering a way to make love to him physically, Arielle did just that, taking possession of Kendra. It was a guilty pleasure for Cedric. Too good to be true, but one of those things you knew you should try to fight, but couldn't. Just like masturbating. It felt good until after you came. Then the guilt set in.

She planted him with one searing kiss after another, bombarding him with French kisses that left him breathless and intoxicated, and which said everything she was longing to say but didn't have to. Cedric absorbed each one with his eyes closed, allowing it to proceed long and slow. And when it was over, he opened his eyes, and Kendra was no longer even there. He was holding and kissing Arielle, who seemed to have materialized completely.

"Christ!" Cedric murmured, momentarily alarmed.

Quickly, she placed her fingers across his lips to silence him, beamed at him and grabbed his collar, bringing him down for another tantalizing kiss. Soon he didn't give a damn what this was all about. Didn't even care how she had done it, whether it was wrong or right, here nor there. He was all into it, a total willing and enthusiastic participant. If there was hell to pay, then he'd gladly pay later. All he could feel now was the burning need to possess her, to have her beneath him. And Christ, this was so illicit, so delicious, the way she was melting all over him. He could feel his heart pounding, and hers, almost as if it were out of their bodies. Trying to calm down, he did his best to relax and just let it all unfold. Unhindered.

Oh, baby! He was finally getting his wish. Making love to Arielle once more. And he was going to enjoy it. Completely.

When he awoke, she was gone. He was naked and the empty space next to him told little of the night they had shared. He was sure it had happened, but then again, he felt confused. Unsure. Maybe, it had not.

***

"What the hell happened last night," he stormed at her when she appeared behind him as he shaved in the mirror, scaring him half to death. Causing him to cut himself. "What are you trying to do? Kill me or land me in jail?"

She said nothing but stood there, beaming. Looking extremely pleased with herself.

"What if she knows? Was I dreaming? Was it real? It felt real."

"It was real," she assured him.

"But how?"

"You know how. You understood last night. Don't bother denying it. You understood exactly what I had done. And you didn't oppose it. You didn't try to stop it. So don't stand your moral ground this morning. If you didn't want to, then you should have refused then."

"I was confused."

She shrugged. "I don't know why? You didn't seem at all confused to me. In fact, you were really into it. You were...well...quite vigorous," she said with a sly little smile, "to put it delicately, ummm...extremely vigorous..." She laughed throatily, "if I didn't know better, I'd be jealous. You never did it to me like that. Poor Kendra, her bottom must really hurt."

Cedric blanched. "You mean she could feel—"

"No-no, she didn't feel it, wasn't even aware of what was happening. Not last night. But this morning, she can certainly feel the aftereffects. It's her body, you know... and Cedric, you are rather...large."

"Shit! Well, I don't care what happened or how you did it. It can't happen again, okay?! She'll have my ass if she ever finds out!"

"Like you had hers," Arielle teased, laughing some more.

"You're enjoying this. You're just perverse enough to actually enjoy this."

She pulled a face, then smiled again. Letting him know for sure why he was wildly attracted to her. She had a harsh, unrelenting beauty and even though there'd be hell to pay, he couldn't be angry with her.

"So what's the deal here? Is she gonna know?"

"She won't. Not unless you tell her."

"What if she had awakened in the middle of it?"

"She didn't, did she... and she won't."

"How do you know? What makes you such an expert? To hear you, you sound like you do this everyday. But the fact is, you're a novice. You don't really understand this any better than I do. Nope, we can't chance it, Arielle. I don't think we should ever try that again."

"Oh, please, Cedric. Don't be such a wuss."

"Uhhh, now I'm a wuss?"

"I really wanted to call you something else. But I thought I'd be kinder?"

"No, why don't you just come out and speak your mind."

"Stop being such a pussy."

"Ha-ha, a pussy?!"

"Yes, a pussy."

"A pussy I am not!"

"Well, maybe you're a prick. Sorry, let me correct myself," she hissed, her eyes glaring daggers at him. "Why are you so worried? I promise you. She's not going to find out. She'll have no memory of anything happening."

"What about the physical pain—or evidence."

"You wore a condom."

"Still, you said she might feel...violated. Sore."

"Well, next time you shouldn't be so..." she grinned, "forceful."

He grinned. "And you shouldn't be so lustful."

"Besides, didn't you like it? Enjoy it," she said wrapping her slender arms around him. Arms that he could see but not feel.

"Baby, she's FBI. And I think it's against the law to kidnap someone—even if it's just their body. She's an agent for crying out loud! We can't just fuck with her like this. And I am literally fucking her."

Arielle laughed. "You're not kidding. But must you be so crass?"

"Oh, I see. First I'm a pussy, now I'm being crass."

"Well, if you're scared...and you think we shouldn't. Then fine, I'm not gonna force you, baby. I can't rape you. I get the message. So you don't want it to happen again?"

"No."

"You didn't enjoy it?"

"That's besides the point."

"Oh, you did enjoy it," she said lifting her hips and rotated it against him in a manner that was absolutely suggestive of the way she had carried on the night before. Reminding him of the exquisitely slow and sensual manner she had enflamed him, where he had felt it from the soles of his feet to the tip of his toes and fingers. All the way down his spine. She had more than thrilled him, and had been quite insatiable.

He closed his eyes, trying to shut out the memories. "Arielle, oh God. This is torture. Why do you tease me so?"

"So it was very enjoyable?"

He sighed deeply. "Yes, very."

She laughed again, torturing him further with her throaty, sexy, sinful laugh that drove him to the brink of madness.

"Promise me that it won't happen again."

"What won't happen?" She asked absently, peering intently at him.

He was getting exasperated. "Last night. We can't do that to Kendra, understand? You can't just snatch her body and do things with it."

"Like what kind of things," she asked being deliberately obtuse.

"Sexual things..."

"You're the one that did the sexual things...not me."

"Well, you're the one that was getting all that good feeling. By the way, was it good for you?"

Her eyes seemed to gleam. "I won't tell..." she giggled.

Cedric shook his head. "You know, Kendra's very uptight, and she would have a conniption if she ever found out. So I'm telling you, Arielle. Cool it. This can't happen again."

"I don't know why you don't trust me," she said defensively. "Kendra's completely under my control. Next time you'll know in advance and—"

"No, Arielle. There won't be a next time. Promise me they'll be no more next times. It's morally reprehensible what we did. It can't happen again."

She was dusting invisible lent off her clothes and looked like she was ignoring him. Examining her fingernails. "Arielle, do you hear me?"

"Loud and clear."

"And..."

"And I heard you."

"And..."

"What do you want from me? I try to give you pleasure and all you do is yell at me! Sonofabitch," she said hotly, her eyes blazing fire at him. "You'll see if I ever go out of my way for you again."

***

Kendra was totally confused that entire morning. She had had her most vivid dream about Cedric to date. One where she was making love to him except it seemed so real. So much so that she could feel a dull ache in her pelvic region, he had been so big.

It was so weird. Her head felt foggy like she had been drinking—except she didn't remember having a drink. She and alcohol didn't mix, and she rarely if ever drank. She went absolutely nutty whenever she drank. Good God, it was something to behold. She became a madwoman. The few times she had ever had alcohol, she had done things she was very ashamed about. She could remember three separate incidents in the air force, which she longed to forget. And now, she never drank. Not beer or wine, not even a wine cooler. Nothing with alcohol for her. She was allergic to alcohol. Her body couldn't tolerate it.

So many times Cedric had tried to get her to drink with him. He seemed to think she didn't drink out of some kind of propriety. Except he was the last person she'd ever agree to have a drink with. She'd never have a drink with Cedric anywhere in the vicinity. Not the way she felt about him. Forget about it! She would never agree to even anything as harmless as a glass of wine. And anything stronger could send her off the deep end.

But she wondered.

Maybe he had slipped something. But he wouldn't have. He wouldn't have to. That wasn't his style. Cedric would rely solely on his charm. Yet, if his charm didn't seem to be working, she wondered if he wouldn't resort to other means…

No. No, she was deluding herself. Yes, he may tease her, might even want her, but she couldn't see him stooping to that level. Even though she felt like something had happened, had transpired between them last night, she shoved it out of her mind. It was probably wishful thinking on her part. A sexual, beyond vivid dream. But only that…a dream. And the pain, the pain she felt in her nether regions, it could be that she was getting her period.

And when she saw Cedric in the morning and he seemed so nonchalant and seemingly oblivious to her, that definitely cinched things for her. Cleared her thinking. No way could anything had happened. She had to have been dreaming. No matter how real it seemed. No matter how bad she ached. She didn't want to believe that he could make love to her the way he had last night and then treat her so nonchalantly the next morning. Like nothing, absolutely nothing had happened. She felt foolish, ridiculous even thinking it. And she was so happy to go home when Neff arrived to relieve her later. She needed rest was all.

***

Meanwhile, Cedric had no idea what he would say or how he should react if the subject ever came up. What a predicament? She would probably absolutely not believe that it was Arielle. And furthermore, she'd think he was nuts as well. He felt relieved that she hadn't said anything. Never brought the subject of that night up. So of course, neither did he.

Meanwhile, Arielle was taking her body and doing things at times. Although he resolved he was not going to do any repeat performance like the last time, it was getting harder and harder. Even though Arielle had promised, well…maybe she had never actually promised, she was relentless. Uncontrollable. She was perfectly awful. Like a spoiled child determined to get her way no matter what.

Nearly every night, she would try to seduce him one way or another, but he was steadfast in his resolve, and wouldn't touch her. No matter what her pranks. Until one night, she got down to business and wowed him in a way he hadn't expected. She had came out without a stitch of clothing except a very tiny G-string. He kept thinking was it hers or Kendra's? He felt so aroused thinking that Kendra might be wearing this under her very conservative suits. But then again…Arielle had always worn them and he had always been so turned on when he saw her in them.

"Arielle, no!" He stormed at her. "You have to stop doing this," he told her, despite his erection.

"Darling, what am I doing," she murmured, offering sex in a caressing tone. "I'm not doing a thing. Shut your eyes if you don't want to look."

Taking her advise, he squeezed his eyes shut against the infusing heat threatening to overturn his resolve, ravaging all of his senses. But he wasn't going through this with her again.

He could hear her taking some small tentative steps towards him, and he knew soon she'd be touching him. He wasn't sure he could bear her touch. That would be too much. He only had so much will power. "Don't take another step," he warned her, his eyes still shut.

He felt sure she moved again. He took a peek and swore under his breath when he came face to face with her crotch, right in his face, only inches away. The tiny lace material of her panties seemed miniscule and covered nothing except the neatly trimmed hair between her luscious, silky thighs. And he could smell her too, the aroma was overpowering. She smelled like sex, so lusty, so sinful. And he was starving for her.

Looking up at her face, he noted the flush of her cheeks and the faint triumphant smile she was not even bothering to hide. "What do you want to do first," she asked breathlessly, her voice was a small, suffocated little sound that drove him close to loosing his mind. His engorged penis surged, rigid and swollen, pulsing now against his stomach, reaching way past his belly-button. His entire body longed to melt against hers. How in the name of God was he ever going to be able to resist her?

She gave him a knowing smile, one with all the wisdom of Eve. She knew the effect she was having on him and purposely allowed her eyes to lower and linger on his raging erection, enjoying herself now, even sensuously running her tongue over her lips in a manner absolutely designed to seduce.

Cedric gulped and then blanched. Then drew in a sharp breath as she swung around and brazenly bent down to give him a bird's eye view of her sumptuous backside—just the way a seasoned stripper would do it. Tawdry as hell! Meanwhile, he was going to come just looking at it, he thought. He lunged for her, his cheek against her cheek, as he bit into her, taking a large bite. She yelped and he shoved her out of the way just in time and ran for dear life towards his bedroom. He wasn't sure, but he may have knocked her down, except he hadn't looked back as he made his way to the master bedroom, locking the door behind him. He climbed onto bed and stayed crouched at the headboard like a frightened little boy, half expecting her to walk through the door. Except she couldn't. Could she? She was flesh and bones. She wouldn't be able, he thought and chuckled, grinning now. God, he was being so silly, but quickly frowned as she began pounding on the door.

"Cedric, you oaf! Open the door, now! You coward! Cedric...," She was pounding some more, making a real ruckus and would soon awaken the entire household. "Stop being so silly, Cedric. You've got to be kidding me...open the door this instant!!!" Her voice was shrill. She was getting piping mad.

"Go away, Arielle," he told her, trying to sound stern, endeavoring to control the laughter in his voice. Christ, this was ridiculous! He was being hunted down! Haunted too. Where was security when he needed them?

"Cedric, I'm not playing. Open the door," she ordered, "or you're not gonna like what I do next."

"Oh yeah, baby. That's a real threat. What are you gonna do, burn down the place?"

"Yes! Maybe I will!"

"Are you serious?!"

She was getting really loud. "Cedric Courage open this door NOW!" She hollered.

Deuce would probably come busting in any minute if she continued, Cedric thought warily, realizing this was getting real out of hand. Also, Arielle just might burn the place down like she promised, he'd put nothing past her. And then next he thought about how embarrassing it was going to be for Kendra if Deuce saw her like this—naked for all intent and purposes and beating down his door, trying to rape him. There was no way he was going to believe or anyone else for that matter that she was Arielle and not Kendra. No one was ever going to buy that.

Shit, that would be too rude and horrible to let Deuce find Kendra like this. How would he ever be able to explain... Hell, he made a quick decision then, deciding to open the door and let her in. He had to let her in before she became hysterical and woke the freaking building. He would have to simply deal with this like a man.

He stalked to the door, pissed now, feeling truly angry at Arielle's selfish antics. "Shut the hell up, Arielle, before you wake everyone."

Wearing nothing but a smile, she pushed past him, once the door was open, moving towards the bed. "All right," she said, hands on her hips, breasts pushed forward, "As I asked before. How do you want me," she said gliding her hands over the flatness of her belly invitingly. "Do you want me on my back, on all fours, how baby?"

Everything about her ready sexuality offended him. But this was Arielle, his wanton, sexually depraved wife. An image of her and Danyel flashed through his mind and suddenly the thought of being with her repulsed him. He wondered if this was what she had done to her cousin that caused him to have such an illicit affair with her. Arielle could be forceful. When she wanted something, she went after it with both barrels loaded. And feeling moody and thinned-skinned thinking about how she might tremble for any man and not just him, he felt hot-tempered and ferociously angry all of the sudden.

"Up," he brusquely ordered, moving purposefully towards her, "on your knees." She scrambled up the bed assuming the position, her bottom pointed out provocatively in offering to him. He slapped her lightly, and immediately felt a rush of unequivocal desire causing him to close his eyes momentarily, dazed from weakness. She looked stunning. Unbelievable. "Are you ready to fuck," he asked hotly, wanting it to be just that. A fuck. One where it was totally physical and his emotions uninvolved.

"I thought you'd never ask," she murmured, gloating. Reacting to the pats he was giving her, soon she was trembling with desire. Cedric climbed behind her, laying a palm on her waist and warmly stroked her spine. He could feel the wetness on her inner thighs. He moved his shaft over the dew on her lush folds, preparing her for his entry. God help me, he thought weakly as he watched her quiver helplessly. She was like a bitch in heat. And bending down, he kissed her slowly, licked her all over her back and neck. Feeling devastated, he felt his arrested breath, and knew from her sexy pant that he was totally and fully involved as he devoured her.

Pushing her down and turning her over, his lips and tongue caressed every curve, every swell and hollow, every cresting peak and luscious plane with long, lingering strokes. Kissing and licking her in every intimate place, while his hands wrecked havoc, roving and stroking her breasts and belly and inner thighs, he brought her to heaven several times before even considering seeking his own release.

After her shuddering stopped, his strong hands slid around

the back of her legs, turning her back over and lifting her in one smooth movement, he shifting her thighs upwards, adjusting her just so, bringing her back up on all fours, readying her for action.

"It's my game tonight," he told her breathlessly, guiding the tip of his ferocious erection to her drenched vulva, sliding it over her warm slippery cleft. "My rules, my pacing, my directions," he drawled, teasing and caressing her with the bulbous tip. "Understand?"

She moaned low, and then panted like a puppy.

"Ah yeah," he sighed in a luxurious murmur. "Are you ready for cock?"

"Always," she answered, pushing her hips back, groaning voluptuously, as she undulated her hips, stretching herself to take him steadily in.

"Uhn-uhn, hold up. Wait a minute." His fingers dug into her fleshy buttocks, and held her rigid under his grasp. "Just so we understand each other, you're my Monday-night fuck.   And tonight, you're gonna get some training on orgasmic restraint," he said and thrust deeply into her. Holding his palm over her pelvis, he pushed down to restrict her movement, wanting her to work for her orgasm. But who was he kidding? This was Arielle he was talking to, and she was coming already. Moaning wildly, undulating her hips and bucking wildly despite his strong grip. Also staring up at him, eyes glazed with pleasure and desire, her smile totally lascivious as her sexual juices oozed down his penis and down her thighs.

His eyes closed and he swore under his breath as he submerged himself to the hilt deep into her shuddering body, striving to pace himself as he began his assault. Gliding fluidly in and out a few times, he started to pound into her, the friction putting an intolerable strain on his heated body.

The raw power in every thrust, urgent and passionate caused another orgasm to wash over Arielle. She was crying now, and he had to bend down and devour her mouth to muffle the sounds of ecstasy until her cries died away.

"You're un-trainable," he told her. "You're not supposed to come until I tell you to come."

Lifting her, he glided her newly sated body up his rigid length with slow deliberation, arranging her now on her back, legs in the air and started anew, grinding into her again in a compelling, maddingly sensual, carnal rhythm, all the while marveling at how warm and slippery she was. She was still breathless and panting but was much more docile now in his hands. He liked her like this. She was the woman he dreamed about, the woman he wanted, the woman he loved. And he wanted to fill her body, her soul, every crevice and groove of her tantalizing body with sperm.

Leaning over, he tasted her lips. "I've missed you," he murmured against the lushness of those lips, "And God, how I love you," he groaned and thrust even deeper, grinding harder, fucking her with heart-stopping force until he felt himself knock against her cervix. She was pushing him back with her hands, it must have hurt, but he couldn't stop himself. He pushed further still, feeding her inches more of him, wanting to give her every inch of him. He convulsed deep inside her womb, but suddenly remembering whom it was he was actually with and realizing he hadn't slipped on a condom before this delirious coupling, he withdrew and came on her stomach instead.

Of course, the guilt came immediately, but he was so exhausted be could barely move, having come for an orgasmic eternity. As he held her in his arms, his hands lazily caressing the curve of her spine, he told her, "This can never happen again, Arielle."

"Ummm," she purred lazily.

"I'm serious, Arielle."

"Uh-huh," she agreed. "I know. It won't. I promise..."

Yeah, right, he thought, wondering what he was going to do, knowing Arielle would never stop. Never relent. She was going to do this all the time, he could bet on it, and unfortunately, she was his weakness, and she more than knew that.

It was all so strange.

He was holding Arielle, and saw her as Arielle. But yet, he knew it was really Kendra. He had to concentrate really hard to see Kendra, but it was Kendra that was laying so contentedly and sated in his arms. Not Arielle. But then again, she sounded like Arielle and really was Arielle. It was too confusing for words, and his feelings were all jumbled and mixed up right now. On the one hand, it was Arielle, but on the other hand, it was Kendra's body, and he was realizing he was enjoying the duality and duplicity of making love to both women at the same time. It was a very weird and strange place to be. One he wouldn't have asked for, but which he was strangely enjoying.

Every time she showed up as Kendra, he would chastise her. Chastise her for stealing Kendra's body. But secretly, though, he was growing to love it.

Inherently selfish, he knew Arielle would most certainly stop if she even suspected he had feelings for Kendra. Perhaps that would put an end to the madness. Yet even in this unorthodox way, he couldn't help enjoying Arielle.

She had eternally placed her stamp on his soul and had ruined him for any other woman. She knew exactly what she was doing, knew how to bring a man to his knees, and he bowed down to her, because yes, he desired her.

Much as he liked and fancied Kendra, it was truly Arielle he wanted. It wasn't enough that she was the one that was there in spirit, he wanted her there in body as well. And although it hadn't fully come to him yet, he was beginning to think there was a way of actually having both.

***

The next morning, Kendra woke up with a really bad headache and a dull ache in her nether regions. In fact, her entire body ached, yet she also felt more relaxed than she had ever felt in a long time. She felt pleasured, the way only a good romp made her feel...languid and calm.

She showered and was truly perplexed by the fact that her sex was swollen and actually stung when she washed it. She smelled like sex too, but didn't want to believe it. Had she drank last night and had sex with Cedric? Had he somehow convinced her to consume alcohol and taken advantage of her? She didn't want to believe it, but the evidence seemed overwhelming—except she couldn't remember a thing...

Everything came to a head, though, when she actually laid eyes on Cedric and immediately started to feel really heated. Her stomach melted and she felt moist between her thighs. Christ, what had gotten into her?

She was distracted too, constantly looking at his lips. At his hands, and several times even sneaked a peek at his crotch, feeling him inside her, stroking her. She ached for him. Actually ached for him, but couldn't believe his absolute indifference to her.

He was totally all-business, wasn't even his usual self. He spoke very little and come to think of it, never met her eyes, and reminded her of a man doing hard penance—like just the fact that she was around, had to be around—bothered him.

For the next few days, she dreaded being around him. He did nothing more than bark orders at everyone, and pretty much ignored her as he immersed himself in his recording. Everyday, bright and shine, they were at the studio and pretty much stayed there till the wee hours of the morning.

In the morning, she'd go home since Neff had the day shift, and fall into a deep, dreamless sleep brought on by the exhaustion of this rigid, grueling schedule of Cedric's.

She was looking haggard, her sister Sophy told her one night when she arrived home early for a change. She had felt so dizzy and weak, that Neff had relieved her much earlier than usual.

That night, she couldn't even sleep. Her mind was consumed with thoughts of him. It was as if he was now all she could think of. Sure, she knew she found him attractive, but to this point? To the point of feeling like she constantly wanted him. To the point where she would daydream all day she was making love to him.

And then to be so ignored when she was with him. She felt so confused. She didn't want to believe he didn't feel the sparks she felt, that she was the only one feeling what she was feeling.

When she finally fell asleep, he was in her dreams and had made love to her in every conceivable way, and she had let him. When he did finally allow her to climax, since he kept telling her she couldn't come until he told her to, she felt rung out and exhausted.

The next morning, it was the same as before. She had felt like she had actually done all those things. She couldn't believe how erotic her dreams had become. But when she woke up, she was at her parent's, in her room, on her own bed, but she smelled like sex and felt swollen again, like she had actually had sex, and simply couldn't understand it.

And of course, she would never in a million years confront him about it. How could she? What the hell was she going to say? Besides, she was too embarrassed—especially since this was all probably wishful thinking on her part.

After all, she did want him something awful. And regardless of how she ached, or what she suspected—which was crazy in itself—she didn't want to believe she was actually carrying on with Cedric like this, making mad passionate love. Nor that he would treat her the next morning as if nothing had happened. In fact, these days, he behaved as if she didn't even exist!

No, Cedric might be a total and complete asshole, but he wasn't a rapist. Cedric could have practically any woman he wanted. Why would he resort to drugging and raping her? It was too weird. She didn't want to believe that he could be having sex with her without her knowledge and consent. Besides, it seemed in these dreams like she was a willing and passionate participant.

This was way too strange! Was she loosing her mind?

Then stranger still was the fact that he was calling her Arielle. It was never Kendra, always Arielle. And even though she hated that she even cared, him referring to his late wife during these intimate moments with her really bothered her. A lot. Him not calling her by her name, regardless of whether it was a dream or not, really sucked!!!

**

Cedric could see her struggling with herself. And he felt bad for her. It was awful what he and Arielle were doing to her, and he felt enormously guilty. He'd really started to like her for herself. She had softened up quite a bit. Sometimes their eyes would meet and he would know and understand just how confused she was and how badly she wanted him. All he had to do was make the first move, because she would never do it, but he knew she was weak for him.

She acted all tough and stuff, but underneath, she was a softy. At least for him. And he wasn't so cocky to fancy she was in love with him, but the desire was definitely there. Sadly enough though, his guilty conscience wouldn't allow him to go near her— not when she wasn't Arielle. It was nice to know he had a conscience—not to mention the fact that he wasn't sure what Arielle would do to her if she even suspected he was soft for her.

So for both their sakes, he kept it real short with her. Squashing any feelings he harbored towards her, he was determined to never let these emotions see the light of day.

And it was a good thing too that Kendra was as repressed as she was. Better for her not to admit how she felt. Better for them both. But it was getting hard, he'd admit, real hard having her around.

For a brief moment, he thought about Veronica. He felt sad now every time he thought of her, and so tried not to think of her at all. Veronica had been determined to have him, but had managed to destroy anything he had ever felt for her.

A few months after the funeral, she had let it slip over dinner how she had been pregnant with his baby but how he shouldn't worry since she had gotten rid of it. Just like that, she had dropped this bombshell over dinner. As he stared at her in total disbelief, reeling over her lack of warmth and human decency, he had known most definitely that she was out. Out of his life for good.

"Why would you even tell me that," he had asked tightly,

meeting her frank, clear blue eyes. It meant nothing. She saw nothing wrong with what she had done. "Why not just keep that tidbit of information to yourself? Did you think knowing this would please me?"

She had paused for a moment then, surprised by his demeanor and the deep scowl that had registered on his face. "I wanted to be honest. I know how you hate secrets and didn't want you—"

She hesitated, at a loss for words as his scowl deepened. The pain of what she had told him was etched right there or his face. And he too was at a total loss for words.

They sat there for several minutes in total silence, neither of them looking at one another until Cedric threw his fork in his place in disgust and excused himself from the table. He strolled out of the restaurant needing some fresh air and a smoke and took a seat in front of the curb watching people as they strolled by. But Veronica came out soon after to find him, unable to leave well enough alone.

"I-I didn't know what to do," she offered lamely as she took a seat next to him. "I felt like it wasn't the right time. I was so confused. I-I'm sorry...I should have told you."

She stopped talking as she watched the emotions play across his face and seemed to hold her breath as she awaited his response. Except he had nothing to say to her. He looked wary, and was expecting her to get all hysterical, and she didn't disappoint him.

"Cedric...I-I'm sorry. I should have consulted you. I should have..." she apologized again and tried to touch him, to reach for his hand, but he managed to move it from her grasp before she could grab a hold of him. She stared at him quite desperately, and did look sorry. Very sorry. She bit her lips. "You look so angry," she gasped. "I've messed up, botched everything up. Please Cedric, give me one more chance. I promise, we can have another baby. Please!"

"Forget it. It hardly matters," he had managed to grumble.

"I hardly matter or the baby?"

"Please, Veronica. What baby? Was there even one? Or isn't this one of your fabrications...you know, the little dramas you make up just to spin my wheels and get me going..."

She started to cry then. "How can you even say that? I can't believe what you're suggesting..."

"Believe it."

"Why would I—"

"I don't know. Maybe cause you're a bitch. Maybe because you're cold, heartless and calculating. Maybe cause you've always enjoyed fucking with my head!!! You tell me, choose one. And maybe because of a hundred other sick things I couldn't even begin to fathom. I don't profess to understand how your perverse little mind works. But just do me a favor, girlfriend, forget about it. Don't ever mention that shit to me again! Cause it's bullshit, and I don't believe you for a second!"

She ran away then, narrowly missing a car.

Cedric had stood up with both his hands holding his head. He shut his eyes tightly, saying a silent prayer that she hadn't been struck. Christ Almighty, that was all he would have needed to push him over the edge.

After that, Veronica had sent him a very professional, well-written note telling him basically to seek other representation, suggesting one, and had never spoken to him again. No contact. Finito. The end.

If only all break-ups could be so cut and dry, so neat and precise. But he did miss her though. Despite everything that had transpired, he had lost a great friend—not to mention a fantastic publicist. Too bad things hadn't worked out.

And now Kendra was his latest headache. What in heavens was he going to do with Arielle stealing her body at every turn, and him unable to resist? No, it had to stop. Something had to be done.

If he could somehow get Arielle jealous of her, she might stop using her body, but goodness, what if she snatched some other, poor, unsuspecting woman. Notwithstanding, the fact that she might harm Kendra in some way. This had become one heck of dilemma.

***

"I think you like her a little too much," Arielle confessed soon after one day.

All I knew was that this was way out of control, and I was caught between a rock and a hard place. What the hell did you do in such a predicament? This was being caught between the devil and the deep blue sea. Either way, you were screwed.

Arielle must have intercepted my thoughts because soon after I thought this, she appeared in her ghostly form, stomping mad.

"Oh, so now I'm the devil right? I'm the devil and she's the sea?" She asked from the doorway and then disappeared.

"So, what's wrong with that? You have me make love to her almost every night. It's her body even though it's you inside of her. I'm bound to have some feelings for her. What did you expect?"

"I think you want to make love to her now even when I'm not around." I heard her say inside my mind.

I hated when she did this, and she knew it. "Let me see you," I said with frustration. "And stop talking inside my head!"

She didn't respond.

"Well?"

"Well, maybe I'm going to do something horrible to her," she whispered this time, still inside my head.

She was in fright-mode. When she got like this, she'd start hurling things around, and get totally hysterical. Pretty soon, my cigarettes were being crumpled and mashed. Next, my aftershave lotion was flung across the room. My keys and cell phone went next. All these things being tossed right at my head.

"Arielle," I laughed. "Are you mad?! Stop this shit this instance! What if somebody walks in? How the fuck do you expect me to explain it?"

Sometimes, I would forget just how crazy she was—especially when she was jealous. And I didn't think for a second, she wouldn't try to hurt me in a very bad way, either. It wasn't just Kendra I was afraid for, but for my own skin as well. Arielle was not to be trifled with.

"I'm going away for good," she wailed. "You'll see. I'll leave you be with your little Miss Prudish and see how long it takes before you're completely and utterly bored!"

"Arielle, please…get a hold of yourself. Let me see you."

"Forget it! Forget me…she's the type you've always liked. I've always been way too fast for you," she said bitterly, appearing clearly for a brief moment and then fading away again until she disappeared completely.

"Oh, Arielle, please!" I said harshly but then softened up when she refused to reappear. "Please, baby. Come back. You know I love you," I cajoled her, wanting desperately for her to reappear. I didn't like her tone or demeanor. "I'm crazy about you. I don't want you to go away. I'll miss you too much. How could you ever think Kendra could ever replace you?"

"She could. I think you're falling in love with *her*."

"Trust me, I'm not. I love you. Please let me see you."

She reappeared, but she was fuzzy, hazy. Normally when she was feeling her oats she was crystal clear. Like an image off a movie-screen, like virtual reality. But now, that signal was very thin and weak.

"Arielle, please. Don't be angry with me. You asked me a question and I answered you honestly and now you want to crucify me for it. Should I have lied?"

"Maybe," she said glumly. "I wish I were alive."

I felt pained now, she sounded so miserable. "I'm so sorry, baby. How insensitive of me. I didn't mean to hurt you."

She was waning. "Oh, Cedric. I love you, you know. And...and as much as I hate to admit it, this is not working. This is crazy! We have no future together. I'm dead. You're alive and...and,"

I gulped, afraid of what she was saying.

"I should stop being so selfish and let you live your life. I watch you two together sometimes and I know you like each other, but I'm in the way. I'm standing in your way and I don't know...I don't know what demon she's fighting and why she doesn't just jump you. She wants you so bad...can't you see it in her eyes?"

"Maybe I don't want to read what's in her eyes...maybe I don't care."

"But you do," she said and sighed heavily. I think you should have a fair chance with her, but you can't do that with me in the way."

"Maybe you don't know what I want."

"I think I do."

"Maybe all I want is you. Only you."

She reappeared then but looked really sad. "Please, Cedric, darling. You have to let me do this one thing. I have to get at least one thing right. I need to move on and let you get on with your life. You're better now. Much better then before. You no longer need me."

"Yes, I do. It's because of these visits, because you're always with me that I'm better. Don't be fooled."

She shrugged. "I think you're wrong. I think you'll be all right now. Even if you never see me again. You'll be just fine."

"Arielle," I was saying much sterner now, "Don't do this. I do need you."

"You'll be fine. You'll see."

"Oh, God. Don't tease me like this, Arielle. It hurts so much. Don't go away. Please, my love. Promise me you'll be back...that I'll see you tomorrow. I can't live without you, Bling. You have to know that."

"You'll be alright," I heard her say again, this time inside my head.

"Baby, please don't even think about going away. I love having you with me. Please don't even threaten me like this. I take it back. I'm not attracted to her at all. You're the only woman I want."

"You'll be fine."

"Promise me, Arielle. You see, I'm actually begging. I have no pride where you're concerned. None. This is what you've reduced me to."

"I promise I'll always love you, my heart. Always..." she said reappearing but starting to fade away again just as fast. "Always..."

She was kidding, joking, I shrugged. She'd be back. She had pulled her disappearing acts before and came back days later—one time nearly a week later. She'd be back, I was sure of it. This was only a test.

She was forever testing my love. But if that was not the case, then Kendra was absolutely to blame. I would never forgive if Arielle disappeared and never returned.

***

The strike happened right on the night Kendra had decided that no matter what, she was going to beg off the case. Even if it meant she would have to quit the force, she was not going to put up with Cedric Courage one moment longer. The man had become quite impossible. Insolent to the point of being unbearable.

They were having an all in all brawl, screaming at the top of their lungs at each other behind the studio in South Beach where he usually recorded when the stalker made his move. As the first bullet whizzed past them, Kendra dove head first, ramming her head into Cedric's belly and knocked him over, covering his body with her as another bullet grazed her on the arm. Feeling the sting and smelling the acrid scent of gunpowder, she knew this shooter meant business and quickly recovered as her hands pulled her semi-automatic out of her shoulder holster and returned fire, firing in the direction that the shots kept steadily coming from.

Cedric struggled with her, trying to turn her over to shelter her with his body. Clamoring to retrieve the pistol at his ankle, but he was just making things more difficult for her. She grunted, "Don't you fucking dare! Anything happens to you, it's my fucking ass. Now stay down!"

She was sure Cedric had never heard her speak so forcibly. She sounded like she meant business and did. She steadily returned the fire, and heard when the shooter ran off, possibly seeking another position to get better aim of them.

Cedric looked wary as she reached for the cell in her jacket pocket and told him firmly, "Call Neff, pronto. Tell him I need back up!"

"Don't be a hero," Cedric said, as she yanked him back behind a dumpster and crawled on her belly to the edge of it, peeking out to see what was going on.

"Just do what I say," she growled, and was soon off, even as Cedric begged her not to go after the gunman.

***

With lightening speed, she was off and Cedric couldn't believe how she had torn out of his arms. He quickly picked himself up and ran after her. But she was screaming at him.

"Go back, goddamn it! Oh God," she cried. "You're gonna get yourself killed. Go back, go get the others. Call Neff or 911, but please don't follow me."

"No! I won't leave you."

"Cedric please," she pleaded. "You're not helping me, please. Go back to the studio."

"No."

"Shit! Shit! Shit!" She said nearly in tears, and that was when he noticed the blood on her arms.

Cedric froze, his heart starting to pound against his ribcage. "Oh shit, you're hurt. Kendra, you're hurt!"

"Cedric, while we're having our little lovefest here, there's a gunman out there that's getting away or who just might be taking aim at us right now. I don't know about you, but I plan on catching this fool, tonight! For the simple fact that I want this shit over and to get away from you. Now go back to the studio now! I'll be all right. Now! Goddammit!" She said grabbing back her cell phone and calling Neff herself.

"Kendra—"

But by then, Deuce and the others had heard the shots and came running out towards them, and Kendra took off again like a shot in the direction the guy had run to. Cedric watched as she peeked quickly around a corner her weapon still drawn throwing a look to Cedric, eyes blazing with anger. Then she turned to address Deuce. "I've called for back up, but call again. Deuce, keep him safe. Sit on him if you have to, but don't let him follow me. The killer's out here. Take him inside now!"

Her words struck against his chest like a cannon.

Oh God, he'd never forgive himself if anything happened to her. He watched her peek first, then turn the corner down the alley and then felt the most unbelievable relief as several uniformed officers appeared from out of nowhere and started down the alley with her. Pretty soon the place was ablaze with lights and sirens, fuck, it was an all out and out manhunt now. There were cops coming from out of the woodworks in every direction. He couldn't believe how fast they had gotten there.

***

Kendra had gotten hurt, and Cedric was going out of his mind. He had tried to call her many times, but she wasn't answering her cell. Neff wasn't answering his either, must be rough whatever was going down. Finally, he had to breakdown and rouse his dad from bed and get him to intervene. His dad called him back thirty minutes later to tell him that Kendra was all right and that she and Neff were busy interrogating the suspect they had apprehended, thus the reason they hadn't answered his calls.

Wow, was his first reaction. Some motherfucker had actually tried to kill him except Kendra had caught him, and not let him get away.

When Kendra arrived to meet him, he was chilling at his place with all the boys, wowing them with the story of how it had all had gone down, pretty exciting stuff. Of course, it was no fun being shot at, but when you had Super Agent Jade by your side, it made all the difference. As she approached, Cedric noted the huge bandage on her upper arm and was immediately at her side checking it out. All the other guys surrounded her as well, crowding her, all of them wanting to see the wound and to compliment her on a job well done.

Kendra was very shy, however, and seemed very uncomfortable accepting all the compliments.

"Ah. C'mon," Deuce urged her. "You can show us."

"Yeah, let us see," Rico chimed in.

Cedric helped her lift the dressing, there was a pretty angry wound, but it didn't look too bad. It could have been a lot worse, but luckily, the bullet had only grazed the skin on her arm and hadn't punctured it.

"She took a bullet for me," he said proudly, boasting to his friends. "Can you believe that shit?!" he told them, shaking his head with disbelief. "Ah, man," he said kissing her roughly on the lips, in a totally non-sexual way. It was simply a kiss of absolute gratitude. "You take this job of yours pretty seriously," he said staring intently at her.

Kendra snorted softly. "It's only a graze."

Cedric grabbed her around the waist and swung her around. "You're a hero, Kendra Jade. Don't be modest."

"Put me down," she told him, scrambling to her feet. "I'm sorry to be a party-poop, but I'm little tired."

"You know what that means," Deuce said. "All right mo-fos, let's clear outta here."

Kendra looked apologetically at Cedric and he smiled taking her hand and walking her towards the bedroom.

"You sure you don't need help taking off that blouse. I can help...don't want you to further injure yourself..."

"I'm sure I can manage," she smiled slightly and turning on her heels made an about face into her room and firmly closed the door.

Later, when she came out for some cocoa, most of the guys had already gone home with only a few stragglers left behind. But Deuce and Rico took their cue and led the gang out to further discuss the events, leaving Cedric and Kendra alone to talk privately.

Cedric caught her hand in his, affectionately. "You know," he began, "you didn't have to come here tonight. You have your man locked up in jail...and what's more, baby, you took a bullet for me. Everyone would have understood if you had headed straight home. I'd certainly understand if you turned on your heels right now and headed home to get some rest. You've been through a lot today. It's been a stressful week and an even longer night. I'm sure, Neff would have come in your place. You got hurt...you need rest."

She smiled slightly, "Yeah," she responded, truly looking deadbeat tired. "But, and so...your point is?"

Cedric grinned. "I think you know..." he let his voice trail. "You came here tonight cause you wanted to be with me."

"Oh, you never stop," she sneered. "You have to push this, don't you. Start back where we left off..."

Cedric chuckled. "But you keep proving my point. Every time..."

"Maybe I'm just a hard-worker, dedicated to my job."

"Oh, and I know you are. I know this is your job. But I think it's become much more than just a job," he grinned, straightening her collar, moving in very close. "So did you interrogate him?"

"He wouldn't talk. Damn, and I don't know, but I know he

wasn't acting alone, thus the reason I'm still here. There's a lot more to this and I'm determined to get to the bottom of it."

"So, you and Neff couldn't crack him?"

"He wants a deal. And we couldn't make any promises, not until we talk to the AUSA tomorrow morning."

"AUSA?"

"Sorry." She smiled. "That's the Assistant U.S. Attorney. So we had no choice but to put this on ice. Tomorrow Neff and I will get another crack at him and with a deal in the works, he'll be singing like a canary."

Cedric looked at her with amusement. "You like all this cop and robber shit, don't you? This is your thing, you enjoy it."

She shook her head, "And you my friend, take this much too lightly. It's your life we're talking about here. Even after tonight, you're still not convinced this is real. You could have been killed," she said tightly, anger seeping into her voice. "You find this amusing, but I don't. Not at all! God, if anything had happened..."

"If anything had happened to me," he finished for her, "you'd have been devastated, because you care about me. Maybe even love me," he teased.

"Somebody wants you dead, and you take it as a big joke!"

"I don't. I get it...I do, baby. But you're here to protect me, aren't you," he said putting his hands on her waist. "And you know, I've grown to like being protected."

"Smooth move," she said slipping easily from his grasp, moving a few inches away from him to evade his touch. "Cedric, I wish you would take this more seriously." She bit her bottom lip in a way that totally reminded him of Arielle. "I don't know why you're so..." she blew an exasperated breath.

"Just for the record, I appreciate your protection," he said a slow grin curving up the corner of his lips. Knowing he was annoying her. He inched closer, slipped his arm back around her waist and pulled her close.

Kendra released her breath as she careened against him. Cedric held her firmly against his chest and smelled her hair, sighing deeply. When he pulled back to look at her face, there were tears glossing her eyes.

"What's a matter," he asked. "Am I being too forward?"

She shook her head, seemingly not trusting herself to say anything. Then she pulled herself away and said, "Goodnight," in a crisp, business-like tone and walked towards her room. And Cedric just stood there, watching her back and bottom as she sauntered up the steps to her room, thinking how sad it was to watch her leave but then how nice it was to watch her go, enjoying the view.

Groaning from the pressure of his hard-on, Cedric flopped down onto the couch, grabbed one of the pillows and stuffed it between his thighs. "I'm not running after her," he said to the air, to himself. If she wants to play games, she'd be playing them with herself. He knew she wanted him in a bad way—maybe even more than he wanted her. But she had remarkable self-control, he'd give her that. However, it couldn't last. How the hell could it possibly last?! Eventually, she'd have to breakdown and admit it—even if it was only to herself—that she was in love with him.

12

Confession is Good for the Soul

KJ: Hello, Mr. Perricone. I trust you had a pleasant night.

Fire: It was okay being that I'm in the slammer.

KJ: So how are they treating you in here?

Fire: Pretty decently. Considering.

KJ: Good. Glad to hear it. You understand that this session is being recorded as well as videotaped to show that you are not under duress and are doing this of your own freewill.

Fire: Yes, I understand.

KJ: This is my partner, Special Agent Neff. He'll be sitting in with us. Is that fine with you?

Fire: Okay. That's cool.

KJ: All right then. That said, shall we begin?

Fire: You are cutting me that deal, right?

KJ: That was what I said. I've talked to the D.A. and he's willing to plead you down, but we have to have a strong solid case against Ms. Champion, who's parents have very deep pockets and who are going to hire the best defense. We need a lock solid case. Dates, times, hard material evidence, you understand. I can tell you right now, if it's only hearsay or circumstantial, it's not going to stick. So whatever you can do to help us is going to help your case in the long run.

Fire: What about the immunity deal?

KJ: Look, we've got you, Mr. Perricone. We have you on all kinds of charges. Now, I'm doing the best that I can, but one thing at a time. Don't get greedy. We're doing all that we can, but like I said, it's all depending on what you have to give us.

Neff: Just try to remember. Be very detailed. Sometimes the most insignificant things turn out major leads. Try to recollect things to the best of your ability, and we promise, you'll get your deal.

Fire: All right. I'll try.

KJ: (Blowing a breath) Okay, Mr. Perricone. Start from the

beginning.

Fire: (Shifting uneasily in his seat). Okay, so it's like this, right? I meet her back in December of last year. I remember cause it was close to Christmas. A week before, I think. Anyway, we met at Space over in downtown Miami. It was raining that night and you think everyone would stay away from the clubs and stay home— except the club is packed. Guess everyone's out celebrating or off for the holidays. I was meeting my friend, Bruce there, who hadn't shown up as of yet. I noticed her sitting at the bar alone and I approached her because she was by herself and usually when a woman was at a club alone it usually meant one of two things: one she was a prostitute waiting for a score. Two, she was a whore, dying to be picked up.

KJ: Maybe she was waiting for someone. Maybe a husband or boyfriend.

Fire: Nah. Not at that club. That place's a meat market. Everyone who goes there knows the score. I get up close and I notice she's real cute. Cuter than I expected. She was small, small-boned. Kind of tiny, everything in miniature size. Even sitting down, I could tell she'd be real short.

I note she's taking shots. Good sign. She obviously had a problem she was trying to forget. Intentionally getting drunk. That helped sometimes. You could always blame whatever you did on all the alcohol you consumed. I had met a lot of women like that. Mostly married women. Figured she must be married. And I liked them best. They didn't bother you. Or expect anything of you. They got what they needed and were out of there. No questions asked. Not guilt trip. No, will you call me tomorrow. Or sometime.

I move towards her and she looks me over real smooth-like. I'm not a bad-looking guy and I was dressed real nice. I usually get my girl. But this one had class. I could tell right away in the way she was dressed. Her posture and attitude.

"Hey," I said to her.

"Hey," she said back.

"What's your poison?"

"Why? You buying?"

"Maybe," I said.

She was quiet for a few minutes. Then she said, I'm having Pinch scotch whiskey."

"Hmmm...so whatcha ya trying to forget?"

She smiled. "Actually, I'm looking for someone. His name is Fire. You know him?"

And here I am shocked, because that's my code name and usually means business. So I'm thinking now she's either a client or heat. In any case, I don't tell her who I am right away. Not until I add two and two together.

KJ: So what finally happened?

Fire: I'm getting to that.   You seem impatient. Do you have somewhere to go?

KJ: No. No, you go ahead. I'm sorry for interrupting.

Fire: Thank you. Like I said, I couldn't put my fingers on it but felt like ummm...this lady means business and smelled of money. So I said, I know Fire. But it's gonna cost you for the introduction.

"No problem," she said. "How much?"

I said, "For now just buy me a drink."

She laughed. "How did it go from you buying me a drink to my buying *you* a drink? So what you're having?"

"Same thing you're having."

"Okay," she said turning to the bartender and asked for two more rounds.

We started conversing, chewing the fat, talking shit. She was kinda interesting. Said she worked for a magazine as a photographer and stuff. But this little lady could drink. For her size, I swear she could hold her liquor. Finally she said after several more rounds, "Ah c'mon. Where is Fire? You said you'd introduce me."

Now I'm looking around and guessed that Bruce was no longer coming. So I told her, "C'mon. Let's go." We left the bar and she followed me to the parking lot. She didn't seem afraid even though she must have figured it strange that we left the club. "Where's your car," I asked her.

"Where are we going?"

"Across the bridge to the Beach," I told her. "I'll take you to him."

She looked leery. "All right, I'll follow you, but I valet parked. Wait for me here."

I watched her walk away, admiring her trim, neat little figure. She had on this little black dress and high-high heels and I was getting turned on.

We got to the SoBe, to my place. I told her I'd have to have to call Fire first to find out what club he was at. And I made her park behind me. She followed me into the apartment and I was thinking this is one brave little bitch. Most women would have been calling it quits already. I figured she must really want Fire if she was willing to risk her neck and ass like this. Like what guarantee did she have that I wouldn't slip her a ruffee and the rape her. But she came in anyway and I offered her a seat. She said she'd rather stand after I told her I was calling Fire on the phone. I told her he lived nearby. Then I asked her, "Now what does a nice girl like you want with Fire anyway?"

She told me a friend of hers needed his services.

So we were getting to the heart of the matter. I thought for sure then she must be an agent. She seemed too sure of herself. Too unafraid. I was on her before she knew what hit her. I was ripping her clothes off, frisking her, checking for wires. But she was clean and fought me off like a hellcat. She clawed me really bad, nearly ripping my eyes out and managed to douse me with pepper spray. She was about to run out when I screamed at her back that I was Fire."

She turned and came back. "What the fuck you attacked me for?"

"Thought you were an agent," I told her. "Are you one?"

She laughed. "Like I would tell you if I was one. No, I'm not a fucking agent!"

"Well, if you want to have any kind of conversation with me, I want you butt naked. I swear to God. Cause I'm not going down like that."

"I have to strip to talk to you?"

"Shit, you know with technology and all, they're making those damn tapes smaller and smaller everyday. You want to talk, take everything off."

"This is really fucked. How do I know for sure you're even who you say you are? First you know Fire. Then you'll take me to him. Then you have to call him. Then you attack me. Sorry but I don't exactly trust you right now. How do I know for sure you're Fire?"

"Well, it's not like I can show you an ID, Fire's my code name. My real name is none of your business, but the way I see it, you're gonna just have to trust me."

"Well sir, the way I see it, you're just gonna have to trust me too. With my clothes on."

"Well, then we can't deal."

"Look," she said softening a bit. "Plain and simple, my husband's cheating on me. I want revenge and I heard you're in the payback business. A soldier of fortune."

"Look lady. I have no idea what you're talking about. There's the door, please use it."

She blew a breath, then raised the dress she had been

wearing up over head and took it off. Next, she unclasped her bra. Then stood with only nylons on. "Do I have to take off my pantyhose too?"

I was rock hard. "Nah, that's pretty see through."

"Okay. So do you think you can help me?"

"So how did you hear that?"

"What?"

"About my line of business."

"Charlie referred me to you."

Charlie was this guy that worked at the I Spy shop I gave a kickback to for these kind of referrals. Nothing to it. Nothing major. Just some extra change on the side. It was usually things like this, domestic problems. But the real money came from elsewhere. So I relaxed more when she said Charlie cause I figured, oh, this is chump change.

All the same, I smiled at her. "Good ole Charlie. Why didn't you just tell me that from the get-go? Got me all fired-up."

"Sorry," she said. "Can I put my clothes back on?"

"What if I said no. I like what you're wearing."

She pulled her dress back on, then and stuffed her bra in her bag.

"So what do you want me to do?"

"Do I have to spell it out for you?"

"Please. Cause I don't like to read between the lines. Not in my line of work. I need you to be really specific."

"Really? I'd figure the opposite," she said smoothing her hair back into place. "I want him knocked off, and his girlfriend too."

KJ: She used those exact words. Try to remember now. Did she say it that plainly?

Fire: (Laughing). She said it that plainly. In fact, the next thing out of her mouth was, "don't tell me I have to be clearer than that?"

"No. I get it. That's two people. It's gonna cost you."

"Name your price," she said making it sound like money wasn't an issue.

"So I told her, 35, meaning $3,500. She whistled and said, "you're expensive."

So I'm thinking Christ. What the hell does she expect. For me to do it for free. But then she says, "Okay. $35,000.00 is a lot of money. But I'll swing it."

I had scored big time.

"Do you require a down payment," she said next.

Meanwhile, I'm making the shit up as I go along. I said, "Ten percent initially, 40 percent the day you order the hit, the balance when the job is done."

"Is that negotiable."

"Well, there's always special circumstances. I don't know. I play it by ear."

She tells me then to meet her tomorrow at the back of the Eckerd's on 5th Street. She said she didn't work too far and would meet me there after work.

But, I still didn't exactly trust her. So I told her, "Nah, let's just make it on the beach on 5th. Be there after five and I'll find you."

Next day, I get there about an hour before our scheduled meeting. Scope it out. Everything seems normal. I watch her approach. Watch as she slips off her clothes. She's wearing this teeny bikini underneath. Hell, I had seen her practically naked, still I'm thinking she's real fine. Everything about her is small and delicate. I find myself getting a rise again. And I'm thinking how I could work fucking her into our little deal.

She's sitting on a towel, rubs on some sun block, then takes out a book. I come out from my hiding place and block her sun. She grins the moment she sees me.

"Thanks for not making me wait."

I sit next to her. "Thanks for making it look real natural. Nice touch, you're sunbathing and all."

She takes out several colored glossies from her bag.

KJ: What size?

Fire: Oh, say 8X10s and show them to me. There's this really hot black chick in them. I mean she's a real looker, tall and slender. Pretty face, great bod. Figure she must be a model. I mean I can certainly see what her husband sees in her. "That's a real beautiful woman," I tell her deliberately being an ass. I figure that has to be the one doing her husband.

But she wasn't hostile. She just said, "She's the one," real business-like, "and yes, she's very beautiful. I agree."

Okay. I thought. At least she's honest.

Then she took out a picture of her man. I'm surprised. I mean, he looks nothing like what I expected. I was thinking the guy would be some schlep, real-douche bag. Figured he must have a nice insurance package and was bothering her with this infidelity shit and she figured a dead husband is more profitable than a living one—especially when he's pulling all this shit. But when I see him, I'm thinking, it's not about the money at all. She must be really in love with him. I mean the guy is stunning. Looks like he could be on the cover of GQ, the kind of guy that women go ga-ga over except usually his type is gay.

"That's your husband," I say with uneasiness. I mean cause like I'm hoping she's not one of these crazy women who's gonna try to back out and demand her money back when she figure she can't live without her honey.

"Why do you ask that like it's so unbelievable," she says now with a little agitation, seemingly annoyed...

"Lady, men who look like that aren't the marrying kind, you know what I mean?"

"No, I don't."

"Forget it then," I told her not wanting to set her off. She hadn't yet paid me and I wasn't looking to start any shit on an empty pocket.

But she was already pissed. "Look, keep your fucking comments to yourself. You know what I'm sayin'. Learn and study their faces," she said giving me a picture of each. "Those are your marks."

KJ: Do you still have those pictures?

Fire: Unfortunately, no. She wanted them back in exchange for her last payment. It was like she was leaving no loose ends. She was smart like that.

KJ: Well...continue. What happened?

Fire: So then she said, "Well, will you do the job?"

"Got the money," I asked.

"Yes."

"Hand it over."

"How do I know you're not going to just take my shit and not do jack? What assurances can you give me?

"Look, baby," I started, but she cut me off.

"Cause like I don't even know if you're who you say you are. You could be yanking my chains. I mean what are the chances that I'm sitting at a club and you walk up to me and you just happen to be the person I'm looking for."

"Yeah, that's some strange shit. But like I said. You just have to trust me."

"Let me tell you something. You fuck me and I swear to God, you won't live to regret it," she said real fiercely. And I was like, whoa! This bitch don't mince words. Shit, my kinda girl. Now I'm thinking I really want to fuck her—just not the way she's thinking. I'm starting to dream what it's gonna feel like being up in all that heat. "Know something, your husband's crazy. He really is. If you were my wife, I'd fuck you till I was tired. I'd be fucking you all day and night, baby. Cause honey, you're bad! I can tell you're tough. One bad bitch! What's wrong with your man, anyway? You want him gone, no problem. I only hope you'll give me a chance when he's gone."

She was smiling now. It was slight, but I could see the corners of her mouth wanting to. "Yeah, you talk a good game, Fire. Why do they call you Fire anyway?"

I grinned. "Care to find out? We'd have to go back to my place. And I'd show you."

"Does it involve sex," she asked bluntly.

And I was surprised again. I mean this broad pulled no punches. She was so frontal, she was making me a bit self-conscious. I didn't know how to respond.

"Fire, do you like having sex," she asked next.

"Does a dog have fleas? Girl, what the hell kind of question is that?"

"Just curious."

"Just curious my ass! Do you like having sex?"

"Yes," she said looking me dead in the eyes. She was freaking me out! I couldn't even remember how we had arrived here, at this point of the conversation—not that I was even complaining. But hell, what if this was all she was about. I was hoping she wasn't just a tease, one of those broads that liked to talk about it, get you all fucked up and excited, just to leave you hanging and shit. There were plenty of those on the Beach.

"But I guess you haven't had it in a while with the situation with your husband and all," I said right on target. "Maybe you should cut him some slack and give him some—for your own sake—even if he has his little piece on the side."

She laughed bitterly. "Fire, you couldn't even begin to understand. He wants nothing to do with me. He doesn't want me."

I shook my head. "Now that's a damn shame, honey. Fine looking woman like yourself. No wonder you want him dead."

She smiled. "Are you married, Fire?"

"No, baby. No wife. I'm a bachelor."

"Do you think I'd be fun to fuck?"

"Oh shit," I breathed. I swear that question almost made me come. "Baby, don't play like that. Don't even play like that!"

"Who's playing?" She said and turned on her stomach then asked me to rub some oil on her back.

"Unh-unh," I told her. "You're not gonna say some shit like that and then...shit, expect me to...Damn, girl. Shit, let's go. And I'm taking you somewhere real nice too."

She gathered up her stuff and we discussed where we're gonna go. She says no way to the Delano. She knows too many people there. Same thing for the National, Albion and the Clevelander. All too close to her job. In fact, she tells me forget about SoBe altogether.

So I take her to the Fontainebleau-Hilton. That's real ritzy. She seems pleased. As we walk into the room, she tells me, "First impressions are deceiving, Fire. You do have class."

"Well, I'm glad you've realized that," I said moving towards her. Although I wasn't sure she'd be singing the same tune after I was through with her. She was leaning against the door and I pressed myself against her, crowding her. She seems to like it.

I fuck her standing up, with her spine pressed into the door, while she stands on her tipy-toes with her nails digging into my back. I'm real rough with her, and it's all right.

I get her on the bed, driving myself between those cute little tits of hers and those cupid bow lips. She's like this little sex doll and I'm totally enjoying myself.

Then I fuck her from the rear, butt raised, head buried in the pillow. Oh yes, I fuck her like a bitch, slap her ass and ask her like that song—*What's my name, what's my name!*"

"Fire," she screams.

Yeah, I'm thinking. Now she knows. Now she understands. I make her come all over the place. She's screaming like an alley cat by the time I'm through with her, which was hours later. I swear, she could barely walk when I was finished.

"Any time you need some good lovin' just call Fire," I told her.

KJ: (Raising a brow) Well, that's quite a story, Mr. Perricone...and although I like the way you're taking us there, could you concentrate on the murder and how that occurred.

Neff: (Clearing his throat). Well, I did tell him to be detailed.

KJ: And he's been very detailed indeed, thank you, very much, Mr. Perricone. It's just that I'd prefer for you to just stick to the facts.

Neff: (Laughing) Is it me or is it really hot in here?

Fire: (Laughing too). Okay. Maybe I've been a little too crass. Pardon me if I've insulted your sensibilities, Agent Jade, but that broad...she was just something else, you know. Anyway, just wanted to say for the record, she was a damn good fuck.

KJ: I'm sure she'll be pleased you said that. And so...about the murders...

Fire: Didn't hear from her for a while.

KJ: What's a while. Let me see the time line here. You met in December, the week before Christmas at Space in Downtown Miami. Met the next day on 5th Street at the beach. Do you recall what days those were?

Fire: We met at the club on a Thursday. So the beach would be Friday.

KJ: You guys went to the hotel. Who paid?

Fire: I did.

KJ: What did you use?

Fire: Cash.

KJ: Would it be too much to ask, too much to hope for? Do you have a receipt? Okay. So you slept together. What time did she leave?

Fire: (He shook his head no.) Trust me, no one was sleeping. I think it was close to three in the morning.

KJ: That late? That long?

Fire: Hey, the woman hadn't had it in a long time. She was starving. I accommodated her.

Neff: (Chuckling). Sorry.

KJ: (Smiling slightly but always the professional) You never mentioned the payment again. Did she give you the ten percent as promised.

Fire: Oh, yeah. She paid all right. In more ways than one. Anyway, she did hand over the money at the end of the night. In this yellow manila envelope, right after I had tapped that ass a few times. I was tired, sleepy. Made me feel like a gigolo.

KJ: Do you still have the envelope?

Fire: Hell no. Why would I keep it. I mean, I didn't think I'd be sitting here and would need it as evidence. I wasn't thinking that far. My mind was just on the money and the money on my mind, you know the song. Oh, and thinking about her ass as well, and when next I was gonna get it.

KJ: How did she pay you?

Fire: In cash, baby. I only deal with cash.

KJ: It's Special Agent Jade, or Agent Jade, or Miss Jade. Anyway, what I mean by that is was it in small bills. All hundreds, etcetera.

Fire: It was all big bills. All hundreds.

KJ: So when did you hear from her again? Try to pinpoint the time as accurately as possible.

Fire: Man, it must have been several months. I think it was mid-April. I don't know the date, but it was on a Saturday night. She called out of the blue because I had put it on the backburner, figuring she had probably changed her mind. Anyway, I heard her voice and got immediately excited, thinking she was calling me again for some good lovin'. Except she says breathlessly, "Fire, it's tonight. I'm ordering the hit tonight."

"Got my money?" I asked. A little disappointed. You know, she had been a little on my mind. I had never met a woman who gave head so good. Then I realized we're talking this shit on the phone. "Look anyway, I can't ...we can't talk about this on the phone. Tell me where you want to meet."

"I can't...look, I can't meet you."

"Then how the hell...look, call me when you got your shit together, when you're ready to do this shit properly. Besides, I had plans for tonight. You can't just call me...look goodbye."

I was about to hang up on her, "Listen, Fire. Just drop everything. This is money we're talking. And you need to do this tonight!"

Click. I hung up on her. Tried to trace her call. Number didn't register on my caller ID. Number untraceable.

She called again and I was becoming irritated. "Look, we can't discuss this on the phone," I told her again.

"Okay. Here's what I need you to do. Do you know where the Miami Sub's is near Bal Harbor Shops?"

"Huh?"

"There's this Miami Subs near the shopping center, between Harding and Collins. No, maybe off of Collins."

"I'll find it," I assured her. "So you want to meet there?"

"In thirty minutes."

"Okay. I'm there. See you in a few."

I get there, and she's already there, sipping on a drink. There's a thick envelope right next to her. A big one this time. I figure that's my money. She says, "I've been holding on to this money for a while now. But tonight is the night." She hands me a piece a paper. "Here's a little map of the marina. And here's the boathouse." She pointed to an X she had drawn. "It shouldn't be too difficult to find. The rest is your problem. But take care of this tonight. I want this business finished. Tonight. Understand?"

KJ: Do you still have that map?

Fire: Nah, she had told me to burn it when I was done.

KJ: Do you always follow directions to the letter?

Fire: I try to...you know...please my clients. That way I get good referrals. And besides, like I said, I didn't figure I'd be sitting here, you know. This was a simple job. I thought it would be no big deal.

KJ (With exasperation) Go on...

Fire: After saying that, she got up and left, and I grabbed the envelope she had left. Got into my car, counted it. All the money there. $14,000.00, all in hundreds, just like before. I liked that. The fact that she meant business, had followed instructions and had somewhat held up to her end of the bargain. I mean, I didn't like her springing this on me the way she had, but I figured she was a good paying customer. Plus, I felt pretty confident she'd have the rest, $17,500.00 to me either by tonight or the next day. I figured this was way more than I usually got paid for this kind of stuff anyway and figured even if she never gave me another dime, I was way ahead of the game regardless...

KJ: You don't happen to have *that* envelope either, do you?

Fire: (Shaking his head) Nah.

KJ: What about the money—

Neff: Kendra, maybe you need to let him finish the story.

KJ: Yes, of course. Finish the story and I'll just jot down my questions as you continue.

Fire: Kendra. I like your name (he said winking).

KJ: (Rolling her eyes) Please continue Mr. Perricone.

Fire: I get to the marina. And her map is on target. I find the place with no problems. Except, they're not there. When I get there, it's all dark.

Neff: Sorry for interrupting you this time, but isn't there security at the marina. I mean a check point you had to go through.

Fire: Nope. I waited for a resident and passed right through, right behind them. Anyway, the guard didn't even notice. He was reading a newspaper or magazine or something. So I just slipped right through.

I parked my car and slipped on board the cruiser, opening it up with the key she had attached to the map. I went in, poked around. It was a really fine craft. New. Smelled good in there—like sandalwood. Left and went to call her.

KJ: On a cell phone.

Fire: Nope. Pay phone. I never talk business on the cell. Don't like to talk business on the phone period. But I called anyway, "They're not there," I told her simply.

"You imbecile," she raves. "They're not there now, but they will be. You lie low and wait. They'll be coming. Hey, and I was thinking, maybe if you should try to make it look like a robbery...you know...instead of an ex-"

"BITCH, ARE YOU CRAZY?! Look, I'll call you. Later." I

hung up on her ass. I mean I couldn't believe she was talking like that on the phone. I was super irritated now. Started feeling bad about this. Like I shouldn't do it. Something was off-kilter, but I couldn't figure out what it was. But then, I thought about the $14,000.00 I had in my trunk, in the tire well, and the rest that was coming and I was thinking, better go through with it. I needed the money.

I had a smoke, waited a little bit, chilled on the hood of my car, listening to some hip-hop. Then I headed back. When I got back, they were already there. I sneaked back on board, using the key again. (And don't ask about the key, cause she wanted that too for final payment.)

KJ: Okay.

Fire: Back on board, they're easy to find. They're in the bedroom cabin already getting it on. When I approach, creeping down the steps, I'm happy to find they left the door open. So I sit on the steps and can see everything perfectly. He has his back to me and is standing there totally naked. Like some bronze god while she's going down on him. I mean and she's giving him some serious head. I can't see her real good cause he's blocking her nearly completely, but I can see she's down on her knees, and I can see her hair a little bit, but mostly I hear all those delicious sucking sounds she's making. Shit. He died happy.

Soon he comes, and I think she was a swallower cause I could hear her gulping it all down, she pulls him down, and they're kissing fiercely. After a while, he stands back up and pulls her up, and starts to undress her. I think. He carries her to the bed, lays her down gently and climbs on top of her. It's beautiful just watching. There's lots of kissing. Lot's of moaning and groaning. It's obvious these two people are very much in love. Even I can see that. It's not just fucking, you know what I mean. It's like in the movies where there's lots of passion, I feel a momentary sadness for them, but then I figure, at least they'll die in each other's arms.

He's kissing down and now he's going down on her. I can see her much better now and she's just fucking out of this world beautiful. I mean she's gorgeous with a capital G! She looks like a fucking angel. That's what she looks like. Like those Victoria's Secret models. The one's with the angel wings that parade around dancing in their skimpy underwear on TV. Anyway, I'm starting to think, I'd better do this quickly before some unforeseen shit happens. But at the same time, I'm thinking, I really want her to get off before pulling the trigger. I'm a little in love with her. Loved the way she looked and was moving. Liked the way she had sucked his cock. So I'm thinking, I don't want her feeling any pain. Figured better to do it right at the point of climax, that way, she doesn't feel it as much. And that's how it went down.

KJ: Okay, so you shot them. We need to be very clear on that.

Fire: Yes, I shot them.

KJ: What kind of gun?

Fire: A .357 Magnum. Him first, right in the head. I saw the blood splatter everywhere, all over the walls and sheets, bathe her all over her chest and face. She'd had her eyes closed, but she opened them then and looks right into my eyes. But what's really strange is the fact that she doesn't even look surprised. Not at all. It was weird, I'll tell you. It was almost a look of resignation, one of expectation. She even smiled slightly. Haunts me 'til this day the look on her face. I let her have it, a bullet right to the chest. I'm an excellent marksmen—expert shooter actually. So I knew the first bullet did the job. Shot her right through the heart. But I wanted to be sure, so I shot her again, twice. Same locale. Didn't want to mess up the face, it was so pretty. So I kept my aim in the same spot. She fell back, after the third shot, with her arms held out, as if she was welcoming death. I felt terrible, like I had just killed an angel. Like I had just killed Bambi.

The blood was everywhere. It wasn't pretty. It's not like in the movies. It looked like a massacre after I was done. I tried not to think about it. About them, their families, and just walked out of there. Real brisk-like.

KJ: Did anyone see you leave?

Fire: I don't think so. There was no one out. It was pretty late. Maybe around two thirty, three.

KJ: Try four. Was it closer to three. Closer to four.

Fire: Nah, I don't know. I wasn't studying the time or anything. But say like the first time I got the call from Leah was right about ten o'clock, ten thirty. I know that cause I was suppose to go out that night. I was meeting a woman friend of mine at the Crobar at around eleven and I was just going into the shower when she called. When I met her at Miami Subs, it was a little after eleven. Got to the marina at about midnight—maybe a little later since I had first counted the money and that might have taken a little time. I believe I came back to the boathouse a little after one, watched them do their thing. But it hadn't taken hours. It was maybe a good thirty minutes. No more. No, I'd say it was closer to two o'clock. Not three. Not four.

KJ: So what did you do after that?

Fire: I left and called her.

Neff: What was her reaction?

KJ: And where did you call her from?

Fire: What, you guys are a tag team now? Anyway, I don't call her from home. Definitely not. I head back to the SoBe. Take the William Leeman Causeway and I go to Lost Weekends to unwind. I play a few rounds of pool to relax cause like I'm a little freaked out, you know. Then I called her from a payphone there.

KJ: About what time would you say it was.

Fire: It was probably close to four by then.

KJ: So what does she say?

Fire: I thought she would be rejoicing. I call her and say, "it's done." But instead of laughing or cheering or being happy, she's like, "Oh God, Oh God! I'm not a bad person, really I'm not. They're dead? They're really dead?"

Fire: She pisses me off again. Talking shit over the phone. I tell her, "You know what I want. Have it ready tomorrow. Same meeting place. Let's meet after five."

"Where," she says. "Which meeting place?"

I'm already freaked and she's acting real funny, asking weird questions. I don't like the feeling I'm getting. I start to wonder if she's not gonna talk. I start to wonder about having done the job at all at the moment. For whatever reason, I don't trust her at all now. From the beginning I didn't trust her. I hang up the phone on her, thinking there might be some potentially serious problems here.

Instead of going home, I hook up with a babe of mine and sleep at her place. And of course, you know what happens in the morning. I don't get up until about close to three o'clock in the afternoon and by that time, the shit's all over the tube. I think, holy shit. I'm fucked! I hadn't known who they were. Had no idea that chick was married to some huge, maga rap star.

KJ: So did you meet her after five.

Fire: Nope. I couldn't figure what to do, and the reports were saying she's in the hospital in any case, that she passed out upon hearing the news. That she'd been hospitalized. I figured, there goes my money. Plus there's so much heat all over the place. It was prudent for me to lay low, figure, let things settle down. I knew she was good for the money. Knew I'd get paid one way or another.

Neff: So how do you finally get your money?

Fire: She calls me the day she's released from the hospital. Tells me she's been out of it. Apologizes. Tells me she's good for the money. I tell her I know and ask if she's all right, you know. She's kind of surprised that I'd even care and she tells me if I can wait until this blows over a little, that I'll get my money. She pays me the day after that highly publicized funeral, the one for Cedric Courage's wife.

But I don't know. I was starting to feel screwed, you know. I realized then I had committed the first deadly sin of making a hit. Know your mark. I'd screwed up, definitely. And I had much cause to sweat.

KJ: What did you do with the money this time? Did you make any bank deposits?

Fire: No way! I had my lady friend put it in her account. Under her name.

KJ: All of it?

Fire: No-no-no. I spoon fed her. Gave her $1000 here, a $100 there. I didn't want her knowing my business, getting all suspicious. So I spoon fed her the money. That way she saw the money accumulating gradually rather than seeing it all at the same time.

KJ: You trust her with your money?

Fire: Oh, she knows what'll happen if any of my money goes missing. Yeah, I trust her.

KJ: So how much money would you say is in that account right now.

Fire: Maybe $10,000.00. I'm not exactly sure.

KJ: That's all.

Fire: (snickering) Well, I have this thing for designer clothes, you know. I also go clubbing a lot. Love drinking Cristale, if you know what I mean.

Neff: So you basically blew the money and have no way really of proving she paid you.

Fire: (Shrugging) I guess...

KJ: Is there anything else you may have forgotten to tell us?

Fire: Well, I hadn't exactly finished. The job didn't end there. Cause later she told me she'd be willing to pay me $50,000.00 if I knocked Cedric over and that she'd throw in a bonus if I'd do his son as well.

KJ: So who's idea was it to send the note.

Fire: Didn't know anything about the note. But what I did know was that Cedric would be a hard mark. I expressed my concerns to her. I knew he had security up the wazoo. Plus him being a bad ass rap star, I knew he was probably packing as well.

Now had I known about the note, I wouldn't have taken the

job at all. I mean cause my whole thing is in the element of surprise. But this bitch had set me up—it's almost like she wanted me to get caught. So I have to say that was the stupidest thing she did. Except maybe she's just too damn smart, cause basically it was like she had sent me on a suicide mission. I would have ended up dead, and you would have found your man, and maybe she's thinking the heat would have been off her. I'd be dead and the bullets from my gun would have matched and connected the murders and she'd never have to worry about me again.

What she fell to realize though was I had no motive. I mean, why would I kill them? What's my link?

Knowing her, though, she had probably already thought about that and had a plan. Who knows how that woman's psychotic mind works?

KJ: Maybe her plan was that you did it out of love. Maybe she could have proven that you were lovers, that you killed Danyel and Arielle because it disturbed her, and—

Fire: Then...why kill Cedric though? I mean, what would be my motive for that?

KJ: (To Neff) Well, we have ourselves a regular sleuth here. No, Mr. Perricone, it would be perfectly explainable. Killing Cedric would just be completion of the grudge. But what if I told you that she had a hit on you too. That she never planned on paying you but planned on whacking you as soon as your job was over—that is, if you didn't die during the mission.

Fire: I don't doubt that. That bitch is stone cold. And even after all I've told you, you can't touch her on any of this, huh?

KJ: It'll be difficult. The way I see it, there's no hard evidence. Everything is circumstantial or hearsay. Your word against hers.

Fire: What if I told you that I pulled a Monica Lewinsky and have the bitch's bikini bottoms. And trust me, there's some nice DNA evidence all over it from that day at the hotel.

KJ: Okay, so she had an affair with you. Big deal. It still doesn't prove she paid you a dime to knock off her husband and his girlfriend.

Fire: Check her bank records. Her phone records. Hell, you guys are the FBI. I'm sure I don't have to tell you what to do, how to do your jobs.

KJ: (Laughing) No, sir, you don't.

Neff: What if we told you that's all been done and she's clean as a whistle.

Fire: What if I tell you that she's a smart bitch. Real smart. But she can't be that smart. She had to make at least one mistake. No crime is perfect, even I know that.

KJ: What if I tell you, you're absolutely right. And I think I know exactly how we're gonna nail Leah Pembroke-Champion. I just need a link...and I'm thinking, we may have one.

Fire: Isn't the bikini bottom link enough?

KJ: No, although it does help. Still, I need a link that will show her intent. Then and only then do we have our case.

Neff: I follow you. Once we establish intent, we have her on at least a preponderance of evidence.

KJ: Not enough for a criminal conviction, but then we work on her, try hard to get a confession, and nail her without a reasonable doubt.

13

Extraordinarily Smooth...
Exceptionally Mellow

Kendra headed to the spy shop on Biscayne Boulevard, near the old Omni Mall. There was this short, balding, greasy looking little man behind the counter. Looking around, Kendra quickly surveyed the premises, inspecting all the gadgets. She picked up some mirrored sunglasses and went to pay for it. He asked for her phone number.

"Oh, I'm not a regular customer," she said wanting to see where this would lead.

"It's okay," he said. "What's the number? We'll have it for next time."

She rattled off her cell number. He finished ringing up the sale and Kendra smiled widely, having what she wanted.

Thank God for point-of-sale computerized registers!

She left the store with her heart racing. She had to stop to take a long, deep breath. God, she prayed, hoping it was going to be this simple, hoping Leah hadn't thought this far ahead?

Okay, knowing Leah, she probably hadn't supplied them with her real phone number. But then again, maybe she had. How had she paid? She wouldn't have dared charged it. She had probably paid in cash. But then maybe she hadn't. Oh, wow. Just maybe there was a credit card record or a cancelled check. If they could be so LUCKY!

This was her best lead yet—other than the full confession from Fire.

She called Neff. Requesting he file immediately for a warrant.

"Be there in an hour," Neff promised, catching her drift.

"You think," she said, giving a nervous laugh. "Okay, an hour."

"Keep your fingers and toes crossed," Neff said good-naturedly. "I'll do the same."

When Kendra pressed end on her cell, her skin tingled with

anticipation. Saying a silent prayer, she next decided to go grab a bite while she waited. She went to lunch at a seedy little Nicaraguan restaurant across the street from the shop. Neff was there about an hour and a half later, with warrant in hand. Minutes later, they invaded the shop.

"Special Agent Jade," she said showing the store clerk her badge. "And Senior Special Agent Neff. We need a print out of some receipts dating back to June of 2001. Where's the manager or owner?"

"I'm the owner."

"That's great! Now, before you even bother doing that, punch in these phone numbers." She rattled off Leah's home number and cell, both of which she had learned by heart. She had done so many phone searches on those numbers until she had gone cockeyed.

"Hello," she turned to Neff when the cell number popped up. Her heart was racing. "Mistake #1," she smiled and next flashed a picture of Leah to the little man behind the counter. "Recognize her?" She asked sweetly.

"Yes, very well. She's a regular customer," the man said innocently.

She and Neff couldn't help the laughter that came pouring out.

"Happy Birthday," Neff said, giving her a huge kiss on the cheek.

Kendra smiled widely. "Yes, and a very happy one at that," she said continuing to grin as the computer started sprouting off stuff Leah had purchased from there. "Now listen carefully," she said solemnly to the little man, trying to hide her excitement. "You're not in any kind of trouble, but do you recall referring this customer to a certain gentleman, a man called Fire?"

He shook his head. "I don't know what you're talking about."

"Look, it's okay. We know about you're little deal with Fire. About the kickbacks. We're not interested in that. We just need your cooperation."

"Look, I don't know nothin' about nothing."

Kendra smiled indulgently at him. "Sir, sir...You see, I'm asking nicely. I asked you a simple question, but if you're not going to cooperate, that's on you. Cause I promise you, I can make you talk and not be very nice. So, here's another question. Do you want me nice or do you want me rough?"

Neff gave a low laugh. Kendra tried to keep a straight face.

She was becoming deliriously happy.

"So what's it going to be? I can make your life really unpleasant. I can guarantee you that. Or you can cooperate and I won't have to come back here with the IRS."

"Oh no, not the IRS," Neff chimed in. "Trust me, they're just awfully nasty. I'd rather fess up and deal with us any day!"

"All right, all right, lady. I'll cooperate," the little man said testily. "What do you want to know?"

"Did you refer this woman to Fire?"

He shook his head. "I did."

Kendra turned sideways and smiled at Neff and then turned her attention back to the man. "Take me through that conversation, would you? I know it's been a while, but try to remember."

"She told me she wanted to get even with someone and did I know anyone in the revenge business?"

"Those were her exact words?" Kendra asked with building excitement.

"Yup."

"Are you willing to testify to that in court, sir?"

"I don't want to, but if I have to, I guess I can."

"Wonderful!" She beamed while the noose continually tightened around Leah's scrawny little neck. They were now building what would be a lock solid case. "So what did you tell her," she continued.

"I told her about Fire. Told her he hung out at Space on the weekends, and that she should go there and ask for him. Everyone knows him, and for her to let him know that I referred her."

"And so what about Fire? Did he bring your cut?"

"Hmmm ..I think about two weeks later."

"How did he pay?"

"Cash, of course."

"Do you keep any kind of record on these...umm...types of transactions?"

He scratched his head, as if considering his answer.

Kendra cleared her throat, looking at him directly. "Well..."

"Yes, I do," he said gruffly.

Kendra and Neff caught each other's eye and smiled widely. "Oh, it's a beautiful day," she couldn't help gushing. And they high-fived.

***

Kendra was sitting at her desk at the SAC Office. It was after ten in the evening, and she was busy working on the paperwork. Neff had left, telling her they could start tomorrow. Besides, he told her, he had a hot date. And although he felt guilty leaving, he urged her to go on home and get some rest.

They wouldn't be arresting her until tomorrow morning. They had organized a whole SWAT team for the raid early tomorrow morning. But Kendra felt too excited and wanted to push on and go over all the details to be sure that tomorrow went without a hitch.

All the pieces had fallen into place. They had placed Leah at the shop. They had physical evidence that she shopped there. They had the man's confession that she had asked and was seeking revenge. They had the referral to the Space Club and the kickback payment between the shop owner and hired hand. But most importantly, they had Fire's entire confession, signed and sealed. Now, the money exchange and payoff was something she hadn't even anticipated, but God, was it beautiful! And while it could not be considered a lock solid case, they certainly had more than enough to place her under arrest and to get a grand jury indictment. As far as an actual conviction, there was nothing more that she could do. They'd just have to rely on the DA and keep digging for more evidence, but Leah was most certainly in a whole heap of trouble. It was going to be difficult for her to wiggle out of this.

She had Arielle and Danyel murdered, and swore she was going to get away with it. But there's no such thing as a perfect crime. Homegirl couldn't have thought of everything. So now, it was time for her to pay. No, this would not bring Arielle and Danyel back, but their families could have some closure and Cedric would once again be safe.

Normally, she was simply doing her job, fitting together a puzzle. Yet none of the pieces ever meant any more to her than a step taken toward a solution. But this was the first case she had ever felt a personal stake in. That she had thoroughly enjoyed solving. Relished, even. She was dying to see Leah's face tomorrow when she placed her under arrest. She was going to really enjoy it, the entire process—from the take down to the fingerprinting.

Just as she wondered why she was having such enormous pleasure in it, her cell phone rang. "Hello," she answered, massaging the crook of her neck. She really did feel tired. She hadn't slept in two days and had no idea where she found the energy to keep pushing forward.

"Hey, girl, what you doing," she heard Cedric's buttery voice. Her heart skipped a beat and suddenly she could feel all her senses whir back to life. Forget about tired. She had just gotten a second wind.

"Working on your goddamn case," she answered, feeling light-headed with love and infatuation all mixed together.

"Girl, do you *ever* go home?"

"Nope."

"I called you there first," he said intimately. "On your private line. Thought for sure you'd be all snuggled up and cozy in your bed. But of course, I should have known better. Now that you're not camped out at my place any longer, guess you're burning the midnight oil at the office."

"Um...you've guessed correctly."

"But you know what, I kinda miss you, though."

"Oh," she said with a huge grin. Thankful he couldn't see her.

"Yeah, can you believe that shit?"

Kendra laughed.

"Can't believe you, though. Hope you get a goddamn medal for this."

"We've got her," Kendra couldn't help sharing. "We've got her, Cedric. But I don't want to go into it too much over the phone."

"Why don't you come over then...or would you rather I meet you somewhere."

"No, I'll come by. Will you be up in a couple of hours?"

"For you, I will."

"Good, then. See you soon," she said clicking off, feeling weird about all the emotion she was feeling. Had she actually let herself fall in love with Cedric Courage? If so, she was a fool. Cause there was no way Cedric was ever going to return that love, when he was still so in love with a ghost.

***

The next morning, Leah was lying back, taking a bubble bath. Eyes closed, enjoying the sensuousness of the bubbles and bath salts, relaxing her body. Even so, she was finding it difficult to relax her mind. She couldn't shake the feeling that something was terribly wrong. Something was off.

Fire had been late in calling her. Real late. A day late. Then last night he had called her at close to eleven in the evening, telling her the hit had been unsuccessful that he had had to abort.

As if she hadn't known. Cedric was fucking walking around, breathing. Of course he hadn't pulled it off. It was strange.

She had nearly lost her cool. Almost. But then she reigned in her anger. Something was wrong. So she didn't say a word to him. Didn't say a thing and hung up.

He called again. "Look lady. We have to make other plans," he said as if he were trying to get her to talk.

"Look, I don't know who the fuck you are. Or what your problem is, but stop your crank calls or I'm calling the police!"

"What?!"

"You heard me, you punk. Don't call me again!" She slammed down the phone.

Oh, fuck. Oh, fuck, she thought in a panic, and traced his call. Untraceable. His calls had never been untraceable. She had always checked. He had always called from a payphone. And he certainly had never wanted to discuss things over the phone before.

No something stunk. Stunk to high heaven!

Fire had probably been apprehended, captured by the police and was now trying to implicate her. What did he have on her, she tried to think hard. Was there anything...anything at all that could connect her?

Shit! Shit! Shit! He had probably sang like a canary.

She had picked up the phone and had started to make reservations to get the hell out of Dodge soon after, but then thought better of it. No, she couldn't lose her head and couldn't start acting guilty. It could be nothing. Maybe he was just grasping at straws. Maybe that was the reason for the call. But if she started overreacting, running away, she might have to keep running for the rest of her life. No, she had to act innocent, behave like someone who had nothing to hide.

So she had put down the phone and decided to ride it out. She kept going over and over in her mind. She had been so careful. Very careful with her entire dealings with Fire. What did he have on her. It was her word against his. But...she was fretting. Anxious. Had she made any major mistakes along the way?

Even in the warmth of the bubble bath she couldn't stop feeling the coldness that was creeping over her, seeping into her skin, causing her to shudder. Her premonitions of disaster couldn't be good news and today, she would cast her chart and from there, she'd know what direction to chose.

But for now, she was going to stop worrying and think about

the meeting she would have with Bailey. It was always nice thinking about Bailey, with whom she now desperately wanted to have a relationship. After that ordeal at Cedric's, when she had gone home with him, she had tried to seduce him. But he hadn't been moved. She had finagled her way into his bedroom, had stood before him, totally naked, and he hadn't stirred. He had explained to her how she was reacting from the shock, that she couldn't possibly want this and that he understood and wouldn't take advantage.

Little did he know!

He had continued being supportive and was extremely comforting—except he had refused to comfort her in a sexual way. Flat out refused, even though she had tried every single trick in the book, albeit, not as boldly as the first time. But she had tried in a million, trillion other little subtle ways, but he wasn't biting.

So she continued playing the forlorn, grievously hurt, distraught widow in need of comfort and healing for his benefit. But she was determined she would have him someday soon in her bed. Every time she met him, she wondered if this would be the day she won out.

She stayed in the water until it began to cool. Then dried off carefully, soothing herself by softly creaming her skin and looking at her body which was tiny and perfect. Then letting the towel slip to the floor, she slipped into a peignoir enjoying its silkiness against her skin.

No question about it. She knew he found her attractive. No one would ever deny that she was a very beautiful woman. With her doll-like prettiness and sexy, pint-size figure, she was an expert at bring men to their knees.

Her skin was the color of honey and she had a dainty straight nose, full rose-colored lips which she didn't even need to color. All she had to do was dab on some clear gloss and she was set. Her teeth were white and she had widely-spaced liquid brown eyes under arched, slanting brows. Oh, she was a beauty. But as her mother often said, if only there was a way of turning her inside out.

Leah frowned as she thought about her mother. She sighed, luxuriating in the agony she inflicted on her holier-than-thou, hypocritical mother. The woman could never be satisfied. If only she could let her in on even the half of it...although she understood well it didn't matter what she did. Nothing she did would ever please her mother.

Sighing more deeply, she stood up and got out to open the

door letting out a flow of steam and scent. Thinking about it, she was reminded she had to phone her mom, who was baby-sitting the twins for the weekend when the doorbell rung and surprised her. For sure she wasn't expecting anyone. Not this early. Bailey she was expecting much later. Immediately her thoughts flew to Fire.

Was that him come to pay her a visit? He could have easily gotten her address. What game was he playing now, she wondered. Her heart was thudding rapidly.

Quickly, she ran to her linen closet, where she kept a strongbox and a .22 caliber pistol. She kept it there for protection. She used to keep it in her nightstand but since the twins had grown into toddlers and were into everything, she had put it away. But now, she grabbed a hold of it, checked the gage and made sure it was loaded.

The door bell rung again. Twice this time. Impatiently.

She ran into her room and quickly donned on some panties and then slipped the weapon beneath her underwear, underneath the rubber bands. She walked slowly to the door, looked through the peephole. There was no on there. Good, maybe he had gone away. She started to walk away, but then it rung again.

Shit! He was playing games.

She started to hyperventilate. Okay, so maybe she was over reacting. Maybe it was Sandra. Even though the girls were with her mother and she had given her the weekend off, sometimes she came by anyway, having forgotten something or another. Maybe it was the nanny.

She checked out the peephole again. Nothing. Nobody there, bloody hell. She tried to look out the window. But there was only shrubbery. She could see the driveway partially. Only her white Land Cruiser was parked out there.

To her horror, the doorbell rung again. She was almost tempted to open the door with her gun drawn, but she held her cool. She swore under her breath and opened the door very carefully.

Special Agent Jade and Neff, along with an entire SWAT Team were there, right on her porch with their guns drawn, all pointed at her.

"Leah Champion," the Jade woman said.

"Yes."

"You're under arrest, and I have a warrant to search these premises."

Leah was fuming and was staring at all of them really hard. "I'm calling my lawyer," she said almost turning.

"Please do not move from that spot," Agent Jade said, creeping slowly towards her, pistol pointed dead at her. "You have the right to remain silent, anything you say can and will be held against you..."

She continued mirandizing her, but Leah heard nothing else. Her hands hesitated, brushing over the pistol in her underwear underneath the peignoir. She thought about going out in a blaze of fire. Oh, they would kill her for sure, but she might get this bitch. She thought about it, but only for a second. Hell no, she wasn't suicidal. More than anything, she wanted to live.

Struggling for her dignity, she tried to pull her robe closer.

"Ah-ah-ah, easy please," Jade told her. Place your arms out and away from your body, palms out and facing me. Legs spread apart and don't make any sudden movements or you might get hurt."

Leah did as she requested. Kendra holstered her gun and moved purposefully toward her, while all the others kept their weapons drawn and right on her.

She came up to her, towering over her, and stepped to the side of her, placing a leg against her and from one side began frisking her, except it was hard because she was so tall and Leah so short. She fluffed her hair, looking behind her ears, making sure there were no needles. She continued on her downward search, running her hand against the mound of her breasts causing her nipples to stiffen which was a natural reaction but embarrassing all the same. Then she got to her waist and felt downward getting really personal with her. "Well, well, well, what have we here," she said then told the others, "She's got a weapon," putting everyone on full alert.

Leah could hear the click of their weapons that were now all half-cocked.

"Wow," Kendra said as she undid her sash and took the weapon from her. "And I was beginning to think you were so smart," she continued leaving her robe open, giving the men a view of all her stuff. "We definitely have you now. At least on a concealed weapon's charge."

"BITCH!" Leah stormed.

"Oh, and now you got her on disrespecting an officer of the law," Neff teased.

Leah was choking back her tears as Kendra stepped to the other side and repeated the same procedure. Then she said, "Now get down. Get down on the ground. Face down. Spread eagle. Legs, arms, everything spread apart."

The guys were chuckling.

"Christ, Kendra. What are you gonna do? Cuff her or fuck her," one of them joked.

Kendra laughed. "Oh, I plan on doing both," she said as she cuffed her arms behind her back. Trying to make the cuffs real tight since Leah's wrist were so small. "Hell, I need someone else's cuffs to put through those. She can slip out. We need to double join them."

Neff handed her his.

She interlinked the cuffs, double-joining them and then helped Leah up.

"I know you're not taking me in like this," Leah hissed. "I know you're gonna at least let me get dressed."

"Right," Kendra said, sarcasm dripping from her voice. Shaking her head, she continued coldly, "You're going as you are. The only thing I'm going to do for you is grab you a jacket. After it's been thoroughly inspected. All right boys," she said. "Go to work!"

Leah watched as they put their weapons away and began going through her home, splitting up the house, searching through all her things like bees searching for honey. "You, come with me," Kendra said leading her out the house, walking her to a police car parked on the curb.

A few of the neighbors had already gathered on their lawns, staring, trying to figure out what was going on. Kendra led her to the marked vehicle where two officers had been waiting. Leah vowed to herself then that if it was the last thing she did, she'd get Kendra Jade. It wasn't so much of even being arrested, but the fact that she seemed to take so much pleasure in humiliating her.

Kendra placed her behind the grid panel, pushing her head down, helping her into the backseat.

"Can I have that jacket you promised," Leah asked, trying to sound docile, but she was sure she was sneering.

"No, I've changed my mind," Kendra said then and smiled. "It's a woman's prerogative, you know. And I'm exercising it. I'm sure you understand."

"You fucking bitch," Leah hissed. "I'll have your badge. You'll see. You have nothing on me!"

"Oh, I have plenty," she said getting into her face. "And you know what, I'm gonna personally see to it that you get locked up immediately with no bail. Murderer!"

Leah stared at her in horror, not believing her ears. Such venom. Why was she taking this so personally? Leah spoke to the two officers who had stepped out of the vehicle and were milling about outside.

"Are you guys listening to this?" she said loudly. "I'm being threatened here by an FBI agent!"

Kendra smiled widely. Something about her smile was vaguely familiar. "And you know what," she continued, "you may not have personally pulled the trigger, but I'm not going to rest until your frying in the chair."

Leah's eyes bulged.

"Oh, yes, and we're gonna go all the way on this. So take this under advisement. I've got your ass, ba-by! And I'll have no mercy. None whatsoever. Cause you see, my heart is just as black as yours. Maybe even a little darker, you little pigmy bitch!"

Then she smiled again, in that very familiar way that Leah had not recognized at first, but which she should have figured out at once. How was it possible? How, she wondered as it dawned on her, had she done it?

As if she wasn't satisfied, just so that she would know for sure, Leah stared on in horror as Kendra came back and whispered so that only she could hear. "This is what happens when you help someone out. You get screwed. You little ingrate! I did everything I could for you. Befriended you, got you a job, gave you some style. And this is how you repay me?!"

Leah was shaking her head with disbelief, not even capable of breathing she was so scared. But Kendra continued relentless. Or Arielle. She was having problems distinguishing the two. One moment it was Kendra's face, but then the next she saw Arielle, but the voice was purely Arielle.

"First you took my man. Yeah, you knew he was my man. You did it on purpose. Seduced him. Got pregnant for him. Probably put holes in the condoms, you little cunt. Then, as if that weren't enough, you had to take my life too. Well, fuck you!"

Leah sucked in air. "No!" she shouted her eyes growing larger by the second. "How do you know all that? How—"

But Kendra eased back out and only smiled. "Sweet dreams, you pigmy piece of shit. I'll soon see you in hell!"

Leah started to scream. Screaming incessantly as the officers rushed to the car, trying to hold her down. Kendra stood back watching, that slight smile still on her face, staring at her with her face but with someone else's soul in her body. Leah was crazed as she realized what was happening to her, becoming unhinged. They would have to call in paramedics and take her out in a straight jacket.

"What happened," Neff approached Kendra. "What set her off like that?"

Kendra shrugged. "I haven't a clue. The woman's insane."

Neff whispered, "Let's keep that on the hush-hush, lest she gets off on an insanity plea."

14

Right, Wrong or Indifferent

It had come as a very big shock to me that Leah was behind the murders, although I wasn't sure why it surprised me. Danyel had been Leah's husband and she was photographer, which explained the pictures mailed to me. There had been much animosity between her and Arielle, for sure, I'd seen it many times. But how was it possible that I didn't connect anything when the truth had always been there, staring me dead in the face.

I was thinking about her a lot lately, that tiny little slip of womanhood so harmless and yet she had gone so far as to pay a hit man to take her husband and my cheating wife out. It just went to show that no one should ever be underestimated. And now she was cooling her heels in the slammer, awaiting trial. No bail was set. She was considered a flight risk.

I thought about the fact that she'd probably be spending the rest of her life in jail. Was her revenge worth it, I wondered. Was anyone worth the price of your life or freedom?

Kendra had let me listen to Fire's confession, thinking it would give me some kind of closure, so I would know exactly what and how everything had gone down that night. Even though she wasn't suppose to do that since it was state evidence, she had bent the rules a little to help me. Except, I wasn't sure it had.

I kept remembering his description of how Arielle and Danyel were making love. He had been an eye-witness, and how they had been so passionate and beautiful that he had waited for them to finish their business before completing his mission to kill them both. It was hard to hear it, but I forced myself to listen to the very word.

Like I said, I wasn't sure it had helped at all. Instead, it seemed to reopen a lot of old wounds.

Anyway, it was all in the hands of the court system now, and there was hardly a thing anyone could do about....except I felt so badly for the twins who would now be deprived of both their mom and dad. That was truly sad. They were the real victims in this whole damn mess...the twins and CJ...

***

Cedric parked his Harley and swung his helmet off and then turned around to smile at his companion. "Well, we're here," he told her nodding towards Lou's Tattoo Parlor. "You're not gonna punk out, are you?"

"Not on your life. I'm as ready as I'll ever be," Kendra said, easing off the bike, and took off her helmet, swinging back her hair.

"Okay, after you," Cedric said grinning.

The tattoo was his way of thanking Kendra for all she had done for him. Hell, he owed her A LOT! And what better way to show his appreciation than to liberate her. Kendra was way too uptight and knowing how she had secretly always wanted a tattoo and since she was constantly eyeing and appreciating his, he made it easy for her and insisted she got one. Told her how offended he'd be if she refused.

The parlor was located in North Miami Beach on a 167th Street, right off I95. Kendra seemed to have really enjoyed flying down the highway, and he was hoping that it would shape up to be a really fun day.

"All right, baby girl, we're gonna get you something nice and sexy," he said as they pushed open the door and went in. The door chimed and the artist bid them to wait, shouting from a back room that he'd be right with them. "Make yourself comfortable," he ordered.

Cedric plopped down on the leather swivel chair that was there, and bid her to follow suit. Kendra's eyes darted around, gazing at all the pictures strewn about and all the tattoos. There was an array of famous people—rap stars, rock artists, models and actors. "Lou must be in the business of tattooing the stars," Kendra commented.

"Hey, you nervous," Cedric asked, touching the small of her back. She was hunched over, looking a little anxious.

Not saying a word, she shook her head, no.

Cedric smiled and continued, "Have you decided on what you want yet? Say a little ivy vine, um...right around your ankle or maybe on your upper arm. But oh no, I'm forgetting, you're with the Bureau. So you might want to be a little more discreet than that. Maybe right here, on the small of your back, right on your bikini line," he mentioned, touching the spot.

Kendra was grinning. "You're really into this."

"Well, aren't you?"

"Yeah. I guess I am. But an ivy vine? I was thinking something more colorful."

"Ummm, I'm scared of you! You want to be real bold. Well, okay, what about a little rose vine." Then he looked at her and said, "You know, something's different about you."

Letting the triumph of the moment settle over her, Kendra laughed and shook her head. "My hair, stupid. I got it twisted."

Cedric was grinning now. "Shit! How could I not have noticed?! Um, well it's good to see the conservative going all out of you. What next? Maybe I'll see you in a dress yet!"

"Don't hold your breath. You know, I'm not even sure I own a dress. I think I might have a couple of skirts, but a dress..."

"That's sick!"

Kendra shrugged. "I suppose it is."

"Well, we'll have to rectify that. After your tattoo, I'm taking you shopping."

"Oh, no! I hate shopping, I really do."

"Kendra, you sure you aren't a dude? Sorry to keep beating that horse, but I swear, girl, you might have a fucking penis between your legs. There's no way possible any woman would ever turn down an opportunity to shop. At Bal Harbor, no less!"

"I don't have the time, money, nor the inclination."

"You're a man trapped in a woman's body!"

"Fuck you."

"No, and I'm not kidding," he said grabbing her swivel chair and spun it around, coming to stand between her parted thighs. "Seriously," he said, quietly. "Pull down those trousers. Let me see. Or better yet, let me feel. I swear, I think I'm gonna feel some balls."

Kendra sucked her teeth and knocking him really hard in the stomach. But he came back and threw one leg over the chair straddling her legs, teasing her, his hands all over. "C'mon, baby. Let me see it. I'm serious. Unzip those pants. Let me take a peek."

Kendra couldn't help giggling. "All right, stop it, Cedric. You had your fun," she warned, not liking his proximity. He was all over her, grabbing and tickling and she was getting more than a little aroused. So was he if the bulge in his trousers was any indication.

The tattoo artist cleared his throat and interrupted them seconds later. Cedric looked up and almost immediately the guy was pumping his hands.

"Cedric Courage," he said in amazement. "Well, I'll be damned. Didn't know it was you—or I wouldn't have kept you waiting."

"Not a problem," Cedric smiled, lifting himself off her. Thank God, she could now breathe.

"Oh shit! You want somethin' done. My boss is gonna go apeshit when he hears you're here. Hey, let me call him, man."

"No-no, this isn't for me. It's for my *pal* here," Cedric said, introducing her. "Ms. Kendra Jade."

Kendra waved. The guy hadn't even noticed her, he had been so keenly focused on Cedric. Now turning his attention to her, he beamed with excitement. "Oh, I see. First-timer," he said, judging her by the fancy navy suit she had on.

"Yeah, she's a virgin, man. So I want you to make it real sweet for her, and for this whole experience to be really cool...know what I mean?"

"Sure," the guy replied.

***

They continued to talk while Kendra stared on at Cedric. She was so busy studying his handsome profile that she hardly noticed when the conversation reverted back to her. She had to shake herself to zero-in on what they were saying. They had started to talk again, but she had continued admiring Cedric's god-like physique. He wasn't overly muscular but was so lean, dressed in all black attire—black jeans and pullover, nice leather belt and shoes—probably everything designer. He had taken to wearing his hair, which had grown out so fast, pulled back in a ponytail.

God, he was good-looking, especially now that you could see his face. But his Eurasian eyes were what stunned her, which were framed by the longest, thickest lashes she had ever seen on a man. The rest of his face was very nice too. His lips were full and sexy and his teeth were white and straight, a real turn-on. For her, a guy had to have nice teeth and Cedric's were fantastic.

She decided to go along with what Cedric had suggested. If he found the rose vine sexy, then that's what she'd have done, right on the small of her back, where he'd suggested.

Cedric was grinning from ear-to-ear. When she went to the

tattoo table, he remained with her, kneeling down so she could focus on his face the entire time the guy worked on her back, sipping on the beer the tattoo artist had offered them.

During the process, Cedric kept on a steady stream of conversation—probably to keep her mind off of the pain of the grievous needles. They covered topics ranging from sports to the weather to the upcoming city elections. Kendra knew what he was doing—and why—and she was so grateful.

The tattoo artist was also jabbering on and on, ecstatic to have Cedric here at his parlor. His friends would probably be hearing about this for a long time to come. Meanwhile, Cedric was being really sweet, holding her hands, rubbing them gently between his, seemingly focused and alert the entire time, wanting to make her as comfortable as possible.

Much later, as they relaxed at the penthouse that was all but packed up—nothing remained but a few boxes and the buttery, leather, sectional sofa in the rec room. Cedric had sold it to a neighbor but was still using to sleep on until he moved to his new home on LaGorce.

Kendra thanked him for showing her such a wonderful day. This had truly been one of the best days of her life! Spending down time with Cedric, gaining up the nerves to get a tattoo, she still didn't quite believe she had actually done it. Then later, she had let Cedric actually talk her into going shopping, and had ended up fighting with him to pay for her things. He had totally ignored her, insisting that he pay for everything—even getting bummed out every time she pulled out her platinum credit card.

"I have titanium. Limitless titanium. Let me pay for it," he kept saying.

Kendra had finally relented but had felt at odds. She was not used to having a man pay her way—not unless it was for dinner or a movie or maybe a small gift. But to have a man pay for her clothes, perfume and other knick-knacks was definitely something new. Something she wasn't exactly sure she could ever get used to.

Cedric was passed out on the couch and all of the bags were spread all over the place. He had gotten a few things for himself too, quite a few things for CJ and had purchased some perfume for Margot and Miss Penny, as well as cigars for his dad. He was going up to Orlando for the weekend, he had told her. He missed CJ, and was inviting her to come along.

"So what are you now, my boyfriend," she teased. "I can't believe you bought me all this stuff—or that you're now inviting me to meet the folks."

He was pensive for a while. "I only bought them cause you get to model them for me, and as for your second accusation, you've already met the folks. Remember...at the wake and the funeral."

"Yeah, but going over with you to Orlando, to their place, what does it mean?"

"Well, if you're going to make a big deal about it, it means nothing. I was only being polite."

"Oh."

"Oh, yeah," he grinned. "And in answer to your first question, not unless you wanna be."

"Oh, could you stop it," she snapped. "If I wanna be...just who the hell do you think you're dealing with? One of your little female floozies?!"

He was up and pulling her down besides him, pulling her into his arms. "Please Kendra, I'm tired. I don't want to fight with you," he said snuggling up, getting cozy. "You either want to be my woman or you don't. It's up to you."

She took a deep breath and tried to ignore the warmth she felt between her thighs as his arms encircled her. She didn't want to think how weak but at the same time how good he made her feel.

"Do you want to be my woman or do you want to continue just being friends. And it's okay," Cedric assured her, "if that's all you want."

Much as she wanted to be his woman, he was saying the wrong things. She didn't want it to be just up to her. Why didn't he care one way or another? That's not how she imagined their relationship would begin—with this lackadaisical attitude.

"If you want, we can continue to be just pals," he continued.

Kendra stiffened and stifled the urge she was feeling. He would never guess how much her arms now ached to hold *him*, how her lips longed to kiss him. How it was taking every bit of resistance not to tear his clothes off his back and beg him to please fuck her. Except, how could she do those things to someone who claimed they could still be just friends? Did he want her to be his woman? Was the urgency to be with her romantically there for him to? Where did sex play in a platonic relationship?

"So when do you have to be out?" She said segueing into a more safer topic, wanting to drop all of this sex-trip stuff. Slowly pulling away and easing herself out of his arms, she moved into more neutral territory.

"The closing's next week," he said with a sigh, curling a lock of her twisted hair around his fingers, seemingly not to lose complete contact.

Their faces were so near, their lips so close. Just a breath away. With just the slightest effort, Kendra thought and nearly closed her eyes from desire, they'd be in a lip-lock. *Damn, I want you,* she thought with remorse. *I want you more than I've ever wanted any other man! And this is crazy, lying here so close to you. But you don't love me, aren't in love with me. It's evident in your attitude and entire demeanor. If I were with you, it would be just sex. Sex with a friend.* So close and yet so far...this was pure torture!

"Why don't you go slip into something more comfortable," he said suggestively. "Oh, and by the way, I really do expect you to model every single outfit I bought you, all right? Meanwhile, I'll go start dinner."

"What are we having?" she asked lightly, feigning indifference.

"Don't know yet, but I'll scrounge something up. Or better yet, we could go out. And you could...wear a dress! The red one."

"The one I promised I wouldn't wear but you insisted on buying?"

"Yeah, that exact one. The one with no back. The one you can't wear with a bra," he grinned. "Yeah, that's the one."

She gave him a steady stare. "But wouldn't that be like going on a date? I thought we were only pals."

"We are...since that's what you seem to want to be. So can't I take a friend to dinner? Like I've never taken you to dinner—"

"I was working then. On duty. Guarding you. This is different."

"To you."

"It's very different now... And anyway, why do you want me to wear a dress? Especially, that particular dress, which just smacks of sex and romance."

He gave a rather elegant shrug and laid a smooth hand over her upper abdomen, sliding it down over the flat of her belly. Kendra's stomach lurched then melted inside.

"Maybe we could be lovers," he said pensively. "You know, maybe we could be hommie-lover-friends," he said grinning mischievously. "Wouldn't you like that? I don't have to be your man. I can just be a friend that lets you have it whenever you want it...baby girl. Whatever works."

Kendra laughed, expelling a breath, "You can't be serious. And women actually fall for that?"

He grinned. "Totally. This is a brand new world, and women want their independence. And hey...that's all right, cool with me, hommie-lover-friend."

"Well, it's a totally new phrase for me, so you'll have to explain," she said deliberately playing dumb.

"That's a guy strong sisters like yourself have on the side that comes around and makes love to her whenever the need arises. He's not a boyfriend and they're both unattached, but when they get together, it's like fireworks! Until the next time..."

"Humph," she said with disdain.

"And..."

"Uh-huh...And ...?"

"That's all you have to say," he asked lifting her up, causing her to topple over him. She was resting right on top of his chest now, her pelvis pressed and aligned with his. She could feel his desire—the warmth, the length and hardness. It was totally unnerving, he was so well-endowed and felt so perfect in every way.

If she made love to Cedric, she'd be the loser 'cause she'd be hooked for life, she thought glumly. She'd fall even more in love than she already was, and then where would she be? No, better she didn't find out. Better to leave well enough alone and get the hell out of Dodge. The saying was true, *if you couldn't handle the heat, get the fuck out of the kitchen!*

"Damn, you know," she said suddenly. "I just remembered there was something I had to do for my mother tonight. I swear it! I know you're not gonna believe me, but I have to go," she said quickly scrambling off him, crawling on the floor, looking for her shoes. "Cedric?" She said, peering under the sofa. "Have you seen my shoes?"

Cedric grunted and next took a large pillow and covered himself with it, and seemed to be squeezing it real tight.

"Cedric?"

A muffled grunt was her only answer.

"Please, have you seen my shoes?"

***

Kendra approached the kitchen door and swung it open, knowing that's where she'd find her sister, Sophy, who was baking or making one thing or another for her family. Sophy was so domesticated, so organized, and just simply everything Kendra was not. Sure enough, there she was, where she knew she'd be—in the kitchen preparing dinner. Chicken pot pie, one of Sophy's best dishes.

Kendra hadn't used the front entrance since she hadn't wanted to disturb Nigel and the kids—not to mention to fact that she felt so unstable at the moment and was quite literally falling apart. The last thing she wanted was for Nigel and the children to see her like this. No witnesses, thank you. In any case, Sophy was used to her coming to the kitchen door.

"Oh boy, look at who the cat dragged in," her sister commented as she quietly slinked through the doorway. "Girl, what's wrong with you? You look like you've just lost your best friend," Sophy said next.

Kendra went over and just grabbed Sophy and started hugging her fiercely. "I'm a fool," she cried softly. "Such a stupid fool!"

Sophy totally startled and caught off guard had no choice but to simply hug her back, consolingly patting her on the back. "Kendra, what's wrong? What's the matter?"

But Kendra just stood there, still holding her sister, unable to tell. Though she felt like crying, the tears wouldn't come. Besides that, Sophy had never seen her cry and might go into shock. Everyone in her family knew she was a tough cookie, a tower of strength. How would it look? Her crying—and over a man!

"I'm a fool," Kendra said again, her voice soft, strangled. "I seriously think there's something wrong with me." Abruptly releasing Sophy, she plopped herself down on a kitchen stool, surprised to feel her eyes moist.

Then quite suddenly there was a stream of tears steadily flowing out her eyes. Sophy looked shocked but still had the presence of mind to hand her some tissues. Sophy continued to hold and soothe her, allowing her to have a good long cry. When she finished, she hiccupped and stared up at her sister.

"I'm so sorry," was all she could manage to say. "Coming over and crying all over you like this."

"That's okay, girl. What's troubling you so? Did you loose your job at the Bureau?"

"No-no. Nothing like that..."

"What happened then? Explain. You'll feel better."

Kendra looked at her through blurry, wet eyes. "It's...it's...Cedric," she whispered.

"Cedric," Sophy said with sudden comprehension. "Cedric Courage? A man?!" Sophy shouted and then immediately placed her hand over her mouth. "Ken-J, you're crying over a man," she asked with too much excitement.

"Why do you look so happy?"

Sophy was laughing now, "Cause frankly, baby-sis, I've always thought... you know...that you might not...well, exactly like...you know...like guys..."

"What?" Kendra shrieked. "You too? You thought I was...gay?!" She closed her eyes, suddenly feeling even more pain. "Well, maybe I am...Maybe I am!"

Sophy was immediately hushing her. "Why do you say that? Don't say that! You were just crying about Cedric. That's a good sign—"

Kendra shook her head, "I was crying because," she tried to catch her breath, "I just left this...this splendid specimen of a man who I find...oh God...so utterly attractive writhing in pain on the couch...wracked with pain from wanting to make love to me...because I can't! I don't feel like I can make love to him and not lose something...and just lose myself completely!"

Sophy was watching her intently. "Well, it sounds like you do want to make love to him too. That's encouraging..."

Kendra sighed deeply, "I desperately want to make love to him!"

"So why didn't you...why don't you?"

"I have no idea," she said blowing a breath. "I have no idea..."

"You have to know why."

"I don't know...but maybe it's because one moment he wants me to be his woman and in the next breath he says he just wants to be friend or doesn't care if all we are is just friends. It's like, he can't seem to commit one way or another, and that bothers me."

"That's a good reason, enough reason to want to walk away."

"But the thing is I want him so much! I really wanted to stay, but something in me...something made me leave."

"Was he angry? "

"Oh," Kendra laughed. "No doubt."

"Did he curse you out or try to hurt you?"

"He didn't have to. I watched him punch a pillow and then tear it to shreds. I suppose that's what he wanted to do to me."

Sophy stifled a giggle. "You're kidding?"

"I had to high-tail it out of there, believe me," Kendra shuddered. "And now I'm afraid I've ruined everything. And I really, really care about him, you know... I do want him, I think I'm in love with him—except, he doesn't make me feel safe. I can't trust him. I think he's in love with somebody else...and I can't go there with him so long as that's the way I feel."

Sophy gave her a warm smile, "You'll figure it out, Ken-J. You're so smart, and strong. You'll do what is best...I know, for the both of you.

After her talk with Sophy, she made her way home all the while thinking. She couldn't stop thinking how she had made a mistake. And it wasn't the insignificant kind that you can forget a few days or weeks later—but the kind that can tear your heart out of your chest and leave it bouncing and floundering like a washed up fish on a desolate shore.

She had gone through most of her life avoiding any kind of deep emotion. Looking at them as obstacles. Normally she'd try to gloss over them— overpower her anger or pain or lust. These were bad, awful things that needed to be squashed or squelched and not allowed to fester. Yet, somehow Cedric had knocked down all her defenses, a formidable challenge, but one he had somehow beat. Somehow he had wiggled himself deep into the depths of her heart—entrenched his god-like little self right there.

How would she ever calm down, keep it under wraps when he was constantly there goading her, taunting her, doing everything he could to torture and overpower her? Sure, before she was in a crucible, had to do her job to protect him and couldn't be rid of him. But now, what was stopping her? She didn't have to agree to see him or spend any more time with him. Except, it was even harder now to stay away from him.

Cedric, without a doubt, was still very much in love with Arielle. She sensed this...no, knew this in her heart of hearts. And perhaps his fascination with her was that she reminded him of Ariello in some way. Yet knowing this from the get-go, how had she allowed herself to get in so deep? She, had known this, been well aware of it, knowing she needed to be on guard and not allow herself and fall victim to his antics. After you'd been around the block a few times and knew the pain a man could so easily inflict on a woman, how could you fail to put up every wall and barrier to block out the ugliness a failed relationship could bring? Getting involved with Cedric smacked of disaster—like leaping off a cliff. He was in love with a ghost, how in the world would she ever compete with a ghost?!

But love him, she did. How had she failed so miserably to guard heart? And what was it about the human condition that made loving and wanting more so unavoidably inescapable?

That night, she cried again. Cried hard into her pillow until finally falling asleep. Hopefully, things would look better in the morning.

***

Cedric knew he been acting really weird lately. Knew everyone who knew him had been walking on eggshells around him. Except by this point, he didn't truly give a shit! He was way past the point of caring. He knew he was taking out his frustrations on everyone, but couldn't help himself.

To relieve some of the stress, he had started playing basketball, every day. He played real hard, and next would go running or to the gym to lift weights or punch out the Every punching bags. At night, he would go clubbing with the boys, where he'd drink hard and smoke excessively, then just pass out and fall asleep—all in an attempt not to think of *her*. He couldn't even bear to dream. All his dreams were totally focused on *her*. It was like he literally couldn't get away, couldn't get her out of her mind. Living without her was proving to be impossible.

It was hard going through all the motions. He wasn't sure it was even a secret anymore, but he felt floored, devastated by her death even more as the months passed. He was just barely making it really, and it was taking everything he had not to stick a gun down his throat and join her. Time was suppose to heal all wounds, but why was he experiencing this acute sense of lost when nearly half a year had already gone by? Why was he even more obsessed and thinking about her now when he should be getting on with his life?

The thought of ending his life occurred to him quite a bit. And though he tried to fight the pain, the sense of loss and sadness by spending time with CJ or Kendra, honestly, sometimes none of that worked. And he was left feeling bereft with no earthly purpose and this one agonizing thought, just end it all...

On a night when he had had too much to drink and Deuce found him nearly passed out in the rec room with a third bottle of Grey Goose, Deuce wrestled the bottle from his grasp, forcing an intervention on him. Somehow or another, Deuce got him to start talking and once he started, it was as if he couldn't stop. He started telling Deuce, hinting about all his dark thoughts. Maybe it was a cry for help, but in a way, that was got him set on a plan. 'Cause when Deuce realized what he was in essence planning, he exclaimed, "Say what?! Now I know you're trippin', boss! You've gotta be shittin' me!"

"No, straight-up, man. I've fuckin' had it. I'm going crazy, yo...I swear it, I'm gonna just do it real soon. It's just a matter of time."

"Nigga, you'se got to be kidding!!! You're Cedric Courage. You musta forgotten who you are!"

"I know who I am, bro, And I ain't about shit—not without her."

Deuce blew an exasperated breath. "Ain't that some shit. I never thought I'd see the day when a nigga was so whipped...by a ghost. She's gone, man. Accept it. You can't do jack until you accept that. She's gone but you still here, and you've got plenty to do...Lots of peeps counting on you, my brother. What you gonna do? Just blow everyone off? That's mighty selfish of you— especially sense you gotta little fellow that loves you very much. Who's he gonna have, man. Don't have a ma and won't have a pa."

"I know man, in fact, he's the only reason I go on...but it's getting to the point where I just can't, bro. I can't. She was everything, my lifeline. It's fucked up, but I can't function without her! I've tried, man. I swear it, but—it's just not working, yo. This shit is just broken now...life absolutely blows, know what I mean?"

"No, nigga. I don't know whatcha mean. I see someone with everything to live for just throwing it all away. Ain't nothin' in the world worse than being ungrateful. My mama always told me that. And Cedric, hate to break it to you, but that's whatcha being— ungrateful! You have everything, man."

"Don't have her. Don't have Arielle."

"Man, bunk Arielle...she was fine as hell, but there's plenty of other fish in the sea."

"No, bro...she was my fish. The only fish I really wanted."

"Nigga, you know what you need, just some T and A. Tits and ass. Yeah, boy. Some vitamin P. That's all a brotha be needing."

Cedric laughed in spite of himself. "Some vitamin capital P."

Deuce laughed, winking at Cedric. "One face full, and BOOM, you're cured," he said high-fiving him. "You've been up in here living like a hermit, man, all shut out from the rest of the world. You need to talk to Stan and Veronica, man. Start planning a tour. Get out there with your fans. Get back into your music and shit. Fuck a few groupies just like in the old days—shit, fuck a room full of them. Remember man, how it used to be. You were the man, everyone respected you."

"And now...I've lost a lot of that respect, huh?"

"No, bro...you've lost your self-respect. That's on you, dude. Nobody can give you that. You gotta do that shit for yourself."

"Hell, don't you think I'd love to do that. I want that so badly to get back to my life, but...something's holding me back, bro. It's like I can't move a step until this..." he blew an exasperated breath and ran his fingers through his hair, "I have to straighten out a lot of shit first. You know...sometimes I feel her, all around me. It's like she's still here with me and she wants me to do something—except I need to figure it out."

Deuce who was Haitian and very superstitious crossed himself. "Don't even kid like that, bro. I knew this place was haunted. Been feelin' that shit for a long time. God, I'm glad we're movin'...Damn skippy. Yep. Yep."

"Hey man, you're from Haiti."

"Yeah, what about it?"

"Think she has some kinda curse on me? Some voodoo...you know she had this fucking little doll of me that was all fucked-up with pins and shit..."

Deuced laughed. "No, man...just because I'm from Haiti don't mean I know anything about that mess."

"Well do you at least know if someone put some voodoo curse on you if there's any way of taking it off?"

Deuce shrugged. "I suppose so...I know some people that are into that shit. Maybe I can put you in touch and they could do something for ya," Deuce said scratching the bridge of his nose.

"Okay, man...you do that."

The very next day, Deuce bought him a book as a joke by some Haitian author called, *Zombi, You My Love: Stories from Haiti.* It was a collection of short stories where Orem, the author demonstrated an intimate knowledge of the customs and beliefs of Haiti. One of the things that fascinated Cedric about the stories in the book was how it was very hard to draw the line between where reality ended and the magic began. Cedric had stayed in bed the entire day reading the book and this constant theme kept reiterating itself in his mind.

What if...what if ...something could be done and he could bring her back?

He started recalling her journal, all the entries she had in there about Florence and magic and about all the special powers she had had and had never mentioned. Was there any validity to any of that stuff? And what about the doll? That grotesque doll she had made of him...surely perhaps this Florence woman might be aware or have something to say about all of this. Could that doll be the reason he was so miserable?

He went for her journals, which he now kept in a wooden antique floor chest at the end of his bed, along with numerous other keepsakes like her old jewelry, their wedding album, videos, and other knick-knacks of hers. The moment he came upon the journals, Florence business card fell right out of the very first one he opened. He didn't recall having ever seen it before. It startled him at first. He had handled that journal plenty of times before and now, all of the sudden as if by magic, upon seeking Florence's number, the card just happened to float right into his palm.

Freaky shit...but then freakier things had been happening all along. Why should this surprise him? He shrugged, feeling as if someone had just walked over his grave as he stared down at the card:

Florence, Mambo Internationale
44 Rue Des Artiste
La Plaine, Haiti, W.I.

There was a telephone number and even a website and email address underneath. Cedric couldn't help laughing, everybody and their momma had a website these days—even voodoo priestesses.

Immediately, he tried calling Florence's number. Ended up calling the number several times, but to no avail. The website was just as unhelpful. So was her email address. Did she ever answer her email? Finally, he decided he would fly out to see her in person.

Why waste time?

With no appointment and not even knowing what he meant to do, he set out to Haiti with the express purpose of seeking Florence out.

Part Two

The Garden of Love

I went to the Garden of Love
And saw what I never had seen:
A chapel was built in the midst,
Where I used to play on the green.

And the gates of this chapel were shut,
And "Thou shalt not" writ over the door.
So I turn'd to the Garden of Love,
That so many sweet flowers bore,

And I saw it was filled with graves,
And tombstones where flowers should be:
And Priests in black gowns were walking their
rounds
And binding with briars my joys & desires.

--William Blake

15

Feel the Heat

If Port-au-Prince got any more oppressive, I was going to have to scratch Haiti off of my "Most Favorite Places" list. The air traffic was getting a lot more heavier now, as was the street traffic. And the crime rate was on the rise too, getting just as bad as the U.S. inner city ghettos.

The second I stepped off my private jet, the heat was horrendous! It was like being in an oven. I could literally feel my skin sizzle and my flesh cooking underneath my skin.

How the fuck did Haitians here even breathe?

And hell, why wasn't there even the slightest hint of a breeze? Haiti was a goddamn island for crying out loud! But you'd be hard-pressed to tell. I had never been hotter my entire life!

Anyway, I was in a foul and fucked up mood to begin with. I didn't like being hot or inconvenienced, and I was both at the moment. The air traffic controllers had kept us circling for hours until the captain complained how we were going crash land right into the fucking tower if they didn't give us permission to land. This trip was much different than when I had come here a few years before with Arielle. We were practically newlyweds then, and I remember flying in and us going straight to Jacmel, this wonderfully little dilapidated village outside of P-a-P (Port-au Prince).

It had been a fascinating trip. Nothing about Haiti had bothered me then, in fact, I had fallen in love with the place. But today, this was very far from the case. I wanted to see Florence and be gone, hopefully by nightfall.

I was already upset about having to fly to a fucking country just to speak to someone who had a fucking phone and email, but who never answered neither. Also, I was angry since Haiti reminded me so much of Arielle, who couldn't be here with me.

I lightened up a little when I walked into the baggage claim area of the airport and saw that the room was fairly empty. Thank

God, cause the last time I had visited there, the P-a-P airport had been an arduous experience. With two to three hundred passengers fighting over 50 luggage carts and the many skycaps milling about, waiting for the bags to come off the plane. Once they did, it was a mad free-for-all of everyone grabbing bags—people taking shit that wasn't even theirs—while the skycaps tried piling bags right next to the conveyor belt, trying to help but unable to effectively do their job with all the madness all about.

Thank goodness I didn't have anything but an overnight bag, and so I just handed the immigration officer my passport and next walked over to the rental car counter that was now conveniently moved to the baggage claim area. I found myself thanking God again for small miracles. Formerly the car rental had been across the street from the main building, and that meant running for half a block, trying to avoid a bunch of bandits that looked like children, shouting "Geeve me moany, my fren! Give me dallah! American dallah, Ahm hoangry! Geeve me yo bag, I carry it!" And it was useless to try and explain that you had already paid one guy to handle your bags, and that you were going to have to pay the two other guys that grabbed your bags and were now dragging them down the rutted side walk—heedless of the fact that you had fucking Luis Vitton's and they were scratching them all up.

I remember how Arielle and I had to finally just toss money up into the air to try and escape. When they all went scrambling for it, we made our get-away, and couldn't stop laughing about it for days. It was crazy—not to mention scary. But that had been one of the highlights of our trip, making that quick getaway. It was a relief, though, to find they had moved the car rental counter into the baggage claim area, equipped with computers and credit card processors and everything.

Hooray for technology!

After an hour and a half delay, which was not bad at all by Haitian standards, the clerk announced my car had arrived. I had asked for a Range Rover or Land Cruiser or Jeep, something big. I knew the streets of P-a-P and a little sedan was simply not going to cut it here.

Nonetheless, I was told that they were all out of cars for the day, but had one left. Would I care to see it?

The only car left turned out to be a shiny green Hyundai. I checked it out, not too bad. The tires were new, the air-conditioner happened to be working. It was even actually cool. Definitely needed that in this heat. I circled around it with the clerk who was making note of all the dings on it to be sure he got everything down. Then I noticed the hole in the windshield.

"Oh no!" I told him.

"Li bon," he said quickly.

"Li pa bon," I told him, motioning to the crack that ran all the way across the front glass.

He pounded on the windshield. *"Li bon, mouin dit-ou.* See...no problem," he said pounding some more. *"Blanc,* if you don't like, you change tomorrow."

I just wanted to move on and decided to just take the car anyway, making a mental note to stay far enough behind trucks that were moving fast so that the next stone wouldn't bring the entire windshield crashing into my face. But then came my lucky break when the guy offered his services as a tour guide.

"After you, I'm off and can drive for you. Be your chauffeur, no problem."

"You can be my chauffeur?"

"Yes."

God was much too kind... "But for how much?" Cedric countered.

"Two hundred dollars."

"American dollars? Or are we talking about, what is it...*gourdes?*"

"No, sir. I talk about American dollars."

"Just for taking me down the street?"

"Gas very expensive here. Some places five dollars per gallon."

"Which I'd be paying for," Cedric said disgustedly, eying him disdainfully.

"Ok, one hundred dollars. Time expensive now in Haiti too. Everything expensive!"

"I see..."

"Yves, *à votre service,*" the guy said, offering a handshake. "So one hundred American dollars, *blanc.*"

"All right, Yves, but you have to drive me around all day, and maybe tomorrow too.

Yves grinned. "Tomorrow, one hundred dollars again."

***

This was his third visit to Haiti, and being good with directions, he could have easily followed the road from "Rue Tabar" to Florence's house. But being that he detested driving, and looking sideways at the little Hyundai, he thought—what the hell. He knew he was being ripped off, but Yves probably needed the money and he didn't feel like the hassle of driving in Haitian traffic in any case.

His pilot had stayed at the airport with his Lear jet, not trusting the ground mechanics, and had wanted to supervise as they refueled the plane. He told Cedric how when he had come there with Arielle last spring, how they had encountered numerous problems. So hopefully, Florence would be home, he'd talk to her and be on his way—by tonight.

After he gave Yves the guide the address, Yves said, "You go to Florence, the mambo. I know her. Many Americans come to see her."

"Really," Cedric responded, reflecting how Arielle had visited Florence the last time she visited Haiti. Although he had been told the trip was to go take care of some foundation business and attend a groundbreaking ceremony of the new school they were building. But he later found out from her journal, the trip had been more to speak to Florence.

The school or rather, the foundation had been the last project Arielle had worked on which involved the building of several public schools in the P-a-P area, the first being in Thomassin. Maybe he could check up on that too while he was here, he thought, realizing that he'd have to stay a little longer, perhaps another day or so to do so. In which case, he'd have to send Yves back for his pilot later.

With any luck, the project hadn't fallen by the wayside or into the wrong hands. He'd have to call Miami and speak to Trey, his personal assistant to get him a contact name and number. Hopefully there were still people handling it. God knows there had been a good amount of money funneled into it, but knowing the character of people in general—not to mention their avarice and greed—it would be prudent to get an accounting of what was going on with these school and how his money was being spent.

Rue Tabar, Cedric discovered from his newly hired chauffeur and quasi-tour-guide, was a road built by Americans in 1995, a wonderful road, one of the most decent in all of Haiti that went from the airport, through the flat lands of La Plaine and winded up the hills into Petionville, a quaint little suburb found up the mountain from Port-au-Prince.

Yves chatted pleasantly as they drove for what seemed a very short distance from the airport, down the paved road built especially for President Aristide. "Lavalas forever," he said patriotically. He also pointed out Arsitide's Famille Ce'st Lavie foundation as well as, Aristide's personal home, which were both on this same road. "Of course, he lives in White House now, but he come all time for weekend on vacation."

"Um," Cedric said nodding absently.

It wasn't too much longer that he took several twist and turns and Cedric could see the street sign for *Rue Des Artiste*. He felt relieved as the car pulled up to a nice tall gate. Yves rang the buzzer then spoke into the intercom in Creole, and soon the automatic gates slid open, revealing a beautiful paved, stone-cut road way, snaking up to a rambling white Victorian style mansion that rose majestically above an array of tropical trees and foliage. He noticed that grounds were immaculately kept and how the graveled driveway was edged with precisely arranged bushes and hedges in array of colors.

"Well, Florence certainly lives large," he said more to himself than to Yves.

"Florence, *gros* mambo. Very popular here in Haiti."

"I see..." Cedric said again, as several youngsters ran up and started chasing the car, as the Hyundai came around the bend and went up the circular driveway that led to the front entrance of the house. Many of the kids looked about the same age, and there were so many of them.

"Who are all these kids," Cedric asked Yves curiously, not sure he even wanted to know. "Are these Florence's kids? Or does she also run a school?"

"No-no, Florence has no children, but she make home for orphans and those with special powers."

"O-kay," Cedric said, as he swung open the door. Almost immediately, he was swarmed by children.

"Blanc...blanc..." They seemed to sing. They were all so friendly.

"Is Florence expecting you?" Yves asked then.

"No, my man. In fact, I'd appreciate it if you'd tell one of the kids to let her know I'm here. I'm not sure she speaks any English. In fact, you may have to also serve as my translator."

The guy chuckled. "Florence speak good English. Better than me. Like I say, she have many American customer."

Thank God for that, Cedric thought, starting to feel much better about the entire trip. He couldn't understand why as of yet, but meeting Florence suddenly felt monumental, like it was going to be a huge turning point in his life.

It was as if he were standing on a precipice, which could

either make him or break him. And even though he questioned Florence and her religion's validity and knew for sure that this could all be a great hoax, one designed to rip people off, still if there was any chance she could help him, he would gladly take it.

***

Florence left him cooling his heels in her cozy sitting room for awhile. After all, he hadn't been expected. Cedric was impressed with the colorful island décor of white wicker, marble floors and green plants. He spent sometime staring at some awesome Haitian paintings lining most of her walls—some artist he was familiar with, others he was not. But the paintings exhibited real talent. Florence had good taste, though, he could tell. When she did finally arrive to greet him, she was not at all what he had expected. In fact, Cedric hadn't known what to expect but felt pleasantly surprised and immediately fell under her charm. She was very gracious and pretty hot-looking too.

Florence's hair was piled on top of her head with long, curly braids falling like ropes down her shapely shoulders. Her sundress was made of ivory and laced with threads of gold. When she walked in, she was shimmering and had a smooth undulating walk that he could only think of as sexy.

Cedric had not expected her to be so young and to have such a hot, sensational bod. He took the slender, dark caramel hand she procured and to his surprise, she pulled him to her and greeted him warmly by kissing him on either cheek. She smelled nice too, like citrus fruit mixed with tropical flowers.

"So you're Arielle's husband," she said with a grin, after asking him to please have a seat. "I've been expecting you," she said, not letting go of his hands. Holding them firmly in hers, smiling prettily at him.

Cedric couldn't help staring at her even white teeth, more pronounced because of her ruby red lipstick. She was a handsome woman, Cedric decided, tall and statuesque, very pleasing to the eye.

"You were expecting me? So you did get the all those messages...but why didn't you answer back?"

She didn't answer but only smiled mysteriously.

"I must attend to some chores, Mr. Courage. Please understand I will assist you in any way possible—just as soon as I can. However for now, I hope you will be comfortable here. Relax, get some rest, regain your strength. I know our airport can be a harrowing experience to those unused to it. So rest first, and soon I'll attend to you."

Her voice was so mellifluous. She had such a rich, melodious voice, one that could hypnotize you if you weren't careful.

Cedric found himself nodding, agreeing to rest even though that had probably been the furthest thing on his mind. But admittedly, he was tired.

"Would you care to refresh yourself? Perhaps have a shower? Some food, a nap on a comfortable bed? You look exhausted...so tired."

Was she always this hospitable?

Something about her regard and warmth affected him. She made him feel comfortable. Almost immediately, he found himself trusting her. There was something about her, a mystique he found himself drawn to.

Cedric nodded again, "Yes-yes, thank you. I would like that, Florence," he heard himself say while she smiled reassuringly, taking his bag and handing it to one of the older boys milling about. She spoke to him in Creole and then bid Cedric to follow him. "Kenau will take you to your room. Please let him know whatever you require. He will attend to you."

Taking Florence's advice to rest, he sent Yves back to the airport for his pilot. Looked like they'd be there a little longer than originally expected.

The boy led him out of the main atrium of the house into a courtyard where a small cluster of cabanas that looked like studio apartments faced the inner courtyard surrounding a nice sized bean-shaped pool.

The boy led him into one of these apartments. Inside there was a neat but tiny living room with built-in furniture, a larger bedroom with wrought-iron furniture and an immaculately-made bed covered with white embroidered linen. The bathroom was white-tiled and had a real tub and white porcelain basin.

"I bring clean towels," Kenau said dropping his bag and running for the door.

"Wait!" Cedric said but it was too late. The boy was already out of earshot, taking off like a shot.

Turning to the dresser, Cedric tore open the colorful plastic wrap covering the large fruit basket filled with bananas and mangoes and other tropical fruit. Cedric picked up a mango and ate it ravenously. He hadn't realized how hungry he was 'til then. By the time Kenau came back, he really did need those towels to capture all the mango juice that was seeping down his mouth and face, unto the white tiled floors. "Would you like some," he offered the youngster, gesturing to the basket of fruit.

But Kenau shook his head, offered him the towels and next said, "Shower?"

"Definitely."

Grateful to have accommodations just fall into his lap, Cedric felt exhausted all of the sudden and couldn't wait to hit the sheets. As Kenau disposed of the mango seed and peel, Cedric removed his shoes, shed off his dusty clothes and headed for the shower. By the time the boy returned, Cedric was stretched out on the bed, stalk naked, deep in sleep.

***

When he finally did awaken sometime late that evening, the boy was still there, waiting...as if he had been there the entire time watching him while he slept.

"Florence, she wait for you," he said, speaking in that funny broken English that Haitians used.

Cedric stood up unabashedly, seemingly unaware of his nakedness and went into the bathroom to take a piss and to wash his hands and face in the porcelain basin there. Smoothing his hair by rote, since there was no mirror, he searched for his bag in vain—since it was already unpacked and the few clothes he had bought were hanging neatly in the closet. He dressed quickly, making himself presentable. Hopefully, Florence would see him now.

He had no idea what to expect, but he certainly hadn't expected the elaborate meal that awaited him. Fresh salad and fried plantains and entrees of fresh shrimp, sautéed conch and succulent lobster served on a bed of coconut flavored rice and beans awaited him, which he washed down with delicious French wine, fresh fruit, cheese and for dessert, lemon sherbet over sliced mangoes arrested his palette. Florence had prepared for him not a meal but a feast. Certainly, this was not a meal he would have expected on such short notice and from someone who lived in a third world country that made a living as a mambo. But then, what the hell did he know? Apparently Florence was doing quite well for herself living as she did. Very well...and he suspected she was quite used to offering these sophisticated little banquets served on impeccable gold-edged china to crazy Americans in need of her services.

He wasn't sure if she had heard about Arielle's death, and

told her somberly over coffee. She seemed genuinely surprised.

She asked all the usual questions that people always asked when you told them something like that. Then she fell silent and simply placed a hand on his arm. The concern in her voice was also tinged with deep remorse, perhaps even regret, and it gave him great comfort. Here was someone who had genuinely cared for Arielle.

"So you want to learn about her. You'd like to possibly contact her?"

Cedric felt a little tongue-tied, unable to pinpoint exactly what he wanted from her. "No," he said slowly shaking his head. "I'm in contact with her already. She talks to me all the time."

"Really," Florence said, again seemingly surprised. "Well, that shouldn't amaze me at all. Arielle was quite formidable. Her spirit must be a worthy one indeed if she can contact you on her own with a medium. Unless, you're a medium..."

Cedric shook his head in confusion and looked at her with a blank face, not comprehending or following where she was going.

"Never mind," she said, looking thoughtful.

"And so...what then would you like for me to do for you?"

"Look, Florence, Arielle wrote about you extensively in her journal. She said you have powers. I have a request to make of you because there's something she mentioned in her journal that has been haunting me for months. She said you could bring back the dead."

Florence smiled patiently. "Of course, I can bring back the dead. I do it every day. But you are apparently in no need of my services since you've just said that she contacts you on her own."

"No, Florence, I'm not talking about your run of the mill séance or anything like that. I'm talking about physically bringing her back."

"You're talking about a resurrection."

Cedric grinned. "Did you just call it a resurrection?"

"That's right. Like Jesus did to Lazarus."

Cedric tried to still his heart, but it was hammering out of control—right out of his chest. "Is that possible, Florence? Resurrections."

Florence was smiling widely now. "Sure...sure...all things are possible, my son. But it will cost you."

Cedric was smiling so hard, it was splitting his face. "Florence, baby, name your price!"

"Well, of course I couldn't do it by myself. I'm not that powerful, nor am I that kind of priestess. I practice only Rada

Voodoo."

"Rada Voodoo," he repeated. "And what's that?"

"Oh...just your standard run of the mill stuff... good voodoo. But what you need is a *bokors*. And not just any *bokors*, but a brilliant one."

"Please explain. What's a bokors?

"Mmmm...you might say that he's a priest but one gone bad—or who borders on the dark side. You see, a regular priest is about as powerful as I am. We call him an *hougan*. But a bokors is an hougan and more. They're normally who you visit if you want to put a curse on someone."

"And you can't do that."

"No, I don't do that. I'm who that person runs to lift the curse placed by the bokors," she smiled.

"Something like the good witch," Cedric teased.

She laughed and nodded her head.

"And so how do you lift the spell?"

"I don't lift the spell. I'm simply the medium...somewhat like a telephone operator—or rather in touch with the operator. I connect you to the spirit you need to get a hold of. Or maybe, you might say I'm the gatekeeper. Your guide to the spirit world. Except I'm friendly only to Rada spirits, the good spirits. The spirits you are in need of are the Petro ones, and so a bokors is what you need."

"So do you know any bokors?"

"Oh yes...but the one you need doesn't live here in Haiti. He lives in Nigeria."

Cedric was trying to slow down his heart-rate, it was still beating so fast. "Nigeria?! But hell, Florence, this is fucking Haiti. You guys are raising zombie's every night. Why do we have to deal with someone way in Nigeria?"

Florence laughed. "Oh, you're funny," she said, wiping a tear from her eye. "Yes, we do. But I don't think it's a zombie you want, my friend. I remember your wife very well. I remember her quite clearly and fondly. You wouldn't want her raised as a zombie. No, *cherie*, I know what it is you want. You want her back in her full glory, spectacular and dazzling, the way she had been in life."

Cedric couldn't disguise his pleasure. "Yes, but is it possible, Florence, to have her back in her *full glory*. Don't get my hopes up if you really can't."

Florence patted his hand. "My son, all things are possible in this world—so long as you have the cash to make it happen. You know the saying, money doesn't buy everything. Well, damn nearly buys most things—trust me."

Cedric closed his eyes, lifted her hand to his lips and pressed his mouth into the back of her hand. "Florence I'll give you all the money I have if you can do this."

"That won't be necessary, *mon chère*. I'm not greedy. No, I'll give you a price after I speak to my Nigerian friend and you come up with it...once you do, you'll have your resurrection, and trust me when I tell you, this *bokors* is good. The best I've ever seen, and you know why?"

"No..."

"Cause he's also a scientist. I've never seen anyone mix both things so well. You can have Arielle back, better than she was before. Splendid. Gorgeous...and here to appease your every pleasure."

Tears were pouring down his face now as he gazed at Florence with pure love. "I love you, Florence."

"I know," she said, as he kissed the back of her hand again.

And he honestly meant it.

16

Lifetime Guarantee

Kendra drove down the meticulously kept winding street, marveling at the fine homes in the expensive prestigious private community of LaGorce, the exclusive island on Miami Beach, where Cedric and Arielle had decided to build their dream house. In those homes, she knew, European heritage would be evident everywhere. Australian crystal chandeliers, sweeping mahogany staircases, and Baccarat crystals peeked from behind most of the drawn curtains. By all appearances, the owners of such homes would probably be mature individuals with great taste and a cultivated appreciation for objects of pedigree. But where would Cedric fit in, she wondered. It would have also taken these people several decades of collecting with a prudent eye to attain such elegant looks in their home, and so she couldn't help wondering what Cedric's new digs would be like?

As she hooked a left on Pinetree Drive, and spied the gate that would lead to Cedric's estate, she took a fortifying breath. Wow, she thought as she entered the driveway. Cedric had told her about this house he and Arielle had had built. He had just moved in that month and had invited her for the weekend.

His penthouse had sold a lot faster than he expected, and with his notoriety of late, he thought it would have taken awhile. Except these days infamy was better than just being famous. And so he was forced to move into a house he was still debating whether to keep.

Kendra whistled and shook her head as she drove inside. The depth of the architectural experience was apparent from every approach. Instead of simply arriving from the street to the house, you were confronted by a winding driveway that with a series of integrated formed squares, rectangles, triangles and circles— arranged in a series of pavilions. One of the first encounters with these forms was the entrance pavilion, supported by four columns leading to a courtyard and on to the main section of the house. To the left, was a freestanding four car garage which connected to the house via a 15-foot-long glass-enclosed bridge. And that was what was so fabulous about this house. All the huge glass plates. Talk about living in glass houses, yet it was beautiful. And private she supposed because of all the ground and all the hedges and foliage surrounding it.

Though attached, the configurations of the three-story multi-leveled mansion jutted out from the main section of the house to enclose the sweeping circular staircase and bent glass tower with a walkway over what looked like the living room which connected to the two upstairs wings. And all of this could be discerned from the outside looking in. It was unlike any other home she had ever seen. Totally unique.

She entered the entrance pavilion and was greeted by the 10-feet entrance doors. Solid mahogany with glass paneling that were etched in gold and which displayed their family crest—Kendra felt like who knew. Cedric told her the same crest was on his dad's gates and doors and was an old Viking crests from ancient times. "Too bad I don't know much about my Zulu roots. Wouldn't that be something," he laughed when he greeted her outside.

"Well, you know something. At least you're aware of being Zulu."

"Not necessarily. Wistful thinking on my part. I just always wanted to feel baaad, growing up. Thinking damn, Viking and Zulu. The best of both worlds!"

Kendra laughed. "Cedric, you're tripping."

"I'm tripping," he turned and smiled at her, coming up real close, unnerving her. "That's the first time I've ever heard you use slang. I like it." He said looking a little too long at her lips.

Kendra played it off by turning her attention to the fabulous house, trying not to wonder too hard at his underlying motives for showing it to her in the first place.

Upon entering the foyer, she took in her breath as the interior laid splayed before her. The first thing that caught her eyes was the champagne colored baby grand piano, which enjoyed a prominent spot in the living room near the built in bar. Behind the baby grand, also on built in panels were displayed his many trophies and awards. Her eyes traveled to the Grammies and gold and platinum records as well as a host of other awards. There were also several vintage, very beautiful looking guitars, probably priceless.

"Come, I'll show you around," Cedric motioned to her.

Indeed. She could get lost in here. It was a beautiful mixture of the old and the new. For instance, glass forms and wooden statues of African warriors and tribesmen fit strategically into niches dispersed throughout the house. Accentuating the positive, eliminating the negative seemed to be the idea for the entire house.

"This is gorgeous, Cedric. You guys had this place built to spec?"

"Yeah, it was our dream home. We worked on it together, Arielle and I. Every aspect. And she never got to see it finished."

"God, but you guys have great taste. I really love it!"

He smiled and continued showing her around.

The main living room consisted of voluminous space, adjacent to a more intimate sitting area. Lattillas above the entry way pierced into the sitting area to become the ceiling. Abundant glazing brought views of the outside bay and natural light to the entire space. The living room was almost totally translucent with large expanses of uninterrupted glass providing long distance viewing of Biscayne Bay and on the Atlantic Ocean. The glass height varied, depending on privacy needs.

There was a consistent use of highly lacquered woods for built-ins and furnishings with gorgeous cream-colored marbled floors, completing the polished and glossy look, complimenting the intricate African art collection. The collection's primitive, colorful and earthy characteristics countered the simple, stark and pure architectural design of the house, adding to the sleekness of its perfection. The geometric symmetry of the home needed to be softened a bit, and the African art did that. Adding texture and richness that contrasted yet brought beauty, making the house simply gorgeous, strikingly beautiful as a result.

She shuddered to think how much a home like this must have cost to build and decorate—not to mention the price paid for the prime location. Seven thousand square feet, Cedric was telling her, such a grand home for a single person. Excessive. Even if it had been built for the three of the them. But as if reading her mind, Cedric said, "I know, it's very large, but Arielle and I had planned on having lots of children." He laughed. "I think she wanted something close to ten."

"No way, not that woman I saw smiling in all those pictures with that awesome body. Maybe if she adopted them."

"Well, yeah, we had talked about adopting some too. But she had actually agreed to have at least four."

"How nice, and I'm sure you didn't mind siring all four kids.

Probably wouldn't have mind having all ten."

"No, not at all. But you're right about not wanting to ruin her body. I wouldn't have wanted that." Next he asked hospitably, "Can I get you something to drink? Some iced-tea?"

"Yes, that would be nice," Kendra said and smiled softly. "So are you keeping it," she asked as she followed him into the kitchen where a massive dark wrought iron pot rack hung over a solid pine lacquered island cabinets. She could see how this would be a favorite gathering spot for favored guests and Cedric himself. She knew how the kitchen was usually her favorite place in a house and this one was definitely warm and inviting. Open and airy, it featured the same lacquered and polished elegance of the whole house, displaying as an extra measure little hand-painted ivy leaves that decorated the crown molding finish of its interior cove that gave it just the right look.

"How do you manage here all on your own?"

"Hell, I'm hardly alone. My security is always around or a couple of the boys from the band—not to mention the fact that one of my friends may be visiting and usually stay over. It gets pretty live around her, believe me, depending on who's here visiting."

He handed her a tall glass of iced-tea and she smiled a thank you as he continued showing her around. They moved from the kitchen to the backyard, where a spectacular aquamarine lagoon-style pool, perfect for entertaining, took Kendra's breath away. There was a bridge that went to a center island with tropical foliage and a spitting waterfall, a veritable paradise. Lushly landscaped and completely screened, the pool lagoon was designed and enclosed with Mediterranean columns and arches that matched the architecture of the home. This flowed into the boat ramp where Cedric's new yacht was docked.

Kendra raised an eyebrow.

"I needed one." He laughed. "Honestly, how else was I going to floss for the neighbors. You see how big theirs is? You can't have a house like this and not have the accessories to go with it."

"I understand completely." Kendra teased, laughing too. "Do you ever take it out?"

"Are special agents special?"

She eyed him, smiling. "I don't know. It all depends."

"Do you trust me enough to go on an outing with me, say tomorrow?"

"Tomorrow? Gosh, that's real short notice."

"Well, you choose a date then, and I'll adjust to your time-table since my schedule is more flexible."

"Ummm…who else would be coming?"

He watched her with amusement. "Why just the two of us."

She looked horrified.

"Okay, I'm only kidding! Christ, you really looked terrified."

She giggled nervously. "You had me there for a second."

"Ha-ha!"

But he didn't look like he was teasing, Kendra thought. She could never tell when he was kidding or being serious about stuff. Nor did she know how to read his subtle changes in demeanor. It was like one moment she would think he was flirting with her, and then the next, she would think it was only wishful thinking on her part. Cedric was still very much in love with his dead wife, of that she was sure, and she wouldn't even entertain the thought of fooling herself. She felt sorry for any woman who taught they had half a chance with him when they didn't have a snowball's chance in hell.

She shuddered, even thinking about her and Cedric, feeling anger and terror and confusion all mixed together whenever she did. Despairing at all the crazy emotions he could make her feel, she felt relieved when he said, "Come, let me finish showing you the rest of the house."

He took her upstairs to the master bedroom, which was the essence of simplicity, with a massive four poster bed with plush, platinum tone on tone satin duvet covering the elaborate bed, there were plenty of toss pillows adding to its comfort. Kendra imagined sleeping on such a bed had to be the epitome of luxury…and making love on a bed like this…did she dare to even imagine.

Fingering the beautiful wooden antique chest sitting at the foot of the massive bed, she said, "This is beautiful," as she ran her fingers over the piece.

"It was a gift from my father's girlfriend, Miss Penny to Arielle. She said it was an old wedding chest passed from generation to generation in her family. Since it looked like my pops was never going to make an honest woman of her, she thought Arielle might as well have it for her wedding trousseau."

"Wow, that's wonderful. So traditional. And so what did Arielle end up using it for?"

"I'm not sure she ever got a chance to actually use it. But for now, I've saved a few of her things in it. Like her dry-cleaned wedding gown. Some of her special teddies that I remember with fondness," he winked. "CJ's christening clothes. Our wedding album. Family album. And all her journals and other personal things."

Kendra was staring at him in wonder. "Damn, you're so thoughtful. But why save all these things?"

"I don't know. I just couldn't throw them out or give them away. I don't know. They felt special."

"Did you save the little voodoo doll she had of you too?" Kendra couldn't help asking, not meaning to sound spiteful, except that was probably exactly how it sounded. Suddenly she felt hot with jealousy—it was that instant. How could Arielle had been disloyal to such a good man?

But her jealousy only confused Cedric, hurting him more. She felt so bad when she saw him flinch. "Oooow! Where did that come from, girl?" Their gazes locked for a few seconds.

"I'm sorry...I didn't mean to go there."

"Yeah, you did. You think I'm a fool."

Kendra smiled at that. "You've forgiven her all, haven't you? You don't even care about all the things she did. The betrayal. The doll she made of you. None of that matters to you, does it?"

"Why does it matter so much to you that it doesn't matter to me?"

Kendra swallowed hard. "I just can't understand...can't get over the fact that you can be so forgiving!"

"Not when you can't be, right?! One man broke your heart one time and that's it for all men. We're scum. Lowlifes. The whole lot of us. Not only would you never give that chump a second chance, but you'll never let any other guy come anywhere near you. At least not for a very long time. So it astounds you other people are more forgiving than you are. Than you could ever be... Well, you're in the right profession, Miss FBI. Attack dog, Stick up the ass, totally straight-laced. Perfect. Never one mistake!"

"You've got to be kidding me" Kendra raged. "You're upset with me?! What did I do? What did I say? Where the hell did all of that come from?" She asked indignantly, her head rearing back as her eyes locked with his. "What could I ever do that would be a third as bad than everything SHE did to you?!!"

"Just something I've been meaning to get off my chest. I'm sorry," he said glumly. "I shouldn't have gone there either..."

"No need to apologize. You told me what you felt."

"I just never realized you felt such hostility towards Arielle. What the hell did she ever do to YOU?"

Hurt you, she wanted to say. But how could she share that without revealing her true emotions towards him.

"I just don't get how you're constantly judging Arielle."

"And I just don't know why you're constantly defending her."

"Well, we'll just agree to disagree about her then."

"Fine by me," Kendra said with an exasperated sigh. "I'm just sick of hearing about her, that's all."

"You're jealous!" he accused.

"YOU WISH!"

He laughed. And soon, she couldn't help joining him

"Well, and I'm totally embarrassed. I've offended you. I've been judgmental, dissing you in your own home."

Cedric shook his head, shrugged and then plopped himself down on the bed. "Shit, this is horrible. Can we start over? Contrary to how it may appear, I didn't bring you here just to slam you...well, not verbally anyway," he joked.

Kendra smiled. "No, I deserved it. I made an uncouth remark and you had every right to defend your wife. Understandable."

"Let's agree to forget this."

"Okay. Forgotten."

"You want to finish the tour?" He stood up, heading to the door.

"Sure," she said following him.

"Are you positively sure." He deadpanned. "I know you...and how you can bear a grudge and shit."

She smiled widely, then brushed her hair back, looking fetchingly at him. He was so close she could see the fine, little nicks on his chin where he had cut himself shaving that morning. "I'm not at liberty to say."

"Cause if you don't, I'm going to have to introduce you to the tickle monster," he said holding out his forefinger, which was bent down at the tip. She could smell his spicy, fragrant cologne.

"The tickle monster?"

"Trust me, you don't want to meet him. He's a real bad cat."

Kendra was giggling now, almost forgetting all the comments he had made earlier. She had seen the tickle monster in action with CJ in Orlando. "You wouldn't dare introduce me to the tickle monster!"

"Mr. Monster..." he said turning the finger to himself, "did you hear that? I think she's daring us."

Kendra stumbled as she rushed to take a seat at the nearby breakfast nook. "Okay-okay. I'm not daring you. I'm pretty sure you would, but can we call a truce?"

"Mr. Monster, did you hear that? She wants to call a truce.

We mustn't forget she's an agent and learned all about hostile negotiations at the academy. We'll probably lose if we go into this trying to reason with her...uh-huh. I know what you mean."

"Ceeedric!" she shrieked as he moved towards her with that bent finger. "Please. I'm very ticklish. I swear, I'm going to hurt you if you come anywhere near me with that finger!"

"Did you hear that, Mr. Monster? Now she's resulted to actual threats."

Kendra was already giggling and bracing herself. "Please Cedric. Don't."

Cedric laughed raucously. "God, Kendra. You look really terrified."

"Please Cedric," she pleaded. "Don't tickle me."

He shook his head, smiling. "Okay, baby. Settle down," he said coming to sit next to her. "I promise, I won't tickle you."

Kendra didn't look as if she believed him.

He laughed easily, settling back next to her, grinning wickedly. "No, really, I promise not to tickle you."

Kendra relaxed somewhat observing how this breakfast nook was the perfect spot for watching the sunrise or for sharing a romantic breakfast. The table had a cloth of antique gold that looked as if it had been sewn with actual gold thread. Kendra ran her hand over the cloth, examining it. The embroidery was so fine.

"Arabic," Cedric supplied.

"Don't tell me, another gift from Miss Penny."

"No, a wedding gift from the family of an Arab prince I used to go to school with. His dad is also an old friend of my pops."

Kendra raised an eyebrow. "My-my, Cedric. You're full of surprises."

"Yeah, and you thought you knew everything about me."

"So where did you go to school? How did you meet this Arab prince?"

He smiled. "Wouldn't you like to know. But I don't feel like talking about any of that right now. I promise to tell you someday though."

Someday. His choice of words jolted her mind. So he was thinking about the future and seeing her in it. That was very interesting, as well as disturbing, considering everything.

She got up and went out on the other side, making her way to the master bath, where slate had been used generously—on a wall inlay above the tub, around the shower and floor for detail. The octagon-shaped bath had a bird's eye view of the bay without privacy concerns. Who could see you? No one. But you could see the sky and entire bay, it would be heavenly bathing in bubbles and oils and staring out the huge picture window.

Kendra picked up one of the two beautifully framed photographs sitting on the marble mantle. The only two pictures she had seen displayed so far. The smaller one was a 5X7 picture of CJ, one where he was blowing out a candle. The other one was an 8X10 of Arielle smiling beautifully with nothing on but a leopard sarong around a neat, tiny waist and a big straw hat, covering her breasts unsuccessfully with her arms.

"She had a sensational body," Kendra admitted aloud.

"Yes, she did," Cedric agreed. "I snapped that of her on our honeymoon in Martinique. That's one of the few pictures I have of her—other than our wedding pictures. You know, for such a beautiful woman, she was rather camera-shy."

"Happens," Kendra said, still staring at the picture. "She was very good-looking, though. I can see why you're still so in love with her. She had the most beautiful smile."

Cedric looked as if he had been kicked in the stomach. Like it was physically painful to even look at her.

Kendra carefully placed the frame down. Christ, he was in love! And it was so beautiful yet so infuriating at the same time. She didn't chose to comment about the state of his discomfort but let her eyes wander instead. She'd simply have to reign in all those jealous emotions and instead channel her energy and attention to the nice time they were sharing.

The upstairs sitting room, just off the master bedroom was a comfortable spot for morning coffee or afternoon tea. But the *pièce de resistance* truly had to be the upstairs terrace, an arched, arcade which looked down into the lagoon-style pool, meandering and dominating the second roof levels, allowing one to take full advantage of the LaGorce waterfront setting.

He followed her out, keeping pace with her until they reached the guard walls. "This is my absolute favorite spot in the whole house," he confessed. "I love coming out here to unwind. The view just totally relaxes me."

With its sweeping view of Biscayne Bay, the terrace inspired a sense of peace and lightness. Even liberation. It was set with a bronze wrought iron dinette, crème-colored folding armchairs and accented with Mexican mosaic insets.

They left the terrace reluctantly and went back into the house. "If she were alive, I know this would be her favorite room in the house," Cedric said leading her down a plush corridor into a beautiful library gallery. The arched ceilings, delightful gold panels, natural wood highly lacquered in-built shelves held colorful paintings, pictures, books, CDs, tapes, and one-of-a-kind artifacts. Kendra loved it too, she could spend an eternity in there and not get bored. There were many African masks, some more of Cedric's gold and platinum album plaques. More awards and statues. Some even for Arielle. *Ah, there, how sweet,* Arielle's Bachelor Degree from the University of Florida. A Bachelor of Arts in Journalism, all framed and nice, "Wow," was all she could bring herself to say. "So many awards and books."

"Yes, Arielle definitely liked to read."

And write, Kendra thought jealously, but she wouldn't go there again.

Strewn in corners were green plants, along with fresh exotic flowers arranged in crystal, glass vases. "I absolutely love this room," Kendra told him.

"Yeah, and I thought you would too." Cedric grinned.

The house boasted eight other very large rooms, one of which was the most complete and creatively decorated child's room she had ever seen—adjoined to a playroom. It was like being on a safari with bamboo panels, makeshift trees hanging stuffed monkeys, lions, and colorful parrots. It was amazing! Yet it looked like CJ hadn't been there. There was also a nicely furnished room, which Cedric said was the nanny's room.

Five more rooms made up the guest bedrooms, all equipped with their own baths and sitting rooms. And there were three more baths located on the first floor—one near the foyer, another towards the kitchen and the one outside, that was more part of the cabana for the pool.

Cedric's new place was awesome, a grand home but she still couldn't get over the fact that it belonged to someone still in his twenties. Nor that he would be the only one living there, basically

"So are you going to keep it or sell it?"

"I haven't decided. So far, the plan is to keep it. I love Miami, and I have no intentions of living anywhere else. At least not now. But the house is so massive. The upkeep is mind-boggling. So far I've had to hire quite a few people to take care of things. I figure I might need house-sitters—preferably a married older couple to see over things. Just the upkeep of the grounds alone is a task, but I think I've found this Venezuelan couple that might work out. He'll do the maintenance and gardening and she'll cook and do the cleaning around the house."

"Gosh, sounds perfect."

"Just wish they spoke more English."

Kendra laughed. "Oh well, this is Miami after all."

"I know...can't have everything. Man," he said with a deep sigh, "just wished she could have seen it. Her work, her idea come to fruition."

Kendra swallowed hard. *Here it was again...*

"It's weird...when we were building it, I never thought once that Arielle wouldn't be here to live in it. I even thought of it as more her house than mine. Not sure I can imagine another women living in it."

Kendra blanched.

"Does it really bother you when I speak about Arielle?"

"No." She shrugged, "it's just that it's always about her. You made her your first priority when she was alive, didn't you? And now, even though she's gone, she's still first."

"Why would you say that? She could hardly be first. Not anymore. But why does it annoy you so, even if she were?"

"I guess it's your business how you choose to live your life.

He was chuckling now.

"What's so funny?"

"You."

"What's so funny about me?"

"You know you want me. Want my ass bad. And you're plenty jealous of Arielle too. But you can't admit it, probably not even to yourself."

She sucked in her breath dramatically. "Aren't we full of ourselves? Goodness, Cedric, am I that transparent?! I want you, I want you, oh, baby, oh, baby!"

"God, I can't believe you. You lifted the line right from that movie.

"Yes."

"*Ten Things I Hate About You*," they said together and laughed again.

"You're too funny, the way you performed it with such a fan's relish," Cedric said grabbing her around the neck and playfully putting her in a headlock and then ruffling her hair.

It was a genuinely playful move, a gesture that a guy would pull on his sister or someone he was totally not interested in sexually. Only a friend, Kendra realized her heart sinking. Cedric saw her as only a friend. And all the sexual tension and all the emotion she felt was solely on her part. Sure, if she allowed him, if she let him make love to her, he would do her. Oblige her. But did he feel *real* attraction towards her beyond her reminding him of Arielle? She doubted it. And for a second, this made her extremely sad.

Perhaps it was best if their relationship was purely platonic, she quickly decided, reigning in her emotions. For sure she didn't need the headache and heartache getting involved with Cedric would entail, and she really needed to pull away from him. Take some time apart. Truly apart. Perhaps she'd even ask for a reassignment. New York was looking better and better every day. 'Cause whatever they were transiting into was toxic. When a relationship started to hurt more than it felt good, it was time to end it.

"You're so cute, though. That's the only reason I like having you around. Why I dig you so much," he said. "You keep things interesting."

"Really?" she said with a sad little shrug. "Is that the only reason?"

He gave her a boyish grin. "No, not actually. I'm hoping too that someday you're going to break down and give up the booty too," he said shamelessly, then winked half-jokingly.

But the truth was, Kendra hardly saw it as a joke, and she was tired of being teased.

They ended up in the living room where the tour had started hours ago and to Kendra, it felt like she had gone to hell and back. Sure, she had enjoyed in part being with him, but Lord, all the talk of Arielle had effectively choked all the happiness out of her. And while yes, she wanted him, wanted him in a bad way, she had to admit to herself that he was reigning havoc on her emotions. One moment he treated her like a friend, the next he was hitting on her, making her feel desired. It was exhausting!

Hell, if she had any guts, if she were half the woman she knew Arielle had been, she'd just grab him by the collar and just plant him with a Mack Daddy kiss, one he wouldn't soon forget and fuck him where he stood.

But she wasn't that bold. She wasn't a bad-girl and didn't have it in her to be the aggressor. And even though Cedric had given her ample opportunities to make her move, nothing would ever happen between them if he didn't initiate it himself. Simple as that. The risk of possible rejection would always make her cower, and she'd never risk the embarrassment it might entail.

All the sex talk could just be harmless banter. It didn't mean that he really wanted to have a relationship or even casual sex with her. What if she was reading him all wrong and he wasn't interested in her at all in that way? What if this was just the way Cedric was, just a flirt, and he only saw her as a friend?

Cedric could have practically any woman he wanted. If he wanted. Whenever he wanted. Why should he want her? What was so wonderful about her?

She stood there and could do nothing but just grin sweetly at him. After a beat, he turned away and started telling her about another piece of furniture, and the moment simply passed. They were back to being pals—and she suspected that's pretty much all they'd ever be.

17

Those Lips...Those Eyes

Against her better judgment, she did go sailing with him the next weekend, knowing it was crazy and dangerous especially since she hadn't been able to get him out of her mind since that day at the house. Luckily for her, Bailey had come along with a girlfriend and she was so grateful they weren't alone. Cedric had probably arranged it like that so she would feel more comfortable.

Regardless, she was clumsy and distracted and had sex on the brain the entire trip. Sex was never far from her mind when Cedric was around, but that weekend in particular it seemed she couldn't stop thinking about it. She even dreamed about making love on that huge four poster bed in his master bedroom. The sex was hot and vigorous. Unlike any sex she had ever had. The things he had said and done, the positions they had tried, she was blushing just thinking about it. How perverted she'd become. If only he knew...about those racy, dirty, intoxicating dreams. She could hear his buttery voice now, *"Yeah, you're a freak, baby. Straight up."*

They sailed to the Keys Friday afternoon, ate at Don Shula's place down there, his Steak House, which was fairly new, only about a year old. It was a pretty pleasant day. They went sightseeing, visited the home of Ernest Hemingway and then went dancing that night. The people in the Keys sure knew how to party. Key West reminded her much of the French Quarters of New Orleans' Bourbon Street.

They slept in real late the next day and then took the yacht out to sea and went deep sea diving, exploring Key Largo's coral reef. They didn't get back in until Sunday evening and Bailey and his girl asked if they'd like to join them and go to the movies. Both she and Cedric rushed to make excuses and then both laughed while they made them up. Kendra rushed to make her excuse to take her leave too, but Cedric wasn't having it. "I have to talk to you," he said.

"Yeah, about what?"

"I have to talk to you. Wait. It'll keep. Let me see the kids off."

They walked Bailey and his friend, Ashley, to the garage and Kendra watched Cedric hug Bailey like a brother. They had gotten really close it seemed. She guessed Bailey was now his only real link to Arielle—other than CJ. She wrinkled her nose as she always seemed to do now at any thought of Arielle. Cedric would never get over that woman, she thought feeling her heart sink.

They walked back to the house, and she felt really uncomfortable when Cedric clasped her hand lightly and walked back into the house with her. She didn't want to admit how nice it felt. How wonderful it would be to get together with him, to be the lady of the manor. It felt so right and being with him, sharing this moment, walking their guest out, holding hands, walking back into the house felt splendidly beautiful.

As soon as the door closed, Cedric pulled her into his arms and kissed her soundly on the mouth. Nothing sloppy. Just a slow, sexy, tantalizing kiss—not even with tongue—that left her breathless. Kendra was too surprised to even kiss him back, but just stood there and let him do it.

"What are you doing," she asked as soon as he broke the kiss. "What did you have to talk to me about," she said pushing him away a little so she could breathe.

"That," he said blowing a breath and leaned against the door.

"You stopped me from leaving so you could kiss me?" She gave him a skeptical look.

"Actually, I'd like more than that...," he said moving toward her, "but I'm not sure you're open to it. Sorry. I was mistaken."

Without saying a word, Kendra picked up her bag that was on the foyer table and stood there as if ready to leave and started to push past him.

"You have a problem, you know that," he said blocking her passage.

"Yeah, well so do you."

"Are you medically frigid or is it psychological?"

"And you, my friend, have a colossal ego. You can't believe that a woman wouldn't want to sleep with you. She'd have to be frigid or a dyke or something. A woman can't just not want to *fuck* you!"

He laughed. "I test for AIDS regularly. Just recently...in fact...and I'm clean. I also have plenty of condoms."

"Oh, I know. A whole drawer full. I've come across them."

"So do you want to get down or not?"

She smiled sweetly. "Really, Cedric, I'm disappointed in you. This is the way you ask a woman to go to bed with you? I would have thought your approach would have been," she searched for the word, "a bit more refined. I thought you'd be a lot smoother than that—with your reputation and all as a die-hard womanizer, a hard-core international playboy. Frankly, I was expecting a whole lot more," she admonished, wanting to put him in his place. "You know, a little more class!"

His face grew serious. "Why do you have to be such a class-A bitch? What are you trying to prove?"

"And what may I ask are *you* trying to prove?" she rebuked. "Like you need another notch on your belt."

He shrugged. "All right then. Suit yourself. You want to play games, play with it! I'm not gonna chase after you if that's what you're expecting."

"Okay, wonderful then. So now why don't you please get out of my way."

He started to move, then grabbed her by the collar, drawing her up against the length of his body, lifting her onto the toes of her sandals as he bent his head to reach her mouth. In total surprise, her body betrayed her by leaning into him, her body taking on a mind of its own. Arching her back and pressing her hips against his thighs, she was conscious of the hardness in his loins and felt how very much he wanted her. Damn, she thought to herself as this time his tongue darted into her mouth, exploring and questing and she returned his kiss tentatively. She wanted to throw her arms around his neck and breathe him in, but she resisted, keeping her hands at her sides. Remaining calm and cool.

When at last he moved his mouth from hers and brushed it along her cheek to her jaw and then pressed his lips to the sensitive hollow behind her ears, Kendra had to close her eyes and still herself not to faint dead in his arms. How long had she ached to have him doing just what he was doing now? Kendra exalted in the low groan that came from his throat and as he pulled away to stare at her, their faces real close, she couldn't even breathe. "Good-bye," Cedric said, letting go of her collar. "Leave now or…I'm not sure what I might do."

She stood there as if rooted to the spot. He watched her and then walked away, going to the door and turned the knob, opening it for her. Still, she made no move to leave, but just stood there watching him watch her.

"You have 10 seconds to leave. One…if I close this

door...two...I'm carrying you upstairs...three...and there won't be a thing...four...you can do...five...to stop me. Six...so I suggest...seven...you take your—"

"Stop counting," she said.

He looked over at her and pushed the door. It slammed shut.

"All right. So here are my rules. If you think you're gonna go upstairs and then renig, pull out at the last second, it ain't happening. And if you think I'm gonna be a gentleman or any other bullshit like that, I'm not. This is gonna be a lights-on, no-cover, slow screw. No romance or any other shit like that. You don't strike me as the romantic-type in any case. It's gonna be all about the biology, okay baby..."

Kendra said nothing, allowing him to continue.

"I like it nasty and dirty and yes, I'll expect you to go down on me too."

"Oh, and I guess you expect me to swallow too."

"Only if you're into that."

"And will you go down on me?"

"You bet," he said, coming back up and circling her. "Most definitely, you have been tested, haven't you?"

"Yes," she said blowing a breath. *"I'm clean,"* she said mimicking what he had said.

"Are there any rules that I should know about," he said coming to stand before her.

"It takes me a long time to come," she said looking him directly in the eyes, as he moved closer invading her personal space. "Also, it's been a while. So I might be..." she bit her lips, and he hoisted her up, grabbing her by the waist. She wrapped her arms around his neck and her legs around his hips, "a little tight.," she finished, and brought her lips down to meet his.

Just then her cellular phone and pager started at the same time. "Oh shit! Oh shit!" She apologized, as he settled her down and she reached into her handbag.

"Don't answer it," he urged her.

"But I have to."

"Please don't answer, turn everything off...please...for me. I need you, Dra, so badly."

She looked at him and then at her pager. He'd call her Dra and she liked the sound of it, but it was Neff.

"It's Neff," she said in a strained whisper, "and it's 911. I have to take this call, Cedric," she said in an agonized little voice, so remorseful, then pressed talk.

Cedric glared at her and snorted.

"Hell, I have to go!"

"Don't do it, Kendra. I swear to God! What would they have done had you not answered? Hell, the shit would have just gone down without you."

"I have to go, Cedric. I swear to God, I have to go!"

Their eyes locked and she understood something very important was happening. He didn't have to say a word, but she understood if she walked out the door that she was destroying whatever it was between them. Something that was just budding—their mutual attraction to each other, which was now so damned strong—it could no longer be denied.

She felt the inner tug that tempted her to run back into his arms as she explored his face, but like an old habit, her training took over and she resisted. She couldn't stay, no matter how much she wanted. Not when it meant her partner might be in trouble. She couldn't let Neff down. It could be his life...and how could she trade his life for sex. Even if that sex came with so much love on her part. She couldn't justify staying. Not to herself. She couldn't do it. And she knew what walking out that door signified. She would be walking out on Cedric for a second time, leaving him wanting her, hurting. But she had to do it. Quickly, before losing her nerves, she walked through the doorway and left him without saying a word. What could she say in any case?

Much later as she lied in bed...alone, she cried incessantly. Neff was okay, and all was well with the world—except she knew Cedric would never understand. The scene of what had happened unfolded over and over in her mind, communicating how this was a life-changing event. It had been a *wake-up and pay attention moment,* but one she hadn't heeded.

The plain and simple truth of the matter was that she had chosen her job over him. And maybe she could have handled things differently. But clearly, she had told him what was most important to her. And God, it wasn't. It really wasn't. Nothing was more important to her than him, but she didn't know how to handle him. She was losing control, losing herself and she didn't know how to go on anymore!

She cried and cried, hiccupping and balling into the darkness of her bedroom. She didn't dare pick up the phone to call him. Maybe she could race over there to finish what they had started. Except, she was such a coward and the fear of possible rejection was too much to contemplate.

***

There was nothing more powerful than having the power of your own convictions. When you could look into your heart and see yourself clearly—with absolute clarity—there was nothing you couldn't accomplish. Nothing was impossible to do.

This was so wrong what I was about to do. It really was. I knew it. Understood it. But ask me if I cared. If I really gave a damn. Did I care about how many commandments I was about to break? Perhaps I would burn in eternal hell—if there was such a place. Yet even if there was, I was going to do this anyway. There was no turning back now. I was going to go through with this regardless of what. Kendra had finally convinced me of what I needed to do.

I was going insane with this news. It was like once I had accepted the fact that this was what I was going to do, I couldn't help myself. I had to tell someone. I'm not sure why I chose Kendra of all people to tell. We hadn't spoken for weeks after the sailing trip. She hadn't called me and I hadn't called her. It was one of those situations that I thought I'd better leave alone. We both had needed a cooling off period, and besides that, Kendra was a great friend and would always be. I wasn't sure what she'd be like as a lover and I was through trying to find out.

She was surprised when I called her and asked to get together. My call seemed to come as a shock to her. She hadn't expected me to want to talk or meet with her after the second time she had run out on me.

"Where do you want to meet?" she asked coolly.

"You name the place."

She chose the Crystal Café, a Manhattan-style eatery on the Beach that served a continental cuisine. Once we were seated and served, I started immediately on my reason for inviting her out.

"Remember all that magic shit that Arielle had written about in her journal?"

"Yeah. All the voodoo and that terrifying doll with your face on it? Sure, I remember perfectly," she said a little bitterly

I gave her a sideways glance. She loved to rub that in, and did so every opportunity she got. "Yeah, all of that. Well, guess who I've been speaking to?"

"Who?"

"Florence."

She took in her breath. "You got in touch with Florence?"

"Yes."

"Whatever for?"

"What the hell do you think? I'm bringing her back."

"YOU'RE WHAT?!

"I'm bringing her back."

"Are you insane?!"

"Nope. This is the sanest thing I'm ever going to do."

"Why would you even—"

"Why wouldn't I? If a person is drowning, is it wrong for that person to try and save himself? Isn't the will to live and thrive not one of the strongest for a human-being?"

"Cedric," she said looking at me with so much pity. "This just makes no sense. There's too many variables. It's..." she seemed speechless, like she unable to proceed.

"There's so many things about life that makes no sense, Kendra. So many things that are totally unfair. Justice is blind. We hear that all the time. But if being who I am and having all this money evens things up a little and open those eyes—then fuck it! You think I wouldn't try everything to have her back?!"

"How do you plan on doing this exactly? Are you having her cloned or something?"

Cedric laughed. "Nothing as inane as that, although that is a possibility if this doesn't work. Nope, I'm having her resurrected."

"Resurrected?!"

"Yes."

Kendra was laughing now. "You've lost it. Oh my God, Cedric, you've really lost it!"

Cedric was grinning from ear-to-ear. "That's what you think. But it can be done, Florence assures me."

"I know you would do anything to have her back, Cedric. And it's beautiful how very much you love and grieve her. I have no doubt you would do anything for her. But you can't do this. This is not the way. It's sick. Repulsive. And it's desecrating to her memory. How can you even think of doing this? It's ridiculous! Like Frankenstein's' monster!"

"It's what I want. And maybe it's not going to work. Maybe Florence is just this big faker, making promises she absolutely can't fulfill. And maybe I'll hate her afterwards for giving me this false hope, but you're the one that's insane if you don't think I'm going to at least try it."

"You can't do this, Cedric. I won't let you," Kendra told me. "Let it go, let her go! I know the way she left was awful. That her murder was brutal and final and that it left you feeling hopeless. I understand that. Given all those dreadful circumstances, if I lost someone I was crazy about—I'd be feeling much the same way you do. But Cedric, don't lose your mind here! You're talking about bringing back someone who's dead. Who died close to a year ago. You're talking about letting this crazy Haitian priestess raise your wife as a zombie. What the hell are you thinking?!"

"Why do you call her crazy. How do you know she can't do what she's told me she can do?"

"I don't doubt that she could raise her. Well, maybe I do," Kendra spoke quickly. "I'm not sure I believe in that mambo-jumbo. But even if she could, would you really want to deal with that? It sounds horrific, Cedric. It sounds desperate. Insane. Why do you even want this? Why? You have everything in the world. It's not worth it. Move on with your life. Let this go, Cedric. You have a great career. You're famous, rich, and you have a beautiful little boy. Let this go. Don't go down this road!"

"Stop your pretty little speeches. You can't convince me and you certainly can't stop me. I'll do what I damn well please."

"Bring her back for what, Cedric. For what?!"

I laughed. "Why, to get even with her, of course."

She was fuming now. "ARE YOU CRAZY?!!!"

I laughed again. "Christ! Calm down, Kendra. You'll pop a blood vessel," I snapped.

"This is wicked, Cedric. I can understand you being driven by love and despair, reaching out to her to seek comfort. I can see you being weak for her. But doing this out of some strange sense of vengeance. No, Cedric, that's sick! It's also evil..."

"Your point-of-view. Not mine."

"I'll bring you to justice."

"Yeah, how? How are you going to do that, my darling? You can't accuse me of murdering someone who's already dead. They'll put you in the loony bin, and you know what, that'll be on you. Why don't you get off my tip, and go on with your life. Forget you even knew me. We're no good for one another."

Kendra looked dumbfounded and then angry. Angry as hell. "Why even tell me this," she spat. "Why?!!"

"Why, to fuck with you, of course." I said, then laughed again. And that was only a half-lie. "Maybe if you hadn't left me high and dry that day at the house a few weeks ago, had you made love to me like any proper woman would, maybe things would have been different. Who knows?"

Kendra was fuming but remained silent.

"Maybe you could have helped me to forget her," I continued

accusingly, loving how I was getting to her. "I don't know. But now, I'm going for this. I feel it in my bones that it might work, so I'm going full-speed ahead. I'm getting my wife back!"

Kendra was staring at me as if totally horrified. And like she wanted to give me a sound thrashing too. Finally she said, "Booze and drugs sure do destroy the mind."

That hurt and I groaned. "Don't start that again. In fact, I've been drinking and smoking a lot less these past few days. "You see, there's light at the end of the deep, dark tunnel. Anyhow, I needed someone to confide in and well, you seemed as good a person as any. I wanted to use you as a sounding board, and now, I'm convinced. I absolutely must do this."

"Yeah," she said solemnly, "why, thank you. Thanks so much for confiding in me, Cedric," she said sardonically and took a sip of her water. "By the way, just for the record, I think you're nuts. Really insane. Leah's not the only person who should be locked up!"

The rest of our lunch was pretty quiet after that. I ate heartily, happy in the knowledge that I was going to totally go for this, Kendra Jade be damned. And she looked as if she was having much difficulty swallowing her food.

So what if she didn't like it or thought me crazy. Her issue, not mine...In fact, it didn't surprise me when she wiped her mouth with a napkin, and got up and left the table without so much as a goodbye or thank you for the lunch.

This was Kendra, I was learning. She fled rather than stayed to fight. But rather than trying to understand the moods or whims and the vagaries of another woman, Arielle resurrected would suit me just fine. Besides, the memories of her lips and eyes haunted me daily.

No, I had to go through with it, had to see this to its conclusion. My struggle would soon be over. I was getting Arielle back any way I could get her. And if that was crazy, then so be it.

***

I had several conversations with Florence before I actually met with her and her Nigerian friend. I wanted to be clear on everything before I started rejoicing. I still couldn't believe what Florence had promised and so I called her nearly every night just so I could be reassured again and again.

"Human beings are suppose to be here for only a certain time," she explained, "and then they pass on. But the moment you find out that you can live forever—that time can be endless—well, it's mind-boggling. Who could refuse that, correct? Except you cease being human and become something else."

"What else is there?"

"Oh, my friend, the world is full of creatures. All kinds of creatures. You think you see a person standing in front of you sometimes, except they're not human at all."

"Florence, this is getting freaky-scary. Will Arielle be one of these creatures if I bring her back? Will she have to drink blood and howl at the moon and stuff like that?"

Florence laughed.

"No, seriously. She won't be turning into a werewolf during full moons, will she?"

"Cedric, I think you watch too much TV."

"I guess what I'm asking is, will she be normal?"

"Very normal."

"Is she going to be able to go out in the sun?"

"Well, not at first because she won't be used to bright lights. At first, you're going to have to keep everything very dim, and then maybe introduce her to candle light, then artificial light, something with low wattage. Then eventually, as she gets used to seeing light again, then you can start letting in a little sunshine until her eyes readjusts itself and she's able to bear the full brunt of the sun."

"Wow, there's so much I suppose I need to know. But is something like this even right? Giving life back, having my own life back?"

"No one has their own life. Not really. We're all connected somehow, don't ask me to explain. I can't. We're all part of something larger. You want to stand your moral ground? Tell me you don't want your wife back? That you don't long to hold her in your arms more than anything else in the world—or that you wouldn't pay me anything I asked if I could do that for you?"

I shook my head in disbelief. Unable to believe what I was hearing. "Florence, I just don't know if I can believe it."

"It's not about the money. It's not about whether it's right or wrong. It's whether I have the power to do it. To make it happen. And I assure you that I do. That I can make it happen. But for what you need, I can't work alone. I'm going to need help. But I promise you, you'll have your woman, your love back in your arms. And this time, she won't stray. I'll instruct you on how to master her. This time she'll be absolutely yours. "

"What do you mean by that?"

"You'll be her master. You're raising her to serve you, *n'est-ce pas?*"

"To serve me," I said incredulously. "*Au contraire,*" I said and laughed. "Um...I'll probably be the one serving her, but that's a very interesting word."

"You will be her master. She will do her all to please you."

"Mmmm...I like that. I like the sound of that. Her master, huh?"

"She will do whatever you wish."

"But she will have her old personality, won't she?"

"Oh, yes, I'm sure. I remember Arielle, she had a rebellious streak. Not saying you might not have to crack the whip—"

"Crack the whip?!" I was laughing again. "That would be the day. I want her to have that same passion, that same fire she had before she died. That's really important. She will be exactly the same personality-wise, won't she?"

Florence giggled. "Of course, Cedric. Of course. She will have the same soul. Therefore the same personality. Except..."

"Except?" Cedric said raising a brow.

"Well, at first she may seem a little younger."

"What do you mean, Florence?"

"Well...some people come back younger."

"Younger? How much younger?"

"Well, some people come out real child-like. They lose a few years."

"Like how many years?"

"Some as much as ten."

I whistled. For her that would be pretty damn young. Ummm, Arielle at sixteen. Gosh, that would be something. "I'm getting really excited here, Florence."

Florence was giggling. "Oh, Cedric. You're perfectly awful."

***

The meeting took place a few weeks later at Florence's estate on the outdoor verandah. The Nigerian witch doctor was dressed in a stylish olive designer suit and looked extra sleek—like a top New York executive. He did not have the warmth and charm Florence emanated, but he seemed knowledgeable and competent. He spoke English with a British accent and sounded well-educated, very professional. But Cedric wondered if he could really trust him.

"Okay, let's get this straight," Dr. Ottawa started right off. "Was there an autopsy done?"

"She was fucking murdered, man. What do you think?" I exploded. I wasn't sure I liked this guy at all. He seemed too forward, too slick and polished. This guy was all-business, which could be good, but then again, it could also be bad.

Florence placed a hand on my shoulder, then started to massage my neck. I was very tense. And this was so important.

"Look, man," Mr. Ottowa said tersely, "I'm prepared to do this thing. I know there's a lot of emotion and money on the line here. But you have to work with me if I'm to do this properly. Just to give you a little information about me," he said pulling out a portfolio to show him, "I'm an M.D, went to Harvard Medical School, graduated suma cum laude, I have a practice in Nigeria. Have been a Board Certified Plastic surgeon for over 15 years. I am also a sixth generation witch doctor. I was born with this incredible gift and even though I am a man of science, I do not shun the old ways. I've embraced them, and made a marriage of them with the science. I want to help you. Florence have told me a great deal about you and how much you adored your wife. I will do the best I can to get her back to you as soon as possible. But you must work with me."

I could not believe what I was hearing. I was thinking it would be all magic, but here this guy was a doctor, a scientist. What the hell—but I was going along. Still, I couldn't help saying, "you're not bringing her back scientifically, are you? Like Frankenstein's monster, are you?" It was probably an ignorant thing to say, but I couldn't help it.

"No, nothing like that. I assure you, there's plenty of magic involved. My being a plastic surgeon and medical doctor is only an added pert. You know, and it pleases me that you understand the significance of the magic since most étrangers, do not."

"Hell yeah! I absolutely want the magic, cause otherwise..."

He laughed. "You've seen too many movies."

"No shit! But good," I said with some relief. "Of course, there was an autopsy done. She was murdered. It was in the United States, and it's standard procedure as you well know. Will that be a problem?"

"Well, it depends on the doctor performing the autopsy. If he worked neat or if he butchered her."

I flinched.

"I'm sorry."

"She looked pretty good at the funeral. In fact she was really beautiful, and looked only as if she were sleeping. But it wasn't like I inspected her whole body, so I'm just talking about her face. Who knows what was doing underneath her clothes."

"Well, I'm referring to her insides in any case. Even had you inspected, her skin would hardly be a problem. Was she an organ donor? Could there be parts missing?"

I grimaced this time. Man, this guy was really hard-core. "No, of course I don't know for sure what they did. But as far as I know, everything should be intact."

"Good. Good."

"Now how was her body disposed of?"

"What do you mean?"

"Was she buried in the ground or in a mausoleum?"

"Oh, I see what you mean. She's in a mausoleum, man. In fact, it's an air-conditioned one. Only the very best for my baby."

Florence smiled, patted me on the back and had a seat beside me, talking one of my hands in hers. She understood how this couldn't be easy, and I appreciated the comfort.

"Very good," Dr. Ottawa said looking very pleased. "God bless America!"

"That's wonderful news, Cedric," Florence said, taking my hand, clasping it in hers. "We were, of course, concerned about the condition of the body. It's been about a year. Of course there are always things we could do, but the condition of the body is very important."

"Of course," I said. "So do you think you can do it. Give it to me straight."

"Mr. Courage, it's more than possible. We can bring her back."

"Swear to God."

Florence and Mr. Ottawa both looked at each other and laughed

"Oh, we swear it. You'll have your Arielle back. I assure you," he said. "Just get the body to us, and we'll take care of the rest. Just remember that the body has to remain in as good as condition as possible. That might mean flying her in on a private plane, and greasing the palms of some greedy Customs officials so that everything happens at warp speed."

"Money is not an issue here. I'll do whatever I have to do."

"Good," he said again.

Florence smiled at me, "Why would you even care? You're getting Arielle back! And she's priceless."

"Priceless indeed," Dr. Ottawa said and wrote down a seven figure number. "Here's my price."

I nodded, agreeing with Florence. Thinking that was cheap

actually. I had been willing to pay a whole lot more.

"Oh, that's just my portion," he said.

Florence wrote down hers. Six figures.

I nodded again—not even thinking about negotiating. Pops would have been pretty disappointed in me, but I wasn't about to squabble over price. "Guys, I think we've got ourselves a deal." I told them both and broke out a stogie. Hell, let the celebration begin!

18

Flesh of My Flesh, Blood of My Blood

The details were very important. Cedric kept reminding himself.

The house was all prepared.

The timing had to be perfect.

Dr. Ottowa said the stars had to be perfectly aligned. The lighting perfect.

There were candles everywhere. Statues. Symbols. Old, dusty books. There was lots of magic involved, he kept assuring him. "You can not be faint of heart. You must absolutely believe. You can not doubt it, if you're to be here. Faith is everything. Do you believe we can do this? Honestly?"

"You said you can do it, I believe you," Cedric said simply.

"We can not have any doubt, any negative energy. You understand that?"

"Absolutely!"

"You might hinder the process."

"I understand. I don't doubt you." Cedric looked around. "Why don't you ask some of these other people here?"

"Oh, they've seen rituals like this dozens of times. They don't doubt it can be done. It's you I'm worried about."

"Look, doc. I'm cool. *Do your thang.*"

"There are certain things we need to discuss first, you and I. Certain things I need you to absolutely understand."

"Go on."

"This is not something to do lightly. Do you understand? I need to know you understand the significance of what's about to impart."

Cedric chuckled. "Understand…"

"Yes, understand."

"Enlighten me, Doc. It may be a bit cloudy," he said

sardonically. "Look, all I know is I've paid quite a bit of money to have my wife resurrected. So the way I see it, I don't have to understand a damn thing. I just want the shit done, know what I'm sayin'," he stated totally in thug mode, feeling as if the good doctor was about to cast some dark cloud, some shadow on his rising euphoria. "And some days, I worry if I haven't gone off the deep end. Hardly matters though. Whatever happens, I'm seeing this through. Now you asked me earlier if I believe you can do this. And I want you to know, I really do. Otherwise, you wouldn't have seen a penny of my money."

The doctor smiled tightly, then snapped his briefcase shut. "Okay, understood. But that is not where I was going, Mr. Courage. I was referring to your purpose."

"Purpose?"

"Your purpose for resurrecting her, as you call it. Cause you see, three-fourths of the entire world think that Voodoo is diabolical and that what we practice is dark and sinister. I will return your money and won't perform this ceremony if such is your purpose. Florence told me you loved your wife. She also explained how your wife was murdered in the arms of another man. Her cousin. Now Florence suspects that your motive might be perhaps to exact some kind of revenge..."

Cedric sat quite still in his chair, reigning in his anger. He was piping mad, and felt his anger flare with the same intensity as the time when he was sixteen and his father announced to him that he was retiring and that they would be moving back to the States. That he had bought a house in Orlando, Florida. "Orlando, Florida!" Cedric had protested. "We're moving to fucking Disney World!"

And God, how he had despised his father! This was further fuel for rebellion, further reason to scorn him for never consulting him about decisions so important and crucial to his life and future. Without his knowledge, his father would make all the plans, and then tell him, as if he required his blessings. But this was usually after every detail had been ironed out, after all the plans had been made and put in motion. His father had always called all the shots, and all he could do was just accept them.

But now, he was the captain of his ship, the master of his universe, and what was this man telling him? He had paid his goddamn money and so now, what was this shit? He didn't believe him one bit about returning the money. Still...he would play it cool. There was no reason to ruffle any feathers and blow this thing. He had to keep his cool and not betray his anger.

He flushed. "Florence thinks that."

"No-no, she thinks there might be a bit of that. However, her hunch is you truly love this woman."

"I do. With every bit of my soul!"

"Good. Then it's really very simple. I don't think you would harm anyone you feel that fervently about."

"Not very likely," Cedric smiled tightly. "It's that simple. I lost her, and I want her back...by any means possible. Now if that's evil, if that's wrong, so be it. But I'm not bringing her back to hurt her, I assure you."

"All right, good man," the doctor said pumping his hand. "No hard feelings. I felt it only right to ask. I hope I did not offend you."

Cedric shook his head. "But can I ask you something? Is it damnable what I'm doing? Will I burn in hell?"

Dr. Ottowa laughed. "I take it you are Christian."

"Hell, I'm nothing, actually. I'm just asking just in case."

"You see, Christianity and most other religions make you walk with your head hung low. You're constantly being told how lowly you are, how imperfect and how you'll burn in eternal hellfire should you get out of line. Problem is, most of the things we desire, they say is wrong. But with Voodoo, you can hold your head high. You can want. You can desire. You have your own personality, your own wants and needs. And that's perfectly fine, no matter what your perversion or persuasion. Whatever your vices, they're perfectly fine. You're not judged. No one cares. Not even God. So long as you're not harming anyone else. From dust you are made, and to dust you shall return. So you enjoy yourself while you are here, cause this is the only life you know.

"So what of the magic...if you gain your happiness through its use is that punishable?"

"No," he chuckled, looking to Cedric like the Devil himself. "That's what the Catholics tell you. They talk of heaven and earth and purgatory and pray to all their useless saints. They're so misled, not even realizing that all those things are right here on earth, and that everyone is constantly going through all those realms right here in their lives. Hell is on earth and so is paradise. And purgatory is all things in between. Life is what you make it, Cedric, remember that."

"And maybe you think it's evil and dangerous what I'm telling you, but let me just tell you one thing. Eat well. Drink well. Sleep well. And enjoy your life, until your last day. *Know what I mean?*"

"Yep-yep."

"Voodoo is the religion before all others. In fact, it's the mother of them all, the most ancient one. The first religion on earth. Now the White man wouldn't want you to know that. No, no, no, the Pope would have a conniption before admitting it. Ahhh," he smiled. "You didn't know that, did you?"

"No, I didn't."

"Not many people do. But Voodoo is one of the best kept secrets," he laughed patting Cedric's shoulder, "But for you, you're about to learn..."

***

The day before the ceremony, my nerves were wrapped up so tight I had to go to through a series of tai chi exercises and meditations to get to even a reasonable calm. The ceremony wouldn't start until well after sundown, and I couldn't eat either. Fasting was good though. I fasted all day, and managed to pray a little too. I wasn't neglecting anyone. Jehovah, Confucius, Buddha, Jesus, Muhammad's Allah, every entity was addressed. Had I known any of the Voodoo spirits, they'd have been addressed too.

Later that day, I watched the sun set into the ocean, watching the gleaming orange ball of light disappear into the water, and stared in wonder. Arielle would be back in my arms before it climbed back out and rose up into the heavens once again. Arielle would be back—if Ottowa and Florence made good on what they had promised. It was hard to fathom. Hard to believe it would actually happen. I was hoping like crazy, but then again, I also had my doubts. Still, I was not planning on admitting this—not to Dr. Ottowa, Florence or anyone else. Truth was, though, I was sacred shitless! Excited too—not to mention confused. Was I doing the right thing, I kept wondering constantly to myself. But as the evening drew nearer, I no longer cared.

***

If I live to be a hundred years old, I'll never see anything as miraculous as what I saw that night. Needless to say, I was nervous as a cat—especially when all the ceremony and pageantry began. We had traveled to a beach bungalow Florence kept on the coast I hardly knew what to make of it: all the drumbeats, chanting and wild, chaotic dancing. All around Arielle's crypt. They had taken the corpse out and had swathed her in bright red cloth, laid her on an altar made of a slab of stone with what looked like scores of candles lit everywhere. The animal sacrifices came a little next, surprising me. They sacrificed a goat and blood was being smeared on everyone and everything, and people seemed to be walking about with dazed—no, perhaps the better word was "stoned" looks one their faces. *Hell, where the hell was I?* I thought at one point, *and how the fuck had I even gotten myself into this mess?!* Especially when the good doctor wrung a chicken's neck and drank its blood.

Even though I had assured Dr. Ottowa I believed a hundred percent he could do it, I realized I had not been totally honest with him until I saw her fingers actually stir and move. My skin crawled and every strand of hair on my body stood on end as I strove to comprehend what was taking place. Her fingers were fucking moving! GREAT DAY!!! I couldn't believe it. I didn't want to dare hope that she could possibly come alive again. I realized then that I had gone through all these lengths, gotten the money, came to Haiti, spoken to these people at length about this entire process, and I had absolutely not believed. Hadn't believed for a moment that they could actually do it!

I knew now that I had been a total skeptic. And if Dr. Ottowa was correct in his presumption of my lack of faith, I could have bungled the whole thing. The only thing that had made me seek out Florence and attempt this thing was my total desperation with life. *Tempt not a desperate man...*

I started to sob uncontrollably when I heard her shrieking. It was a miserable, pitiful sound. It sounded as if it was coming out of someone who was over a hundred years old. It was weak and feeble. She was croaking, as if she couldn't feel her lungs up with enough air. And I flinched as I watched her body go through these convulsions like a heroine addict in need of a desperate fix. I shuddered, and a stillness, a sense of peace seemed to descend upon me as I watched her calm down. Her body soon stopped its violent jerking after a time and started to just tremble instead. She continued crying though, as if she were still in horrendous pain. I could hardly bear to hear it. Still, I sighed, feeling deeply relieved. Felt as if I had slipped out of my skin, my heart was close to bursting, I was so deliriously happy. Something utterly miraculous had just happened. Arielle was born—again.

And yet I reigned in my happiness. I couldn't let myself get too joyous. *Would she remember me? Would she hate me for doing this? Oh, God, what if she were really suffering? What if this was all very painful? What if something could still go terribly wrong? Did I have the right to play God and bring her back like this?*

I had played God and now I was sobbing, tears were streaming down my face as Dr. Ottawa commanded her to sit up and she actually did. This occurred with some assistance, but she was up—Christ in heaven—she was up! I was hoping this wasn't some magician's trick, but she was moving. I saw her raise her hand to her face, covering her eyes and I couldn't stop weeping.

Dr. Ottowa was right. Heaven was definitely on earth...I thought as my heart rushed with a mixture of excitement, happiness and pure adrenalin.

"Quick," I heard the good doctor say. "Blow out some of the candles. It's too bright in here," he commanded as some of his underlings rushed to do his bidding. Florence was still holding on to her, and seemed to be soothing her. "Does the light hurt your eyes?" the doctor asked her.

She nodded.

"Jesus," I swore under my breath. She understood. She had her mind and seemed to have control of her facilities. I felt so relieved.

They undressed her, and were rubbing an ointment on her arms and body. It was greenish and slimy and had a pretty foul odor too, or maybe that odor was coming from her. Hope she didn't reek, I thought but then smiled to myself. No, if she reeked, I deserved to smell it for the rest of my life. And I would never complain. I was prepared to accept her in whatever condition she was in. I made this happen and I had to accept the consequences regardless of what.

They continued rubbing the salve all over her. It looked like mud. Still chanting and saying incantations I didn't understand, they continued rubbing the salve. I couldn't tell what they were speaking. Whether it was Creole or some other African dialect. It seemed to be working, whatever they were chanting, since Arielle was shaking less and less. The chanting seemed to be soothing her. Once she was covered in this mud from head to foot, when I could no longer recognize her, Florence explained this was a life-giving salve. It was made with all natural components, she explained: natural beeswax, pure honey and lanolin, rich wheat germ oil, fresh herbs and spices that would create a rich emollient. She said it was a disinfectant, moisturizer, a calming balm and beautifier for the skin. She had been dead for nearly a year. Her skin was dried out—no doubt. Anyway, they had her covered in this salve for a few hours as they made the preparation for the ceremony. They had a prepared a bath that she would be put in later that was a concoction of seaweed and other leaves. I watched all the preparations with curiosity, and although I was hoping with all my heart it was going to happen, I still couldn't believe it even when it actually did.

When they were ready to introduce her to me, a strange feeling came over me. It was this weird awareness that something miraculous had just happened. One of those things, those mysteries that you would never be able to explain or have anyone who wasn't there believe. Arielle came back to me—in the flesh—and I felt whole again.

They were chanting loudly now, reading incantations, it was hot and humid, and I could barely breathe. But the candles were flicking, and the moon was full and shinning brightly through the curtains even though they were drawn. She lied there totally hapless, keeping a hand over her eyes.

After their little ceremony, the doctor came to her again and started speaking to her. "Greetings, Arielle, welcome back."

Her voice was frayed and so soft, you could barely hear her, but he seemed to have understood what she said.

"Your name is Arielle," he told her gently. "That's what we call you. And this is Cedric, your master," he told her, pulling me to her.

"Doc, maybe you should tell her I'm her husband. I don't want—"

"No, don't worry about the words. They're nonessential. But we want her to feel is as if she belongs. As if she's not alone. She needs to feel she has an owner. That she's protected. That she's loved. When a child is born, the child has a mother and naturally feels the ownership that way and feels the love it needs to survive. It's the same for this situation too. Humans are social creatures and it's important she understands she belongs to someone. We need to establish that she belongs to you."

I nodded, seeing his point.

She peered at me rather shyly, seemingly afraid. And all I could do was grin at her from ear to her. I was so happy to see her. I sent up a grateful prayer. She was still covered in that mud but everything seemed fine, intact. She looked frightened though, her eyes looked haunted. Wild. Like she had come from a deep, deep, deep, deep sleep. She looked so groggy and tired, it was a small wonder she didn't fall right back to sleep. My face was teeming with heat as I looked at her. Her lips were dried and cracked. She moistened them. And I marveled at that one little act, was dazed by it. My heart started to sing. She *was back. She was back, oh*

God! How was this even possible?!!

I stood there motionless, following everything. Trying to absorb the reality of everything that had taken place before me. The incredulity of it all was mind-boggling, yet it was real. Pinched myself, ouch, I felt that. It was real. I couldn't be dreaming.

The doctor took out a stethoscope and checked her heartbeat and pulse, and then tied her arms with a rubber band, found a vein. Using a puff of cotton, he cleaned the area with alcohol then shot her up.

"Hey, what is that?" I could no longer keep quiet, nor could I keep the edge out my voice.

"Morphine."

"Morphine?!" I said loudly, startling her a little bit.

"Sssh," he protested. "Quiet. She needs it," he said simply. "It's going to help her, help alleviate the pain as her body gets regulated."

"Don't tell me she's going to be a junkie."

"No, she'll only need it for a few days. She'll be fine afterwards. Unless you need to calm her down."

"Calm her down?"

"Sometimes, she might go a little crazy."

"How crazy," I asked.

"To the point where she'll have to be restrained. This will calm her, get her into a euphoric state."

"Shit! What else, doc, what else haven't you guys told me?"

"Nothing. Just have some of this prepared just in case. Maybe it'll never happen."

"Why does it happen?"

"We don't know. Maybe it's a bad memory. Nightmares. We're not sure."

They carried her to the bath where Florence and the other women bathed her. Later as they tried to dress her, she couldn't stand.

"It'll be a while until she can have her motor skills back. It's been so long since she's used them that the muscles might have atrophy. We'll have to exercise them, maybe give her acupuncture to strengthen them," the doctor explained.

"So when will she be normal, Doc?"

"All in due time. Rome was not built in a day. Good things come to those who wait."

"Three clichés all lined up in a row. You go, doc!" I joked.

"Glad to see you still have your sense of humor. You'll need it. The next few days are going to be hectic at best. We have to do our best to keep her stabilized. It's touch and go. The key to it though is making her comfortable, keeping her grounded so she doesn't go."

"You mean, she could still go? Die?"

"Well, technically she's already dead, but she needs to want to stay in order to stay in the state she's in now—which is in a sort of limbo. Right now, she's neither here nor there, but we need to make her want to be here. *Know what I mean?*"

19

Slippery Curves Ahead

The next few days were chaotic at best and I was gripped by uneasy feelings. So worried was I that something would go awry. That she'd slip away once more. I couldn't stand it, felt uncomfortable in my skin, couldn't relax one bit until she was in the clear. I refused to be robbed of her again.

Florence and the doctor cleared out after a few days. I had paid them the balance of their money and Florence told me she'd be leaving me three of her people to help. A woman that would cook, a man as my steward/butler, and another guy who'd be my chauffeur and security.

"You have to be careful around here, Cedric. This is Haiti and the country is really crazy now with Zinglen-dou, a fearsome Haitian gang who goes around robbing and pillaging the countryside. Lots of bad things happening all the time. If you need me, you have my number. But I'm going to leave you with her now. Let you two get to know each other again. She won't be sick anymore. I think she's all-better now. You just need to have her get stronger before you can take her anywhere. So I'd say hang around here for at least another two weeks before traveling. A month would be even better."

"Thank you, Florence. For everything," I said kissing her cheek.

"I'm so happy for the both of you. Please come and visit with me before you leave. And remember, it may take her a little while until she recovers her memory. So be extremely patient with her."

"Sure thing."

Meanwhile, Arielle was still in bed, peeking at us from under the sheets. I kept catching her staring at me whenever she thought I wasn't looking. She was so shy. So maidenly. Virginal. I was touched by her innocence and child-like manners. Loved the startled little gaze constantly on her face as she discovered one thing or another.

She hadn't talked much, although I knew she spoke and understood English. Also Creole. Florence and the doc had said she would know all the languages she had known when she was alive, have the same level of intelligence and so forth. It was just at first that everything would come slowly. Words, speech patterns, reading, writing, memories, but that eventually it would all come back in a flood. How fast, they didn't know. Everyone was different. But the more the person was around things once familiar, the easier the transition would be. The faster the memories would return.

Actually, I had been thinking a lot about that. It was going to be really hard to get Arielle back into that kind of environment because I had sold the penthouse, her old apartment was now owned by Bailey who still lived there. She couldn't go to my dad's or her grandmère's, she couldn't see Margo or CJ—or at least none of these people could see her at least not yet (maybe not ever). Oh God, who would ever understand? And how would she ever get her memory back if everything was new. And everything would be— except me.

It was going to be very difficult to get her into her old environment, so I suppose it might take a while to get her to remember. Basically, I had planned on taking her to LaGorce Island, to the house that she had helped design. Maybe that might stir some memories.

Florence went to the bed and talked quietly to her before leaving. I noticed how attentive she was to Florence. Also how affectionate. Maybe she thought Florence was her mother. They hugged briefly before Florence took her leave.

As soon as the others left, that's when the fun began. Arielle who had been quiet and shy and sometimes downright gloomy since she had awakened got all rowdy. She had been peeking at me from under the sheets, watching my every move. She was so cute about it, that at one point, I winked at her and blew her a kiss. She blushed and turned away quickly, and then smiled and started peeking again. I came over to the bed, and gently pulled down the sheet to her chest so I could see her entire face.

I marveled at how beautiful she still was. Her skin looked so smooth and soft. Translucent, just like new. Like newborn skin. Man, I marveled, she had always been great-looking and had pretty skin, but she looked even more beautiful now. She positively glowed. There was this innocence, this radiant, wonderfully refreshing newness about her that made her all the more alluring. I was thinking it must have been the salve that they had kept rubbing on her all those days. But it was probably a lot more than that. I still couldn't get over the fact that she was dead and now alive. I smiled gently at her and she smiled back, wider now.

"Can you talk," I asked her softly, touching the tip of her nose, then her mouth.

She giggled and it was the most beautiful, miraculous sound. Quickly, she grabbed my hand and then stared at it, placing her fingers against each of mine.

"Bigger," she said then.

My eyes opened wide. Great! She was speaking. "Bigger and longer."

"Bigger and longer," she repeated. "Spell it."

"What?"

"Spell longer."

"L-o-n-g-e-r," I spelled it.

"Longer," she said then smiled at me again then sat up abruptly. Heavy, luxurious hair spilled over her shoulders, across her chest. She was in a thin slip and her breast came spilling out too. She stared down at her breasts for a second. Fascinated. "What's this," she asked cupping them. "Feels good," she said next squeezing them. Giving another gaggle of laughter.

Now I was blushing. "No-no. Don't do that," I said taking her hands away, and fixed her slip so it would cover her breasts back up. "Those are your breasts."

"Why you say not touch them? Feels good," she said cupping them again.

I was becoming aroused. "It's just that...um...they're for me to touch. Not you," I told her for lack of anything better to say.

"You have to touch them," she asked curiously, her eyes blinking, seemingly distracted by what I had just told her.

"Are you hungry," I asked wanting to change the subject.

"You have breasts?"

I nodded. "But not like yours."

"Let me see them," she demanded. "I want to see them."

I looked at her for several minutes, then stood up and pulled off my T-shirt. She was staring at my chest really hard. Then she cracked a small smile. "My breasts bigger...much bigger."

"Well, that's because I don't really have breasts, but a chest."

"Chest? Spell it."

"C-h-e-s-t. Chest."

"Ahhh," she said with sudden comprehension. "I have breasts, you have chest."

"Yes."

"Why?"

"Cause I'm a man. You're a woman."

"Different?"

"Yes, we're different."

"Man. Woman. Chest. Breasts. What else?"

I couldn't believe we were already having anatomy lessons this early on, but I supposed we had to start somewhere, but leave it to Arielle to get straight to the point.

I came back and sat down next to her. "Well, I have hair on my face. Whereas your face is smooth," I said feeling her cheek with the back of my hand.

"Hair? Smooth?"

I took her hand and placed it on my jawbone, running it up and down, marveling at the fact that her hands could be this soft. "Hair. You feel... I have to shave, but there's still hair. Stubble." Then I placed her hand against her face. "Your skin is smooth. No hair."

She smiled and then placed her hand back on my face, feeling my jawbone again. Then she placed a finger against my mouth. "What's that?"

I shook my head, not wanting to believe that in a crude, child-like and very simplistic way, that she was actually flirting with me. *She was unbelievable.* "That's my mouth. You have one to," I said tracing hers. Her eyes darkened when I did that.

"Feels good," she said all serious now. "Mouth feels good too...like breasts. Don't touch?"

My heart contracted. I thought I would die. Surely, this was heaven and I had gone straight there. I started to rumble with laughter and she looked frightened at first. "Laughter," I told her. "Funny."

She started giggling too. Then her hands traced its way down my chest. That was when she noticed the heart tattoo. She touched it, staring intently at it. I saw a flash of recognition pass across her face. For a few seconds she said nothing. She looked at me then smiled but didn't ask me about the tattoo which I was sure had intrigued her. Strange, I thought. Maybe she had remembered something. How I had had this done on our wedding day in Vegas.

She jumped up abruptly, stood on the bed. Her legs were long, colt-like, and all of the sudden, she started dancing. Stretching her limbs in graceful ballet-like movements. "Can you do this," she said out-stretching her arms, and squatting down on her legs in a classic arabesque pose."

"Nice. I told her. Yes, I can do it only because I'm a dancer."

"Dancer? Spell it."

"D-a-n-c-e-r. Dancer. I'm also a singer."

I started to sing for her. At first it seemed to scare her. But then, I grabbed her up, and started swinging her around, and pretty soon she was pealing with laughter. And I was laughing too, laughing and singing. I felt so incredibly grateful and happy to have her back. I was actually holding her in my arms, and it felt so incredible. So surreal.

Afterwards, as I settled her back on the bed and held her in my arms, as she gazed up at me with wonder, her lips curled in a sweet, angelic smile. "You my master," she said rubbing her hand against my chest.

"No," I started, but then remembered what the doc had said. "Yes, I'm your master, but also your husband. You're my wife."

"Master...husband. Me, wife."

"Yes," I said, running my fingers through her silky hair, rubbing her scalp. "Feels good?"

"Not good as breasts and mouth. But yes, feel good."

I squeezed her, kissing her cheek. She was a symphony of slender limbs and feminine curves with the most luscious, perfect breasts. I marveled how nothing had changed. She was my angel. My precious Bling. Oh, and how excited I was that she was back. I kissed the top of her head this time.

"Why you do that?"

"Cause you're sweet."

"Sweet? What's that?"

"You're an angel straight from heaven."

I realized that everything I said, I would have to explain. So the next few hours I spent trying to teach her what everything in the room was. And then luckily for me, I discovered she could read. Upon discovering her ability to read, which I should have known since she had been asking me to spell everything, I tried to get her to write. After all, she used to be a journalist. But writing was too high a skill for her, she couldn't control the pen and was getting frustrated. So I wrote her name and asked her just to practice that for a while, until the rest came to her. That kept her busy for several minutes. But then she mastered it and got bored and wanted me to show her other things. She was a voracious learner.

"Why your chest moving in and out?"

"I'm breathing."

"Breathing? What you breathing?"

"Air."

"Air? What is air?"

"It's all around us."

"I don't see nothing around us."

"It's invisible. You can't see it but it's there."

"I don't believe it's there. Where it goes?"

"It's all over. Where doesn't it go, would be the right question. It's everywhere."

"What's holding it? Why don't it all go away?"

Cedric shook his head and laughed. They had moved from anatomy to physics. "Gravity. I think that's what holds it down, or else it would float away into space, but because of the earth's gravitational pull, the atmosphere stays in place, as do us all. This house, the plants and animal, us. Gravity is causing us all to have weight and helps us to stay down. It's like this huge magnet holding everything down. Keeping us from floating into outer space."

Her eyes opened wide, and she remained quiet, seemingly soaking up all that I had told her. I had probably said too much. I could see her computing all the information, and I was wondering what word she would ask about first.

"What it mean, float?"

"Escape. Vanish, glide away. Your feet leaves the ground."

"Other word for it."

"Yes," I said with genuine excitement. She was learning already there were many ways of saying the same thing. She had higher order thinking skills. Good, I thought. But all her endless questions were certainly going to tire me out.

"What is magnet?"

"Can I explain it to you later?" Maybe she'd forget. I was exhausted already.

"Why not now?"

"It's a pull. It's an attraction. It's...it's very complicated, Arielle."

"Complicated?"

"Difficult to explain. It's scientific." Oh boy, I thought. I was in trouble. I had never spoken or explained so much in all my life.

She was quiet all of the sudden, digesting it all. She was going to short-circuit pretty soon. Too much information much too fast. This couldn't be good for her either.

"So much I don't know," she said softly. "I don't know much."

I was touched, and felt sad for her. She was already feeling bad. Maybe I was going about this the wrong way. "Don't ever be afraid to ask me any question. You're learning, and learning so fast. You'll see, you'll understand everything soon."

"Like scientific? What is scien...tific?"

"Science is another one of those complicated words. But it's the study of nature and of the universe and everything in it. Like air. It's the study of everything in the physical universe."

"Physical..." Tears came pouring down her face, out her eyes. She was crying which totally alarmed me.

"Arielle, what's wrong," I asked with great concern.

"I never know all things like you, my master. I sad cause I know nothing."

"Arielle, please. You're going to learn and understand everything. You hear me, everything that I know, I'm going to teach you. And...and you're going to know everything too. Wait and see. Learning is suppose to be fun, baby. Don't worry. Soon, you're gonna know everything. Just you wait and see, you'll be teaching me."

Oh boy, I thought to myself. I'm in for it.

"The only problem is we're going about this the wrong way. We have to tackle the basics first, before we get into all of these other things, which are so complicated. Believe me, a lot of people don't even understand them. People that have been here for a lot longer than you. And they get on...and the world keeps spinning and they keep living and breathing. So, it's going to be all right. Okay, baby. We have to take it slow. Aw'ight?"

She sniffled, wiping her eyes, but then smiled. "Aw'ight," she mimicked me.

"Good girl. That's my girl?" I said twining myself with her. She seemed to like that...our bodies close together. And I was dying...I was enjoying it too much!

After lunch, we went through the alphabet and then onto numbers. Soon she could count to a hundred. She saw the pattern pretty quickly, understood the concept and was soon adding and subtracting. Wow, I was thinking as I watched her calculating and learning everything so rapidly. The mind was a really powerful thing. But then when we started on colors and I pulled out a red dress from the closet, she started screaming at the top of her lungs. At first I couldn't figure what was wrong with her, what was frightening her so. Soon, I realized she was terrified of red. Or anything too bright or colorful.

"I'm afraid," she cried.

"Why?"

"I don't know. I don't like it! Makes me scared."

Okay. Only muted colors for her. Luckily I had heeded what Florence had said and had kept the curtains drawn. Light would have to be introduced very slowly.

I was by no means a teacher but I was dumfounded by her. She had excellent retention and this intense need for mental stimulation. She had a rapid learning rate, intellectual curiosity and exceptional reasoning abilities. She was insightful, would immediately grasp the essential elements of any situation. I hardly knew what to do with her.

Dinnertime rolled around and our servant had set up the dinning room table with candles and brought our food, serving it to us. I noticed she was very quiet when he was around. Looking at him, as if she didn't trust him. The cook came and she reacted in much the same way, staring at them but not saying a word. Only soft foods for her, mashed potatoes and butter, steamed carrots, she barely touched her meat. I didn't force her. She pretty much played with most of her food, but she drank lots of the mineral water. Then she asked for milk.

"Milk?"

"Yes, I like milk."

"Milk does a body good. Okay, why don't you ask for milk," I told her.

"No, you do it. I'm scared of them."

"Why?"

"I don't know. I don't like them."

"Well, they're nice people, Arielle. They haven't done anything to you and you should like them."

She shrugged, spooning a tiny bit of the potatoes into her mouth. "I like you."

"Well, I'm glad, cause I like you too."

She smiled then. "So you ask for the milk for me?"

I was amazed how fast she was learning. She was already trying to manipulate me. "I'll ask just this one time, but next time, you're going to have to ask for yourself."

After dinner, I filled the tub for her with warm water, put oils and liquid soap that made lots of bubbles, which she seemed to love. "Bubbles," I told her.

"Ohhhh, I like bubbles!" She exploded with glee, trying to get into the tub with her clothes still on.

"No-no, you have to take your clothes off first."

She didn't know how to, so I had to help her, and I realized I was going to have to stay in the bathroom with her while she bathed, lest she drown in the tub. She was like a baby and couldn't be left alone, there was so much she didn't know or understand.

I undressed her with chivalry and reasonable detachment. Let me repeat that, reasonable detachment, but that didn't mean that I didn't notice. *Get real!* Arielle was so gorgeous, she made my eyes hurt.

Good God, death became her and had done nothing to her. She was fine as ever! Her body was unblemished. Creamy. Flawless. My eyes followed extraordinarily silky hair that cascaded down her back to the gracefulness of her curving backside. She had two deep dimples right at that curve below her tiny waist. This gave way to exquisitely curved hips, which were pure perfection. Her ass was the shape of an upside down Valentine. Christ, and how I loved that ass. I continued my appreciation, moving down to her long, sleek legs and shapely calves. I knew from memory how silky and satiny those legs could feel, wrapped around me the way a bow would wrap around a package. I didn't stop paying my homage, admiring her ankles that were nicely delicate, culminating with her pretty feet. I inspected her toenails that were unpolished, and thought how they had always been. Since I had known her, never a chipped nail. Everything always perfect. I'd have to rectify that, I thought, get one of the women to give her a manicure and pedicure. Or maybe I'd do it for her myself. Thinking about it, I thought about how much I'd enjoy that.

I felt elated. I had my wife back and she was in mint condition. Christ, it was a miracle. And I didn't even care about the morality of it all. Today all that mattered was that I had her back. In the flesh. On my own terms. In my arms.

I turned her around to face me, then bent down to peel off the tiny little lace panties she had been wearing while she held unto my head to keep her balance. Needless to say, I was staring straight at her crotch, that fleecy curly hair that gave me an immediate erection. She bent her head to look at it too. "Hair," she said touching herself.

"Yes, now get into the tub," I said thickly, somewhat gruffly. I was getting aroused, wanted her bad. But felt like a real perv too, realizing she was way too young to even contemplate having sex with.

"You have hair there?"

"Yes."

"Let me see."

"No!" I told her sharply and stood up abruptly.

She jumped at my tone, then looked all sad, starting to pout.

"I'm sorry," I said stroking her hair gently, helping her into the tub.

"You mad at me," she asked looking perplexed.

"No, baby. Not at all."

"Then why you...I don't like your voice just now!"

"I know. I apologize. I didn't mean to sound like that. I'm not mad. I'm mad about you, though, but that's besides the point."

Of course that went clear over her head.

"You don't get in and take a bath?" She asked more gently.

"No, I'll take a shower later," I said putting the toilet seat down, and getting comfortable there.

"Women take baths, men take showers?" She asked curiously.

"Yeah, something like that," I said watching her from under lowered lids. All of the sudden I felt really tired. Drained. She had exhausted me with her million questions and incessant talking. She was quite a handful. A genuine chatterbox.

She was playing with the lotion bottles, humming and trying to sing the way I had that morning except she had no idea what she was saying. Maybe I ought to teach her some nursery rhymes. But I was tired now, so I'd maybe do that tomorrow.

After her bath, I rinsed her off and toweled her dry and put one of my over-sized T-shirts on her, making sure it was a neutral color. Baby blue. Then had her pull on some clean panties. They were the plain cotton kind. I had never seen her wear anything so big or plain. Another thing that needed to be rectified. Lastly, I brushed he hair, which felt so incredibly silky. I plaited it into one long, thick braid. It looked like a rope, which she started whipping around. Giggling as she'd strike me with it.

"What you call that?"

"A braid."

"You teach me, braid."

"Yes, but not tonight. Tomorrow, I'm so tired now, sweetheart.

"You tired?"

"Very tired. Aren't you?"

"I'm not tired," she said with a deep yarn.

"Yes, you are. It's bedtime for you. Sleep time."

"I don't want sleep."

The butler had already changed the sheets and turned down the bed while we had been in the bathroom, and I made her get under the covers to tuck her in.

"It's night now and time to sleep. Until tomorrow."

"No," she said, but I could see that her eyelids were heavy. Drooping. "I don't want to sleep," she said with another yawn.

"Yes, you do," I said grinning at her. "You're tired. I can see it in your eyes. Now go to sleep, my sweet baby. We have so much to do tomorrow," I said brushing my lips against her cheek. Then kissed her on the lips, drawing her into a nice, long kiss.

"Mmmm," she said snuggling down into the bed, purring like a kitten. "What's that," she asked groggily.

"That was a kiss."

"Kiss?"

"K-i-s-s. Kiss. Feels good?"

"Um-hum." She sighed and closed her eyes. "I like kiss." And just like that, she was out.

I looked at her in the semi-darkness and pondered her beauty, basking in the comfort of being so near her. Celebrating the fact that she was with me once again. I breathed her in, she smelled so fresh and clean. Like the world after rain.

I thought about where I was going to sleep tonight. How nice it had been sleeping with her the night before, smelling the scent of her body, her hair, feeling her warm flesh against mine, her silky hair on my face. Christ, it had been so nice. But I wasn't sure I could take sleeping with her like that again tonight. Not the way I was feeling. Tired as I was, the memory of how her body had looked moments ago, lingered in my mind. She was exquisite and I wanted to corrupt and violate her a hundred thousand ways. Even though I was tired as hell and could scarcely keep my eyes open, I still didn't trust myself not to wake up in the middle of the night and...

No, better I sleep somewhere else. She was too tempting.

With great effort, I raised myself to my feet, still staring at her. She looked so peaceful, like a little angel sleeping so soundlessly. Again, I was floored by her beauty, except she looked too peaceful. For a second, I felt a blind panic, thinking she might be dead again. Pinching her nose together, she shook her head, pushing my hand aside and settled back to sleep. "Thank you, God," I said quietly, grateful to a God I was starting to believe in. 'Cause surely this was a miracle. Arielle was back, she had died and now she was sleeping in my bed. Inconceivable. So there had to be life after death. There had to be somewhere that we went when we died. I was an absolute believer now. Death was not the end. It wasn't just oblivion. Arielle had been somewhere and the doctor and Florence had summoned her and called her back, and she was back. Right back in the same body. Inconceivable, I thought again, as I walked over to the couch and just fell into it, passing out right away.

***

The next morning, I had the security guy go into town to get me some books. I asked for an English dictionary and some children's books. Magazines. Anything he could find in English I told him. Meanwhile, I was getting everything prepared while sleeping beauty continued to slumber. I was thinking about taking her for a swim, after the sun went down. The bungalow was right on the beach, in fact the lapping waters of the Caribbean sea was less than 50 feet away. I'd take her for a walk later this evening.

I took out my I-Walk. I was going to have her listen to some music as well. *My Bring It On* CD. Maybe it would spark her memory a little. Too bad this place didn't have a TV.

I took a quick shower, brushed my teeth and shaved, and then had a smoke after getting dressed. I was savoring my cigarette, realizing I hadn't smoked the whole day yesterday, she had kept me so busy. That was when she got up, right as I was blowing rings.

"What's that?"

Here we go again, I thought to myself. Except today I was prepared.

"Smoke. S-m-o-k-e."

"You have smoke in your mouth?"

"No, there's a cigarette in my mouth, which I'm inhaling smoke from. It goes through my lungs and then I exhale it through my nose or my mouth."

"Why you do this? Feel good?"

I laughed. "No, not exactly. I suppose it tastes good."

"You taste smoke?"

"No, yes, I'm not sure. But I guess I do it really cause it relaxes me, and I like doing it."

"Feels good."

"I suppose so."

"Can women smoke?"

"Yes, of course,"

"Can I smoke?"

"No."

"Why?"

"Cause it's not good for you."

"But you smoke."

"I know. And it's not good for me either. I'm trying to quit," I said, putting the cigarette out in the ashtray. She was following every move I made just like she had yesterday morning. "Well," I smiled, "good morning to you. I need to teach you some manners, I see. When you wake up in the morning, you say good morning before saying anything else."

"Good morning?"

"Yes, you wish the person you are with a good morning."

"What does that do? Does that make them have a good morning?"

"Not necessarily, but it's polite. P-o-l-i-t-e."

"What about the afternoon and night?"

"You wish people that too. Just depends on when you see them."

"Why don't you just wish the person a good morning, afternoon and night all at the same time? That way, it doesn't matter when you see them?"

"Well...that's a very sensible idea—except people don't do that. You wait till the appropriate time to wish them."

"Good morning, master-husband," she said then with a smile.

I smiled back, "Good morning to you too, my beautiful wife."

"What is beautiful?"

"You. You're beautiful."

"I'm beautiful," she said raising herself off the bed, getting on her knees and sitting back on her haunches, giving me a glimpse of her satiny thighs.

"Ah, yeah, baby. You're really beautiful."

"I want to see. Can I see me?"

Going over to her, I took her hand, helped her off the bed and took her to the bathroom. Turning on the light, I let her stare at herself in the mirror for a little while. She was touching her face, playing with her hair and was cupping her breasts again.

"Don't touch? Only you touch," she asked turning to me.

"Go ahead. You can touch them if you want. They're yours."

"But I want *you* to touch."

Oh, God. It had started again. There's only so much I could take.

"I don't want to touch," I said huskily, feeling aroused as I watched her stroking herself and saw her nipples become erect.

"Why? Don't feel good when you touch?"

"Feels *too* good when I touch."

She took my hand and placed it on one of her breasts.

"Feels good?" I asked but didn't do anything but held my hand there.

She shrugged. "I don't know. I like better when I touch," she said turning back to stare at herself in the mirror. Her eyelashes fluttering, lips smiling.

"Ummm...yes, I remember how vain you were. Of course, you'd like it better," I said snaking my hand around her waist and hugging her back to me and sighed deeply.

She purred like a cat. "Ummm, what's that?"

"It's called a hug. Feels good?"

"Feels soooo good," she shuddered. And I could feel myself growing hard again.

Quickly, she turned around, stared at my crotch. She looked scared. "What's that?" She asked curiously. "There's something in there. Something move in there...in your pants. What is that? Very warm."

I couldn't stop laughing. And soon she was giggling too.

"That's what makes me a male. That's my penis."

"Penis?"

"P-e-n-i-s. Penis."

"Let me see it!" She said with excitement. Quickly getting on her knees to see it up close."

"No," I said, trying to stand her back up.

"Please," she pleaded. "I want to see it. Felt good. Real good. Want to see it. Different?"

"Yes, very different from you."

"Have hair there too?"

She had remembered from last night.

"Lots of hair. Much more than you."

"Oh, please," she said excitedly. "Let me see it!"

I realized she was going to badger me all day about this if I didn't let her see it. So I unbuttoned my jeans, unzipped the fly and pulled down my shorts and showed her. At first she stared at it in wonder, then tried to touch it.

"No, don't touch," I warned her.

But she ignored me and grabbed it between her fist and nearly jumped back in absolute terror when it grew harder.

"It move! It scare me," she cried, holding her heart.

"It's a monster. Don't play with it, or else it might..."

"What does it do?"

"Lots of things."

"Oh, I want to play with it. It's fun! You play with it?"

"All the time."

She was giggling now. "Oh, I want to play with it too."

I pulled my briefs and pants back up, and zipped up. "Not now. Later."

"Later you let me play with it?"

"Yes."

"What time? In the afternoon? At night?"

"Maybe tonight."

She looked skeptical, as if she didn't believe me.

"Promise," I said.

"Promise?"

"That means—"

Just then the chauffeur came back with the provisions. Thank God!

"A promise means I have to keep my word," I said over my shoulder, leaving her to go see about the things. When I came back she was still staring at herself in the mirror.

"So, now it's time to brush your teeth. This is a toothbrush," I told her, demonstrating for her, "And you put toothpaste on it." Happy it wasn't red gel or else she would not be brushing her teeth. Then I showed her how to brush. I had her open her mouth and examined her teeth. There was no decay. No sign of wear and tear. They were white and perfect. Just like before. After brushing, I showed her how to floss and then what to do with the green, minty mouthwash.

"I have to do every morning?"

"And at night before you go to sleep. And at other times when you've eaten something gross and want your teeth properly cleaned. Then also if you're going out."

She looked perplexed. Then she asked, "What's that on your tongue?"

I grinned and stuck my tongue out and did something naughty with it.

She seemed to like it and tried to do the same thing.

"Oh no, don't do that. People will think you're a little freak."

"Freak?"

I chuckled. "Kinky, baby. Hot stuff. Hot to trot. Not that you're not, but I don't want everyone else knowing that. You understand? That's only between me and you."

"Secret?"

"Uhm-hmm. It's our little secret."

She looked at me. "So what's that," she asked doing it again. "It's freak?"

"No, you say it's freaky."

"It's freaky?"

"Ah, yeah, it's freaky, ba-by," I said teasingly and winked at her. "It's off-the-hook!"

She blushed lowering her eyes. "I want freaky on my tongue too," she said sticking out her tongue again.

I lowered my mouth and took her tongue, sliding it into my mouth, shocking her. "Ummm, that's what happens when a young lady sticks her tongue out like that. Other more serious things can happen too. Keep your tongue in your mouth," I warned her with mock sternness.

That seemed to sober her up and would hopefully make her think twice before sticking her tongue out like that again. She looked alarmed, incredulous. Afraid to even speak now, lest I see her tongue. She had me rolling, cracking up, but I stifled my laughter and remained serious.

"Now, no more talk about tongue rings or any other piercings," I said. "You never liked them—or else you would have already had them. Now I'd like to show you how to wash your face."

Her face looked flushed and she was avoiding eye contact but I could hear her uneven breathing. She was excited and my heart fluttered thinking how I might still move her. Of course, she had no idea what it was she was feeling, but I had gotten her all hot and bothered, and could hardly wait to explore that with her. But I had to be patient and wait until she was a lot more mature.

"I know how wash my face. Let me show you."

She sloshed water everywhere, getting it all over the mirror and floor.

"Um, that's nice Arielle. You did a nice job, but next time, can you make sure the water goes into the sink and not everywhere else."

"I not do it good?"

"No, baby. You did great! Just a little messy, though, although I'm sure you'll do better next time."

Next I introduced her to the shower.

"But you say men take showers," she protested.

"Women take them too."

She screamed when the water came splashing down hard on

her body. Her nipples immediately stiffened.

"It's okay. It's only water," I said soothingly, not wanting her to bolt out of there.

She took several deep gulps of air to steady herself and then blushed even more and smiled at me.

"Feels good," I asked.

She didn't answer. I figured it must feel really good since she didn't say a thing, but continued savoring that good feeling. I had to smile. She was something else, my Arielle. Sensual as hell!

Later after her shower, she toweled dry then refused to put the clothes on I had laid out for her.

"I don't want clothes. I'm hot."

"Those clothes are cool, Arielle."

"I don't want clothes."

"Look, you can't be walking around naked—especially not around other men. You must wear clothes at all times. Except..."

She cocked her head, listening intently, waiting for me to finish.

I gazed at her. "Must keep dressed, because I'm jealous. I'm jealous. Your husband won't permit it. You keep your clothes on, always. Understand? No other man is to see you without clothes except me. In fact, while we're at it, no other man is to come near you or touch you but me. Understand?"

She nodded her head. "Must wear clothes always. Bad if other man see me or touch me. Only my husband, my master to touch me."

I smiled. "Good. You got it," I said taking her hand and twining it with mine. I was really hoping everything I had said would really settle and soak in. With the proper conditioning, she'd be the perfect woman.

We spent nearly the entire rest of day pouring over books. She read very well, and when she encountered words she didn't understand, I'd make her first try to figure them out through context clues. Next I showed her how to look it up in the dictionary and had her make sentences with them herself, so I'd be sure she understood them. Just the way my dad had done with me. She was insatiable in her quest for knowledge. And we practiced more with her writing. Breaking only for lunch, and then hit the books again. As the sun began to set, I told her how I planned to take her outside to the beach.

"The beach, is that other word for ocean," she asked.

"Yes, very good. What did I tell you we call that?"

"A synonym, word that mean same thing," she said pleased with herself.

"Yes."

"And there many words that mean same thing."

"What's another word for ocean?"

"Sea," she said with relish.

"Oh, you're so damned smart. My baby is so smart," I praised her.

She giggled with delight, and my heart simply filled with joy hearing that laughter, seeing how much she was learning and the bold steps she seemed to be making.

"Okay, so now we get ready for our walk."

She didn't have much in the way of clothes, and since she refused to put anything with bright colors against her skin, she ended up having to wear one of my plain white T-shirts and a pair of my khaki shorts, which looked pretty sexy on her. The waist was way big and so I folded down a few times and it came down to hug her around her hips. She didn't even have any shoes and had to wear my leather sandals, which were also too big, but...oh well, we had to make do.

I'd have Jean-Louis pick up some clothes tomorrow morning. Oh and some women sandals too.

I swear it was pure heaven, walking arm-in-arm on the beach with the sea breeze kissing our faces. It was really pretty out there, and she was staring at everything in absolute wonder. "I'm not beautiful, this is beautiful," she said solemnly as she looked at the ocean, watching the surf roll in and out. "This is beauty."

"You want to go for a swim," I asked her.

She shook her head. "I'm scared."

"Why?"

"It's so vast. So big! And I'm so small. It scares me, the world. It's so huge!"

I took her into my arm, and hugged her fiercely. "You don't have to be afraid, cause I'll always be right here beside you. You're not scared when I'm holding you so close, are you?"

She shook her head, holding me tightly. Then she kissed my cheek and whispered, "I like hug."

She was too adorable, off-the-hook. I gave her this great bear hug which lifted her into the air and swung her around. She laughed with glee.

"Sing for me," she requested.

"Sing?"

Yes, I like your voice. It's beautiful. Like an angel voice."

"Wow, what a compliment. I'm flattered. But what should I sing?"

"What you sang before."

"I love you...for sentimental reasons," I sang to her, "I wish that you'll believe me...You'll always have my heart." Then I kissed her real hard, using my tongue which seemed to delight her. She couldn't get enough of it, so I lowered her down into the sand and I ended up kissing her for close to thirty minutes straight. It was like that classic beach scene from the movie, *From Here to Eternity*. and indeed, we were making our own little movie.

Afterwards, she gave a rich chuckle that reverberated against my chest, then slid her knee between mine and relaxed with a sigh of pleasure. I didn't want to believe how sumptuous it felt to hold her in my arms again.

20

The Wench Who Stole My Soul

The second we got back to the house, as our food was about to be served, she grabbed my hand, and staring intently at me, she asked, "I can play with it?"

I rumbled with laughter. "You didn't forget?"

"You promise."

"Not now. We have to eat."

"After we eat?"

"Then you have to bathe."

"After I bathe?"

"You have to go to sleep."

"Before I sleep?"

"Maybe right before you sleep."

She smiled widely. "You promise?"

"I promise."

Shit, what had I gotten myself into? I would have to distract her in some way tonight, so she would forget about the penis thing, although looking at her, I knew that was exactly what was on her mind. She could have a one-tract mind when she wanted something. That was when I remembered the I-Walk. I'd let her listen to music. Maybe that would distract her enough to make her forget.

Like yesterday, she wouldn't speak at the dinner table, looking on curiously as everything was served, and still refused to say a word to any of the help. After dinner, she asked politely, "May I have some milk?"

"You ask for it," I told her, "just like you asked me."

"No, you ask for me," she protested.

But Jean-Louis brought it out without our even asking. She smiled slightly at him as he set it down, and he averted his eyes and tried not to look at her. They were probably just as afraid of her as she was of them.

She watched as I prepared her bath the way I had yesterday,

and she started undoing her clothes. I was pleased she had learned to at least undress herself. Constantly having to peel off her clothes was becoming a bit too much for me. There was only so much my heart could take without my jumping on her and going buck. When she stood naked before me, she said, "Please take a bath with me."

"The tub is too small for the both of us," I said quickly.

"No, the tub is big. It can take us!" She insisted.

I shook my head. "I don't think so."

"Why don't we *try*."

Amazing! I was now being controlled by someone who was only a few days old. "You just want me naked so you can play with it," I told her accusatorily.

And she actually blushed. "Please," she said laying her hands on my chest, rubbing gently, awakening the monster. "Please," she said again smiling prettily up at me. She was a master manipulator already.

Reluctantly, I took off my clothes and got into the tub to her delighted pleasure. She was ohhing and ahhing, as her legs slid over mine. "Oh, hair!" she shrieked, rubbing her smooth, satiny legs against my hairy ones. She slid her knees between mine and gave a deep sigh of pleasure. "Ohhhhh, hair feels so good!"

I was fully aroused by then listening to all her ohing and ahing. Not to mention how satiny her own skin felt sliding against mine. When she slipped her hands down and grabbed my cock, her eyes opened wide. So did her mouth. In a perfect O. I looked at her parted lips, at her half-closed eyelids with pleased surprise, loving the way she looked. So sensual. I groaned loudly. It was sinful for someone to be this lovely, this attractive. This...God! Words could not describe. I tried not to think about how much I'd like to ravage her. It felt like ages since I'd had physical fulfillment. I wanted to wait until she had gotten her memory back, until she was fully mature, but her enthusiasm was proving too much. Yet, I didn't want our first time to be like this.

"Bigger!" she exploded loudly. "Much bigger!"

"Ummm," was all I could manage to say, as I closed my eyes from the intensity of the pleasure her hands were unwittingly giving me.

"Why you close your eyes," she asked, peering curiously at me as she stroked me back and forth between both of her fists. Yanking on it like it was a sinewy rope.

"Oh God," I moaned, licking my lips. "Oh baby!"

"Feel good," she asked huskily, watching the expression on my face very intently.

"Yes!" I hissed. "It feels real good." I was breathing real hard. And so was she. She was now on her knees, and moving over me. "Arielle, what are you doing," I asked gently, feeling weak. "Easy, baby. Easy." She was grabbing me tighter now, and the sheer ecstasy of it. Although I was begging her to be gentle, it was a perfect balance between pleasure and pain. The oils and bubbles in the water made her hands smooth and slippery, and the friction she was building going faster and faster was simply killing me.

"Touch me," she whispered with emotion. "Touch my breasts."

Oh shit, I was being seduced by someone who was barely out of diapers. She was a baby still, but hell, when it came to carnal knowledge, she seemed very much to know what she was doing. She was way ahead of her time, on top of hr game. I reached out and touched one of her breasts and the nipple tightened making me grow even larger in her hand. She shrieked and I laughed. She squeezed and it grew even more. She shrieked again, giggling this time.

"It keep growing!" She said with delight. "It grow so big!

"Mmm-hmm," I murmured my delight, loving the feel of her slender hands.

"Oh, I like it!" She said tugging on it some more. "I like your penis."

Oh, man, and she was going to like it a lot more in a few minutes. But then again, I thought half-heartedly about how this was no good. This was not how I had planned on introducing her to lovemaking. I had wanted champagne and dinner, flowers and dancing, candles and soft music and a big comfortable bed. I had wanted her to have fully recovered. To have her memory back. But she was proving too much for me. I couldn't fight this little hell-cat that had risen out of her spot and was now trying to straddle me.

Presently, she had her hands locked around my neck and was trying to slip my cock between her legs. Shit! How had she known how we fit? Was it purely instinct—or did she remember? I grabbed her around the waist with one hand and then her head with the other. "No, baby. No, not like this...not like this, sweet darling."

She was grabbing my head and was trying to shove her breasts into my mouth. "Touch them please. Touch them with freaky."

I was trying to struggle, but Christ! She was driving me CRAZY! Her body was oily and slick and felt so velvety soft against my skin. She felt too delicious. Like one large vagina. I couldn't take it. I groaned and opened my mouth, covering one of her nipples with it, starting to suck on it. She sobbed and started to shudder, arching her back, touching the tip of my cock to her inner thigh. She was grinding her hips too, trying to take it in. It was as if she was determined to have me right then in there. I felt like a fool trying to stop her. It was fast becoming a loosing battle as she grabbed my head and pressed her lips to mine. I was shocked as her tongue plunged deep into my mouth.

I grabbed her, knocking her hard against me, driving the breath out of the both of us. She was looking at me through half-closed lids and her lips were moist, trembling. The raw desire I could see on her face just pushed me over the edge. I lifted her up, stepped out of the tub with her, laid her out on the carpet on her back, and then just gave it to her, kissed her with all the pent up passion of a man just back from war.

"Oh, God in heaven this feels good," I murmured. "So good."

Her femininity seemed to blossom in response to my sheer virility. I wanted to take her, to have her surrender, to make her shudder helplessly beneath me. My lips settled at the corner of her mouth and I moaned deeply as she responded to me with feathery light kisses. I responded with harder strokes, teasing her with my tongue.

"Ohhh," she groaned, which enflamed me even more.

"God, you're sweet. Baby, you're so goddamn sweet. And it's been so long since I've tasted you. Let me taste you again..." I brushed her face and lips with quick, random, desperate kisses.

She giggled. "Master...oh, Master! Feel so good."

"So good," I murmured, agreeing with her. Roughly grounding my lips into hers. This was becoming too much. I now couldn't help myself. I wanted to fuck her bad.

I claimed her lips again. Boldly. Evocatively. She was gasping, trembling. "Tell me you want me."

"I want you," she whispered fiercely.

I kissed her all over first. Starting with her face—kissing every inch of it, her forehead, eyebrows, nose, lips, cheeks and neck, moved down to her breasts, cupping them. They felt full, nice, like ripe plums. I kneaded them then pinched her already erect nipples, watched them grow into little cherries beneath my thumbs. Then I licked them, sucked each one thoroughly and well.

At first she was quiet, just breathing hard, taking her punishment like a woman. This surprised me, her silence. Arielle had always been loud, quite vocal. She used to let you know real properly when something pleased her. So this quietness I didn't yet understand, but I continued. Licking down the valley between the breasts, traced that light colored line that went down her abdomen to her navel. She was panting now, her breathing shallow as I smooched her stomach, squeezing her waist and hips.

I looked up at her and her eyelids were heavy. Her long pretty lashes brushing her cheeks. She looked so sexy. Kittenish. That look used to always drive me crazy, and things hadn't changed much. Still I couldn't understand the change in her attitude. All this quiet. I wanted to hear some moaning. Some serious moaning.

She watched me as I held her lower body in my arms, legs spread apart, parted by my opened arms and chest. I bent down and rubbed my face against her pelvis, breathing her in, wallowing in all her femininity, feeling her soft, moist pubic hair tickle my nose and caress my cheeks. She moaned then, grabbing a hold of my hair, pressing my face to her sex. I glanced up and smiled at her. She poked the tip of her tongue out between her lips and smiled at me. I melted completely. Shit, she was still nasty. I loved that.

When I slid my tongue in for the first lick she went completely rigid and a cry tore from her throat. "Unngh!" *Ah, that's what I'm talkin' 'bout,* I thought. *Yeah boy, this was the Arielle I knew and loved.* Nonplussed, I buried my face between her thighs and went for broke, caressing and teasing her mercilessly with my tongue. She was trembling as I continued nibbling, kissing, sucking, even biting her real gently, lapping my pierced tongue against her clit the whole time. I knew the small metal ball must have been a nice sensation against her velvety softness. Used to make her cry and whimper just like a baby, and nothing had changed.

She wound her hands into my hair, pushing my face into her, grinding her hips up to meet my thrusting, questing tongue. Hers was the sweetest pussy I had ever had in all my life. I could eat her all night long and into the next day. I loved the way she tasted. The way she smelled. The way she was squirming and grinding her pelvis against my face. The sexy, desperate, amazing sounds she was making, I was sure the household staff outside was getting an earful.

The first time she came, she went absolutely wild. She was screaming like I was murdering her, she was so loud. I could only imagine what they must have thought I was doing to her. I had wanted her to moan, but this was ridiculous. I was sure her shrilling scream could be heard all across the island. God, she was wailing like I was killing her. Still I kept at her, making her writhe with pleasure and sob like she was in pain.

Finally, I made my way back up, took her mouth and swallowed her cries. She was trembling real hard, convulsing. Knew it had been a while, but she was one hot little piece of ass, I swear to God! She made me want to holler. I could come just hearing her sounds and feeling her hot, delicious little bod trembling against mine, endearing as hell. Not to mention the effect it had on my ego, I felt ten feet tall.

Once I had quieted her down, I brought her hands down to my painful erection. I was beyond hard, pure marble by now. Her hand slipped over it but could barely hold it in her grasp. Even so, her slender little hands felt so wonderful. I was groaning as she touched me, feeling like I could come right between her warm hands.

I had to concentrate real hard, remove my mind, think about something else in order not to release. Don't think about how hot and soft and small her hands were as she glided her fist up and down my cock. Don't think about how much I wanted to slip it between her thighs. But pretty soon, thought turned into action. Her eyes grew several sizes when I adjusted our positions. "Relax," I told her soothingly. She was panting and I could feel her heart beating faster. I was pushing her legs farther and farther apart and I was knocking but she wouldn't let me in. "Please baby, relax," I urged her feeling her start to squeeze me out. "What's wrong," I asked her gently, rubbing the head against her moistness. "Relax and let me in. I promise, it's going to feel so good."

But she was shaking her head. "No, I'm scared. I don't like it!"

"It feels good, just let me put it in, baby. Please!" I told her, shuddering with pleasure as my cock stroked and caressed her moist, swollen, warm velvety folds. "Ohhh," I groaned, closing my eyes. "Feels so good," I half-sobbed.

She put her arms around my neck and cupped my head and then brushed her lips against mine. "Feels good," she asked but didn't seem convinced. I was grinding my cock against her, I was starting to ache real bad. Needed relief. I grabbed her bottom, cupping her globes of exquisitely squeezable flesh and opening her legs a little wider, "Oh, baby. Feels really, really good," I murmured, grinding against her.

I massaged her bottom, loving how perfect she felt, kissed her again as I ran my hands down her body, stroking her thighs and hips, and ground my cock into her some more. She was making little noises again, little sounds of pleasure. I opened my legs slightly to get her to open hers wider. Felt pretty confident that her legs were spread as far as they could go now. I took one of her breasts in my hands and started rolling the nipple between my finger as I sucked on the other one with my mouth. Her legs started to tremble. "Don't be scared," I whispered huskily to her. "Relax," I said riding her gently, tenderly. "Relax and let me in," I coaxed her.

She was panting, holding me real tight, and I could feel her body slowly start to open up to me, felt her body trying to take me in—except the head of my shaft seemed too big, not to fit. I felt as if I might tear her or hurt her if I pushed any harder. Why wasn't I going in? I was having the hardest time getting into her. No matter how wide I opened her legs and even though she felt warm, real moist, I couldn't get my cock into her.

"What's wrong?" She asked sensing my frustration.

"It won't go in," I told her, starting to laugh now.

There was a mixture of delight and anxiety on her face. "Funny?" She asked smiling gently.

"No, not at all," I said seriously. "It's not funny at all!"

I stood up, grabbed her up, and carried her from the bathroom to the bedroom and deposited her on the bed, laying her gently on it. The floor was too uncomfortable and it felt like she might still be tense. I noticed how she was now staring at my shaft, which was pointed straight out all by itself. I was very pale in my groin area and did tend to get red when I got excited. Arielle was staring at it in absolute amazement. It was red and huge and looked really angry now. Because I was fully erected and super excited, I knew it was probably close to eleven inches, very thick, real veiny— normally a pale pink but now crimson, a deep red. Felt pretty sure it must have looked like a monster to her. As I climbed over her, positioning myself between her legs again, she looked on in terror, "I'm scared," she said in a small, agonized voice. "It's red. Very red."

Oh-oh.

"No, it's okay. Feels good. Touch it," I said taking her hand.

But she shrieked. "No, I'm afraid," she said pulling her hands back.

"Oh God," I moaned. I was going to have blue balls. She wasn't going to go through with this. My penis was red and she was not going near it now. I attempted to go down and place it back between her thigh, but she froze up. I could feel her shrinking back in repulsion. Oh God, that's what I got for trying to make love to a kid. A Baby. Albeit a very well-endowed, over-developed baby. But a baby all the same. I got up abruptly and headed to the bathroom and shut the door, locking it. She was immediately at the door, knocking.

"Master. Master-husband. I'm scared."

"I'll be right out. Just go lie down. Put some clothes on."

"Master. I'm scared," she cried, sounding as if she was about to cry.

"I'll be right out," I said again, letting the water down in the tub. I needed to take a cold shower. A very, very cold shower. Icy even. And more than anything, I needed to distance myself from her a little bit and calm myself down. I was aching, I wanted her so bad.

"Please let me in. Please! I'm scared!" She continued knocking.

"ARIELLE, go lie down right now!" I hollered. I had had just about enough. "I will be right there as soon as I'm finished. Just listen to the noises I'm making in here. I'm right here. I'm not going anywhere. You're not alone. I'm just in the other room."

"I don't see you. I need to see you."

"But you can hear my voice."

"Please. I need to see you," she pleaded. "Just let me see you."

I opened the door and poked my head out. "See, I'm here."

She smiled. "Oh, there you are."

"See, I'm right here," I said looking at her. She was still naked and looked so incredibly good. Staring down at her lush, bobbing breasts and delectable bottom, I was aching even more.

"Can you leave the door open. I want to see you."

"Okay, just go to the bed. Go to the drawers and get something to wear."

"I wait for you. There's colors in there," she said turning on her heels and walked back to the bed, rounded, tiny-waisted, totally appetizing, shaking her fine sexy rump across the room.

Umph, I thought to myself. I was up shit's creek without a paddle.

***

I think the sight of my huge, red, angry cock must have really scared her because after that night, she wasn't trying to play with it anymore. Now she was deathly afraid of two things: the color red and the bulge in front of my pants. She tried avoiding both things. She wouldn't touch any food that color, didn't want anything that color touching her skin, she had a serious aversion to even seeing anything red, my cock included. Even though I tried showing it to her again, explaining it was no longer red, but she only said, "Oh, but it gets red. It gets real red." She wanted to be sure it was always covered. Protected. Nowhere near her. Sex was pretty much out after that. I mean, but like it didn't matter anyway since I couldn't get into her regardless.

Meanwhile, I was really concerned about why I hadn't been able to have intercourse with her that night. I honestly couldn't get it in, and man, how I had tried. Also her fear of colors and damn nearly everything else was problematic as well. I called Florence with my concerns.

"Well I told you it would take a little time for her to adjust. And I knew she wouldn't like anything too bright. She's more accustomed to darkness and muted things right now. So bright colors and sunlight you'll have to introduce very slowly."

"Okay, so what about the sex thing?"

"Well, what's the problem?"

"Florence, it wouldn't go in. My penis. I couldn't get it inside her."

"Well did you try your fingers?"

"Ummm...well, I tried my ton—" I started to say but stopped. "Something else..."

"Yes, you tried your tongue," Florence said, "and did it go in?"

I grinned, unable to talk to a woman I wasn't intimate with so freely. But Florence seemed pretty cool with it. "I think so."

"Well, maybe she's just very tight. Maybe you need to try lubricants or something next time. Make sure she's very excited too before trying it again."

"Believe me, Florence. She was more than excited. I really think that the doc should check her out."

"You sure? She may not liked being handled like that. Especially now— that she's a little more aware of herself. Also, the doctor will be leaving for Nigeria tomorrow, so if you want her examined, you'll need to bring her tonight."

"Could there be something physically wrong with her? I'm really concerned. I mean so far, she seems perfect, but I just know that something's bound to be wrong. Like maybe she was sewn up or something."

"Don't be so pessimistic. Think positive and thank God that she's so perfect."

"Of course, you're right."

"Okay. Call me when you make up your mind what you want to do. Maybe you should try bedding her again first before you have her see the doctor."

After my phone call with Florence, and watching her from the corner of my eyes reading quietly, flipping through her little dictionary, writing things down now, she looked so studious and beautiful. My eyes drank in her velvety brown skin, her lithe, curvy limbs, her chiseled, sculpted face. She looked up and saw me watching her, smiled and continued what she was doing. She was an angel, straight from heaven, and oh how I wanted to corrupt her. I wanted to violate her 50 million ways. She was growing more and more independent and could entertain herself for hours at a time now—without looking to me. I wasn't sure I liked this. I sort of enjoyed when she was so helpless that she couldn't bear to be without me for a second.

I was probably going to be taking her for that examination because I didn't have the heart to try and make love to her again and not have it work out. And I couldn't play doctor and examine her. How awkward would that be. Really, the way I saw it, I had no choice but to let the doc examine her before he left. I didn't want the doc leaving then come to find out that there was something really wrong. So we were probably definitely going for a visit to Florence's. Tonight!

21

Springtime in Haiti

Arielle gave me so much problems simply to get into the car, and then clung to me for dear life the whole drive there. She was scared of the speed at which we were traveling, afraid of the street and traffic noises and the lights. "So many people," she murmured in disbelief. "So many people," she kept saying. She was traumatized by the time we got to Florence's place in La Plaine.

She went straight into Florence's arms as soon as she saw her and huddled besides her, totally ignoring me. I think she was mad at me. She told Florence she was scared, that I was mean and had scared her, and just kept peeking at me from the corner of her eyes and wouldn't even look at me or acknowledge me when I spoke to her too. Her attitude had change 180 degrees. At one point when I touched her she even shrieked, "Don't touch me! I don't like you!"

I was stunned by the venom in her voice and the heat in her eyes.

"Arielle," I said pushing a lock of her hair behind her ear and then squeezed her shoulder, but she glared at me, shrugged off my hand, and then stuck her tongue out at me. Then she ran away, going to huddle again near Florence. I could hear her selling out to her, telling her everything I had done to her. She even told her about freaky, which was supposed to be our secret. Florence was laughing her ass off.

I couldn't believe it, but I actually felt jealous that she preferred Florence to me. The way she was always all over me and now she wanted nothing to do with me. I'd get her, I was thinking. It was silly but I was going to punish her for this, I vowed, as I watched her from the corner of my eyes, while the doctor tried to explain some medical term to me. Florence was talking softly to her, cupping her face and she was listening attentively, nodding her head. Florence was like her mother or something. But I was still going to get her. She was way too fickle!

I signed some paper for him to examine her. I was surprised he was being this formal, but I didn't care. I needed him to get to the bottom of this asap. I was kind of pissed right now and felt like I wanted to bed this little hellion immediately. She was very distraught about the doctor handling her. Florence was right. She didn't want him touching her at all. Florence said she was very mistrustful of people.

She had to be strapped down and held down to be examined, and she was hollering and screaming and carrying on like we were killing her. Later, she was crying, and didn't want anybody to come near her, at all—not even Florence. She was huddled in a corner by herself. She wouldn't look at neither I nor Florence now, who I guess she felt had betrayed her as well. Florence tried to soothe her and so did I but she kept crying uncontrollably.

"She's fine," the doctor told me. "I think what you have is something close to virginity here. Her body has formed a hymen again, and I can take care of it by surgically removing it or you can break it the old fashion way, my friend." He smiled at my incredulity, "But I'm thinking you'd like the honor."

"Hymen? But she's had my baby."

"Even so. Physically...she's now technically a maiden again."

I was grinning from ear-to-ear. And the doctor laughed good-humoredly, slapping my back.

"It just keeps getting better and better, right? I'm so happy for you. Enjoy," he winked. "You lucky bastard!"

She was sleeping when I carried her to the car and was grateful she was asleep as we rode back to the bungalow. Florence had given her this tea that acted like a sedative, and she just continued to sleep as I put her to bed. Afterwards, I stared at her for a long time as she slept, pondering her mystery, wondering about all the perplexities of this thing I had done. What would she think once she truly understood what had happened to her, what I had done in resurrecting her. She might not like it. In fact, she might totally freak out on my ass!

I was beginning to think, HOLY CHRIST, what had I done? What if she wasn't happy? Not being able to see her family. EVER. Even though they were all alive. Or her friends. Or anybody from her previous life. I mean everyone had seen her in that coffin. She was dead to all the rest of the world except me. How much comfort would she give her? I mean given the fact that she had even decided now she didn't like me. I realized she probably didn't mean it. Still, it hurt. I didn't like being treated the way she treated the staff. So mistrustful. With such disdain. I felt dejected.

I had brought her back from the dead, and right now, as happy as I was, I realized too I'd never be able to share this happiness, this triumph, this victorious miracle or whatever it was, with no one else but a handful of strangers that meant nothing to my life. All my other significant others could never find out about this. She was a secret I would have to keep to myself forever and take to the grave. And right now, I was scared to death of what significance that would bear on *her*. Apparently I hadn't really thought about any of the consequences beyond just having her back in my life, but at this moment, I was dreadfully aware of how unprecedented this action of mine truly was.

Christ! I was basically in the same moral dilemma she was in when she was with Danyel. *You love this person more than life itself, but no one can know about it. No one will understand. Morally it is wrong. Reprehensible. But this person makes you happier than anything in the world! This is your soul mate, the person you would die a millions death for, the person you'd be willingly go to hell for.*

Was it possible that I now understood completely what she had gone through? How torn she had felt every day of her life. Honestly, I got it now. This was my a-ha moment (borrowing a phrase from Oprah Winfrey) and I could forgive her all. Forgive her anything...

***

I awakened to the most erotic sensation. Her mouth was on my nipple sucking and licking greedily. I grabbed a hold of her and swung her around, knocking the breath out of her as I threw her on her back and climbed on top of her. She was serious as she gazed up intently at me, apparently not at all intimidated by me.

"What do you think you're doing," I asked her roughly. Sounding a lot more gruff than I actually felt.

She said nothing but started stroking her hand up and down my back. "Good morning, master-husband," she replied.

"Good morning, my baby." I melted.

"Mad with me?"

"Whatever for?"

"For last night."

"What did you do last night?"

She shrugged, kissing my shoulder. "You look mad last night."

"I may have been last night," I said kissing the tip of her nose, "but I can't stay mad at you."

She gave a small smile.

"What about you? You mad at me?"

"Yes!"

"Yes?" I said rolling over on my back, and brought her with me. Letting her climb over me.

"You let that man touch me," she said accusingly. "You and Florence. I don't like that man!" She pouted. "You told me not to let no other man touch me!"

"He was a doctor. You needed to be examined. It's okay if a doctor touches you."

"Why?"

"Because a doctor takes care of you if you're sick."

"Sick?"

"I'm not saying that you are sick, but I had to be sure."

She was still pouting.

"Still mad at me?"

She turned to me and snuggled against me. "No," she said softly. "I love you!"

My heart nearly stopped.

"Love?" I said, touching her chin to look into her eyes.

"Love. L-o-v-e," she said and bent down to claim my lips.

***

I now smiled at every sight of her. I could hardly believe that the same woman who used to fuck me raw three or four times in a single night had now become this demure and pure little girl that I was now dealing with. This woman was also my wife and the mother of my child and now how in the world could this be? It was hard and I had had no idea how difficult this was going to be. All of the sudden, probably because I now knew about her physical condition, it made the pressure of having her all the more intense. Perhaps a natural reaction to the situation. But being in such close quarters wasn't making it any easier.

I was diligently making plans to go back home. She seemed fine to me now. I felt fairly confident she was going to be all right, that nothing would go awry at this point. Day-by-day she grew stronger. Her speech was steadily improving, as well as her maturity level. She was doing great. I was the one not fairing as well.

Every day having to look at those sensational legs, and that incredible body. So perfect. Those tantalizing, perky breasts always being thrust in my face. Or bobbing up and down when she walked. (I hadn't introduced her to the idea of wearing a bra yet. I was enjoying the freedom of her breasts too damned much). Then there was that questing tongue she enjoyed sticking down my throat. The first time I had kissed her, I had been so excited and delighted that I had tongued her thoroughly, sticking my tongue all down her throat. It had been one of those deliciously sexy kisses that you gave to someone who you wanted to have an orgasm. Yet now, she thought that was the only way to kiss. And did it often. It was only embarrassing when she kissed me all nasty like that in front of the help or around other people—who would stare at us with much amazement. Then at night, in bed, she was all over me, hugging and squeezing, loving. It was all good for her. It came natural, and was all rather innocent. But she was killing me. She had no idea the enormous effort, the painstaking effort it took not to stick my big, red cock right between her lusty little thighs no matter how much she protested.

I had taken her into town with me a few times. We had to get provisions for the voyage to LaGorce. I was planning on taking off before the weekend.

I had my arms around her waist and she had her hand around mine. Everyone kept staring and I wasn't sure if it was because word had spread about her or if it was simply because we looked like foreigners.

The marketers kept referring to me as *blanc* and Arielle became curious about what it meant.

"Why everyone calls you *blanc*? You not their master?"

I had to laugh at just how ironic her entire question was. "No, I'm not their master. And *blanc* means white."

"White?"

"They probably think I'm white because of my light complexion and the color of my hair."

"You white?"

"No, I'm Black—like you."

"You not like me."

"I'm just a lighter shade, but yes, I'm like you."

"You only my master," she asked next.

"Arielle, I'm your husband. And you're my wife. I thought I explained that."

"You not my master?"

"Only if you want me to be. You want me to be your master?"

She nodded her head, smiling like morning sunshine. She was too precious, and my heart lurched in response to her genuine innocence.

"All right then, I'm your master."

She kissed me sweetly, and I returned her kiss. But soon, her kiss deepened and got real intense, causing everyone to stare even more and whisper.

I attempted to break the kiss gently, but she was being really frisky. "Arielle, goodness, girl. You can't kiss me like that in public—not unless we're alone. Only when we're alone."

"But you kiss me like that."

"I kissed you like that at first because I was excited and happy to see you. But it's indecent to do that in public. We can only kiss like that in private.

"Indecent? Private?"

"You can't kiss me like that around other people."

She looked perplexed. Totally confused.

"Look, baby. Let me show you the right way."

I demonstrated by giving her a chaste kiss on the lips. "See...real sweet. Nice and decent."

She followed instructions to show me she had learned.

"Oh, that was lovely. Real nice."

"But why can't I kiss you like this?" She did it again, blowing my mind—making all my hair stand on end this time—not to mention my shorts.

"Ooooh, God, that felt good, but you can't kiss me like that unless we're alone and you're willing to back it up."

"Back it up?"

"Yeah, unless you plan on giving me some pussy right after."

"Pussy? Spell it."

I laughed and spelled it, feeling like a dirty school kid.

"Pussy. I like that word. What it means?"

I grinned. Yeah, she would like that word. "It means sex. Your vagina," I said discreetly touching her crotch. "So unless you plan to get down, don't kiss me like that, aw'ight?"

She smiled. "I want the sex."

"Oh, no. Trust me. You don't want the sex. Cause having the sex means having that big red thing you don't like touching you—in fact, inside you. So, look, let's drop it, okay?"

"Oh, like the night in tub. On floor?"

"Yeah, exactly."

"Oh," she said with sudden comprehension. And I knew there'd be no more discussion on that subject.

22

Shacking Up at the Crib

They left Haiti on a hazy Wednesday morning. Arielle was so sick the first day of the voyage. So much so that Cedric thought about turning back. She had sea sickness—or so he had thought at first, until he caught her wiping white stuff off her lips and found several boxes of chalk stashed in her bag. Half of one box was already gone—and this was after a long lecture he had given her the first time he had caught her eating chalk.

"Arielle he asked her calmly after dinner. She could hardly hold anything down, she was vomiting so bad. He hated to even bring it up, but he was concerned. "Have you been eating chalk again?"

"No," she said quickly. Shaking her head, "I didn't eat no chalk."

"No?"

"No, I don't eat chalk no more."

"Sure about that?"

"I don't eat no chalk. Sick. But not because of chalk."

"Oh."

"I don't know why I'm sick. Just sick!"

He groaned, wanting to squeeze her. This was her first lie to him. She was learning to be deceitful. And he didn't know how to proceed, how to react to it. Did he confront her or let her think she had gotten away with it? It was difficult deciding what to do. He gave her a sweet smile.

"Arielle," he said taking her hand, "sometimes we make promises we can't keep. For whatever reason," he said gazing into her eyes, wanting her to understand the gravity of the situation, but also not wanting to scare her. "Maybe because we were coerced into making them. And maybe even because we never had any intention of keeping that promise in the first place...I just want you to know though there's nothing in this world you can tell me that's going to change the way I feel about you. You never have to lie to me. I'll forgive you all. Just...baby, if you've done something you're not suppose to and you don't tell the truth, and if that something is hurting you and I don't know about it, it could really hurt you. You know? Cause then you put me in the position where I don't know how to help you. Understand?"

She nodded her head.

"Okay. So now, I need to know if your vomiting is simply seasickness or if it's because you've been eating chalk again. You need to tell me the truth. The truth is what really happened. Okay? What actually happened. Now what happened, baby? Did you eat some chalk. Tell the truth."

She looked fearful, peering shyly into his eyes.

"Don't be afraid. I'm not going to hurt you or beat you or be mad at you. I simply have to know."

"I ate the chalk." She said very quietly. "I eat it and it make my stomach hurt and I got real sick. Maybe I eat too much."

"Ohhhh, and so now you see, chalk is no good for you."

"I see...I see," she cried. "I'm a bad girl. I disobey."

"No-no, you're not a bad girl. You're a good girl, you told the truth." He kissed her on the top of her head, and hugged her fiercely. Then, letting her go reluctantly, he pulled out the two chalk boxes. "I found these two boxes in your bag. Now Arielle, be truthful. Is there anymore chalk?"

She started to shake her head and then stopped as he held her gaze, not letting her turn away. She then took out several pieces from her pocket and presented them to him.

Cedric took them from her. "Anymore?"

She nodded.

"Where?"

She stood up and walked to the drawers and took out several more pieces and next took out a couple she had hidden in a pencil box she had stashed in her back pack.

"Arielle," Cedric exclaimed, and then couldn't help chuckling. "Is this all of it?"

She nodded.

Cedric took all the chalk and walked with her to the railing. "Now baby, what I want you to do is toss all of this chalk overboard, so that they'll no longer be a temptation."

"Temptation," she said curiously.

"Yes. If you don't have the chalk, then you won't be teased and tantalized by them. We're removing them so you'll be free of the thought of them."

"I will still think of them," she said matter-a-fatly. "I like them."

"Even though they made you sick?"

She nodded. "I still like them."

"Arielle," he admonished gently. "What's so good about eating chalk?!"

"You like cigarettes. I like chalk. Cigarettes you said not good for you either. But you smoke anyway. We throw your cigarettes away too... in the water?"

"Oh shit," he laughed. "When did you get so smart? Oh-my-God," he exclaimed with a wide grin. "Anyway...well, I guess then we'll have to throw my cigarettes overboard as well."

"You won't smoke no more?"

"Not if you don't want me to."

She wrinkled her nose, then beamed up at him. "It's okay, master-husband. You can smoke if you want to." She threw the chalk overboard, then giggled. "I won't eat the chalk no more."

Cedric hugged her fiercely. *Yeah, because I'll never let you get your hands on them again*, he thought smugly, but was so happy she wasn't pressing the cigarette thing. "For you I'd give up anything, baby. I love you." *So fucking much*, he thought with relish, not believing how good it felt holding her in his arms again.

She leaned into his embrace, accepting his affection eagerly. "No more chalk, I promise," she murmured. "No more."

His arms tightened around her.

***

She was sleeping when they arrived on LaGorce island. He had wanted to pinpoint some sights to her, but hadn't wanted to wake her, she looked so peaceful, so angelic laying there. He carried her into the house with her hardly aware that they were somewhere completely new.

This was the house Arielle had taken painstaking care to have built. She had been involved on all levels of planning—from location choice to architectural design to construction and finally the interior design. He was hoping that being there would rev-up her memory, fast-forwarding it to the present. And though she had made leaps and strides in maturity since her rebirth, he calculated that emotionally, she couldn't be more than fifteen years old. And this was beginning to concern him. Just how long would it take to get her fully functional and at a reasonable level of adulthood?

After paying his yacht's captain and the two hired seamen for the trip, he was quite alone at the house. He and Arielle would have the entire nine-bedroom estate to themselves. No one knew he was there and in fact knew of his whereabouts. He had been very cryptic about where he would be a few weeks ago when he had given his entire staff of servants, security and musicians a 3-month hiatus. He had told them something to the effect that he needed space and needed to be completely alone, how he wanted to go on a spiritual journey and explore things on his own.

It had sounded very *Zen*, extremely New Age, and although he knew his boyz thought he was tripping, what could they do but relent and stop bothering him about his music and career. He had been more than generous with their vacation pay, so no one complained too loudly. No one except Deuce who had told him, "I knew you'd go Hollywood on us someday, but hell...look at this shit...you did!" Later, as he said good-bye, he was a little gentler and had told him, "Hope you get better soon, man." Like he had some illness or disease he needed to fight to overcome.

If only he knew, Cedric reflected with a smile. Perhaps Deuce was right, and this was some illness or disease he had to struggle to overcome. Some days, it certainly felt like it.

So now, the only person he'd have to deal with in the morning was Manuel, his gardener and caretaker for the estate grounds, who he knew regularly cared for the house and Manuel's wife, Consuela who had been doing the cooking and cleaning. He and Arielle were going to need them now. And what was great was that they had both moved from Venezuela only recently, and so would not be familiar with all the commotion of the murder last year.

But they'd have to make do tonight—no one was expecting them, and it was really fine with him. Cedric changed Arielle without waking her into one of his large T-shirts and tucked her in nearby room across from the master bedroom, adjacent to CJ's nursery—Margo's room. He showered and had just fixed himself a cognac before settling down, relishing the fact that for the first time in a long time, there was no one there to do his bidding. There was absolutely no one and it felt great! No one, but him and his lady love...

After downing the cognac and slipping beneath the crisp, Egyptian cotton sheets, he was just about to turn off the lights when Arielle came waltzing in.

The cotton t-shirt he had dressed her in was gleaming white, and her nipples were like little beacons, pointing at him.

"What, Arielle. Why are you out of bed?" He demanded

moistening his lips. The last thing he wanted was any temptation tonight, horny as he was.

"I can't sleep by myself. You never come back. You sleep in here?"

"Yes, baby. This is my room."

"I don't sleep with you. Like before?"

He looked helplessly at her. "Baby, it's better if you sleep in your own bed. It's better like that." Besides, he wasn't sure how much more he could take. He was positively aching right now. He had planned on watching a good porn flick and taking care of his aching groin before going to sleep.

"No, I sleep with you."

"Please, Arielle. Please go back to your room. I don't want you sleeping with me," he nearly hissed.

She ignored him, and hopped on top of him regardless. He moaned in agony as her crotch slammed down on his aching balls. She snuggled down on top of him like a giant cat, her erect nipples digging into his chest. "No," he groaned rather loudly.

"Feels good," she asked, now planting butterfly kisses on his face and neck, being overly affectionate.

He could barely speak. "Arielle," he said struggling beneath her. She had him pinned down and he felt aroused and weak. He had had a permanent hard-on for weeks, and this was pure torture.

She was looking at him through half-closed lids. He could tell she was about to kiss him, and her kisses were nothing nice. Totally indecent. Designed to drive him wild!

"No!" he protested and roughly shoved her off him. "Stop it! Stop it right now! You need to leave right now and go to your own bed. I mean it. Leave, right now!"

Slinking off onto the other side of the mattress, she looked bewildered, like her feelings were hurt. But Cedric kept his resolve, and pointed her to the door. Snorting at him, she rolled her eyes and sauntered off to the direction he had pointed, but not before turning back and casting him a quelling look.

***

"Ceeedddriiiccc! Cedric! Ahhhhh! HELP ME!!!"

I nearly broke my neck, taking the stairs four at a time, trying to get upstairs to see what was going on with her. My heart was racing as I rushed to the master bath and found her sitting on the toilet, screaming hysterically.

"Cedric! There's some red stuff coming out my ass!"

I collapsed on the floor. If I hadn't nearly broke my neck, it would have been funny.

"Cedric!" She was sobbing, staring in between her legs, looking absolutely horrified.

I looked down into the water at the blood.

She was staring at me with terror. "What is it?!"

"It's blood. You have your period, baby. It's only your menstrual cycle."

"Menstrual cycle?"

"Yes, every twenty-eight days, you bleed for three to five days. It means that you can still have babies.

"Babies?"

"Reproduction. You can give me another son or daughter."

"But you said I already have a baby."

"Yes, and this means you can have others."

"You want me to have another baby?"

"I didn't say," I said kissing her on the thigh, breathing her in, loving the smell of her—even with her period.

She bent her head and looked down into the toilet again. "Blood."

"Yes. Blood."

"Eeeoow! I don't like blood!"

"Of course not. It's red. I know."

Then, she grabbed me by the hair and tried to push my head to her crotch to go down on her. "Whoa, whoa, whoa, baby. Uh-huh, I'm not down with that."

"Suck it," she demanded.

"What?!"

"Take the blood off."

I had a real good laugh. "Do I look like a tampon to you? No baby, I love you and all but that shit is nasty. I promise to lick it real good though as soon as your period is off, and you're nice and clean. But right now, we need some toilet paper and I need to go get you some tampons from the store."

"Tampons?"

"Yes, a feminine hygiene product, designed expressly for this. I need to get you a whole shit load of that stuff. And teach you some manners too."

"Why?"

"Cause you don't grab a man's head and attempt to shove it..."

She was staring up at me with her big beautiful liquid brown eyes looking all innocent.

"Forget it. I need to go get those things for you at the store. I need you to sit right there until I come back."

"I can't stay here by myself," she said bolting up, splashing blood all over the place.

"Christ, Arielle," I said pushing her back down. "Gosh, you're getting that damn period blood everywhere. Now just stay put," I said, rolling out a wad of toilet paper and handing it to her.

"I'm not staying here by myself," she told me again. Just in case I didn't hear her the first time. Then she stared at the paper I had placed in her hand seemingly perplexed, like she had no idea what to do with it.

Taking it from her in disgust, I shoved it between her legs. "You have to put that here, and keep your legs closed so it doesn't fall out."

"Keep my legs closed? How do I walk?"

"Look, I think your panties will hold it in place," I said with an exasperated sigh. "Okay, I don't really know. Maybe there's a belt or something—maybe—or tape. Hell, I'm a man...I don't know about these things. Shit, why couldn't you have had your period in Haiti where Florence could have helped you! Damn inconvenient, I'll tell you," I mumbled.

She stared at me blankly like she didn't care or couldn't understand.

I thought about what I could do.

I could order it and have them deliver it. Yes, all I'd have to do is go on the web and see if I couldn't get one of those companies to bring the stuff directly to me. But that might take too long. Meanwhile, Arielle was soaking up the wad of toilet papers. She kept changing them every few minutes, because she didn't want the red against her skin. And she was having a real hard time sitting down, fidgeting. Not to mention the fact that she would clog up the toilet flushing all those huge wads of toilet paper one after the other like clockwork. At least once I got her the tampons, she wouldn't have to see it.

"Okay, look, I'll take you with me, but you have to promise to wait in the car when I go into the store. Also, baby, make sure that you have the toilet paper real thick. I don't want blood all over the seat of my Ferrari, know what I'm sayin'. It's a white leather interior." *Like she was paying attention to anything I had said. Like she gave a damn about my car or the color of the interior.*

She rolled her eyes at me, which meant I was talking to her ass. She had such a little attitude, although I admit I loved it. She was beginning to act more and more like her real self lately. More and more like Arielle.

"So do you agree to stay in the car while I go into the store?

She shrugged.

"I need a yes or a no or you're not coming."

"Okay."

Thank God for small miracles, since she wasn't going to fight me on this.

I left her in the bathroom to take care of her business and she came back out. I let her walk in front of me and checked out her ass. She was wearing a pair of Levi's and I wanted to be sure she had put on some padding, but I couldn't tell through the jeans.

"You did put on some tissue, didn't you, Arielle?"

"Yes, yes, yes," she said in annoyance. "I put on that paper."

I shrugged, this was quickly becoming a nightmare.

The car ride seemed to cheer her up. She was momentarily distracted from the blood situation, and was hanging out the window, soaking in the gorgeous South Florida view and sun. "Wheeee!" she was screaming out the window, all happy, no longer afraid of the sun and cars, nor the fact that I was driving so fast.

Several young punks passed next to us and started hollering at her, signaling me to pull over. I had half a mind to pull over and whip some ass, they were being so disrespectful. But Arielle, always the flirt was laughing and giggling and having a good time, waving and smiling at them.

At the store, I donned some Pilot shades and pulled down my baseball cap before going into the store. I felt uncomfortable as hell, and had never had to purchase this type of stuff before. As a precautionary measure, I grabbed a gallon of milk, some yogurt and two boxes of tampons—one for heavy days, one for light, and some panty liners. Then I grabbed a box of Summer's Eve, remembering how Arielle used to always douche after her period. I wondered when and if she'd ever know what to do with all this stuff.

At the check out counter, the cashier looked at me several times. Looked at the items I was purchasing and kept sneaking peaks at me. It was getting me really nervous. Hell, this was how rumors got started. Then when I started to pay, she looked dead at me and said, "S'cuse me, but are you Cedric Courage?"

I smiled and gently shook my head.

"God, if you're not, you look so much like him. Has anyone ever told you that?"

"Yeah-yeah, I get that all the time."

"You sound like him too.

"Um...wish I had his money."

"Don't we all! Well, if I were you, I'd try to make some money off him. You know since you look so much like him. There's this agency I know—"

"I'm sorry," I said cutting her off. "I'm really in a hurry, but I'll take that under advisement," I said, grabbing the shopping bags and got the hell out of there. Luckily for me, she had been so interested in trying to figure out who I was, and had not been too interested with the items I had purchased.

Okay, so I was beginning to miss having underlings—people you could send out to get stuff. People to do unpleasant things you had no desire to do. People who could drive you everywhere...who knew you couldn't park in the fire lane, directly in front of a supermarket—especially when there was plenty of parking spaces further back.

As I approached the car, there was a cop circling my Ferrari. Arielle had her head tucked out the window and the cop seemed to be carrying a conversation with her.

Oh-oh.

"Oh," she laughed as I came into earshot and giggled. "Here's my master now."

The cop looked me up and down. "You're her master?"

Shit, here it was. He was going to bust my ass with all kinds of tickets. Not mention how he'd think I was into some kinky shit.

"Ah, she just calls me that. It's just a pet name."

He snorted. "Some weird, sexual-stuff, I'm sure. No need to go into details. Anyway...you do realize you are parked in a fire lane."

"I'm moving it right now, officer."

"If it weren't for your very lovely companion, I'd writing you out a ticket."

"Thanks," I said, climbing in, revved up the engine and next eased slowly out of there, being sure to obey the 20mph speed limit in the parking lot. Soon after I turned the curb though, I was tearing out of there. Too many close calls today.

Once back at the house, I put the milk and yogurt in the fridge and handed Arielle the boxes of tampons and other products, instructing her to read them and follow directions. Arielle took the boxes and headed upstairs. When she took an eternity to come back downstairs, I went to investigate what she was up to. I walked into the bathroom and Arielle had several of the tampons open and had made a mess of them all over the counter. She had no idea what she was doing.

I swore under my breath. Christ, this was a nightmare! Leading her to the bidet, I made her sit on it, realizing I was going to have to clean her up, and insert the tampons for her myself to show her how it was done. "Okay, I think we're gonna have to start from scratch. Take your jeans off completely. Your panties too."

"Everything?"

"Just leave on your top."

I could do this...if I approached it clinically, like a doctor, all impersonal. But as I watched her pull off her pants and observed all the blood that was on the pad she had on, I felt repulsed. "God, you're bleeding so much. I never realized you bled so much," I told her.

She held her stomach. "Hurt so bad."

"You're cramping too?"

She nodded.

Shit, I had forgotten to buy some Midol. But Extra-Strength Tylenol might work just as well. That and some hot tea. I'd be sure to make her some later.

"Okay, so now pay attention. I'm going to show you how this works...this is called a bidet, and it helps to clean this part of you. Understand? Women use this to clean their privates."

"Bidet? Privates?"

"Yes, some fancy French name, but it washes you real good. Feels good too...the water pressure. After today, you'll probably be in here all the time using this thing." I laughed. "But anyway, I'm gonna show you how to put in the tampon, and then I want you to put it in. Okay?"

She gave me a weak smile.

Poor thing, she must be really hurting.

"This thing," I said holding up one of the tubes that looked like a very thick cigarette, "you have to slip this in there, but this part, you trash," I explained double-checking the instructions. "This part is called the applicator and is made of plastic, so it helps glide the cotton absorbent in there. You see," I said, demonstrating to her how to do it, then trashed it. "Now, go ahead and take this one, and glide it right up there."

"How I'm gonna stick it in there? Hurt."

"It's not gonna hurt. It's small. Just like my finger. You like when I stick my finger in there. Does my finger hurt?"

"No," she smiled. "Feel good."

"Well, this isn't gonna feel good like my finger. It's not suppose to, but it won't hurt either."

She looked doubtful.

"I'm sure it might be a little uncomfortable at first, but you'll get used to it. Here. Take it."

"Unh-unh."

"Unh-unh? What? You're not gonna put it in?"

"No, you do it."

"Know what? Today is the day you grow up, Arielle. You're not a baby, but a grown woman who has her period. Now I'll be goddamn if I'm gonna put your tampon in for you. Forget it. Never gonna happen. No way! You either put this on the way I explained to you, or you get red stuff all over your legs and body. You decide which you'd rather," I said and shut the door on her.

There. *I'd told her!*

Half an hour later, she came out looking fresh as sunshine and came and sat next to me on the couch, and placed her head sweetly on my shoulder. I felt my heart contract. She could be so sweet sometimes.

"So did you do it?"

She nodded, and smiled gently. "Yes, I did. I touched the red stuff."

"Did you wash your hands?"

"Yes, I used bidet. Warm water was very good. Feel much better now."

I put my arms around her and hugged her real tight. My baby was growing up...

23

Kiss from a Rose

Perhaps there were good and bad rhythms in life. And for me, this moment was one of total beauty. My life had become a pleasant landscape, where the grass was green, the bush was thick and the lake was very calm. For the first time in a long time, I was loving life. I felt blessed, truly happy.

It had been over thee weeks since we had arrived at LaGorce and so much had changed—for the better. Arielle was learning things at an alarming pace. Sometimes I would wonder if she had gotten her memory back. Her speech was now nearly perfect. She had lost her fear of bright colors and was slowly adjusting to the color red. She still hadn't embraced it, but she could now stand to look and maybe touch it and wasn't totally repulsed by it. Thank God!

She was also getting on much better with people too. She was now on friendly terms with Maria, the cook and her husband, Manuel, who took care of the grounds and pool. She was fascinated with gardening, and several times, she had gone out to help Manuel with the yard work, asking about all the shrubs and flowers around, enjoying the simple pleasure of raking, after he had cut the lawn. Her very favorite place though was the rose garden, where she would visit nearly every morning to cut roses to place in some of the vases around the house. And never did she forget to place at least one bud in a little vase she'd place on the breakfast tray she'd bring to me after Maria had prepared it.

I'd come to love our early morning breakfast and conversations. We'd sit together in the breakfast nook in the master bedroom, very private, and have toast, drink coffee, sip orange juice and talk, talk, talk. She did most of the talking, but I enjoyed listening. It was becoming my favorite time of the day. Afterwards, I'd coax her back to bed for an early morning smooch-fest and it was totally everything I had ever wanted. The only thing that would have made my happiness more complete would be having CJ and Margo here with us.

CJ, ah, I really missed the little tyke.

When we weren't in the room or on the terrace, we were in the library-den. I watched her from across the room as she sat, cross-legged on the sectional sofa, her nose buried in a book. She was a voracious reader, even so... she still managed to watch entirely too much TV. She especially loved the movie channels and the DVR—we had Tivo and she could devour entire seasons of her favorite shows. She watched her favorite ones over and over again.

I knew I was totally smitten by her since I actually sat there and watched them with her sometimes—even if it was for the tenth time. I didn't mind, since it meant we got to spend time, laugh and be entertained together. Before that, I'm not sure I had watched more than 30 hours of television in a year.

There was something else I was enjoying too. She was completely uninhibited. I still hadn't taught her too much about dressing, and even though she now tended to always wear panties—must be an instinctive woman thing or maybe she felt the need to protect her privates from me—she still wasn't too up on the art of wearing a bra. So I got treated to having her go around braless and in the skimpiest bikini's I could find. Being with her in all her naked glory all the time, I got used to seeing her body. And even though I was always aroused, it made it easier for me not to pounce on her when we did fool around. And although it was hard to even fathom it, I still hadn't made love to her properly. Her hymen was still intact.

I no longer minded it so much. It was old-fashioned, but now I could understand why in the olden days men and women weren't allowed to have sex before marriage and had to go through a courting period where they'd have to get to know each other first. I found myself enjoying the acts of romancing her. I wanted to win her heart. I was enjoying it immensely. Being with her like this and not having sex be an issue.

I couldn't help feeling that the fact that we hadn't consummated our love was making it all the more special now. *Who knew? Who's have ever thought...?*

I could have gone for months at this slow, sumptuous pace with hardly a complaint. My wife was beautiful and interesting and delightful. I was learning all the layers that made her Arielle and hopefully, she was learning a lot about me as well. I was noticing things about myself too in the process, I had never paid attention to before. Realizing how fragmented my life had been.

How much it still was, and knowing it was something I wanted to rectify.

I had never felt I needed anyone to complete me. I had written a song for Arielle right before we married called *You Complete Me*, which hadn't been written to mislead her, but the truth was, deep down no matter how close I allowed anyone to get, there would always be this last vestige, this last ingredient I would never be able to give. In other words, I would never be able to give completely of myself to anyone. That was an impossibility, I had always thought, before now.

Growing up, I had always felt like a loner, and was a loner by nature. I think it was being an only child without a mother, having a man like my dad for a father, and growing up in different boarding schools all over the world, it was difficult for me to form close ties.

The fact was, I didn't know how to share myself with anyone else. So I shouldn't have been surprised that Arielle would turn to someone else for whatever it was she had found lacking in me. And there had been so much lacking, I realized now. I had never given Arielle what she had needed the most. *Me,* minus all the bullshit. So it was no wonder she had sought someone to give her what she was missing.

So I was coming to terms with how lonely I had always been—despite the fact that I had always been surrounded by a multitude of people. How I had never really had a true companion, not in the real sense of the word. Sure, Arielle had been my wife, my mate, but there were so many areas in my life she had never entered. She had had her little corner, her compartment, and that had been all, and I had thought that was enough. Yet now I could see it so clearly. It hadn't been.

I felt myself opening up to her now. Being completely honest. Being who I truly was. Screw the fame, the public persona, being the person others expected. I realized many people, even some of the ones who called themselves my closest friends, did not see me as a person really. To them, I was this idea, this famous face, this larger than life notion, a perception, which could not be contained. Sure, they honestly believed they could separate who I really was from what I did. But the reality of it was they didn't. And I couldn't say I blamed them completely because I played that trump card. And I did so deliberately to further fragment and push away and not let anyone get too close. Close enough to hurt me. Yet Arielle had still managed to creep in somehow. And now, she had forged in completely.

Being one on one with Arielle who wasn't as yet tainted and who perceived only what I directly projected, made me feel joyous. Gave me hope that I could be something other than and separate from Cedric Courage, public domain, the singer/songwriter/ entertainer. I was ready to let her in and wanted badly to really mean that song I had written to her, which seemed so long ago.

Yes, how much I was learning. Like the perfection of this moment and how fleeting it actually was. Loved the simplicity and beauty in my life. Appreciated it. But the downside to this was the realization that it couldn't stay this way. The day would soon come when I'd have to delve back and go back into the world. And how then would I be able to live openly with my lady? How in the world was I going to make that happen? Was anything like that even possible now?

I wasn't sure. But I was keeping faith, attempting to forge a plan.

***

I came to know my wife again in the biblical sense on a rainy afternoon when it was pouring out. She was downstairs watching a movie and I was upstairs listening to some demo tapes when I slipped upon a tape entitled Arielle, a tape that I had long forgotten but which got me thinking about her and how we had made it that night. Hell, I became totally aroused, I knew exactly what was on the tape and I trembled as I held it. Did I dare watch it and get myself all riled up? I thought about watching it and pleasuring myself to it while she was downstairs amusing herself in the library-den. Figured I could just do my thing, spank my monkey, and no one would be the wiser.

I went to the bedroom, got some lotion and popped in the video, getting nice and comfortable on the bed, and watched our homemade skin flick. She was hot. Naughty. Making all those wonderful sounds I loved to hear and I started to touch myself. Right at the climatic moment when she was having an orgasm and I had unzipped my fly ready to get into some real action, guess who the cat dragged in?

She came waltzing in, breasts all pointy, in the skimpy little lace panties I liked to keep her in, asking, "Watcha watching?"

I fumbled with the remote control, clicked it off real fast, and then tried unsuccessfully to zip myself back up. *Oh shit! Oh shit! Goddammit, she had caught me red handed.*

"What were you watching," she said coming over to the bed—

naked for all intent and purposes—all curves, brown skin and slender, coltish legs—doing dangerous things to my already raging libido—not to mention my quickly diminishing sense of restraint. "Turn it back on," she said, flopping herself next to me.

"No, It's just work. Anyway, I have to go finish—"

She grabbed the remote from me and flipped it on herself. I was so embarrassed. She turned over upside down, trying to understand the picture. "Is that me," she asked in disbelief. "Are we having sex?"

I could do nothing but fess up.

"Yup."

"You videotaped us having sex?"

"That's correct."

"Why?"

Because of moments like this. But I didn't say it. "I don't know. I...we just did it once. I—"

"You're a pervert," she told me, shaking her head. Her vocabulary had grown big time, and she was as sassy as ever—especially since watching all those Hollywood movies.

"So what were you doing? Masturbating?"

Shouldn't have been surprised by that one since one of her favorites movies was *American Pie.*

She turned back around and started watching the tape, then flipped back over and caressed her exposed breasts. Then turning to look at me, she asked, "How come you've never tried to make love to me again, Cedric?"

"I figured you'd let me know when you were ready. Also, I thought it would be nice if you got your memory back."

I watched her hands glide down her thighs and them move up her hips to rest of her waist. Her every movement was getting me really turned on, unbelievably hot!

"What if I never get my memory back? Does it mean we'll never make love?"

I laid my palm on her sleek, slender stomach. Her flesh burned. There was a quick intake of breath on both our parts, and I felt my cock swell even more. "Do you want to make love, Arielle? Please think very carefully before responding. You understand what happens if we really make love. It's not just my using my tongue on you."

"I know. You put the big, red thing inside me, where the tampons go."

"Yes," I answered. A bit surprised she could be so clinical.

"Well, do you want me to put it inside you, where the tampons go?"

"Yes," she murmured, touching my arm, running her long fingernails over my biceps, tracing the tattoo on my arm and caressing my chest with her fingertips. Next, she kissed the heart tattoo with her initials in it.

Well, I'd be darned, I thought in anticipation. My heart was doing somersaults. I took her hand and brought it up to my lips and sucked gently on her middle finger. She closed her eyes to better savor the sensation.

I gazed down into her face, thinking how outrageously beautiful I found her. I wanted her so much.

I took her other hand and slid it over my erection, sliding it down my shorts. All the while still sucking her finger but thinking how I wanted to take my time in pleasuring her.

She moaned softly and started touching me, grabbing hold of me powerfully. Masterfully. Stroking me steadily. Lovingly. Just the way I remembered.

"Oh God," I cried out, loving her touch. I had been waiting so long for her to hold me in her hands again. She raised herself into a more comfortable position to pleasure me better. When I started to become so unbearably aroused that I might have my release without having given myself to her properly, I maneuvered out of her grasp and got completely undressed and started to inch her panties off as well.

But I was playful, wanting to tease her a bit first, knowing how she liked to be teased first. All women did. So I would inch her panties off and then pull them back on her again, or gently raise myself up to, massage her breasts, and then tug her panties back up until I felt her frustration grow and her passion rise.

I did not want a repeat of the last time and had something to prove this time in any case—even if it was just to myself. I wanted her panting and begging me before I let her have it. I wanted her out of her mind with anticipation.

When I finally peeled off the tiny flimsy panty she was wearing—just the mere look of her was setting me on fire. I loved the lust beaming from her eyes too, as she looked me over. She had this totally hot-blooded, wanton look. One that said she totally appreciated my maleness.

"So..." I said as I laid her back against the pillows, and climbed up and positioned myself over her, loving the bold way she just yanked me to her, grabbing a hold of my cock and showed me she knew exactly how we fit. I bit my bottom lip from the rapture and the anticipation of what was to come. Soon I felt the sweet pressure of her warmth against my swollen flesh and winced from the excruciating pleasure I felt. "You're something else, you know that, Bling?"

She laughed but not for long, as I started to kiss and lick the tip of her breasts like they were globes of cherry-dipped candy.

"Ohhh," she groaned in sweet agony.

I wanted to taste her inside and out. I wanted to bury myself inside, but I knew I had to make her go wild first.

I bent over and started kissing down her neck, down her stomach. She opened wider to allow me access, as I licked down her thighs. Grazing her with my teeth, getting closer and closer to her center, but purposefully missing the mark time and time again, until she screamed and shoved my face between her crotch demanding I lick and suck what she wanted the most.

Ah hell, she was too sweet. Her juices were so hot and potent, I could scarcely breathe. I licked her from top to bottom, gliding and sticking my tongue everywhere, sucking and lapping, caressing and endeavoring to drive her insane. Finally, when she arched her back and rubbed herself all over my face in sweet agony, moving her hips so erotically, it made me want to rage, I wanted to fuck her so bad. It took everything I was not to come. Instead, I made her come—like a volcano.

She actually squirted me with her come and was crying from the sweetness of it. The sound of her explosive ecstasy did things to my male psyche I never knew were possible. I was so charged and so happy, I could burst.

She slid her hands over my shoulders and chest, and while she recovered from her orgasm, I hung back. Not penetrating her yet. I kissed her deeply, drinking her in as my hand played with her tiny opening, caressing it, squeezing it, then I slid a finger inside. She was nice and slick when I started fingering her, rubbing her clit with my thumb, while stroking her in and out with my index finger, playing out what was about to happen with my penis. I brought her to the brink of orgasm that way, but stopped right before she could come. I wanted her to save her energy and not to slack her lust, but wait for the big one that was to come.

She was panting. Moaning. So was I.

Damn, she felt amazing! So fucking wonderful! She was my heaven. In her arms, I would love to die. I eased her legs a little further apart, coming to rest between them. "Tell me you want it," I murmured, "that you want me, Arielle. All of me."

She moaned loudly, her eyelashes fluttering and began to speak. "I want you," she whispered fiercely. "I want you...deep inside me. Make me come just like you did in the video, with your penis buried deep inside me," she groaned, undulated and grinded her hips against mine for emphasis.

Fuck, I hadn't asked for all of that. In fact, the fact that she could still speak in complete sentences told me she wasn't that gone. I had to rectify that. I wanted her speechless. But all that sexy talk had made my head spin.

I grinned at her, loving the way she was moving beneath me, so erotically. Loving the softness of her breasts against my chest, the silkiness of her skin slipping against mine while I remained poised between her thighs. For a moment, I rubbed the tip of my cock against her velvety folds, feeling a nice little jolt, a shock of pure pleasure and excitement when I touched her moist opening.

"Feels so nice," she murmured, as I rubbed against her a little longer, wanting to make sure she was nice and wet and ready before I attempted to enter her this time.

She moaned her pleasure, but then gasped as I thrust suddenly and started to penetrate her slowly, carefully, kissing her face, her neck and breasts to lessen any pain she might experience. I wanted to give her only pleasure. She undulated beneath me, swaying her hips provocatively, welcoming me deeper and deeper and deeper still, until I could go no further, and I was only half-way in. Watching her reaction, the sexy smile that touched her lips and the sensuousness of her heavy lashes, I felt an indescribable sensation at finally being inside her.

"How does that feel," I murmured, kissing the side of her face.

"Ugh!" She gave a throaty little laugh. "Good. Um, real good," she assured me, sliding her hands up and down my back. "Wonderful!"

"So-so wonderful," I agreed, starting to slip out to push back in, but she grabbed me, flexing a little with alarm. "Baby, does it hurt?"

Her eyes were wild. "No, where you going? Stay...I like it. Don't go out!"

It was my turn to give a throaty laugh. "Oooh, God!" I was grinning from ear to ear. Then grinding my hips deliciously against her, I told her, "But I have to move, sweet love. That's the way I make it better. I go in and out and round and round and you go wild. Doesn't it feel better when I move?"

"Mmmm," was the only sound she could manage. Her eyes had rolled to the back of her head, her mouth opening in an orgasmic O.

"Yes, much better," I said deliriously, feeling faint as her tight, warm, little womb enveloped me in a sumptuous embrace.

She was delectable, and I had to steel myself by trying not to think about how good it felt. But hell, it was incredible! I had never been with a virgin before, and to have what I was having now, to have her and be inside of her, goodness, it was unbelievable!!! Slipping out of her with some effort, I glided back, and repeated the process a few more times holding my breath, stroking inside of her with controlled expert thrusts, wanting her first time to be perfect.

I was digging for gold and had started to stroke her clitoris while I was still buried inside. Her head fell back and I could see her eyes, and gazed deeply into them, losing myself, my soul. She cried out loudly, her eyes pleading, begging for release as her body responded with a trembling pleasure that nearly snapped my resolve. Though I was unsure she had come, I knew she was almost there.

Pressing down lightly on her slender hips, I spread my legs and forced hers to open more, so I could drive in deeper. Whimpering, breathless, she clung to me, her arms and thighs gripping me tighter, while the sexy little sounds she was making told me she was enjoying this completely.

I backed away and lay her back against the pillows, and bent my head to kiss her nipples. She moaned and I could feel the small, delicate tremor of her muscle ease, which allowed me to plunge a little deeper. Inch by inch, I would breech her, all the while as I plundered her mouth with my tongue, kissing and tasting and savoring her until she could give no more.

Nibbling and licking, I now glided my tongue down her neck, plunging down to suck on her tender peaks. Her breasts felt full and lush, ripe to the extreme. I weighed them in one palm then squeezed. That first exquisite spasm of her climax that gushed fluid all around me allowed me to bury myself further still. And I had died a thousand deaths, as she thrashed and moaned and writhed beneath me. Kissing her lips tenderly, I laughed, smiling, "Ahhhh, that was good, wasn't it?" I smiled.

She gasped, her grip tightening as she seemed to come again, impelled on my naked lust. I could feel her muscles contract, her body convulsing again, and this time, I drove home, burying myself to the hilt.

She screamed. And I thought I might pass out, it felt that

incredible "Sorry, that couldn't be helped. Does it hurt?"

She shook her head no.

I kissed her.

"It's like a game," I told her, "where you try your hardest to make me come. While I try my hardest to make you come. And so far, I'm winning," I grinned and kissed her again. "But I always do. Except once I come, game over."

"Why?"

"You'll soon see," I told her, "or maybe not so soon. Are you enjoying this? I can make it last for a long time."

"I love it," she whispered.

"You want to come again?"

"Again and again."

I laughed. "There's my Arielle. Greedy girl!"

Carefully heightening her pleasure, pacing myself, deliberately quickening the strokes and then slowing down, until they deepened and became maddeningly faster, I drove deeply inside her. She bucked, and then lifted her hips and started to move against me, thrust for thrust. "Oh, yeah, just like that," I told her, as she raised her hips to welcome my every thrust. Some things you just learned instinctively.

She groaned, quivering, on the brink of another orgasm and clung to me. I lowered myself and pressed her down into the bed, driving into her hard and fast. She let go of me, needing to grab a hold of something, anything. I could see her fingers digging into the mattress, grasping the sheets. "Aggghhh," she expelled, arching up to meet me as I penetrated the very depths of her. "I want all of you inside me," she demanded fiercely. "Ohhh! Mon dieu...mon dieu," she moaned in French.

I tightened my grip, driven by savage impulses, amazed at her audacity. She was now actually giving me orders. Well, I thought, right now she might be speaking French, but soon I'd have her speaking in tongues.

Breathlessly, I pounded into her, rhythmically dancing inside of her, gyrating my hips, knocking against her, crushing her with my weight. Trying my best to be gentle, but then again, she was becoming so wild, her response so hot, it was making me lose control. Her tight little cunt was so deliciously, maddeningly sweet. So tight. I could feel the muscles squeezing, caressing, holding me firmly. And I was loving it!

Nothing had ever felt this good.

I was making love to her and she was a virgin again. I was going to come so hard, and this gift of ecstasy would be like no other. Like nothing I would ever experience again. And I was going to enjoy shooting my load inside her. I would never get enough, never stop loving her.

"You feel like heaven. So fucking incredible," I moaned, thrusting deep, forcefully, giving her several long, deeply penetrating strokes, in and out and in and out, back and forth, riding her until I could hold on no longer. I felt myself begin to crest, especially when I realized I had her upside down and she was holding onto the edge of the bed for dear life. *Heaven was on earth,* I thought, having reached the limit of my endurance. Putting my mouth to her ear, I kissed her and murmured, "Bling, baby, I want you to come now. With me! Right now!!!"

She started screaming, opening herself further by wrapping her legs around my waist thrusting up to meet me, despite practically being in a headstand. Her head was hanging down from the bed, practically touching the floor. "Cedric," she cried, her thighs beginning to quiver, her body totally intoxicating me.

"Fuck!" I moaned loudly, grinding myself harder into her hot, tight pussy, giving her inches of me still. Her pliant flesh gave way to me and all of my muscles tensed up. I could feel the first convulsions deep in my guts. "Oh, God! Jesus fucking Christ! I'm coming, baby. I'm coming real hard," I told her breathlessly. "You win! It's all yours, Bling..."

She was panting, crying, making all these wonderful noises I loved so much. Holding on to her for dear life, I gathered her to me, brought her back up to my chest and held her real tight as we came together in a violent rush.

I was howling and tears seeped from my eyes, it felt that good. It was the kind of orgasm that skyrocketed your entire body, where moisture seeped from every pore. I was soaked, completely. Sweating buckets from head to feet, so overwhelmed by all the emotion I was feeling. I had fallen completely in love all over again.

She was the most precious gift. Never could I let this woman go. I'd have to have her for all eternity. This maddeningly good loving, it was unlike anything ever! I felt L-O-V-E in my heart, my body and deep in my soul. Nothing, no one, would ever mean more to me. She would have forever my undying love.

Then later, lying entwined with in each other's arms, all tangled up between the sheets, I couldn't stop kissing her. I couldn't keep my lips off of her. She was giggling, loving it. That was when she corrected something I had said earlier. "No, we both won."

I laughed. "Yeah, I guess we both did." Then I asked her to kiss me.

She did.

"Again!"

She obeyed.

"Now give me your sweetest kiss."

She smiled and then closed her eyes and did her best.

"Your hardest kiss."

I helped. We did this for quite some time, pushing our lips real hard, bruising each other.

"Now give me a good-bye kiss. One where you won't be seeing me for a very long time."

"You going somewhere," she asked gently before proceeding.

"Never. There's no getting rid of me! This is just for fun."

She clung to me on this one, and it lingered on and on, as if she didn't believe me.

"What about a tender kiss?"

"That wasn't tender?"

"Mmmm...maybe you ought to try it again."

She acquiesced with a another searing kiss that made my head spin.

"Your sexiest kiss."

"Your shortest kiss."

"Your slowest kiss."

"Your most annoying kiss."

"Kiss me real nasty—nice and wet. Like you desperately want it."

She stuck out her tongue and touched it to mine, and kissed me mostly with tongue.

"Ummm...I could really get into the nasty kiss," I remarked as our tongues twirled and entwined together, where it was only our tongues touching and not our lips.

"Now," I told her with a deep sigh, rolling her over and getting on top of her. "I'm gonna kiss you and make you burn like fire." I did my best, but had to stop. I wanted her very badly... again. "Ahhh, your kisses can almost make me come."

She giggled and rubbed noses with me.

"Now that's how Eskimos kiss. That was sweet."

She looked at me with wonder and then her mouth slid down over mine again. This was the kiss to end all kisses. A kiss that bruised and sealed a deal.

24

Dancing on Fire

Her pink silk undies lay in a gentle heap atop his robe of black silk in the master chamber. A fine lace netting draped over their canopy bed like a fine mist, a veiling from heaven protecting the lovers from the care of the outside world. Every night they would fight over who got to be on top. Play a game of chess to settle the matter. He usually won.

Even though he could have introduced her to a plethora of Kama Sutra positions, lately, he found his favorite to be the classic missionary position where he could hold her in his arms while joined in coital union. Their mouths could exchange the deepest kisses while his hands caressed her face and hair as he gently explored her bottom.

Finally, he had what he had always wanted. An end to his loneliness, to the yearning of his loins, to the suffering he had gone through after her death—the whole ordeal with the FBI, the press and the police, all of that had been worth it since it met they could be together living here like this. None of that mattered now. It all seemed so remote, so removed from his reality, it was as if it had never happened.

He could make love to her all night long and usually did. He would wake up and take her or wake up and find her taking him. It was as if they never slept. Not completely. So hungry were they for each other's love. So much loving. So much tenderness. The more he got of her, the more he wanted. He felt so happy—except there was one thing missing from this equation.

CJ.

***

It was tearing me apart thinking about what I was going to do about this whole situation. On the one hand, life was now beautiful, but on the other, perhaps truly fucked! I was in a quandary. What were we going to do about our child?

More and more, Arielle was asking questions about him, wondering aloud where he was and why he couldn't come here and live with us. Several times, I had caught her moping around in his room. Touching his furniture, daydreaming over his pictures, refolding some of the baby clothes she had found in his drawers.

I knew pretty soon, she'd be making demands. Demands I wasn't quite sure I would be able to deliver. How much longer could we pretend that CJ, our son, was not part of our lives. Sure, the memories she had of him were scanty, and more a part of her mind because of the things I told her about him and the pictures I had shown her.

And yet, seeing CJ and hearing about him had not done the trick of rendering back her memory.

Meanwhile, CJ the little tyke was growing up. Every time I saw him, it seemed he had grown at least an inch. And he was smart as whip too. He had picked up my father's and Miss Penny's British accents. And there was even a hint of Caribbean-Irish accent present also, thanks to his nanny, Margo from Barbados.

Without proper influence, I thought, I might have a little Euro-American gentlemen on my hand, and how could I live with that? I needed to temper this very proper upbringing he was receiving with a little thuggishness, no? That, or he would be lost in my world. And in my world was where I wanted him to be.

Could I be greedy and dare to think I could have him and Arielle both? Could I have it all after everything that had happened?

Maybe not here in this country, I was beginning to think, but if we moved, if we ran away to somewhere else in the world, where people weren't so in tune with the media, where no one knew who we were, maybe we could have a chance. A chance to start over, a chance at a brand new life.

There were plenty of places we could go and live, where no one would know us or care. To be a real family again—just the three of us. That was my goal, my dream.

I would give up the fame and go into retirement in a heartbeat. I could do it, I was beginning to think. And I could still make music, because that was who I was. But did I need the recognition, the high that playing to a multitude of people brought? Did I need the fame? And as for the money, I had more than enough and could live off of just the royalties I made for decades.

The hardest question was, however, could I give up my family and friends and just drop off the face of the earth? That was the hard part.

But Arielle had to remain a secret, my secret. And how was I going to keep her under wraps living here in Miami, in this fishbowl called the United States? Or living where any number of people could just drop by unannounced for a visit? Or even if announced, how was I going to keep this secret and not sacrifice other ties?

The three month hiatus I had given to my crew was nearly over. Soon I'd be getting calls, people would be dropping by. I knew the gang was anxious to get back into the groove of making music and touring and making videos? How on earth was I going to be able to have a career and live a normal life with Arielle back in my life?

It couldn't be.

I had some hard decisions to make about exactly how I was going to disappear, and how best to handle CJ and that whole situation. Sacrifices. Yes, those had to be made. Unfortunately, life rarely allowed you the good fortune of having your cake and eating it too. And whereas my entire concentration had been centered around Arielle, it was time to snap back to reality, and think out this situation…carefully.

***

How best did I tell her I was leaving her?

Even though it was going to be for a short time, how did I tell her? We had never been apart, and she was going to put up a fight.

Although I was still formulating my plan, one thing was clear. I had to go to Orlando for a visit—one because I hadn't seen CJ and missed him like crazy and two, I needed to talk to my father about regaining custody of my son. I knew he would still argue that my life was not stable enough and while that was probably true, we had to start talking about when and how this transition was going to take place.

Arielle was definitely not going to like the idea of my leaving her. Even though I wouldn't be gone for more than a couple of days, and though Orlando was only four hours away and I could go there and turn around and come right back, I needed to spend time with our son. That was important. I didn't want it to be where he didn't even recognize me anymore. And for a child, two months of being away was like an eternity.

That night, I decided to make some martinis. I wanted to

butter her up, well...actually...liquor her up. Martinis used to be her favorite drink, and I wanted her nice and soothed when I delivered the news about my Orlando trip, which would most likely encounter much resistance—especially when cold sober.

My father made a perfect martini. I had watched him prepare it many times, mixing drinks with flourish. As soon as the clock struck 5:01p.m., it was politically correct at our home to kick back and enjoy cocktails before dinner. I had been enjoying this family ritual since turning 16. Screw the States and their over 21 bullshit. Good thing my dad was European and thought nothing of my drinking before being legal.

The classic martini was made with gin and if you wanted say, a vodka martini, it usually meant adding just a hint of vermouth. I filled our martini glasses with ice and water, added some Grey Goose Vodka with just a few drops of dry vermouth. Then I shook it with attitude, dumped the ice water from the waiting glass, straining in the perfectly blended drink and garnished our glasses with a slice of lemon peel and added some fancy olives.

I brought her the drink, "here you are, Bling," and watched her take a sip. "You used to love these."

I had made her drinks before. Mostly the sweet, fruity kinds like smoothies or daiquiris. We also sometimes had wine with dinner. After smelling the drink, she took a tentative sip. Next she smiled and then touched my face. "Nice."

Nice, I thought, feeling hopeful. Perhaps this was a smart move, I reasoned, as I watched the peaceful look that came over her face as she continued to sip. A little booze, a little sex, and maybe she could sleep the whole day and not even notice I was gone.

Maybe I wouldn't even have to tell her, I thought wishfully.

No sooner had I sat down with my drink, starting to feel a bit more relaxed and less anguished then the doorbell chimed. I hadn't heard that sound in months! My heart raced. Who could that be? No one had any idea I was here.

Arielle who had never heard the door chime before was even more startled. "What is that?" She asked, looking wide-eyed.

Trying not to seem panicked, I waved her off. "I'll go see."

Next, I ran to the security room to see who it was via my home security cameras, and couldn't believe my eyes. My heart froze in my chest, as I watched the person standing on my doorstep.

My jaws obstinately set, I grounded my teeth while my mind reeled. *What the fuck!*

The only person I had confided to about my secret plans. Of course, I had had no idea that it would be possible, and for the life of me, I now couldn't figure why I had even told her. To hurt her perhaps. To try and get her to talk me out of it. Whatever my reasons, I realized it was pure folly now. Of course she had came to check on me. Of course!

If I ignore the chime, soon she'd have no choice but to go away. The lights were turned down real low. And anyway, people left lights on for security purposes—even when they were away. She'd realize I wasn't home and would soon leave. There was no way she was coming in here. No way she could...

But then, Kendra did the most surprising thing. She started to open the front door with her own set of keys, and that was when the awful realization struck me. I had given her my house keys during our brief courtship—telling her how she was to use them *whenever*. Meaning whenever she felt horny. "Wake me up and make me happy one of these days," my words came back to haunt me. And here she was...using them. Hopefully not because she was horny, God Help me, but nosy. Except I wasn't very happy to see her. No, not at all!

I stood there frozen with incredulity as she let herself and in, wondering what I was going to do. How was I going to handle this colossal problem? What spin could I possibly put on this? This was a wipe out, a total disaster, and growing worst by the second! Standing there, I realized it was too late, as I watched in total terror Kendra walking into the foyer while Arielle stood erect and furious, and gloriously naked in nothing but her lace panties, staring at the stunned interloper. Running towards the living room...I knew I was too late, but wasn't prepared at all when Arielle started to hiss at Kendra, like she was a trapped, cornered she-cat.

***

Kendra stood there stock-still, thunderstruck by what she was seeing. Time and space seemed suspended as she tried to comprehend what her eyes were registering, though she could scarcely believe it. The image that stood before her in naught but the skimpiest panties had to be Arielle—and yet, how could it be?

She might have begun to groan, if she hadn't had to cover up her shock, refusing to betray her emotions. How could she let them see how afraid she was...or how disappointed.

Cedric had actually done it! He had actually done it!!!

Just went to show that the saying was wrong about money not being able to buy you everything. *Money could actually buy you just about everything.* Including bringing back the dead.

She was trembling with apprehension and something bordering on hysteria. Afraid to utter the name Arielle for fear that the scantily clad siren standing there, hissing at her in a manner non-too-friendly, might actually respond.

Then, from the corner of her eyes she spied Cedric approaching, who looked guarded—perhaps even scared. He had been standing by the door with his arms braced across his chest with one hand cupping his chin in contemplation of the situation, but now, he dropped the stance and went to take his place next to his demon. Smiling at Arielle in a soft, appeasing way, he calmly took her by the shoulder, saying: "Now-now, my darling. Is this anyway to greet a guest?" And immediately, the demon seemed to comprehend and stopped her hissing.

She and Cedric had not spoken since that luncheon date, where he had announced his horrifying plan. And here it was in fruition. He had gambled and won. Arielle was here with him, still her lovely self. He had gotten his wish.

Kendra stood, still unable to move, peering at Arielle's face in the semi-darkness. She was absolutely stunning. Exquisite, and unabashedly beautiful. She invited veneration, and for minutes, Kendra was struck by her vivid beauty and could do nothing but stare—understanding why Cedric was risking the wrath of God to have this lovely creature back.

It was hard not to hate, not to compare, not to stare. Arielle was heart-thumpingly gorgeous. She had the kind of beauty that could render other woman invisible in broad daylight. It was difficult not to envy or resent her.

Hearing Cedric give a low sigh, Kendra turned her attention from the beatific creature, momentarily turning her gaze to him. "Kendra," he started, "I wasn't expecting you."

She heard herself respond, "Is that so," and turned her attention back to Arielle. Transfixed.

"We were having martinis, and though I'd love to have you join us, as you can see…we're not dressed for company."

Indeed, they were certainly not. And she felt stupefied, still trying to believe her eyes. But her eyes weren't lying and Arielle was really standing there, nearly naked and looking on. Were they actually having this conversation?

"Does she talk?" She felt compelled to ask Cedric, "or is she capable only of making hissing sounds?"

"Yes, she does talk," Cedric responded. "Rather well. And she absolutely understands—everything. So please discontinue talking about her as if she's not standing right beside me listening."

"It doesn't make sense, you see..."

"Of course, I completely understand. I know it's hard to fathom—very difficult to wrap your head around. But, as you can see, it is so."

Arielle moved then, away from him and started to move towards Kendra. Circling around her, staring at her from head to foot, inspecting her the way she had been studying her from afar.

"Be calm," Cedric told her with some concern. Kendra was not sure the concern was for her or for the demon. "She means you know harm. She's just curious that's all."

Kendra smirked, he was probably afraid that she might shoot her again—dead. Unfortunately, she would probably need a silver bullet this time.

"Call her off," Kendra ordered now, getting the distinct feeling that Cedric had very little control over this she-devil, and probably had no idea what she could or could not do. "Make her stop," Kendra whispered, standing there trying not to make any sudden movements.

This was strange, and Arielle gave her the creeps. There was something hostile about her, like she could spring up and attack her at any moment.

"Arielle, leave her alone. Come back here!" Cedric called to her.

She ignored him completely but rather started to hiss at Kendra again, causing all the hairs to prick up all over her body. She was horror-struck because of Arielle's close proximity and because of the look she saw on her face. At one point, she could swear, her eyes had actually gleamed with an unnatural light. She was a demon for sure, from the furthest recesses of hell, and Cedric had called her back into an earthly body. Improbable it seemed.

"Arielle, stop this! You're scaring her. Come, go sit down over there!" Cedric pointed to the ottoman chair.

Kendra could see Arielle's contrary smile, as she barred her teeth at her. But after hissing at her one last time, she turned and obeyed and went over to sit in the chair Cedric had pointed to.

"Thank you," Kendra whispered, relieved. "I'll be leaving now."

Cedric gave a low chuckle. "I'm sorry about that. She's simply making sport—"

"Look," Kendra said cutting him off, feeling mortified, appalled, and miserable all of the sudden. "No need to explain. And you don't have to worry. I'll never bother you again."

"Now-now, come on," Cedric said softly. "I owe you my life! And though I know you don't approve of this..."

"Approve?"

"I know this is difficult to accept or understand, but...does this mean we can no longer be friends?"

Kendra felt further stunned, revolted even. Lifting her eyes from his demon, she stared directly into his eyes, "I will keep you in my prayers," was all she could get out. And goodness, he'd need it!

***

"I want to remember, Cedric. I can't stand living like this anymore. I want to remember everything," Arielle said as she sat on the edge of her boudoir chair, brushing her hair before her mirror that same evening.

"Bling, you will...it'll come. Florence said once it did, it would all come back in a flood, and you'll remember everything. Just give it a little more time."

She shook her head, "No, I need to remember everything now. Right now! Who was she?!"

"I told you, you don't know her. And she only knows you because...well, she knows of you from pictures, but until tonight, you had never met."

Arielle rolled her eyes. "I don't believe you. Why did she look at me like that? And why was she so angry at you? You hurt her? You say you're my husband, but what about her? You're her husband too?"

"No, I was not...I am not her husband. I am married to you. I've never done...well, nothing ever technically happened between me and Kendra. It's a long story, but...once you get back your memory, you'll understand everything."

"Is that her name?" She said coming over to the bed, where I had been sitting, contemplating her. "Kendra, is that her name?"

"Does it really matter?"

"What's her full name."

"Kendra. Kendra Jade. She's an FBI Agent. Are you happy now?"

"Why were you mean to her?"

"I was mean to her," I stammered. "You're the one who was

hissing at her, trying to scare her to death and you're accusing me!"

"But, you were not welcoming of her."

"Well, I wasn't exactly expecting her. She came here uninvited and unannounced."

"Why?"

"How the hell do I know? Perhaps to spy."

"Why would she come to spy?"

"I don't know," I shrugged. "Because she's nosy like that, and that's what agents do. They spy. They're snoops. They always want to be in the know."

"This Kendra, she knows many things?"

"I suppose."

"Maybe she could help with my memory..."

"How? I told you, she doesn't even know you!"

"She seemed to know me. She couldn't stop staring at me."

"She was just surprised is all."

"Why?"

"She's never seen you in person. Only in pictures..."

"But why does she seem so familiar to me. Why do I feel like I know her?"

"I told you, it's a long story."

But Arielle was still adamant. "Well, it doesn't matter. I don't care! I still want to remember now! I have to!" Next she was practically in tears, "Cedric, why can't I remember? Why don't I remember anything?"

I felt helpless, hapless. Raking my hands through my hair, I told her, "I don't know what else to do, Arielle. I don't know how to make you remember."

I tried not to think about the journals. There was no way I was showing her those journals. No way!

But then she came up with a bright idea that momentarily quelled her rising hysteria. "What about videos? Don't you have more videos of us?"

I smiled. "Yes, as a matter a fact, I do."

Why hadn't I thought of that? Maybe if she saw people—CJ and Margo, Bailey and her grandparents, my father and Miss Penny, perhaps that would jog back her memory. The problem has been not being in her old environment and not having contact with things once familiar. The videos might work. And there were plenty of them.

Soon I had dragged an entire box out from the closet into our bedroom. Gleefully, Arielle stuck in the first tape titled: *CJ's Special Moments*. Surely seeing CJ's christening and birthdays was bound to have some effect.

Arielle seemed to be really into it, smiling and giggling, all excited about watching CJ take her first steps. I, for one, felt myself nodding off after the first tape. Especially since I was lying down propped up by fluffy, goose down pillows. Next she wanted to watch, *Our Wedding*.

"Who are all these people?" She kept asking me as she watched, seemingly mesmerized by the grand event.

"Friends. Family."

"Where are they? How come one ever calls or come over? Why are we always alone?"

Hard questions.

This night was not going well at all, and it was bond to get worse. I still had to tell her about Orlando. And now there was this thing with Kendra and her insistence on getting her memory back.

What was I going to do?

I needed a shower...one where I could have a little quiet and have time to think. I waited though, and finished watching the wedding video with her, but then excused myself as she pulled out another video, *Parties*.

"I'm going to take a shower," I announced to her, and kissed the top of her head. "You continue watching though. "I'll be back."

After my shower, my head was no clearer than before. But what greeted me as I entered the bedroom nearly stopped my heart. For a few seconds, I do believe my heart skipped several beats.

Arielle was kneeling only inches away from the big screen TV, holding the remote control and rewinding a scene from our 2001 Christmas party, where Danyel was talking, wishing us a "Happy Holidays and a fantastic New Year." The scene would finish and she would rewind, and watch it again and again. She must have done this a dozen times, before I finally had to step in and stop her.

Thin-skinned, resentful, battling violence, by the time I approached her, I'll never forget the stricken look I saw on her face. I felt literally punched in the gut. Her eyes had slayed me, cut me into a dozen filleted pieces.

"What is his name," she spat, her jaws obstinately set, her rounded breasts raised high from the stiffness of her spine.

I could barely speak. I was aglow with such incredulous

jealous fury.

"What is his name," she demanded again, her voice falling to a hushed resonance.

"Danyel."

"Who was he to me?"

I could not bear this, I thought. I couldn't. I couldn't. Much as I loved her, if she...if she remembered because of him, I would never forgive her.

She had turned her eyes from me and had frozen the frame, and was staring at him again. The expression on her face pained.

"I loved him," she said then, quite simply. "I loved him."

And there it was. Brutal honesty. Her words were like a picking goad. I wanted to scream. I wanted to rage. I wanted to bash her head in. Squeeze her neck.

"No!" I screamed, yanking the remote from her grasp. "Stop this! You loved me. He was...he was... your cousin, Arielle. Family."

She shook her head, her eyes blazing. "No, you lie! You said you were my husband, but that's not true. I know it's not. He was my husband. Danyel, he was my husband!"

"No-no-no," I said, wanting her to stop. With one purposeful stride, I was on her, my right hand closing around her wrist like steel. Yet I kept my voice soft, "Please, please don't say that. Please...Bling. Stop saying that!"

She sniffled, her eyes cold. Unrelenting. "Let me go!"

"Please, Arielle. I'm the one who loves you."

"Where is he? Take me to him now. I have to see him, this Danyel."

"I can't."

"You can't or you won't?"

"I can't and I won't!" I screamed violently, seeing red. How dare she?! Oh, God! I was living this goddamned nightmare all over again...was this what I had brought her back for?

"You are mine," I said, grabbing her firmly by the shoulders, "you hear me. Mine!" I said forcibly. "I am your master—or have you forgotten that— and no man is your husband and ever was or will be your husband but me. Only me!"

"Where is he?" she hissed this time, unshaken by my damnable arrogance. "What did you do to him?!"

I glared at her and she returned the look, visibly upset while I was becoming murderously angry. Our gazes locked, I could see the anguish in her eyes. And I could feel the torment deep in the depth of my guts. I felt like my heart had been cut out of my chest, and felt the most excruciating pain. I was in actual physical pain! "He is dead," I told her finally. "DEAD!" I hollered, wanting to lash out at her. Wanting to punish and torment her, the way she was tormenting me. She had ripped out my heart, thrown it on the floor and done a Mexican hat dance on it.

"You killed him," she cried. "You killed him?!"

"And I'd kill him all over again if he were here!" I taunted.

"YOU KILLED HIM!" she screamed, beginning to gulp and sob in spasms.

"No," I shook my head, wanting to mollify her, but my jealousy was overpowering. Jealousy and rage the likes of which I'd never before experienced assaulted my senses, and it was difficult to even admit this, "Somebody else did, but you know what? *I'm glad.*"

She jerked back and with a sweeping movement, rushed and snatched with one hand the heavy silver mirror from her boudoir table, aiming for my head, before I could reach to grab a hold of her. Miraculously, I twisted out of the way, but barely in time to avoid the mirror's returning swing. The blunt edge had grazed the top of my head.

I grabbed the mirror, or tried to wrest it from her grasp before she could do more damage with it. But she was strong and refused to let go. Meanwhile, she was like a storm out of control, and it went on for a long moment—lunge, feint, thrust, twist, punch— she was trying to kick the hell out of me. But my fingers never relinquished their grasp on her wrist or on that mirror she was trying to gorge me with. After minutes, I was finally able to tear the mirror from her grasp.

Angry as a hornet by now, all of the crystals and perfume bottles went next, hurled with more fury and more success right at my head. I wanted to lunge at her and knock my head into hers, but was afraid the force might break her nose or shatter some bones. So instead, with my free hand, I swept the marble top clean with one mighty stroke to get rid of the missiles that she kept flinging continually. Undeterred and near hysteria, Arielle began to strike out blindly now, furious that I refused to loosen my grip on her.

Right when I decided to slacken my grip, hoping she had somewhat calmed down, her hand reached around and closed around a lizard belt tossed carelessly over the back of her boudoir chair. Expertly snaking it around her hand and wrist, this belt soon became a formidable weapon as she whipped me like I was and errant slave that had vexed her to the utmost. The metal buckle, the end she was whipping me with cut sharply over my shoulders, causing me to grip her wrists even tighter—just short of breaking bones. Of course this only made her rage all the more. I watched her fury rise to dangerous levels as she struck the belt with a mighty stroke, which split open my left cheekbone.

That was the end for me. Did she have any idea what she was doing to me? Had she the foggiest notion how I felt about her?

I had constrained myself admirably, I thought, considering the beating I was receiving. But enough was enough. Arielle seemed uncaring of the pain she was inflicting, in fact, cold, outrage radiated from her eyes bespeaking her murderous intent. The blood was already tracing a path down my cheek when I ripped the belt from her hand and flung it across the room, and quickly captured her other wrist, yanking her to me with such force, it knocked the wind out of her.

"That's enough," I told her, seething with rage, trying to squeeze her half to death to calm her rage. But she continued to struggle while both our hearts pounded against each other, our nerves taut from our shackling embrace. "You calm down right now, or I'll have to fucking hurt you." I promised her.

Flushed, trembling, enraged, Arielle stood captive in my steely embrace, breathing hard, eyes flashing fire, seemingly exhausted, but not tired enough to stop her antics.

Next she screamed, an ear-splitting, blood-curling scream, her breasts heaving from the exertion. "LIKE YOU HAVEN'T HURT ME ENOUGH!" She stormed, but by this time, she was rasping and hoarse, starting to loose her voice. "How can you *possibly* hurt me more than you already have?!" she whispered.

I regarded her for a moment at a loss for word. Excruciating seconds passed where I cautioned myself inwardly not to cry. Don't cry, don't you dare cry, I told myself. And only a long, drawn-out breath gave any indication of my tremendous effort to overcome the most terrible urge to weep.

Why?" she asked more softly now, seemingly perplexed. "I loved him."

"And I love you, and you see…in this world, we don't share."

She was sobbing again. Limp, broken…but I didn't dare let her go.

"Where is my brother, Bailey? And where is my grandmother? And how come they never call or visit?"

The cut on my cheek and back were aching, but not as badly

as the rip she had rendered to my heart. And now, I could no longer stop the tears that were pouring down my cheek, mixing and pouring salt into my wound—seeing the folly in everything I had tried to do.

"Cause you're dead too," I said very quietly. "You're dead too."

She looked at me, unable to fathom what I was saying. I could see the confusion in her eyes, her lips quivered. "I'm dead?"

I stood looking at her, my gaze traveling across the beautiful planes of her stunning face. "Yes," I said with a deep, exhausting sigh, resigning myself for whatever was to come. "To everyone but me."

How can I even explain how I felt in that moment? How can I explain the depth my emotions had plummeted to? I was in the deepest recesses of hell. I was in a chasm so deep, so dark, so completely indescribable. Dr. Ottowa had been right. Heaven and hell were truly on earth.

She fixed her gaze on me and smiled with a satisfaction that bordered on maniacal hysteria. She staring daggers at me, the expression on her face malevolent. I could feel her scorn like a physical thing, absolutely felt the depth of her hatred. It was as if she were inside of my mind. "*Die*," she whispered. Except her lips hadn't moved. "*I want you dead too.*"

She flicked her hand, and suddenly I was thrown clear across the room. She flicked her wrist again and I could feel her hands wrapped around my throat even though she was standing at least eight feet away. I was choking, I couldn't breathe. In that moment, all my rage, all my fears, all my hatred coalesced into a warbled cry that I was afraid hadn't reached the earshot of Arielle, whose soulless black eyes seemed to be tracking my every moment. "Die," she whispered in my head once more.

I gasped for my last breath of air as my gaze settled on her eyes. She smiled at me with those eyes, long-lashed, sensuous as hell—taking me in, trapping me in their self-assured, possessive way—squeezing my throat without seemingly lifting a finger. Reminding of the erotic power she held over me, of rumpled sheets, of flower-filled rooms. And goodness, even though she was killing me, I still understood why I had gone through such lengths to bring her back.

Her lips curled into a bitter sneer, and I heard her voice once again inside my mind, "Die..." she whispered before everything went black.

***

When I came to, I wasn't sure what time it was, but it felt like morning. The house seemed deserted. I sensed she was gone, but had to check the house for her anyway. I looked everywhere. Then I checked the grounds. The cars were there, my motorcycle, all of her clothes were still there—the little she had. Nothing was missing—except her.

My throat felt choked up, and I was still finding it difficult to breathe. All that had transpired between us came to me like a rush. She despised me. And she was gone, I thought glumly.

Where to, I had no idea.

How did I even begin to look for her?

What did I tell anyone?

Briefly, I thought about Kendra, whose job it was to find missing persons—except, Arielle was no longer a person. How did you track down someone who was dead? Oh God! What had I done? And besides, Kendra now hated me as well. She would probably not help, regardless.

I was stuck, I thought as I sat out in the middle of my lawn, feeling all weird inside. It was like a scene from the *Outer Limits* or *Twilight Zone*.

I was screwed.

Completely.

And Arielle was gone again...

***

I lay at home in bed with a high fever. I had constant pain shooting through my muscles and joints. I had never felt this sick.

I kept calling for her, but she never came. And although at times, I recalled she was gone and therefore couldn't come, at other times, I was furious with her. That I could be this sick, and she not be here for me.

My mouth felt dry and I was flustered. My body was deeply fatigued. I couldn't figure what was going on with me.

Still, the night brought on insomnia. I couldn't sleep a wink during the night and I feared I was beginning to have hallucinations. Horrible nightmares while I lay awake.

I had never been this sick in my life! For days, it seemed, I just lay there, too weak to move, sometimes having to force myself to get up and go use the bathroom. Forget about food. I hadn't eaten in days.

I thought about calling my father. Maybe he could send

someone to help me. Thoughtlessly, I have given Manuel and his wife a week off, after Arielle's disappearance. I hadn't wanted them to know or to ask any questions, and so to avoid any problems, I thought it would be best to tell them we were going away, and that they could have a week off.

Of course, now I totally regretted this.

I thought about some other people I could call, surprised that none of the crew had tried to call to find out what was going on yet. Then I remembered my edict of "Don't call me, I'll call you." They were just following orders.

How had I mange to screw my life up this bad?

And what was I going to do about Arielle, this unnatural creature I had unleashed on the world. I still couldn't understand how she had knocked me across the room and choked me, with just a flick of her wrist. And would never forget what she whispered in my mind.

Visions of Frankenstein's monster flickered through my head. Christ, it was true, I had perhaps created a monster. Albeit, a very beautiful monster, but all the more deadlier because of it. Where was she? Where had she gone? How had she fled?

The days merged into each other, and after awhile, it was hard to figure how many days I had been laying there? One day? Two? Three? Four? A week? I was unsure of a lot of things.

At some point, I started to think about calling 911. I should try to get some medical help, because try as I might, I truly could not get myself up. It was as if my body was in atrophy, from lack of use, and now, it was impossible to stand or walk.

Towards the end of the day, I was determined to stand. Besides, if I didn't try to make it to the bathroom soon, I was going to go on myself. I tried standing up and my legs couldn't support me. I fell on my face and broke the bridge of my nooo—or at least it felt like I did. More pain.

I was now laying on the floor, and literally had to crawl on my belly to the bathroom. I ended spending the night in there, too weak to make it make back to bed. Laying on the cool tiles brought on the shakes. I was cold. I was in pain. I was miserable. And now, my body couldn't stop shivering.

It was either I die here on the tiles or try my damnest to crawl back to bed, where there were covers, a down comforter to at least keep me warm. It was hard though, as if all my joints were now locked up, and the pain was becoming more and more excruciating. I was stiff, couldn't move. Much as I tried. I was like a frozen piece of ice. I ended up spending another entire day and night in the bathroom.

By then, my mind had gone.

I could no longer think. I knew hunger like a unspeakable horror. I had a refrigerator full of food, and yet I couldn't get to it. Oh, the irony of it! I had water though, at least. I had to drink from the bidet, like it was a fountain. By now, the water was the only thing keeping me going.

I was utterly debilitated. Surely it had been a week, and Manuel and his wife would be back. Surely, God would not let me die like this. Like some miserable, mangy dog. Right in my own home.

But I was alone. Truly alone. No one in the world knew I was here. No one in the world who cared—but tow women—both of whom hated me for one reason or another.

***

Days passed into night and night into day. It was hard to recall now how much time I had been there, but I knew I was doomed. This was my payment, of course, *time to pay the piper*. Arielle had left me, and she could be anywhere by now, and I was going to die this horrible death. I would starve to death due to this paralysis. Right here, right in my master bath. I could not move for the life of me—it was as if I was made of stone and could not budge not even a muscle.

What had she done to me? I tried to remember what exactly what she had said. I couldn't help feeling like Arielle had everything to do with the way I was feeling. It was as if she had willed it so, and it was so.

My mind was going. And I had no basis on which to judge my rambling thoughts, on which to base my logic. Some days I would dream of things long past. Other days I would imagine I was in another place, caught in another time. Was this how it was when you died? And I was very near, very close to death. Several times, I thought I saw my mother, waiting for me, smiling at me, beckoning for me to come and join her.

Other times I would see myself in a forest, where the oaks and dark trees reached into the heavens. I would wander through, gazing at the wild flowers that grew in profusion, arrested by the dancing gusts of yellow, lavender and blue. When not entranced by the beauty of the trees and flowers, I would stare at the moss, afraid of the little rodents darting through the shadows, afraid of the snakes and other predators that might be lurking in the giant trees.

These were my thoughts, the ramblings of a feeble mind, preparing for death. I was paralyzed. And yet in my dreams, I walked and waited. Waiting for death to come.

I thought about this strange forest, this place I had come to inhabit, remembering this poem I had read in high school. A poem about a savage garden. Possibly Eden. An ancient place that rivaled the beauty of my forest.

Was this heaven?

I continued to dream, but became unsure of whether I was dreaming or whether this place was real. I was still in the forest. Walking. Watching. Enjoying. But all alone, solitary. By myself. Like I was the only soul in the world.

The forest shifted, and the mammoth tress gave way to slender, graceful branches. Here in there, there were water springs and little ponds sprinkled with water lilies and jumping tadpoles. And off in the distance, there were fields of high, waving grass. They made a rusting noise, a noise I would forever associate with this place.

I was enjoying the breeze, and the sound, not to mention the pleasant smell of it. The breeze smelled heady and heavy, like it had water in it. And I could feel it, lifting up my hair, smoothing it back and away from the side of my face. I felt it cool on my head and on my hands, but not on my heart.

I felt peaceful. Yet beautiful as this place was, if this was where I was going to die, I didn't want to be there, and didn't want to die. Not just yet. *I don't want to die*, I said to myself, in my mind. Even as I peered down the ledge at the end of the forest, and gazed down the green slopes, and saw the distant, pink crested mountains. This was beauty incarnate, I thought as I contemplated the ragged and rambling wood, the dipping valleys and hills, from which peaked the glitter of the twinkling light of the deep blue sea.

Suddenly I was stricken with sadness. So this was the end of my journey. Here in this beautiful place, a landscape of rolling hills, and rising mountains, of forest glens and fields of vibrant-colored wild flowers. I was stricken with grief so dark, it nearly obliterated the sunlight, closing the view I had of the far horizon, where the mountains came as if to close in the waters, only to be forced to let the waters flow out beyond my sight.

I needed to get to the water. I needed to let go, to float beyond this place. I needed to be free. I didn't want to die, and if I stayed here, I would surely die. So I started to walk again, throwing caution to the wind. A child of danger, immune to whatever perils might await me. I had to reach the bank and make it out to the sea. The sea was the only means of escape from this savage garden that had imprisoned me.

25

On the Eighth Day, God Created Courage

One year later...

Madison Square opened its gates at four in the afternoon and was quickly filling up. Cedric was kicking off his Genesis U.S. Tour there and HBO was covering the event.

The press was thick. Cedric hadn't given a live performance in nearly three years. The last time anyone had seen him live was in Manila during his *Bring It On!* World Tour.

Although Cedric had come out with a multi-platinum album and several videos since then, everyone was itching to see if he still had it, cause his strength had always been that he could absolutely rock a crowd and kick it live.

The media had been speculating. Did he still have it? Could he deliver? Many believed he didn't. He had gotten rusty. Had stayed away too long. However, the fans weren't listening to the critics and didn't stay away, but came out in droves to judge for themselves.

Cedric wished the label execs had as much confidence in him as the fans did. Even though he was doing this live concert for HBO, they had been hesitant about securing any actual dates for the tour. Everything had been tentative and riding on this performance tonight.

And Kendra wasn't missing this for the world. She'd be there for him no mater what, she had promised. It didn't matter where she was in the world, she'd be at Madison Square by 8:00p.m. on time for the start of his concert.

Except she hadn't shown up yet, and he was beginning to worry she wouldn't. And the fact that he needed her to be there to make it through the performance was beginning to terrify him as well.

He'd never forget how it was her that saved him again. Twice. She had saved his life that night with Fire. And she had saved his life again, at the house in LaGorce when he had practically died right there on the master bath floor. If it weren't for Kendra, he certainly wouldn't have made it out of there alive, and wouldn't have gone through months of therapy to be able to walk and gain the use of his limbs again. But Kendra there as his personal coach, there as a constant reminder to never give up. And now, he needed her to be here tonight. To watch what her precious gift of life had garnered.

***

I would never forget the day that she found me. The bright overhead lights of the room burned my eyes. I could still hear the ambulance siren blasting in my ears. Not to mention the screams and sobs that had came from Kendra ricocheting and bouncing off the walls. She had punched and screamed and raged and knocked life back into me. And I remember thanking God for Kendra and promising him a whole lot of other things for allowing me to come back.

At first, lying there in the sterile hospital room, it was hard to distinguish what had occurred first, what happened next or last. And even though it felt like a century had passed, it may have only been a matter of hours. I had lost all sense of time. All I knew for sure was that I was terrified and exhausted but also very glad that I had been found.

Later at e hospital in the O.R. I had been poked and prodded endlessly. And if they took anymore blood, I might not have any more left. Happy still to be alive, I tried to look to the bright side. My dad was there, Ms. Penny, CJ and Margo and Kendra...I was also relieved to see a couple of my boys, Deuce and Rico. I had no idea how much I had missed them.

If only they would come with a prognosis and stop with the endless questions. At first, the line of questioning had surprised me. What the hell were they talking about, *were they on drugs?*

"I'm not on drugs," I kept telling them. "No dope," I kept reiterating, unsure they understood English.

Finally one doctor was merciful enough to tell me, "Your blood pressure is very high, and your eyes were completely dilated even though you were found with your eyes closed and in a dark room. There seem to be no medical reason for your paralysis, and though we've tested you for all drug traces that could cause your particular symptoms, everything has come up negative. We're drawing a blank. Did you shoot up with anything? Did you ingest anything, any toxins or poison?

In other words, did I try to commit suicide?

All I could answer to all those questions was a resounding no. No-no-no.

And what had followed was perhaps the most painful, but most therapeutic time of my life. I had to give up everything and throw my entire strength into getting better, to moving and walking again. I refused to remain a cripple, even after I had been diagnosed with MS a few months later, all my hard work had paid off. And now I was back in the mainstream, getting my life back.

***

Kendra arrived at the square at about half past seven. She had just come from Quantico where she had been lecturing on police procedure. She jumped out of the cab and paid the driver, giving him a generous tip for getting her through the thick Manhattan traffic in record time. She breathed in deeply, relishing the smell of New York, smiling gently to herself. Yeah, she missed it here, but she didn't have time to dwell of its significance. Cedric was waiting and she could hardly wait to see him!

As she made a mad dash for the gates, running as she made her way through the crowds of people wading through the gates, she was late and she hated not being prompt. Flashing her badge all the way to the back, hustling through several security points trying to make her way backstage, Kendra was desperate to see Cedric before he went on stage. She knew it was important she be there for moral support. Besides, this would be the first time she would see him kick it live and perform with his band.

And God, she was so proud of him. They had made peace and though she wouldn't lie and say she was completely over him and knew she still carried a torch for him, for now his friendship was enough. What more could she ask for considering the circumstances.

Most of Cedric's personal security and body guards knew her well—except tonight there were tons of hire-ons—NYPD and private security too. Not to mention the press, that were like a pestilence, crawling all over the place.

She felt so good when she saw the look of absolute relief on his face when she finally reached his dressing room and popped her head in. It had been a feat, muscling her way in there.

Flashing her badge, mustering all the authority she had. And now there he was, larger than life, looking every bit the star in his black Versace leather gear. It was well worth it, when he ran for her, grabbed her up and swung her around. "You made it!"

"Told you I would," she gushed.

"Yes you did it. And you've never let me down. Ever. Don't know why I doubted you."

Kendra smiled.

He smiled back, then ruffled her hair, and gave her a big bear hug.

Then it was back to business. Everyone was moving super fast in preparation. Stan was busy barking orders, while Cedric had a smoke. Kendra was happy to see that he wasn't holding a drink and that there was no alcohol anywhere. And she prayed that he had given up the drugs.

She would never forget the anguish she had gone through after finding him half dead. She had called 911 and had him rushed to the hospital and later on, they had come to learn some very troubling things. She had gone along with his father, participating in this intervention he's set up where they had ambushed him, forced him to check himself into rehab, strong-arming him with the threat of losing custody of his son in order to get him well.

Thankfully, Cedric hadn't held this against her and was actually grateful once he got better that she still cared.

She had also been there to console him and motivate him after they had learned he had somehow contracted MS. Cedric had truly wanted to die then, and rehab somehow didn't seem that big of an issue after that. It was a very rough year for him, but somehow he had gotten through it, and she felt so proud that he was about to have a second shot at his music career.

Tonight was going to be his great come-back concert, and she was rooting for him all the way! He was crazy to think she wouldn't show up. She wouldn't have missed it for the world, and apparently, many of his fans felt the same way since everyone, including many of his celebrity friends had all come out in droves to support him.

Kendra was happy for him, proud of all his success. She was grateful too that they had become such good friends over the past year. They spoke at least twice a week, sometimes more. Yet she would never forget the broken state she had found him in—undone by horrendous events he had yet to share with her, gaunt and near death from lack of food and trapped like an animal on the bathroom floor. She would never forget the stricken, heartsick incredulity she had felt when she had realized how much she desperately loved him and understood then with clarity why he had fought and sought so hard to bring Arielle back.

This was love she had thought, impervious to the pain. Aware of the fact that her love, ardor and desire would never be fully returned but understanding the significance of this revelation, he was her love. The love of her life, in fact. Yet like Arielle, it would always have to be her secret.

And so now it felt strange every time she saw him, but in a good way. Seeing him in person. Remembering. Though the good part was—or maybe it was the sad part—neither of them could ever mention Arielle or what had happened. Even though she was forever etched in both their memories and monumental in their minds, she was something they'd both have to carry to their graves.

Kendra had had to seek therapy to deal with the entire situation, and had urged Cedric to do the same. Although he had refused, she was happy to see him doing so well. Though he was now leaning more towards producing than performing, Kendra could feel his excitement and was praying the crowd would receive him with open arms. Giving her a small peck when they called him out, he caressed her cheek with the back of his hands in an affectionate gesture as she whispered, "Break a leg."

If only...she always found herself saying where he was concerned. If only...

She followed not too far behind them as Cedric and his band made their way to the stage. The lights were blazing hot and the air was crisp with anticipation. Titanium, a new group that Cedric was producing had just finished performing. The lights went off and the crowd went crazy, roaring, out-of-control. The emcee came on:

In the beginning, God created heaven and earth.
And the earth was without form, void and dark.
So God said, let there be light, and there was light.

On the second day, God separated the heavens from the earth.
On the third and fourth day, God gathered the oceans and
made dry land and brought forth grass and herbs to the earth.
Then separated day from night.
On the fifth and sixth day, God created all the living

creatures, creating man in his own image.
And God saw that it was good.
So on the seventh day, God rested.

But on the next day, God said,
Ooops, I goofed.
On the eighth day, God said, Let there be Courage.
And it was ON! All the way LIVE ever since!
Ladies and gentlemen, please welcome,
Mr. CEDRIC COURAGE!

The crowd went berserk as the lights started to flash and the music started to play. Cedric and his band were coming down, descending from the heavens, amongst a blast of cloudy smoke. Charging forward to the front of the stage, Cedric began his rap:

I'M BACK!
Courage's the name.
Got my life back!
So let me kick my rap.
I'm back on the scene, on the stage, here to stay
Back on the case, like an attorney at a car crash.
I'm BACK!
In the groove, in the mix, in effect mode.
Here to rock, here to sway, here to move,
Make you groove...
More powerful than before.
So take pleasure and abide,
And let me kick it again
With all of you!
I'M BACK!
Heir to the throne
Back it up and give a brother his due
Rhythm, Blues, Rap, Hip-hop
Enable me to enlighten
As I reincarnate and replenish my material
I'M BACK!
More than a man,
I'm like an entity
Giving life and giving hope
From deep within my soul
So welcome me back y'all, back to the fold!

There was mad applause as the crowd cheered and indeed welcomed him back. Strapping on his guitar, Cedric began talking to the crowd: "HELLO NEW YORK!"

The crowd went berserk, wild with applause.

"I just want to take a moment out to thank those of you who supported me when I was down. Never giving up on me even when I had given up on myself. Thank you!"

The cheer grew even louder.

"I have a very special song I wrote called, *Tomorrow is a Place Where There's Love*. This song is dedicated to all of you—my fans!"

And Kendra watched mesmerized as Cedric made love—yes, love—to a crowd of 90,000 people. Watching him perform was tremendous, especially since she had never seen one of his live performances. His voice, his presence, dancing, everything combined made her realize just why all those fans were chained together that afternoon on the lawn at the police department protesting his release that day they first met. Nobody that talented, who could touch such a multitude of people deserved to be locked up—no matter how heinous the crime. Yes, he was an entity, truly a phenomenon. And the crowd was in agreement, in a frenzy, screaming his name. The girls were crying, fainting, and even she felt like dying. He was that potent. That good. He inspired reverence. Adulation, wielding so much power on that stage. All the charisma and charm he had on a personal level was magnified several hundreds times over on the stage. And by God, his voice. His voice was hypnotizing, making her feel things she wasn't prepared to face. Things she didn't want to feel.

She was standing off to the side, in the wings, slightly behind the paneled barriers of the elaborate set, but several times he seemed to be looking directly at her while he sang, strong and powerful, his voice wafting up into the night or as he performed and danced. It felt personal, like this was all for her, even though she knew there was no way this was possible. But his music, his voice, his energy, everything about this evening was making her feel special—like it was all for her.

As he went into his forth number, *Losing my Mind Over You*, the song stabbed her hard in the chest. She was still in love with Cedric, and probably had been from day one. As she watched his fluid movements, gliding across the stage in unison with his dancers. Graceful and sensual, lithe as a panther, she knew the sacrifices he had made to get there. A pleasure to watch, he was so incredibly hot. Smooth as silk.

How could Arielle had walked away and turned her back on him a second time, she wondered. Guessing, after all, there was no accounting for taste.

Just then, he slowed it down a bit, going into a ballad, the one he had written and sung at Arielle's funeral. "This song is in memory of my wife, Arielle," he announced, "and my friend, Danyel." You could hear a pin drop as he began, *Life Carries On*.

Tears were welling in her eyes and looking around, she could see that almost everyone was crying. How he got through the song and not break down completely, she would never know. But the rest was history...

The concert was a triumphant success, tour de force. He was back in the groove in peak form and she was sure he would sell a gazillion copies of his new CD. And being that it was being filmed live on HBO, he had a hit on his hands. Sales would soar, no doubt, and the Genesis tour would be sold out worldwide, an all in out SUCCESS!

Kendra watched in amazement as the press that had lynched him a few years before, were kissing his butt now. Cedric could do no wrong, he was back at the top of his game, and now with his MS and his struggle to fight the disease, the press had their heads so far up his ass, they exhausted every sensational adjective to describe him and his HBO Live performance. Not that they would even need to, the nation would see for themselves when the concert aired that not only could Cedric walk, but he could still dance his ass off. Though she knew what a personal price it would be for him afterwards and had seen him from time to time wracked in pain when his joints locked up, she knew the dancing was something Cedric was determined to do.

His family had come—his did was there with his girlfriend, Miss Penny, CJ and his nanny, Margo. Kendra's heart fluttered as she watched him play with his son after the concert. It was a beautiful thing to see, the two of them together, laughing and playing, having a good time. CJ now looked exactly like him, especially since he had long, twisted curls, which was starting to look like little miniature dreads, like his daddy. They had the same complexion and hair coloring as well. Looking at Cedric's tanned face that was lightly sheened with perspiration, her own romantic thoughts obsessed her for a moment.

"He looks just like you," she told him. "He's beautiful."

"Why thanks for the compliment," Cedric said grinning gloriously at her, "regardless of how back-handed it might have come," he finished flirtatiously, giving her a quick wink.

Hmmm, she thought. He must have been getting much better since he was up to his old tricks.

"So what are you going to do now?" She asked him.

"Tonight?"

"I mean in general?"

"You ask as if you're about to take off or something."

Kendra shrugged, since that was precisely what she had had in mind to do—especially considering the heavy pounding in her chest and the little butterflies that were causing her stomach to lurch. She had to fortify her defenses, and lately, being around Cedric seemed to chatter her nerves. Now that he was fit and doing so much better, she could no longer bear being in such close proximity and not touch him. Or kiss him. She wanted his arm around her waist. She wanted to hear the lies. Anything, and wanted desperately to think that maybe he was a little in love with her too.

"Well, we'll be going on tour for the next four and half months," Cedric said, his words breaking into her irrational thoughts. "And I suppose after that, I'll be in the studio. back to the drawing board to weave some new magic." He smiled widely.

Kendra's mouth curled upwards as well in a bright smile, ecstatic to see him happy once more.

"But tonight...if you'll hang out a bit, I'd like to chill with you," he said somewhat provocatively. "I have a press conference, a couple of interviews, but I promise not to be long."

"What about your family?"

He grinned sheepishly. "Well, it's way past CJ's bedtime. They're about to head back to the hotel. I'll see them tomorrow morning. But tonight, Miss Special Agent, Kendra Jade, I want to spend all alone with you. Is that cool?"

Kendra's face burned, not wanting to read too much into what he had just said, but then also understanding the implications of that last statement. She scarcely knew what to think or how to feel, but one thing she wanted for sure. *Please God,* she thought, *please let him find me beautiful.* And with that, her last illusion, the talisman that had kept her dream alive, that had sustained her through several long, dreadfully lonely years and nights—lay in shattered fragments at her feet. The moment had come to step up to the plate and she was going to knock that ball right out of the stadium.

She smiled and nodded. "Yeah, that would be totally cool."

26

Slow Fade to Bliss

Cedric struggled reluctantly out of a deep slumber, completely disorientated at first, so drowsy he merely wanted to roll over and fall asleep again. Not having slept so well in ages, he painstakingly endeavored to remember what day it was, where he was and even what his name was. He had to struggle to answer every question. The only thing he was entirely sure of was that it was raining good and hard. The downpour was so heavy it had roused him from sleep. And now listening to the rolling thunder, the splatter of thick rain against the windowpane and the heavy pounding of it on the roof, he felt a sublime contentment.

Squinting at bit, he noted his lush surroundings, first noticing the plush Renaissance furniture scattered about, the hand-frescoed walls, the eyelet comforter, and finally, the comfort of the colossal mahogany four-poster bed he was in. Wherever this was, he acknowledged, it was certainly elegant, but time and place was slow to register.

A soft murmur turned his attention to the woman lying beside him, and slowly the fog began to lift. Curled up in a little ball, legs tucked in a fetal position, she slumbered peacefully, her dark, silky hair streaming down her shoulders to fan the pillowcase. Cedric was overcome by an immediate rush of unequivocal delight as he registered her warm, steady breathing, and now snuggled against her, spooning her from behind, breathing in the sweet fragrance of her mussed hair, savoring the delightful pleasure she had given him the night before. Wrapping his arms about her slender waist in a tender embrace, his lips touched her soft hair. Like heroin to a junkie, this was what she'd become to him. She was everything: powerful, pulsating, passionate, painful. She was love, and she was his.

He sighed contentedly as his hands continued to caress her, kneading her breasts, sucking on the jutting tips. "Mmmm," she purred, making him feel glorious. Wickedly, wondrously delicious!

Reliving what happened between them only hours before, every delightful moment came pouring forth like an unspeakable pleasure. He wanted to bask in the sheer joy of it. He was naked and on top of her now, his muscled body intimately positioned between her splayed thighs. Bringing with her the surest hopes in her own magical arts and charms, he'd be forever her willing victim.

Was this happiness?

Last night, he had been engulfed—body and soul—consumed by her flames. She had propelled him to another time, another place. Kisses. Caresses. Shadows of lips and teeth against luxurious brown skin; bodies and limbs slipping in and out of bends of skin; tongues tracing patterns, mouth to mouth and heart to heart, dancing and swaying, drinking plum wine—if only he could relive the moments, where he had meticulously placed strawberries, white grapes, and little melon balls in the crescent round her vulva, then partaken of them from there. Last night, all of the unspoken promises had finally been fulfilled. He had found heaven—on earth. And the ecstasy of it was too magnificent for words.

He closed his eyes to better savor the completeness of his happiness, as he snuggled against her, content to just lie on top of her for all eternity. Soon though, he opened his eyes again because he loved to look at her. Even while she slept, she captivated him—so riveting was she to watch, not to mention, touch.

Lifting himself off her, he pulling her to him, his sinewy arms wrapped more firmly around her. And though he had no specific definition for precisely what he was feeling at the moment, he knew he loved this woman with a wrenching desperation that knew no bounds, nor humiliation. It was merely a pleasure to gaze at her face, to have her wrapped in his arms.

Contemplating her tenderly, gazing at her stunning face that while she slept gave the illusion of transparency. To him she was peerlessly beautiful, and therein laid her irresistible charm. Brilliant to look at and to listen to, she had the power to subjugate him—in every way.

This was a delicious moment, he decided as he stroked and savored the texture of her protruding nipples. He couldn't believe that he had finally won her, conquered her, and that she was laying right there beside him. Winning her had not been easy, but that was what made the occasion all the more joyous. Feeling deliriously happy, he listened to the pattering rain while holding her fabulous sleeping frame against him. Outside the rain fell in sheets, like a water fall, but inside this room felt safe and warm, delightfully sunny.

Would he ever be this happy again?

Her breasts were like pomegranates, he thought to himself. Ripe and bursting with their sweetness, and the nipples like little cherries crowning the top, he mused, lowering his head to tongue and kiss and lick at the peaks. How could she sleep through this, he grinned mischievously as he kneaded her breast. His happiness at that moment was so clear, so strong. So free of ambiguity. There was no question or doubt in his mind that he had done the right thing in bringing her back. It didn't just *feel* right. *It was right.* This was what life was meant to be, should have always been; and he welcomed the labyrinth of limitless possibilities now open to him and could hardly wait to explore them. She was his prize...his possession...and finally he could embrace that. Finally, he had balance and felt perfectly satisfied with himself. And his contentment was more than just finding love, but also had a lot to do with the fact that he had finally accepted himself. Completely. For what he was.

Good or bad.

Right, wrong or indifferent.

He was what he was, and so why bother fighting it or denying it? And yes...life was about choices. The choices you made. And he felt justified and embraced the ones he'd made.

Nothing or anyone would ever affect him this deeply.

Sighing deeply, he whispered sweet endearments in her ear. Hearing her mutter and knowing she was now smiling—even though he couldn't see it—he dragged her sleeping heart to where his mind had gone. He longed to make love to her again, to feel her heat. To be cloaked in her softness. Yet at the same time, he hated to disturb her.

His body ached from the searing memories of the night before—not to mention the mindless pleasure he was receiving from caressing her body.

Suddenly, she swiveled her head and his eyes locked on her delicate features. Imperceptibly, his arms tighten around her, she looked so beautiful and peaceful, angelic and pristine, despite all that had transpired the night before.

Her little hand reached up to stoke his face. Catching her hand in his, he turned it over and placed a burning kiss on her palm.

They exchanged a heated glance, while the back of his fingers casually moved up and down her velvety skin. He loved the hollow right below her lowest rib, that silky, sexy little cliff of skin right above the concave of her belly.

"Mmmm," she purred like a sated cat, "Were you just sucking my breast? Continue...I liked it," she said groggily and turned back around, laying her head back on the crook of his shoulder and immediately fell back to sleep. His heart fluttered as he gazed down at her. She was as sweet as she was treacherous, and yet he had entrusted her with his most intimate and private of possessions—his heart.

Longing to do her bidding, but knowing it would make him too hot, he listened instead to the patter of rain intermingled with her steady breathing, which lulled him and made him want to fall back to sleep. Closing his eyes, he attempted to do just that, right after giving her a lovebite on the neck.

What did it matter what day or time it was, or even where they were. It was raining so hard, he'd just as soon spend the entire day in bed. Except the second he closed his eyes, the visions returned, sweeping their wave of terror over him.

He had this recurring nightmare...that never quite seemed like a dream at all, but which was always so incredibly real. It was more like an old memory...horrible as it was...but a memory all the same. He hated remembering the drenching cold...the acid sweat...the bottomless tears...the violent rain and dirt streaming down his face. And whenever he did remember, it brought on migraines that continuously racked his brain.... But worst of all, was the snapshot memory of her lifeless, bloodless body and the ashen, grey lips that forever haunted his dreams.

Why couldn't he forget? Why did he constantly remember?

Suddenly, his heart began to behave strangely. Setting off like an explosion of gunfire, it leapt around unevenly in his chest, pounding at one moment and then stopping irresponsibly at the next. As if it had hit some inward nerve and then quiet...all quiet...as if it had just stepped outside of his body. It was forever this way lately, anytime he tried to fall asleep.

A lone tear fell. Then another...so hot and so caustic, he wondered how it didn't burn straight through his skin. Although he believed he had found what he had been looking for...still, he couldn't be too sure...

Was this moment even real? Was he actually experiencing this or was this his "Vanilla Sky," and just wishful thinking on his part?

This was now forever the question.

Epilogue

It was hard to believe it had all come to an end.

Seven years gone.

Finished.

That chapter of my life closed forever with Arielle vanishing into thin air. Even now it was difficult to believe any of it had actually happened, as exciting and perfect as it had been when it all began. Like an acute pain that seemed to have no physical source, her absence persisted, more real than her presence.

Yet Kendra was right.

You eventually had to put tragedy behind you. What else could you do? Surely, what didn't kill you made you stronger. And while I was still trying to cope, trying to come to grips with certain things and accept what had happened, I still had a ways to go.

Thank God for the fans, though. For family. And for my many, many friends.

Especially Kendra, who reached out to me in so many wonderful, beautiful ways. Ways that helped me examine the pain, face it, and finally move on and grow.

People say that time heals all wounds, but that's not true. The wound never really heals. A scab grows over it. And you find ways over and around it, or find ways to bypass it...but the wound never truly heals. It remains...always...throbbing, however dull.

Don't miss the 3rd Installment

No Good Deed
Goes Unpunished

Coming soon in the not so distant future.

***

Also pick up a copy of

Just One Night

Written under the pen name of

D.M. Coupet

Visit www.darlinedorce-coupet.com for more details...